THE RICHEST HILL ON EARTH

**Center Point
Large Print**

Also by Richard S. Wheeler and available from Center Point Large Print:

Snowbound

This Large Print Book carries the Seal of Approval of N.A.V.H.

THE RICHEST HILL ON EARTH

Richard S. Wheeler

CENTER POINT LARGE PRINT
THORNDIKE, MAINE

This Center Point Large Print edition is published
in the year 2012 by arrangement with
St. Martin's Press.

This is a work of fiction. All of the characters, organiza-
tions, and events portrayed in this novel are either products
of the author's imagination or are used fictitiously.

The text of this Large Print edition is unabridged.
In other aspects, this book may
vary from the original edition.
Printed in the United States of America
on permanent paper.
Set in 16-point Times New Roman type.

ISBN: 978-1-61173-271-9

Library of Congress Cataloging-in-Publication Data

Wheeler, Richard S.
The richest hill on earth / Richard S. Wheeler.
p. cm.
ISBN 978-1-61173-271-9 (library binding : alk. paper)
1. Copper mines and mining—Montana—Fiction.
2. Butte (Mont.)—History—19th century—Fiction.
3. Large type books. I. Title.
PS3573.H4345R54 2012
813´.54—dc22

2011033702

To all those of inquiring mind,
who abandoned youthful visions
for something more profound

One

John Fellowes Hall fretted about his middle name. He had changed it from Frank. He couldn't imagine why his parents had inflicted that loutish name on him. Frank has such a pedestrian aura about it, but that had eluded them. Fellowes had just the right tone for a person of his stature, so he had arbitrarily switched it. What's more, it was sonorous, unlike a string of one-syllable names. Anyone of any sensitivity knew that there should be different numbers of syllablcs in one's given names and surname.

He doubted that his new employer would fathom any of it. The man was a bumpkin in a silk hat. John Fellowes Hall had suffered a string of miserable employers who hadn't the faintest idea of his gifts. Maybe this time things would be better, but he doubted it.

The narrow gauge train from Helena slowed as it entered the flat below Butte, and slowly ground to a halt, hissing steam and belching cinders. Hall could see from his grimy window that the Western city was just as ugly as it was proclaimed to be, and maybe worse, but that didn't faze him. Butte was the place to get rich. It wasn't money that Hall was after, though he had bargained for as much as his new employer could manage. It was reputation. Here was the place for a distinguished newspaper editor to turn himself into a legend.

On this cold and windy spring day of 1892, the smoke pouring from Butte's mine boilers and mills scraped downward, catching the city in haze. Far up, on the naked crest of the naked slope, stood a forest of headframes and rude sheds, which seemed to catch the eye because they didn't belong there, and insulted the dark grandeur of the forested mountains stretching north and east. The russet hill was burdened with a cancerous mélange of buildings, cramped into gulches, teetering on slopes, while Butte, as far as his eye could see through the jaundiced smoke, seemed to seethe.

Well, he had been warned. The train, down from Helena, squealed and sighed, while passengers collected their Gladstones and duffel, and stepped down to the gravel of the station yard. There would be a trunk on the express car, but he would get that later at the depot. He had everything he needed in his pebbled leather overnighter.

The sulphurous smoke struck him and irritated his eyes. Was there no escape from it in this mountain vastness? He located a hack, operated by a skinny gent with a full beard, and engaged the man with a wave of his hand.

"You got any more luggage?" the cabby asked in a ruined voice.

"Trunk I can leave in the express office."

"Moving here, eh?"

Hall was offended by the man's familiarity, and didn't reply.

"I can carry the trunk if you want."

"I will send for it when I need it."

"You headed for the company?" the driver asked.

That secretly pleased Hall, but he would not confess it. That would be the headquarters of the Anaconda Copper Mining Company. The cabby had taken him for an executive, as well he should. Hall wore a fine three-piece gray broadcloth suit, a fine polka-dot cravat, a lean shirt with a starched white collar, and polished hightop shoes.

"Call me Fat Jack," the cabby said. "Where to?"

Hall hated to disillusion the man. "I'll be stopping temporarily at the *Butte Mineral*," he said. "Of course, before going up the hill."

Fat Jack eyed the editor, and nodded. The man was anything but fat, just as Hall was anything but a copper executive, even if he looked the part. The editor extracted a dainty handkerchief and mopped his face. The harsh wind had already deposited a layer of soot on it, which Hall noted on the clean white folds of his handkerchief. Ah, well, he thought. To live is to suffer.

"You seeing Clark?" Fat Jack asked, as he steered his lumbering dray north, up mud-soaked thoroughfares.

"Clark?"

"Himself."

The cabby was referring to William Andrews Clark, owner of the *Mineral* and other rags, owner of many of those mines and reduction works up the hill, owner of the street railway, owner of a bank, owner of surrounding forests, owner of thousands of mortal souls, and about to be the owner of John Fellowes Hall.

"I am planning to interview him, yes."

"I think he'll do the interviewing," Fat Jack said, slapping the lines over the croup of the dray to hasten him uphill.

Hall considered the hack man insolent and resolved not to leave a tip.

In a rude part of town below the commercial center, Fat Jack reined the dray to a halt. This appeared to be newspaper row, with the *Butte Mineral* sandwiched between some others. There was no sign of prosperity emanating from the weary storefront. At least cobblestones paved this street; others appeared to be mire.

"Two bits," Fat Jack said. "Want me to stay?"

That was extortion, so Hall simply handed the man a quarter and smiled icily. He lifted his knobby bag and eased to the grimy pavement. Fat Jack eyed the quarter, stared hard, and slapped the dray forward. Hall eyed the *Mineral* with vast distaste. No one had washed its windows. There was no brass on the door. The name had been stenciled in black on the windows. There should have been a gilded sign above. The street had not been swept and was deep in dung. A wave of disdain swept the editor. What sort of rag was this?

He would make short work of it and seek employment elsewhere. He smoothed his three-piece gray broadcloth suit, adjusted his cravat, eyed his hightops, and then pushed his way through the creaking door, to the sound of a bell.

The familiar smell of hot lead, and the bitter smell of ink, caught his nostrils. He heard the clatter of Linotypes. That was good. The new machines made quick work of typesetting and printing. No one showed up at the counter, so he hunted for a bell to clang, but found none. The interior was as grimy as the exterior, and he hesitated to touch any ink-sprayed surface, knowing his hand would be smeared. These things were not good omens.

At last a printer emerged and eyed Hall.

"You're the man," he said.

"John Fellowes Hall."

"You'll want to talk to Mr. Clark. The old man's not here. He's up at his bank."

"May I see my office?"

"We haven't got them. But Louis the Louse could steal one."

"Never mind. I'll just look around."

The printer eyed him. "Without a smock?"

Everything in a print shop stained clothing black.

11

"I'll interview Clark first," Hall said. "Steer me."

"Two blocks uphill, and left."

"Will this bag be safe?"

"For ten minutes. The next bandits are due at four."

Hall intended to fire the man.

He settled his knobby black bag in an obscure corner and headed into the cold smoke. The spring weather did nothing to improve the looks of Butte. He might have enjoyed the stroll but for the foul wind, which drove ash into him as he toiled upslope. Butte seemed to be a thriving town, with solid brick commercial buildings everywhere, a streetcar system, and electric wires strung in a crazy quilt pattern. He wondered how Amber would react to it, not that it mattered.

He found the bank, W. A. Clark and Bro., readily enough. This enterprise at least was gaudily announced with gilded letters across its brick front. He pulled open the polished brass door, eyed the lobby, decided that Clark would be upstairs, ascended stairs of creaking imported oak, and found himself at a reception desk, with a comely lady in charge. She had a typing machine before her.

"John Fellowes Hall to see Mr. Clark. He's expecting me."

"Oh, the newsman."

"Editor."

She retreated to a corner office, vanished, and then reappeared. "He will see you in a little while," she said. "Do have a seat."

Which was a polished walnut bench resembling a pew, and probably was. The worshipers of this god required pews.

But Clark surprised him. Moments later the dapper man boiled out of his lair, greeted Hall effusively, shepherded the editor into the sanctum, and settled Hall in a quilted leather chair.

"Ah, so it's you, Hall. I've been awaiting this moment with more anticipation than buying a new smelter."

John Fellowes Hall had never been compared to a smelter, and didn't quite know how to respond, but his wit saved him.

"Ah, yes, I get the bullion out of the ore," he said.

"Well, the *Mineral*'s not going to be doing that. I've hired you to cut off the tentacles of the octopus. You will hack away, one by one, without remorse, and without surcease. You will win the allegiance of the people of Butte and you will support the Democrat Party and you will discreetly remind the public of who it is who wants to keep Montana independent, free, fair, and honest. We will elect Democrats this November and they will make me senator."

"It sounds like a job made in heaven."

"There is divine purpose in it," Clark said. "We

must rescue Montana from the octopus. We must not allow a single corporation to own the government, own the governor, own the legislators, own the regulators, own the tax collectors. I'm determined to fight to the last, so that the people of this state are free. I will be honored to become a senator."

Clark was so earnest it surprised Hall. Did the little tycoon actually believe all that?

"I can see you doubt me," Clark said. He headed for a window. "Up there are a dozen properties of the Anaconda Company. The best mines, reduction works, mills, and a little railroad too. Over in Anaconda is the most advanced smelter in the world. That's Marcus Daly's empire. That's his town. He built it. He erected his smelter, platted the streets, started the houses, built his fancy hotel. Now he wants to put the state capital in his backyard. He wants to own the government, just like he owns most of that hill up there, owns his own city, owns half the forests in Montana, owns a railroad, owns a horse racing stable, and owns every Irishman in Butte. He wants Montana's public buildings, its governor, its legislators, under his thumb. He wants to see them from his office windows. He wants to tell them how to tax and regulate. He wants to own Montana. He cares nothing about the farmers and ranchers and all the rest of the people. And he doesn't want me in office. You will stop him. He may own papers across the state, and a deluxe paper in Anaconda, and another here, and more in every town that can support a daily. But you'll stop him, and when you do, God will smile on you."

Hall debated whether to sound reassuring and confident, or whether to sound a little more modest.

"Let me at him. What's a newspaper for? I'll show you what a bulldog is."

"I don't want to own a bulldog. I want a shark."

"You've bought one," Hall said.

"Good. Now, I imagine you'd like to bring your wife and children here, but I will require you to hold off for the time being. You have more important things to do than raise a family. Keep her back East."

That took Hall aback. "But Mr. Clark—"

"And you may consider that your lodging is taken care of, Hall. I will supply it."

"Well, I'll take a room tonight."

"No need. You are going to board with me, Hall."

"With you? I wouldn't want to intrude in your private life, sir."

"Oh, pshaw, you haven't a notion about me, do you? I have a house with so many rooms I've lost track of them. There are rooms for an army. You will stay in my house. You will enjoy the most modern plumbing in Montana. A half dozen indoor water closets. Not even Daly's plumbing can match it. Not that he cares about plumbing. Any old outhouse will do for Daly. But let me tell you, Hall, you'll live in beauty and luxury. You might live there but you'll not see me. Not that I will avoid you, but our paths won't cross. You'll be in the servants' quarters, of course, where life is lived entirely beyond my gaze. If I invite you for breakfast, you'll come, and bring a notepad so you will have my directions on papers. Agreed?"

"I'm your pet shark," Hall said.

Clark stared. "Hall, I am very good at reading men. You are taking this much too lightly, making smart jokes. I don't know about you. Are you the man I want? Pet shark. I don't know at all about you. A serious man wouldn't make bad little quips. A serious man would know exactly what I mean, and dedicate himself to the cause. I'm going to put you on probation for a month, and then we'll see about a job."

"Well, I'm not sure I'll work under such conditions. I find them rather heavy. If you think you can buy my loyalty as well as my pen, sir, then—"

"Oh, pshaw, Hall. You're hired. Get to work. The miners have ten-hour days, but you don't and never will. I will own you twenty-four hours of every day including Sundays. And call me Senator. Senator Clark. I'd like to get used to it in advance."

Two

Hall studied his new digs, more amused than angry. He had been consigned to a monkish cell on the third floor, which was entirely the realm of the household servants. Clark's redbrick mansion rose importantly west of the central city, announcing its owner as one of the grandees of the mining town.

No sooner had Hall climbed the endless stairs to the third floor, from a rear servants' entrance, than his trunk arrived and two draymen toted it up the narrow stairway and deposited it in his austere white room.

Hall discovered an iron bedstead, a washstand with a white vitreous washbowl and pitcher, a wooden chair, and an armoire. An incandescent light hung on a cord from the ceiling. A single toilet served all the servants. The best thing about the room was its dormer window, which opened on a northward view of the numerous headframes and the mountains beyond. That's what Butte was all about. Wealth yanked from the bowels of the city. Those headframes sat over shafts plunging thousands of feet into the mineralized rock below the city, and each day those shafts coughed up a fortune in copper ore laced with zinc, silver, and a little gold. That mass of rock was known as the

17

richest hill on earth, and with good reason. It had already created some of the greatest fortunes in the United States, not least that of his new employer. Even as he watched, the clatter of the mines drifted to him, and he saw moving ore cars, stubby engines leaking steam, and the bustle of fierce industry.

Or master. Hall wasn't quite sure whether he was an employee or a slave. To William Andrews Clark it made no difference. Other human beings were there to be exploited; most for their muscle, but Hall for his brain. Hall was discovering some advantage in all of this: his family could wait. He'd send them some cash now and then, and maybe in a while he would decide to bring them to Butte. But just now, he was furtively and deliciously pleased to be freed from all domestic burdens. If Clark wanted a crusade, he'd get a virtuous crusader—more or less. Hall had heard a few things about Butte.

He hung his spare suit in the armoire, hung some shirts, lined up his older hightop shoes, and settled his small clothes on its upper shelf. The room was oddly pleasant. A manservant had taken him to it and had answered a few questions. Yes, there would be meals there in a separate dining area served by a dumbwaiter from the kitchen below. Breakfasts at six, lunches at eleven, suppers at five. One ate what was served. It was not a restaurant.

The afternoon was already far gone. Hall glanced at his turnip watch and decided to skip servants' supper and head for the newspaper, blotting up the city as he went. By the time he reached the street, a chill had already settled, reminding Hall that Butte was located almost on the Continental Divide. The street teemed with wagons and carriages and pedestrians, swarming this way and that. Butte was alive. Some towns lay inert and sleepy, but Butte seethed with life, and never slept.

The city was only twenty years from being a shantytown, a place of log and frame structures built to abandon the day the ore ran out. But here was a metropolis of stone and brick, with cobbled streets, trolley lines, a forest of utility poles festooned with wire, and gaudy advertising that commandeered the eye.

Hall thought he knew how to get to the *Mineral*, but nothing looked the same in the spring twilight. It didn't matter. He wanted to see William Clark's city. Marcus Daly's city. The Anaconda Copper Mining Company's city. The city with ore cars rolling through it, sometimes on streetcar rails, pushed and pulled by stubby little engines. Wealth, unending, blasted and shoveled out of the resisting rock. Metals of great worth, and minerals of more dubious value, such as arsenic. Clark had once said that the arsenic in the air of Butte put a lovely blush on the cheeks of Butte's women.

The great schism between Marcus Daly and William Andrews Clark had erupted a few years earlier when Clark was running for the office of Territorial Delegate to Congress, Montana not yet being a state. Daly supported Clark—they were both Democrats—and then, suddenly Daly no longer did, and the vast armies of mill men and miners employed by Daly's Anaconda Mining Company had voted for the Republican candidate, Tom Carter, who won the election in the heavily Democratic territory. Betrayal, treason, perfidy, screamed Clark's paper, the *Mineral*. And now Hall had been hired to sharpen and deepen the feud, and to use his mighty pen to whittle away at the Irish immigrant boy, Marcus Daly, who had learned hardrock mining and made good.

It was going to be entertaining. And no one on earth was better qualified than John Fellowes Hall. At least Hall could think of none other.

Hall paused at a downtown street corner to examine a yellow dog. The mutt seemed to own the corner. People passing by were obviously familiar with the dog, and some paused to pet it. Hall could find no sign of a master, but one probably was around in a saloon or getting fitted for a suit of clothes. But then a man in a white apron emerged from a restaurant with some bones and scraps and fed them to the dog, which yawned, and settled into some happy gnawing. People approved. Maybe the dog belonged to the man in the beanery. Hall thought it was disgusting, letting a dog occupy a busy street corner while its owner was busy. The odd thing was that every passerby seemed to know the mutt and approve of it.

Hall found the *Mineral* easily enough and entered to the rattle of the Linotype machines. A newspaper never slept. Clark had kept it reasonably up to date, which was necessary if it was to compete with Daly's propaganda sheet, the *Anaconda Standard*, financed by Daly's deep pockets.

A compositor in a grimy apron materialized, a question on his face.

"I'm Hall."

"It's the arsenic in the air," the man said.

"I'm the editor."

"That's what I was afraid of. I'll get you a beer."

"Mr. Clark hired me."

"The taller they are, the harder they fall," the skinny man said. He pointed to a cubicle off to the side of the composing room. "All yours," he said.

Hall found another compositor in there, and a copyboy, and a mutton-chopped reporter at a desk in an alcove, hammering on a typing machine.

"Where's the newsroom?" Hall asked.

"Newsroom? Why don't you quit and go back East?"

"I'm John Fellowes Hall," he said.

"The new copyboy?"

21

"What are you writing?"

"A story about Anaconda's railroad. It'll run ore trains from here to Anaconda."

"Another arm of the octopus. Who'll they put out of business?"

"No one."

"Well, invent someone. Pretty soon the Anaconda will own everything. Say so in the story. The railroad is another sinister Daly business."

The reporter stared. "What's it to you? It's just a virgin little railroad."

"I'm Clark's shark."

"Call me Grabbit. Grabbit Wolf. That's because I grab the story before anyone else, and the name stuck."

"Well, Grabbit, grab this: it's a new monopoly. This is Marcus Daly's sinister new ploy to own Montana. Get the whole story. If you don't have answers, publish the question. How did it happen? Who financed it? Who got paid off? Was the octopus playing some sort of game? And for what?"

Grabbit frowned, and Hall thought the man was a bit dense, but it turned out to be something else entirely.

"Hey, I write news," he said. "This is just a virtuous little railroad."

One of those, Hall thought. The only question was whether to fire him on the spot or wait a few days. He decided to wait.

"Grabbit, get this straight. If you don't have answers, ask questions. I want twenty questions in this story when I see it in the morning edition. You can also tell readers that the *Mineral* was unable to check the facts. Got it?"

Wolf cocked an eyebrow, stared out a grimy window, and grinned. "I always wanted to write editorials," he said.

"Grabbit, I think I'm going to like you," Hall said. "And so will Mr. Clark. And Grabbit, I only employ people I like."

"I am now a pundit," Wolf said. "I've been promoted."

Wolf was a pale man, so white that Hall doubted he had any acquaintance with the sun. He looked like he had crawled out of an abandoned mine somewhere. But at least the man could operate a typing machine. Half the reporters in the country still wrote in longhand.

"The *Mineral* have any other reporters?" Hall asked.

"A few stringers," Wolf said.

"Who gathers the news, then?"

"You do," Wolf said.

"I'm the editor."

"You're the new gumshoe. Your predecessor wore out a his brogans every six months."

Hall wasn't about to spend his life collecting news. That wasn't his job. His job was to shape the news, fit it to Mr. Clark's needs and whims. He decided to talk to Clark about hiring a few more reporters, plus a cartoonist or two. A good cartoon burrowed into numbskulls' noggins better than a lot of words. If Clark wanted an engine of influence, there would be some changes.

Hall thought he'd write editorials, but those weren't important. Anyone could mouth off, and it didn't affect the thinking of anyone else. The whole deal was to shape the news, turn every scrap of information into something that would help Clark.

"Wolf, what do they pay you?"

Wolf stopped his typing and thought about it. "Not enough," he said. "It keeps me in nickel cigars."

"Mr. Clark has political ambitions. How are you going to help him?"

Wolf pondered it. "I could go to work for the *Anaconda Standard*," he said.

"Comedian, are you?"

"So fire me," Wolf said, and returned to his typing.

"You're not worth getting rid of," Hall replied.

Hall examined the cubbyhole that was supposedly the editor's brown study. At least he could keep an evil eye on the rest of the bunch. He'd know every slacker within a week. He meandered through the rest of the place, watching a bald Linotypist compose lines of type, that would be fitted into forms.

He found stacks of back issues, and pulled one off of each pile, wanting to see what the advertising looked like. He found plenty of it in every issue. That was good. A paper without ads had no impact. This was no rich man's toy, but a working newspaper in a brawling and prospering town. There were clothiers' ads, haberdashers, shoe stores, cobblers, wine and beer dealers, saloons, restaurants, doctors and dentists, but not many classified ads. Only two funeral parlors were advertising, and those ads were in the classified section. Tomorrow he would talk to the ad salesman. Lots of people croaked in mining towns, and the *Mineral* should get a lot more business out of it. There should be big ads, listing the departed, with funeral times posted. There appeared to be only one desk with advertising order forms on it. He'd find out who the joker was and put some heat under him.

A boxed classified ad caught his eye.

See into the future. Know your fate. Know the day and hour when trouble might come. Know when illness might strike, and what it will be. Learn if you have a secret beau waiting to meet you.

I have been given clairvoyant powers. I am in touch with the other world. I have the gift of vision. Stop in, and let me tell you how all this happened, how a suddenly widowed woman with only a few pennies to her name was given profound gifts. And how I can help you, share with you what is given to me. I charge nothing but donations are welcome. If I help you see your future, and you are pleased or rewarded, then you might think of rewarding me.

—AGNES HEALY,
317 WEST MINERAL STREET, REAR.

There might be a news story in it, John Fellowes Hall concluded.

Three

A well-dressed, even natty, man stood at the door. Slanting Agnes eyed him narrowly. She didn't let just anyone into her kitchen. She gave him a closer look. He wasn't even from Butte. No one in Butte dressed like that except the pimps.

"Miss Healy?"

"It's Missus. Are you from the city?"

He seemed puzzled. "You mean, employed by the city? No. I saw your notice and I was curious."

She felt a faint relief. The city kept trying to move her to Mercury Street, but that wasn't her business, and she didn't intend to move there. She

26

was a good woman, period. She did not peddle anything but whatever sprang to mind when someone wanted answers.

"All right," she said, admitting this natty man into her grim kitchen, which was falling apart from neglect. She couldn't help it. A widow didn't have the means to do much, especially one with two grubby boys. He eyed her closely, and she found herself dabbing her stray hair into place. Usually it didn't matter.

"You want something? Advice?"

"What I want is just to listen to you. It might be worth something to you. I read your card in the paper, and it made me curious."

She caught him eyeing the drainboard, the battered table, the sagging yellow muslin curtain at the window, which overlooked an alley.

"You are?"

"Oh, it's unimportant. A newcomer here."

"You're a snoop."

"That's my profession, ma'am."

"I thought so. A detective." She felt better. Snoops were fine with her. "I'm fey, you know."

"You have me there, ma'am."

"Fey. I sometimes see into the next times. Like death. I told Emmett not to go to the mine—the Neversweat—that day but he did. He just smiled and picked up his lunch bucket and that was the last I ever saw of him. He knew I'm fey, but he didn't care. I told him don't go up the drift that slanted like that. Don't go up it because rock will roll down. But he did, and rock came down, and now he's buried in Mountain View. Wouldn't you know? I can see it and tell people but I can't change fate. So now I'm without a man and I'm forced to do this."

"Fortune-teller?"

"I don't tell fortunes! What do you take me for, anyway?"

"I'm sorry. I'm on new ground here, ma'am."

"They called me Slanting Agnes because I told Emmett not to walk up the slanting drift. That's how Butte is, you know. Everyone's got a name. My name is Agnes and now they call me Slanting, and I have lost my dignity."

"How do you foretell these things? Are you a medium? Do you consult with spirits?"

"Oh, no, sir, that would be a mortal sin. I don't hear voices, I don't listen to whispers. I just . . . things come to me in a flash, and I know I've seen something, like lightning in the darkness, a flash of something. That's me."

"What did you think when you saw me?"

"Nothing. You're just a man who doesn't know anything about here."

"That's certainly true, Slanting Agnes. Is that how I should address you?"

"I'm used to it. At least they don't call me Flat Agnes or anything like that."

"You charge something for this?"

"I am a widow with two boys. But I'm not for sale, and make sure you know that and behave proper."

She eyed him. It wouldn't be the first time a man had made advances. But he didn't seem inclined, and spent most of his time glancing furtively about, reading her wants in everything that lay about.

"Who comes here, Agnes? And what do they ask?"

"Why do you want to know?"

"You have had some successes, obviously, or people wouldn't come to see you."

Agnes was secretly pleased. "I won't name anyone, but I'll tell you a little bit. One regular is a shifter, a shift foreman. He comes to ask me if the pit will be safe that day. He lost some men and is very sorry about it, and wants to know beforehand if there's trouble in the rock. I told him one day to get men out of a drift because there would be a gusher, and that's what happened and three men drownded dead from hot water."

"He didn't do anything about it?"

"I see what I see. If a gusher's gonna kill men, it's going to kill men, and there's nothing a shifter can do about it."

"Then why do they come? If it's foreordained why bother?"

"Beats me," she said.

"Who else?"

She knew this was really why he had come, and it made her a little huffy. "Wouldn't you like to know!" she said.

"Do stock brokers and jobbers come calling? Do they want to know what stocks are going up or down?"

She smiled but didn't nod her head.

"How about big-time people? Do mine owners stop by and get a whiff of the future from Slanting Agnes?"

"Aren't you the nosy one."

"Do miners' widows come wanting to visit with their dead men?"

"I tell them to go away. That's wicked. The dead are dead, and I am not a messenger woman running back and forth like that. I tell them to go to church and pray to join them, if they want to get together with them again. Me, I miss Emmett sometimes, but he drank too much and we had to live on three dollars and fifty cents a day, except when he wasn't working, and then we starved. So why should I itch to see Emmett? All he wanted was more babies, but I had too many, two live, three dead, and don't want any more. Just in case you want to know."

"I bet some big shots show up here, sneaking in, too, from the alley so no one sees them. I'm right, aren't I?"

"You sure are nosy."

"Who?"

"I won't say, but they're some as own the Anaconda. I don't like them. After Emmett was killed, they gave me one month's wage. A few dollars. They left me with two boys. The union, it took up a collection, and that was good for another month, but then I was on my own, with nothing at all, just being fey and having a door on the alley."

"Who?"

"You get out of here."

"Who?"

She stood, arranged her skirts, and pointed toward her door. He seemed reluctant. Not even when she ordered him out of her house was he willing to go.

"I'll call the coppers," she said.

He got up, started out, saw the money jar on the table, withdrew a ten from his pocket, and dropped it into her jar. Then he smiled, tipped his hat, and stepped into the gray light outside.

She hadn't seen ten dollars in a long time. But it wouldn't do him a damned bit of good. People came to her with fears and needs and hopes and terrors, wanting one of her lightning flashes on the future, and she'd never named names, except for Emmett. So let him roast in hell, this snoop.

She could feed the boys and pay the rent and buy some kerosene for the lamps.

She wondered about the man. He wasn't the sort to search out his own death. He would be more interested in stocks and bonds and things like that.

31

She felt some relief. The worst part of her life was telling people their fate. Sometimes, when she saw the doom of a man sitting at her kitchen table, she went faint with grief, and she couldn't speak, and she would shoo the man out if she could. But the persistent ones wouldn't be shooed away, and would sit stubbornly until she told them what she saw, in a clipped low voice. Oddly, the doomed were the ones who tipped her the most. The doomed stuffed the empty glass jar with bills. The rich were the worst; they didn't really value fate, and just wanted to see what stood in their paths. Like Marcus Daly, who rode up in a carriage and parked on Mineral Street, or William Andrews Clark, the heathen who drove his elaborate trap up the alley and parked half a block away and sneaked in at twilight.

So far, at least, she had little to tell them. Clark wasn't interested in death; all he cared about was tomorrow's prices on everything: stocks, copper, art works, real estate, water, mine timbers. He sometimes sat and waited, oddly patient for such a busy financier and great man. He had smoothly tried to befriend her, thinking that he would get at the future if he buttered her up, and she despised him for it. He was another Protestant, and blind to all sacred things. She wished he wouldn't visit her, and ached to tell him some bad news, but mostly she had nothing to offer. It was as if her gift fled her when he came around, yet that never deterred him. Once she did see the stocks of one of his smelters being sold in great amounts and for more than it had been selling for. She told him, and he told her he had profited greatly from her glimpse into what would be.

She began scrubbing the kitchen. The boys were at school. She would have enough now to buy Tommy some knickers. He was sprouting so fast she couldn't keep him clothed.

No one came for a while, and that was good. Then Andrew Penrose came. He was the night shift boss at the Anaconda, suffering miner's lung but gamely keeping on. He was a Cornishman and Methodist but she forgave him for it. Most of the bosses were Cornishmen, even in Marcus Daly's company, because they knew all about mining, having learned their trade in the tin mines of Cornwall.

"It's you, is it?" she asked, pouring some lukewarm tea which she served in a chipped cup. "Going to try your luck again?"

He settled in her kitchen chair and just nodded. He looked more tired than usual. At four, as the mine's whistles blew, he would descend to the eight-hundred-foot level in a triple cage and begin his daily ordeal far from sunlight.

"It's not for me, Agnes."

She knew. He had been haunted by accidents on his shift. Men working for him had died. A cave-in caught five. A runaway cage loaded with seventeen men had plunged a thousand feet and killed them all. A delayed charge had killed three muckers. He had come to her broken and ready to quit. She didn't know whether these disasters were a failing of his; whether he had been careless or let his men act foolishly. All she knew was that these things haunted him, ate at his heart, took years off his life, and filled him with a desperate need to keep his men safe. It didn't matter that when she saw the future, fate was sealed and he could do nothing at all to stop it. He came to her, wanted that flash of light, and hoped somehow to save lives and prevent wounds and spare future widows. Like herself.

She sat down across from him, took his rough hands in her rough hands, and held on tight, and waited for the lightning to strike. It seemed a long time, this transport from the now to the infinite, but she waited, and he waited, and then she saw what she saw.

She didn't want to tell him.

"What?" he asked.

"I saw a coffin, plain wood, and a face in the coffin, and a Dublin Gulch widow in black, and three children, girl and two boys, and if anyone had looked, the face had no legs."

"When? When?"

"Whenever the future comes, Mr. Penrose."

He slumped in the wooden chair. "I must stop it," he said. "That'd be Brophy, you know, two lads and a lass. I'll tell the man to stay away the next shift, I will."

It would do no good, she thought.

He rose, agitated, and headed toward her door, remembered that he had left nothing in her jar, found two quarters and tossed them in.

Then he plunged into the quickening afternoon.

Four

Brophy, then. Andrew Penrose fumed. That hag would be wrong. What right had she to point a finger at someone, the finger of doom? It was all nonsense. No one could see into the future. It mocked science.

He wondered why he went to her. He didn't believe in anything supernatural, especially visionaries. And yet he went, helpless to resist his own obsessions. She was just another fraud milking money out of the gullible.

Not Brophy, not the lad from County Clare brought over by Daly himself. The boss had offered to help any of his countrymen cross the seas if they would work for him in Butte, and some came, including that singing man who had started as a mucker four years earlier.

The Anaconda Hill wouldn't claim him if the shift boss Andrew Penrose could help it. He'd spit in the face of Fate. He'd send Brophy topside to work in daylight that day and the next. The man should get some experience unloading country rock.

Penrose scorned his own thoughts. The Hill was getting to him. The Hill killed people so regularly that he could hardly count the dead. He didn't know why these things obsessed him. His task was to pull as much good ore out of the pit as he could each day, as cheaply as possible, and send it off to Daly's smelter in Anaconda. He was good at it. He was the best in the business. Other companies had noticed, and tried to hire him away. But he was a Daly man, an Anaconda man, and he earned enough to buy a few lace doilies for his wife, or take her out to Meaderville for dinner now and then.

His weapons were rarely fists; they were sarcasm and fear. There were all sorts of males in the pits, ranging from quiet and timid ones to bristling damned fools. There were reckless powdermen determined to blow themselves up, and muckers who itched for a fistfight, and quiet family men who only wanted their three-fifty a day and would work hard for it. Penrose watched them closely. He didn't boss from aboveground, with rare trips into the pit. He stayed down there most of every shift, showing muckers how to muck rock, showing timber men how to brace the drifts, showing other men how to lay a turn sheet. He could do it all, and he took the time to make sure his men were doing it right.

The only thing was, men died. They got silicosis, miner's lung, drawing all that dust and dynamite fumes into their lungs, deadly fumes after each blast, with lethal bits of rock hanging in the air, ready to dig into a man's lungs, including Penrose's own lungs. He was no more immune than the rest. He could hardly count all the ways men died in the pits. He'd seen them all. And fought them all. Every time a man on his shift was killed, it struck him in the gut. Other shift bosses didn't give a damn, but he did. He might be the best shifter in Butte, but he wanted one thing more: to be the safest shift boss in Butte. And he was far from that.

He was still an hour away from the shift, plenty of time to find Brophy and keep him topside. Brophy lived in Dublin Gulch, a warren of miserable cottages jammed between steep slopes, mixed with corner pubs, mining machine dealers, stained trestles, shining rails, and equipment yards. There was always laundry flapping on lines there, absorbing grit and smoke from the mine boilers. That's where a lot of the newcomers collected. They had to start somewhere, and most often they found rooms with others of their kind. And Dublin Gulch was just a skip or two from the mines on Anaconda Hill, including the Neversweat. It all worked out. There were plenty of Brophy's countrymen to lend a hand to anyone in that miserable gulch.

As Penrose walked east, Butte seemed to grow more crowded and tired and worn. Women in babushkas trudged wearily on their daily rounds. By God, Butte was a city of muscular and tough people, and Singing Sean Brophy was just such a one, raising three children and keeping a wife fed, and still finding time to sip some Guinness and throw darts in Shannessy's Shamrock Ale House after his shift.

Penrose wasn't quite sure where the lad lived, but there would be dozens of people to steer him. High above, smoke streamed from the seven stacks on the hill, where boilers powered stamp mills, generators, and hoists. It was never silent in Dublin Gulch, not with the heart of the Anaconda's mining just up the hill. Mines were noisy; stamp mills nosier, ore trains and whistles and the rattle of rock shook the air at all hours.

But the wail he heard was not from the mines, but from a crowd of weary women before a small, well-kept frame house. There were a dozen, not a man in sight, all of them huddled at the stoop of the gray house. Spring breezes drove the mine smoke off this morning, and seemed only to amplify the wailing. Andrew Penrose had a moment of premonition, and savagely rejected it. There was no such thing as fate. He found a boy in ragged dungarees, who was staring at the commotion.

"Tell me lad, where does Sean Brophy live, eh?"

"Him that got killed?"

Something sagged in the foreman. "No, the living man, damn you."

"He cashed in. That's the widow lady in the doorway."

There was indeed a young, rail-thin woman with strawberry hair loose on her head, standing stolidly in the doorway. She wasn't crying. A boy in knickers clung to her skirts.

He approached warily, and halted before the women.

"It's Sean Brophy I'll be looking for," he said.

"You'll not find him now. And you're from the company?" asked a young woman.

"I'm his shifter, and I came to put him topside today."

"He's never going to go topside, sir. He's beyond sunlight now."

"I probably have the wrong man. I'm looking for Singing Sean Brophy, not Walleyed Brophy or Three-Finger Brophy."

"That's Singing's widow there, and don't you be disturbing her. She's got a hat pin she'll stick into you."

"There's no widows here. I want to talk to Sean, my shift man. I've got a new spot for him."

"Are ye blind, man? Can't you see she's not saying a word? Go away," an old crone said.

Penrose stood awkwardly, one foot and the

other, barred from further talk with these women by some mysterious unity among them.

"Go talk to him, the copper there," one finally said.

Indeed, a man in blue, with a helmet on his shaggy head, sat nearby, writing something in a pad with a pencil. Penrose knew the man: Big Benny Brice.

Penrose hastened that way, glad to escape the wall of women. "What's all this?" he asked. The copper eyed him warily. "I'm the shifter at the Neversweat," Penrose added.

"Lost a man, then. Got run over by an ore train. Empties going up the hill. He tried to hitch a ride, slipped, and ended up cut to bits. Train run straight over Brophy, cut off his legs like a guillotine had chopped him in two."

"But why?"

The copper shook his head. "Who knows, eh? Going to work, maybe. Things happen. Right on the street. Same rails as the streetcars use. It was Anaconda's train, sir. Taking those empties back to the mines. Who knows, eh? Happens all the time. A man wants a ride, puts a boot on the iron step, misses, and a dozen people watch him tumble under the wheels, and then there's blood all over the cobbles and the ore train halts a few blocks down, and I get to tell the widow."

"It's not fate," Penrose said. "It's not predestined. Nothing happens but by what

40

precedes it. No one wiggles a finger and says it's your turn now."

The copper stared.

"I'm sorry. I need to give my condolences to the widow, and make sure she gets a little, and hire a new man."

"You do that," the copper said. "You fix it all up good."

"It's not fate," Penrose said. "It wasn't ordained."

"He's been taken to Maxwell's," the copper said. "In three pieces. That's as ordained as it gets."

The widow sat mutely on the stoop, surrounded by her neighbors. Conversation had ceased. Penrose approached reluctantly, hat in hand.

"I'm sorry, ma'am."

She stared.

"I'll try to get you something. It didn't happen in the pit, you know. That makes it hard."

"They killed him," she said.

"A company train, yes. Maybe that will do."

"You some big shot?"

"I was his shift foreman."

"I won't get anything," she said.

"He wasn't watching where he was going," the copper said.

"We've lost a very good man," Penrose said.

"Cannon fodder," one of the neighbors said.

"Mountain View's like a battlefield cemetery," another said.

41

"They don't die for their country, they die for three-fifty a day," the widow said.

"I need your name, Mrs. Brophy."

"What good is that? I won't get anything." She paused. "Alice. Like thousands of Alices."

"I'll see what I can do."

She nodded.

Penrose stood awkwardly, but the mourners had retreated into their private world, so he tipped his hat and left. It wasn't far to the mine. Brophy should have watched out, he thought. It wasn't fate. There's only cause and effect, one thing leading to another. The more he thought of it, the more agitated he got. He'd not go to see Slanting Agnes again. He'd not succumb to such ignorance and superstition, and he hated the impulse within him that had driven him to visit her over and over.

There was a single hiring hall for all the company mines on Anaconda hill, so he stopped there, pulling the creaking door open. The place reeked of tobacco smoke, and maybe vomit. He steered around a battered desk to a rear office, and nodded at the fat walrus sitting there.

"I need a mucker," he said. "And don't send me bad merchandise."

"The union controls it," the walrus said.

"I'll control it," Penrose said.

"Who quit?"

"No one," Penrose said.

He felt weary even before the whistle blew. He

42

hadn't brought his lunch, the usual richly seasoned pasty his wife made so faithfully. But he could fetch a lunch. He wasn't imprisoned in the pit until the shift was done, like his men.

His men collected in the changing room, where they left coats and hats and gear and got themselves ready to descend nine hundred feet down, where no light ever shone but the light of candles or carbide lamps. His men would squeeze into the lifts and plunge with sickening speed down the black shaft, and then the lift would bounce on its cable and the men would spread into the workings.

The shift whistle wailed, and Penrose was reminded of a dirge. Just superstition, he thought. When the shift ended, the whistle sounded like a fire alarm. He couldn't explain it.

He stayed topside, awaiting the new man. He heard the whir of cables and drums in the hoist works, the steam plant that yanked men and ore, and sometimes worn-out mules, out of the earth, and dropped empty ore cars and weary men into the hole in the hill.

The new man came looking for him. He was black haired, squat, with slavic features, and assessing eyes.

"You the new mucker? What's your name?"

"Red."

"Red who?"

"Red the Socialist Gregor."

"You got a first name?"

"That's it."

"Where've you mucked?"

"All over."

"You been fired?"

"Everywhere. I usually last a week."

"Then what?"

"Someone doesn't like me."

"Why?"

"I stand up for the downtrodden."

"You're hired," Penrose said. "If you don't stand up for them, I'd not want you."

"Three dollars is below a just wage."

"You'll get more as soon as you prove yourself."

"Meanwhile you exploit me."

"Don't cause accidents," Penrose said.

"Accidents happen."

"No, accidents are caused. Everything is cause and effect. They don't just happen. It's not fate."

Gregor smiled. "You're the first boss who's ever said that. Maybe I'll work for you."

"Nine hundred level." Penrose watched the man stride toward the lift.

He had to talk to the super about Brophy's widow, and try to get the widow a couple of weeks' pay. Then he'd go give Gregor a close look.

Five

Royal Maxwell eyed the brown-soaked remains on his zinc-topped table. One thing about Butte, he thought. He never had to worry about his next meal. Butte was a mortician's paradise. The widow couldn't pay, but it wouldn't matter. Someone else would. There was opportunity in it.

He eyed the stack of pine boxes, and selected one without varnish or handles. The varnished ones cost two dollars more. Handles would add five. This would be easy. He'd load the beloved departed in and nail it down, and save all the work of undressing and dressing the deceased, or patting a little rouge on his cheeks, and all that. The widow wasn't going to see anything but a tight box.

The coppers had summoned him, and he'd gone with his ebony handcart, properly attired in a black swallowtail and silk stovepipe, and the pine box, and with white gloved hands, lifted the three parts of Singing Sean Brophy into his conveyance, covered Brophy with a gray silk sheet, while two or three hundred citizens of Butte watched. Then he had stood reverently, silk hat in hand, the cold breezes toying with his jet hair, and after a moment wheeled the handcart the six blocks to the rear of the clapboard Maxwell Mortuary.

He wouldn't need to wait long for the widow. They usually showed up in minutes, and indeed this one, Alice Brophy of Dublin Gulch, made her appearance with the sound of the door chime.

She was bone-thin, and had a little boy in tow, and wore a brown Mother Hubbard.

"I'm so sorry to hear of your misfortune," he said.

"What's it going to cost?" she asked.

"Oh, we won't worry about that now. Come sit down here and tell me what you want for your beloved husband."

"I haven't got anything anyway, so you can't stick me."

"He was a splendid man, Singing Sean was, and I know you'll want the best for him."

"When he wasn't drinking," she said.

"I hear he had a fine tenor voice, and a great repertoire."

"He was more interested in lifting my skirts," she said. "Now I'm stuck."

"Ah, yes, your little ones will want to remember their father, and visit his grave one day soon. You'll want a fine headstone, something that will endure through the ages, and you'll want the finest casket money can buy, and a double lot so when the time comes when—"

"I want to see him," she said.

"But that's not possible. You wouldn't want to see him. You'll want to remember him just as he was, loving and kind."

"I want to make sure it's him, and he's not skipping."

"But the casket's been sealed."

"Open it."

"No, madam, it would be too much for mortal eyes to bear."

"I've seen men that fell a thousand feet down the shaft, so I'll be looking at Sean."

"Well, let's deal with that later. We'll want to set an hour for visitors, and get some lots, and choose a coffin, and arrange a service of your choice. Shall I summon Father McGuire?"

"I'm not ordering a thing I can't pay for. Now show him to me."

"Ah, I'll need time to unseal the box, madam, and I don't think this is wise."

This was turning into a standoff, but not anything that Royal Maxwell could not deal with.

"Madam, my heart aches for you, and I think the best thing is to put all this off for a day, and for you to return in the morning when we can proceed in peace. Take this lad to his fatherless home, and think reverent thoughts and blessings and tomorrow we'll proceed according to your every wish."

"I knew you'd not let me see him. He's mine, I own him, and you won't let me see him."

"May I offer you a conveyance back to Dublin Gulch?"

"I'm not yet thirty," she replied.

He watched her sweep out, into the cold wind, and the door jangled behind her. He waited a few moments, found his placard saying he was out briefly, placed it in the curtained window, and slid into the biting spring air. The Butte Miners Union hall was just down the street, and Big Johnny Boyle would likely be right there.

The hall was stark, with cream-colored paint and stained brown wainscot, and a few handmade desks. Plus a lot of wooden chairs. Big Johnny Boyle, head of the Butte Miners Union, wanted it that way, and was oblivious to comfort anyway. He could stand up or sprawl on the floor as well as settle behind a rude desk, and not know the difference. Most of the time he was out of the place anyway, but the door was unlocked and any down-and-out person on earth could find shelter there. Boyle's real office was the Trelawney Tavern next door, where he conducted nearly all his union business and received visitors from a chair in the far corner, which may as well have been a throne.

Maxwell found him there, a mug of dark ale before him, staring at the racehorse lithographs on the wall. The place was not quite a restaurant, but there was always enough stuff on the bar, such as hard-boiled eggs and pumpernickel and big salty pretzels, to feed any beast.

"I know, and I've already started a collection," Big Johnny said.

"You'll want to give him a good send-off," Maxwell said.

"You kidding? Singing Sean Brophy, he was a lousy brother, hardly paid his dues, was always complaining. He'll get your pine-box special."

"His poor widow's distraught. You'll want to put the beloved into a good honest walnut coffin, you know. She hasn't got a dime."

"She'll get a month's pay."

"No she won't. This didn't happen in the pits, and the company won't pay a nickel."

Boyle stared, pondering that, blinking his brown eyes. "It's the company's fault. That was their ore train."

"And Sean tried to hop it on the streets of Butte and died undcr it."

"They'll pay," Boyle said.

"I don't think so. Alice Brophy's depending on you."

Boyle stared into his ale. "I'll shake it out of some pockets," he said. "And I got other ways."

"Enough to keep her going? Three children?"

"That was always his excuse, got to feed my kids so I can't pay dues. He got it exactly wrong. You pay your dues so you've got a union that'll get you enough to feed your kids. So my heart don't bleed one damned bit."

Royal Maxwell saw how it would go. "I'll give him a good send-off," he said.

"I'll send a few brothers over to console the widow," Boyle said.

There was yet another place to visit, but it would take a bit of luck. Marcus Daly was usually available if he wasn't in Anaconda or out at his stock farm in the Bitterroot, and was a soft touch. The top man for the whole Anaconda Company was often in town, working from his Daly Bank and Trust office, though more and more he relied on his cronies to run the company. Still, it was worth a try.

He tracked Daly down at the Butte Hotel, where he was in the saloon surrounded by people wanting something from him.

"You, is it?" Daly said. "Want a drink? How's business?"

"Improving every day, Mr. Daly."

"You're looking for some funeral cash."

"Singing Sean Brophy, yes. He leaves a widow and three children with nothing."

"It didn't happen in the pit, now, did it?"

"No, sir, but it was a company train."

"My shift boss Penrose was here a bit ago. He wanted a month wage for her. I said no, buy her a nice new gown and call it good."

"Gown?"

"She'll remarry in a week or two. That's how it goes. Give her a gown for the marrying."

There were a lot more males than females in Butte, and a new widow was a prize half the lonely miners would pursue even before Singing Sean was planted. The lady would do just fine.

"That's just right, Mr. Daly, but can I count on you to bury the man? The company man?"

Daly smiled. "Good work, Maxwell; I'll give you an A for effort."

"Then you'll accept the bill?"

"I like men who go for a profit," Daly said. "Send me the invoice."

Royal Maxwell worked his stovepipe hat around a little, and bowed. "It's a fine day, sir."

"It's never a fine day when one of my men dies, Maxwell."

Maxwell retreated, plunged out of the hotel into bitter sunlight, and hastened back to his funeral parlor. It had cost him an affront, but now he had some cash from the union and a hundred from Daly, and it had been a profitable spring day. He was lucky the big man was in town.

The newsboys were on the street, hawking the evening papers, so he invested a few cents in all three papers. The only one that interested him, though, was the *Mineral*, Clark's noisy sheet, which always had its own slant on the news. Including the death of an Anaconda miner.

The headline read: "ACM Train Claims ACM Miner."

The rest fit the bill: "This morning an ACM

51

miner, Sean Brophy, perished while trying to avoid an ACM ore train operating recklessly on city streetcar rails. Brophy was unable to escape the train, rolling at high speed through the heart of Butte to return the empty ore cars to the mines on Anaconda Hill. As usual, safety was not a consideration in the operation of the ore train, not even while it was rolling through Butte neighborhoods lying between the ACM mines and the railhead on the flat. Mr. Brophy is survived by his widow Alice and three children. The *Mineral* determined that the widow will receive no compensation, because, as ACM officials explain it, the accident didn't occur on shift or in the pit. The destitute widow says she has no plans, nor the means to feed her children."

That's the *Mineral* for you, Maxwell thought. He set it aside and hunted for the story in the *Butte Inter-Mountain*, the Republican paper operated by Lee Mantle, an editor with ambitions.

"Miner Dies Hopping ACM Ore Train," went the headline.

The text went a different direction: "A Butte miner employed by the Neversweat, Sean Brophy, attempted to hop a string of empty ore cars en route to Anaconda Hill this morning, slipped, and perished beneath the wheels of the cars.

" 'Employees are forbidden to hop the cars,' said mine manager Cyrus Wilkes, 'and do so at their own peril.' A flagman riding the lead car waved Brophy off, but the miner ignored the command and attempted the dangerous hop onto a moving train. The Butte police determined that Brophy died instantly. The company noted that the tragic death occurred on off time, and not during Brophy's shift, and not on ACM property, and has declined further comment. Brophy is survived by his widow Alice, and children Timothy, Thomas, and Eloise. Services are pending at Maxwell Mortuary."

Daly's own paper, the *Anaconda Standard*, which circulated widely in Butte, said nothing at all. Maxwell was annoyed. It meant he would need to buy a funeral notice in the *Standard*. ACM had a large hand in controlling the news in Butte, as well as the rest of Montana.

Royal Maxwell always enjoyed the rivalry, and especially enjoyed the *Mineral*, which was becoming the least scrupulous rag in the city, if not the state. He wished the other sheets would go out of business. But meanwhile, he'd make around two hundred on a hundred-dollar planting, and that always put him in a good mood. He might head for Mercury Street this evening, and spend a little even before he got it.

He scribbled out some funeral notices, setting the time as ten in the morning, two days hence, and summoned a messenger to deliver to the papers. Filthy McNabb showed up, and Royal was happy because Filthy was more reliable than

Watermelon Jones. He gave Filthy a dime and told him to deliver the notices to each of the papers in town.

Tomorrow, he would inform the widow that all the arrangements had been made, courtesy of Sean's union, and she would be free from the burden of arranging her husband's funeral. He remembered to set his two grave diggers to work. They would each get two dollars to dig the hole, wait out the funeral, and fill it up again. He'd order a wooden headboard, no sense fooling with granite, and that would take care of things, except for summoning a priest. Alice Brophy would be grateful, of course. Service was what Maxwell's was noted for.

Six

Big Johnny Boyle stood at the stately door with a small hitch of unfamiliar fear roiling him. He'd never been in the bank. He'd never met William Andrews Clark. In all of his dealings with Clark's mines and smelters Boyle had dealt with Clark's hounds, the cronies who turned Clark's commands into reality. But this time Clark himself wanted Boyle, and had sent Watermelon Jones from the Messenger Service with the message.

Boyle had heard a lot about Clark, and knew much more about the great man than Clark knew about any Irishman named Boyle. Clark was Scots, and that explained everything. Boyle knew exactly what Scotsmen were made of, and Clark was no exception. Clark would be dour, short, thin, and grim. It was not known whether anyone had seen Clark smile, much less laugh. You couldn't be a Scot and smile; that would be a contradiction. It was an odd thing. Scots were Celtic, Irish were Celtic, but the Scots got all the bad Celtic and the Irish got all the good Celtic.

Boyle couldn't understand the fear in himself. He was never fearful. He didn't rise to the top of the Butte Miners Union being afraid. He was as big as his name implicd, big enough to smack grumblers, knock heads, boot whiners, and shake dollars out of pockets. But this time fear roiled him. Well, if worse came to worst, Boyle could lift the little captain up by the scruff of the neck and shake the daylights out of him—and then fight off the dozen goons that surrounded the little Scot.

He guessed what this was about, but he would have to wait and see. He straightened up, plunged through the doors of Clark and Bro. Bank, headed up some creaking stairs to the second floor, and headed for the unmarked pebbled glass door that would admit him to the sanctum sanctorum. The note, written in a fine script, said simply that Mr. Clark requested the presence of Mr. Boyle at once. That's how it was with Clark. At once. Boyle had read it slowly; he wasn't a top-flight reader, having barely finished sixth grade, and he read at all only because he had designs larger than shoveling rock.

Much to his surprise, the owner of a dozen mines and mills in Butte sat alone behind a plain desk, the chair and desk on a platform. There was a door leading to adjacent offices, where his lackeys no doubt did the great man's bidding, but here, in a modest corner office with modest views of the bustling city, William Andrews Clark pulled his levers.

"Mr. Boyle, my good man, do come in," Clark said, extending a hand and offering a smile. So much for the lousy stories, Boyle thought, shaking the delicate white hand of the little fellow, who was most of a foot smaller. Boyle estimated Clark's height at around five seven, maybe eight in platform shoes, and a hundred pounds wet. His eyes were bright, his gaze penetrating, and Boyle felt himself examined from head to heel.

"You're Irish," Clark said. "A noble race."

Another myth tumbled into dust. Boyle had heard that Clark had nothing but disdain for the citizens of the Emerald Isle.

"Came here direct, and on Daly's dime," Boyle said.

Clark nodded. Butte was heavily Irish. Boyle's union was even more Irish, save for a few bleak and gloomy Cornishmen. Scots weren't popular with anyone in Butte save for the dozen or two Scots themselves.

"You may sit. When you stand you have the advantage of me," Clark said.

Big Johnny settled in a plain wooden chair. That's how this office was. There was not an ostentatious item in it; no gilt-framed oil portraits of fake ancestors, no walnut wainscoting, no velvet drapes, no Brussels carpets, no gold-plated spittoons.

"That's better. Now, let's cut to the chase. In a few months I will be Senator Clark. I'm going to take the seat. That means there are matters to negotiate. Namely, what I can do for you, and what you can do for me. You and your union."

Clark waited for the union boss to absorb that, but Boyle had already absorbed it before stepping into this austere throne room.

"Mister Clark, it's not easy to buy a labor union. Or sell one. And the brothers, we decide things together. Maybe you should talk to the brothers."

"Senator. Call me Senator Clark."

"Yeah, and call me Big Johnny, boyo."

Clark's attentions seemed to drift elsewhere, and settled upon a fly buzzing at the window.

"Kill it," he said.

Big Johnny didn't budge. The fly sailed through space and alighted on another pane.

Clark rang a little ringer on his desk. A plunge of a lever chimed a summons, and instantly a gent in a white shirt materialized.

"A flyswatter for Big Johnny," Clark said.

The weasel in white vanished and reappeared, carrying a wire-handled flyswatter and handed it to Boyle.

Clark was studiously eyeing the window.

"I think the time has come, boyo, to pay my brothers a four-dollar wage."

The going rate in the mines was three-fifty. Daly resisted. That was an odd thing. Daly had been a hardrock miner and spent plenty of his early life in the pits of the Comstock in Nevada, and Utah too. He still drained a mug of ale with his miners, and looked after them. And paid three and a half.

"If I plunge, Daly will follow suit, and then what?"

"The brothers will know who was first."

"Will that obtain their solidarity?"

"Nothing but the union does that, boyo."

"And you won't guarantee a thing, I suppose."

"They're Irish, and they mostly work for Daly."

"I'm American," the boyo said. "I've created thousands of American jobs for Americans. And in the Senate I'll do even better. I'll help repeal the silver law. I'll support eight-hour days. Eight hours for all who toil. If it's federal law, everyone must comply. Even Anaconda. I'll be known as the Friend of Labor."

That silver stuff was too much for Big Johnny to figure out, but Congress was lowering the price of it compared to gold, and that made everyone in Butte mad.

He shrugged. "No skin off my back," he said.

The fly circled Clark's desk and bombed Clark, messing around Clark's hairy face. Some men had handsome beards, well trimmed. Clark's was a mass of long hair surrounding his mouth, with hair drooping over his lips to strain any soup the man spooned into himself. It was a thick, matted, symbolic beard surrounding a voracious hole in the man, guarding his mouth like a forest of needles. The boyo's wife must have suffered.

Clark probably weighed not much over a hundred pounds, but he liked to eat, and he liked to conceal his eater behind all the shrubbery he could manage. Who could explain it? The boyo was beyond explaining.

"The brothers shouldn't have to go into the pits for less than five a day, boyo."

Clark twitched. His bright gaze fixed on Big Johnny a moment, and then followed the buzzing fly back to the window panes.

"Marcus Daly would take a strike before he'd go that high."

"Daly lifts some ale with the brothers. His company isn't Scots."

"You're a good man, Boyle. If ever you want to work for me, I pay a good wage. Some of my young assistants earn five thousand a year. You certainly have the makings of a man who gets things done, my sort of man. You show me what you can do with your brotherhood, and I'll show you what I do for rising young executives."

The windows blotted out street traffic. Not even the grind of the trolley cars penetrated the rich silence of Clark's chambers.

Big Johnny yawned, picked up the flyswatter, waved it a few times, stood, headed for the bright window, and dispatched the fly. Clark studied the fly on his maple floor. Then Boyle placed the swatter on Clark's shining desk, and stepped out of the sanctum.

An odd breeze lowered smoke from the smelters and boiler rooms over the city, stinging nostrils and throats. It was mostly wood or coal smoke, now that Butte was connected by rail to the coalfields of the state. The mining outfits had quit the open roasting of ores in town. They used to build giant bonfires over heaps of ore, to roast the ore before milling or smelting it. The smoke was laden with arsenic. Everyone in Butte coughed then, and old-timers still did.

Half the old guys he knew would trade a lower wage for anything that stopped miner's lung. They lived out their short lives panting for breath, every wheeze of their lungs hurtful and sad. They'd hopped the immigrant boats thinking that anything was better than starving in Ireland, but in Butte they put food on their table and rock dust in their lungs and were half dead ten years before the wake. That was mining for you. Long days shoveling rock in the dark, twenty years of being unable to breathe, and nothing much for your widow and babies.

Boyle found Eddie the Pick in the union hall. Eddie was a hothead. His plan was to storm the corporation offices, slit the throats of the big cheeses, take over the companies, and dole out wages instead of profits. That wasn't a bad idea, but Boyle thought the time wasn't ripe yet. In a few years, maybe.

"I think I just sold out," Big Johnny said.

"My price is a million; what's yours, Boyle?"

"I don't know yet. Those Scots have a way of ruining the rest of us. He offered to fight for an eight-hour day once he gets in."

"He's calling himself senator already."

"He had me kill the fly," Big Johnny said. "Doesn't that mean something?"

"You got me there, boyo," Eddie the Pick said.

"I didn't give him any answer, but I killed his fly," Boyle said. "Now he's going to call it a contract."

Eddie the Pick wheezed with joy. He was far gone with miner's lung, and his real goal was to take the world down with him when he went.

"You gonna put it on the table?"

"No. It's no one's business. But maybe I'll see what Daly's up to. I'm thinking politics is good business for the brotherhood."

"Nah, them captains of industry will think of a new way to screw us."

"It's a lever," Big Johnny said.

"Clark, he's a strange one. When he wants something, nothing stops him, including us. He's got no laugh in him. If he laughed once in a while, it'd be different. But he's as grim a man as ever walked the earth, boyo. That kind scares me. What does he want to be senator for, eh? Not to help anyone in Montana. Not for the money. He's got all the money he needs the rest of his life. Not for anything except looking at himself in the mirror and seeing a senator in the glass. He can buy anything, castles, railroads, men like us, women, fancy clothes. But a Senate seat takes some buying. First you got to put your own men in the legislature and then you got to have them make you the senator. That don't come cheap, boyo."

"Neither do I, Eddie, neither do I," Big Johnny said.

"I got the money for the widow," Eddie said. "Enough to pay Maxwell and a little left over. That's work, shaking it out of miners. They don't have but ten cents in their pockets, and that's to buy a pint after the whistle blows. But I got it. Maxwell's bargain burial is ninety-seven and there'll be some left over."

"So give yourself the change, Eddie. You made the widow happy. When is it, tomorrow?"

"Yeah, at ten. Maxwell, he told her to show up,

because that's what the notices say, so she'll be there. After that there'll be twenty brothers in line wanting to marry her. I wish they'd abolish marriage. It's the ruin of a man. And what business is it of government? Why should government care, eh? It's none of their business. When we take over, we'll abolish marriage. All it does is ruin men and wreck women and label half the children in the world bastards. Share all and share alike, that's my motto."

"But it doesn't work," Big Johnny said. "I ain't sharing with anybody, ever."

Seven

Alice Brophy stormed into Royal Maxwell's mortuary, found the undertaker sipping from a brown bottle, and lit into him.

"Tomorrow is it? And without asking me? Well, it won't be tomorrow. It'll be the next day. I'm sewing shirts and pants and a little dimity dress. I'll not have Sean's own babies going to their pa's burying in rags. I'll get them dressed proper, and you'll just have to wait a day."

"But madam, that's not possible. The notices were published. It's all set."

"No it's not all set, and you'll delay it a day. Tommy's going to get new britches, Eloise is going to get a white dress, and Timmy, he's got a clean blue shirt coming, and that's that."

"Why, I don't see how we can alter a thing."

"Without a word with me you set the day and the hour and now you can set a new day and a new hour."

"But I have another service scheduled."

"Well, that's too bad. I'm not coming to the one tomorrow, I'm not. I'll not bring Tom or Tim or Eloise either. You'll bury my man without the widow, without his children. And then what'll Butte think of you, eh?"

"They'll think nothing of it. They'll think you're being, well, a bit emotional, madam. Now please accept my sympathies, and we'll seat you at the service with a black veil wrapped about all of you, and no one will see a thing."

"And that's not our priest. What right have you to make these arrangements? I've never met this man. I won't be having a stranger blessing my husband, or saying words over him."

Royal Maxwell smiled, gently, out of long experience smoothing out the uproars of last rites. "We'll send a carriage, madam, at a half hour ahead, and you'll be settled nicely for the service."

She stared. "You're going to switch."

"No, madam, these things are settled."

"Go to hell, then," she said, and wheeled away.

She felt Maxwell's bland gaze on her back as she stormed out. She wondered if she could kidnap Sean and bury him on some hilltop somewhere. Let them gather without her. Let them do it without Sean's own widow and little ones. Just let them.

She needed to talk to Sean's shifter, Penrose. If not one of Sean's friends from the pit showed up, maybe that would show Maxwell a thing or two. Finding Andrew Penrose wouldn't be easy, but in an hour the second shift would begin, and he'd be up there somewhere. She headed up Dublin Gulch toward the Neversweat, but didn't see anyone about except for the topside men lining up an ore train.

But there was an office, and she penetrated it. The presence of a woman there startled the clerk, who wore a white shirt with black arm garters.

"Where is Mister Penrose—the shifter?"

"Madam, if you'll turn about, you'll see him behind you."

The shift boss eyed Alice Brophy, a quizzical look on his face. She spilled out her story in swift angry bursts, while he listened restlessly.

"Why, there's a remedy, madam. I'll stand the price of some readymades, not only for your children but for you. Go where you will, and take this," he said. He began to pencil a note on a sheet of yellow payroll paper.

"I can make my own clothing, thank you," she said. "What I want is for you to tell the men that worked with Sean not to go tomorrow; not a one

65

show up. Let Maxwell run his funeral without one living soul."

Penrose shook his head. "I can't do that, madam. I won't discourage any man who wishes to pay his respects from doing so. Those who want to bury your husband, they're free to do so and I'll not stand in their way. They'll go there to honor their friend Sean Brophy, and that should please you."

"But I want Maxwell to suffer."

Penrose simply shook his head.

She knew he was right, but that wasn't going to slow her down. She'd get the funeral she wanted or embarrass Maxwell's Mortuary, and that was how it was going to spin out.

Penrose stood quietly, his note written.

"No thanks," she said, ignoring the note, and whirled into the cold wind.

She'd make Maxwell stew in his arrogance one way or another. She picked her way down the worn trail, and headed straight for the union hall. She knew what she wanted, and she'd have Big Johnny Boyle do it for her.

Johnny was in the pub next door to the hall, which is exactly where she expected to find him. She entered, and won the scowls of the bartender and all the males standing there with one foot on the brass rail, sipping ale. She knew Big Johnny. Everyone in Butte knew him. He made sure of it. And a few had discovered his brass knuckles, too.

She marched straight toward him, but he caught

her arm and led her straight out of that male sanctuary and into the bright spring wind. And there she delivered her ultimatum. "Tell your men not to show up tomorrow. The widow won't be there. I'm going to strike, that's what. It's a widow's strike against Maxwell, treating me like that."

Johnny Boyle was grinning. "You got it wrong, dearie. I've ordered every brother who's not in the pits to show up. We're going to give our brother Sean a fine send-off, and maybe there'll be a few you'll want to visit with afterward."

She knew what he was talking about. The Butte Miners Union was a marriage mart, and she'd have her pick of a dozen after an appropriate week of mourning.

"I'll not have it your way, Johnny Boyle. Go ahead, fill up the funeral parlor, but you won't see Scan Brophy's widow or his three children there. Let them celebrate that, and if they're planning to look me over, and making plans without my consent, let them think that I don't love, honor, and obey anyone unless I choose to."

Boyle's black eyebrows arched.

She left him, and felt his gaze on her as she hurried away. They didn't want to help her. All they thought about was politics and money and ale. Well, she'd go back to Dublin Gulch and sew, and if she wasn't done in time for the funeral, too bad.

She spotted her neighbor Kegs O'Leary parking his wagon in front of his house. He operated a beer wagon and there was always a little spillage or a faulty keg that he needed to take care of to keep the beer from going to waste. Now he wiped his hands on his once-white apron and lifted a sweating keg to the dirt.

"So it's you, is it? My condolences to you, Mrs. Brophy."

"They're going to bury him tomorrow and never asked me, and I'm not ready, I'm sewing a dress for Eloise. And shirts for the boys."

"Maxwell's didn't?"

"Not once. They didn't even ask me what priest. Am I supposed to send off my own man with his children in rags?"

"That's a venial sin, I'd say, Mrs. Brophy. Rags at a funeral."

"And the union wouldn't help me and Sean's shift boss, he at least cared a little."

The beer man stared at the smoke-shot sky. "Would you be wanting a wake for poor Sean, Mrs. Brophy? Would you be wanting to bring poor Sean back to his own little cottage one last time, and keep him there until you get the sewing done?"

She stared at him, and finally nodded.

"I think I'll just drive over to Maxwell, Mrs. Brophy. I'll put this keg in your kitchen for future use. And I think I'll let Sean's brothers come and mourn this evening if it pleases you."

Maybe the world would be made right again, she thought.

Kegs O'Leary snapped the lines over the croup of his big Percheron and drove off, turning west toward the funeral home.

"There now, he's a man who knows his way into a woman's heart," she said to Tommy, who was clutching her skirts.

She settled down to sew on the dimity dress, and had just hemmed the skirt when she heard the clop and rattle of Kegs's beer wagon. She hurried outside and found him removing two sawhorses from his wagon, which he carried into her small parlor and spaced about five feet apart. "I don't have a thing to cover them," he said.

But she did. She had two white sheets. By the time she had these draped over the sawhorses, Kegs was settling the plain pine box on the sawhorses, almost as easily as he hefted kegs of beer.

"I'll put out the word, Mrs. Brophy," he said.

"Please do." She couldn't think of what else to do, so she kissed him. He turned bashful and wiped his cheek.

"Maxwell wasn't even there, so I just backed up the wagon, lifted Sean here, and drove off. I think it's Sean. He weighed about two kegs. There was another, but polished oak and all."

"That's Sean here," she said. "Oak is for heretics."

"I'll put the word out, Mrs. Brophy. This evening, will it be?"

"This evening, Mr. O'Leary."

"I'll be stealing a kiss," he said.

She watched him climb onto his beer wagon and haw his horse ahead.

Everything was right. She settled in a parlor chair, a few feet from the pine box, and began sewing industriously. Everything was perfect, as much as a widow could want.

Sean's union brothers would be on shift, but his brothers from across the sea would come, and maybe that was best. County Clare brothers, County Galway brothers. And there was even an untapped keg in her kitchen, so that she could be hospitable. She thought of her good luck, and Sean's good luck, and how the world was a good place. Even Butte.

She sewed furiously, adding a collar and cuffs to Eloise's white dimity dress.

"There now, go try it on, dearie," she said.

"Is that Daddy in there?"

"It is. Sean Padraic Brophy."

"Why is he there?"

"So his friends can remember him and send him off."

"Where is he going?"

She smiled. "He's going to be with the angels. Maybe, anyway."

The girl took her dress and headed for her

alcove, where she had a bunk. The boys had bunks in the other alcove. Alice and Sean's bed stood behind two hanging drapes in the corner of the parlor. Alice eyed the brown drapes, and decided to take them down. She didn't need them anymore. She clambered up on a wooden chair and undid the cords, and the weary cloth tumbled. The room looked different somehow with her bed in it. She felt exhilarated, now that she could live without curtains hanging around a part of her life. Suddenly her whole life was contained in one large room: the kitchen and parlor. She could see the boundaries of her life from where she stood.

She fussed with Eloise's white dress for a while, unhappy because one side seemed to dip below the other, and she finally decided Eloise was lopsided, her left side smaller than the other, and she would leave it be.

The boys barged in. What they did out in the gulch she was glad not to know, but they were uncommonly clean this time, for which she was grateful. She fed them some porridge, and had just finished up when the first of her guests arrived. That turned out to be Kegs himself.

"I thought I'd get the keg pouring right, Mrs. Brophy, so the brothers have more than suds to sip on."

"I don't know what I'll do for cups and mugs," she said.

"They'll bring their own, madam."

She watched him tap the keg and screw in a faucet, and settle it on a counter, and try a few golden swallows to draw off the foam.

And then at twilight the first guest came, and she saw through the glass that he was bringing flowers, and she wondered what she would put them in. She opened up, and beheld a man in a gray suit, cravat, and fedora, standing solidly before her.

It was himself, Marcus Daly.

Eight

One swift glance told Marcus Daly everything. The coffin rested on its sawhorses with a silken green cloth over it. The Dublin Gulch house barely held a family. Alice Brophy was work-worn, bone-thin, freckled, and with spun-gold hair.

"Sir?" she said, fiercely wiping her hands on her apron.

"Marcus Daly here. I can only stay a bit, Alice Brophy. Here's a few daisies to remember Mr. Brophy with."

She took them timidly, and attempted to curtsey.

"Word came to me that the funeral home wasn't helpful. Here, take this card. It's a way to reach me. Whenever you say, I'll send a carriage for the remains, and I'll have a grave ready at the cemetery, and if I can manage it, I'll have your parish priest present for the burying. All this will be at the time and place of your choosing. Send a messenger boy to the place here on the card, ask for my subaltern Hennessy, and he'll make it be."

"But sir, how can I repay you?"

"Name your next boy Tammany, Mrs. Brophy."

"But—lord, how did you know? And why me? Us?" She slid her hands over her children, who clustered at her skirts.

"The Anaconda Company has risen out of Ireland, Mrs. Brophy, and we look after our own."

She nodded. "But we've tapped a keg. Won't you stay?"

"You make a bouquet of daisies for Scan Brophy, and I'll be going now."

"Oh, sir . . ."

He smiled and left, walking the bare-dirt path to the rutted grade, where his ebony trap stood, with one of his fine trotters in harness. She watched from the door. Her house had been whitewashed once, but that was gone and what remained was gray wood.

He drove off, through one of the most twisted thoroughfares in Butte, so bleak that nothing but flame could remedy the ugliness. He felt that yearning for which there was no word, something akin to loneliness even when he was surrounded by his closest friends. It was something he couldn't explain. It was that yearning that drove

73

him to the widow's house, and the yearning that had inspired a company that was almost an outpost of Ireland.

He'd heard about Maxwell's affront to the woman soon after it happened. Maxwell treated the Irish as if they were sardines. The mortician would bury Sean Brophy in the morning, keep the flowers, and stage a fancier funeral in the afternoon for someone with another kind of surname. But let it be said among Butte's Irish that Marcus Daly spared the widow a little grief and shame.

Just up the hill were his three best mines, a ramshackle cluster of headframes, boilers, and sheds, all working the same massive seams of copper, laced with silver. Just keeping them going and profitable consumed his energy and his life. There was no stability in a mining operation. Whatever bad might happen probably would, no doubt all at once.

He had risen to every challenge, expanded and enriched his company even while building an idyllic life for himself raising blooded horses in the Bitterroot Valley. He thrived on the competition, including the competition of horse racing, and his stock farms had produced a succession of winners. He thought he was like his prize Thoroughbred Tammany, who kept his nose ahead of the pack because he had to.

Always trouble. There was pressure in Congress

to repeal the Sherman Silver Purchase Act, which provided that the federal government buy several tons of silver each month. Without those purchases Butte would sink into idleness if not depression. Then there was the Montana Union Railroad, charging monopolistic prices to haul Anaconda's ore from the mines to the smelter thirty or so miles away. Daly had his remedy for that, his own Butte, Anaconda and Pacific Railroad, but that wouldn't be finished until next year.

He had erected the enormous upper and lower smelters over there because that was where he found the nearest water, in Warm Springs Creek. Rival companies had claimed all the water around Butte, and every drop of Silver Bow Creek. Then there was the problem of getting timber enough to run his mines and smelters. He needed four hundred thousand board feet a year to fire his boilers, supply mine timbers, and build his buildings. He and various lumber barons had been cutting public forests, mostly sections interlaced with the Northern Pacific's railroad lands, but the Cleveland administration was putting a stop to it. His own Democratic Party was threatening his livelihood and that of all his miners. What could a man do but buy coal anywhere in Montana and Wyoming he could get it, and build rails to get it to Butte and Anaconda?

There was trouble in Butte. To get his ore off the

hill he had to share his right of way with the trolley cars. There were apex lawsuits to deal with from rival mining companies. Copper prices were low and declining. There were elections coming up, and he needed a slate of candidates that would look after the company's interests.

And now he faced another effort by William Andrews Clark, the dour Scots genius who was not content to own much of Butte Hill, but wanted to wear a senator's toga as well. Wherever Daly sought to make a move, there was Clark checking him. The election of 1888 had started it all. For business reasons, Daly wanted to form an alliance with certain Republicans and elect someone who would oppose the administration. He and Clark were both Democrats, but there was a difference: Clark was a rigid loyalist, while Daly was a man to go after coalitions that would do what the company needed. And in the end, Daly rescinded his support of Clark, and had his numerous employees vote for a Republican, Tom Carter, who won the seat by a narrow margin. Clark never forgave him, as rigid in his anger as he was in his politics.

Daly never thought of it as a personal struggle, although he didn't care for Clark. The dapper dandy was a distant relative by marriage, so Daly had avoided contention, while quietly undermining Clark's support among the coalitions that owned Butte. It was all for the company, he thought. Just business. Not for himself, not to punish Clark. Just for the company, and all those men he was responsible for, the men whose pay envelopes put food on their tables and sheltered their families from the brutal winters on the Continental Divide.

But that wasn't the limit of his ambitions either. The new Montana constitution had left it to the citizens to choose a state capital. Helena was the temporary capital, but Daly had other ideas. His shining new city of Anaconda had been laid out to perfection, with broad boulevards and generous lots and sweeping views. It was rising at the foot of Mount Haggin, named after the California financier and major owner of the company, who had underwritten the whole expansion of the Anaconda Mining Company into the dominant business in the new state. It was the most beautiful place on earth.

What better place than Daly's own city of Anaconda, with a grand capitol building at the foot of Mount Haggin, and a welcome proximity between state officials and the company's own directing class? But William Andrews Clark had no intention of letting that come to pass. So it was all politics, politics, politics, from mayors and aldermen on up. And Daly had not forgotten that Butte was Irish, and Daly himself had made it so, and the numerous Butte Irish were the key to all the state's elections to come.

And that brought him back to the story he discovered in that evening's edition of The *Mineral*. It was all about the woes of the widow Alice Brophy, whose late husband had been employed at the Neversweat, and who had been denied a pension by the ruthless company that had employed him. And how the Butte Miners Union members had dug deep into their pockets to give the brother a funeral, and how an Anaconda ore train had taken the life of a hapless miner.

Marcus Daly had thought to protest, to tell the editor that a few facts were missing. But he knew better than that. He wasn't quick with words, and whatever he said would be turned into fodder for another twisted story. Still, he wanted to do something about it, and decided it was time to meet the new editor, the one William Andrews Clark had hired to do whatever jobbery he could do and in any way he wished so long as it tore at the fabric of Daly's company, and Daly himself.

No, he would not get into a sparring match with words. Instead, he would simply meet the bloke who called himself John Fellowes Hall, as if his name were a three-piece suit. He would ask questions. He'd do the interviewing. It was time to take the measure of the thug whose bludgeons were words and phrases, and who stole a man's honor and a company's good name. There would be things to find out: was Hall simply Clark's goon? And maybe he could find out what Clark hoped to get out of this barrage of character assassination.

Daly steered his trap back toward central Butte, which rose proudly on the slopes below most of the mines. The newspapers were all cheek by jowl, and he found a place before the *Mineral* to park the trap and keep the horse tethered to a carriage weight.

He remembered that newspapers were inky places. The ink jumped at you. Leapt from distant presses and typesetting tables, smeared you as you dodged your way through, and ruined the clothing of innocents. He was greeted by the acrid smell of the Linotypes, but he was used to that. His own paper, the *Anaconda Standard*, had nothing but the finest equipment that his money could buy.

Daly eyed a window-lit corner at the rear, and the sunlit gentleman in the alcove who radiated brightness, and decided the man looked like his quarry, so he dodged his way through the smoky plant and presented himself at the gate.

Hall, dressed nattily, especially for a newsman, stared up, recognized the man at his door, and stood.

"Mister Daly, is it?" he asked.

"I'm Daly. You're Hall."

"John Fellowes Hall, yes. What may I do for you?"

"Nothing at all, Mister Hall. I just wanted to

79

stop by and welcome you to Butte. You're new, are you?"

"Not to journalism, sir. I've been editing newspapers in the East for many years."

"Well, that's fine. What papers did you edit?"

"Oh, names you wouldn't know, sir, New York, New Jersey, Pennsylvania, Ohio, all splendid papers."

"What brought you here, sir?"

"Well, I bested the competition. My employer—ah, Mr. Clark, searched widely for the sort of talent he wanted, and finally settled on me, after looking at several dozen applicants. Of course I was greatly honored. He's offered me unusual remuneration, which I have taken to be a sign of his confidence in me."

"I've started up a paper of my own, you know, over in Anaconda, and got a good man there. What did Clark look for in an editor?"

"An ability to penetrate to the truth of things lying just under the surface, Mr. Daly. He wanted a man who'd be a natural skeptic, a good man with words and ideas, and a man who might know how to advance Mr. Clark's many interests in public affairs, business, politics, and theology. He's a devout Methodist, sir, and a knowledge of scriptures was paramount with him. He told me frankly, a man who knew the Bible was a man who would have the inside track to this position."

"What's your favorite verse, Mr. Hall?"

"Why, I'll paraphrase here. Don't stick it to others when you don't want them to stick it to you."

"Very interesting, Mr. Hall, a motto worthy of Caesar. Well, I was just passing by, and thought to take the opportunity to introduce myself."

"I'm happily employed, Mr. Daly, and not ready to accept any change in my circumstances. But it was kind of you to inquire."

Daly stared, and thought to make something of it. "I tell you what, Mr. Hall. You've got splendid credentials. Put your credentials down and send them to me by messenger so I'll know where to look for such outstanding talent if I should need to find someone. I may be buying more papers, you know. Maybe one in Helena, maybe one in Missoula. And probably Great Falls. And I'm always on the lookout for a gifted, loyal man."

Hall seemed to light up a little. "I'll prepare a little package for you, sir. Read it with care."

Daly scarcely knew whether to shake Hall's stained hand, finally did so, and made his way safely out of the building. The air was much better outside.

Nine

The burying was perfunctory, and Alice Brophy was driven to Dublin Gulch in the black carriage and deposited at her cottage. That was fine; the wake had lasted into the wee hours, and that was fine too except that her outhouse stank worse than usual. She only wanted a nap.

Someday she would put a marker on the grave. But she knew where Sean was, and maybe she'd go see him sometime. He didn't deserve it, but she would.

Her children vanished into the spring afternoon, and she settled down in an old morris chair where she could see the daisies that Mr. Daly had brought. She was glad there weren't a lot of neighbors around, trying to solace her. She didn't need solacing. But she had hardly got her feet up when she was summoned to her door by knocking. Wearily she slid into slippers and opened up.

She knew the man slightly. He was Edward Petrovich, Eddie the Pick, of the Butte Miners Union. She didn't want to invite him in.

"You settled and all right?" he asked, brushing aside her and entering unasked.

"I wish to rest now."

"I'm sure you do, but Big Johnny's got some business with you. You want to come along?"

"Big Johnny Boyle? Me? What does he want with me?"

"He paid for Sean's funeral."

"Mr. Daly did."

"The union brothers did, and now the chief wants to see you."

"I will go some other time."

"No, this is a good time." He grabbed her arm and forcibly steered her out of her home and directed her toward downtown Butte. She tried to work free, but his clamp on her was nothing she could resist, and short of tumbling in a heap there was nothing she could do.

"All right, I'll come, but lay off me," she said.

He nodded and let go. Her arm hurt. She wished she had a handbag so she could whack him with it. He walked beside her, plainly ready to grab her if she bolted. But she knew better than that.

"Finc way to spend this day," she snapped.

A while later she found herself in the Butte Miners Union hall, face to face with Big Johnny.

"The widow lady's here. He's planted, is he?" Boyle asked.

"No thanks to you. Mr. Daly's kindness did it."

"Is that how your treat the brothers? No thanks to the ones that dug into their britchcs to bury their brother Sean Brophy?"

She thought about Maxwell and all that and decided not to say a word.

"Good news, sweetheart. I've got a husband for you, Alice," Big Johnny said. "He'll take you and the brats."

"I don't want a husband. At least not now."

"Well you've got one. The union did right by you, so you got to help the union. His name is Mickey Metzger. He's got a lot of seniority, and was first in line."

"First in line, is he? Well he's not first in my line."

"Ah, now, you and Sean, the union gave Sean his job and made sure he was treated right, and now you'll want to treat the brothers right. Mickey Metzger is a good man, a little bald and he's got yellow teeth, but otherwise real bonny."

"Is that what you think? I'm union property? Well let me tell you, Big John, I'm not going to marry anyone. Sean, all he did was climb all over me and then I had more dirty diapers to clean. I'm not going to marry any Mickey or Freddie and have him hand me more dirty diapers, and that's that."

She glared at him hard. He might be the boss, and there might be about ten union men for every available woman, but she wasn't going to let him boss her around.

He smiled suddenly. "You owe the brothers for a funeral, sweetheart. I'll come collecting."

"Ha! What do you know about marriage, Big

John? Whatever you catch down on Mercury Street, that's what."

He shrugged her off, and Eddie the Pick steered her toward the door.

She stood outside in the wan sun. It wasn't over. They'd come knocking. They'd find a way. There'd be some grimy galoot busting her bedsprings in a day or two. It made her mad. She could probably go complain to Father O'Toole, but he'd likely tell her to do her female duty.

She made her weary way back to Dublin Gulch. The smoke was lowering over town again, searing her throat. She found Eloise curled up inside, staring at the flowers.

"Did Daddy go away?" she asked.

"He's dead and gone," Alice said.

"Are we poor now?"

"Yes. We'll just have to stick together more."

Eloise stared. The sawhorses still stood in the room. "Pa got took away," she said.

The boys burst in, and studied the sawhorses which now carried no burden.

"Tom, Tim, you take these sawhorses out. Then you wash," she said.

"He croaked," Tom said. "He got run over and bit the dust."

Alice didn't rebuke him. Let the children work it all out on their own terms.

"Will he go to heaven?" Tim asked.

"If he had a four-leaf clover on him," Tom said.

"Of course he will," Alice said, not at all certain of it.

The boys took the heavy sawhorses out the door, and then poured water into a washbowl from the pitcher beside it, and scrubbed.

There wasn't much to eat, but that was nothing new. She scouted the cupboards, looking for anything, but a tapping on the door interrupted.

She found her neighbor, Mrs. Cantwell, with a basket on her arm.

"I thought you'd not want to be frying cakes on an evening like this," she said.

She pulled away a napkin, revealing a tureen of chowder, the scent savory.

"Oh, Claire," Alice said. "Oh, dear Claire."

Mrs. Cantwell swiftly ladled her chowder into bowls, and set the children to eating.

Alice wasn't hungry but she found comfort in seeing the children spoon the thick soup into their mouths.

"There now," the neighbor said. "That's the way. I knew you wouldn't want to cook. It's bad enough cooking for a man, but worse when there isn't one to cook for, Alice. But you'll find someone. They always do, especially here. I could name a few men if you want. I know one especially, a fine lad, Algernon, and he doesn't even work in the pits. He drives the streetcars."

"I don't need a man, Mrs. Cantwell."

"Why, that's like saying you didn't need Singing Sean Brophy!"

She was right, but Alice thought to keep silent.

The children licked the last of the chowder, Mrs. Cantwell refilled their bowls until the tureen was empty, and then the neighbor retreated into the evening.

It struck her that she needed to make an unusual decision, and one she would never tell anyone about. She needed to decide whether to grieve for Sean Brophy. She wasn't sure she grieved for him at all. Wasn't sure she missed him. Wasn't sure she would ever yearn for his attentions in their bed. Wasn't sure but what he made her life harder. What did he give her but pails of dirty diapers? Sometimes he drank up the pay before she saw it, and then they could hardly feed themselves.

On the other hand, he had a quick smile and a quick hand when it came to grabbing a handful of her, and she liked that. And most of the time he did bring the brown pay envelope home. And he did no harm to the children. He didn't beat them or anything, even when he yelled at them. And once he took her on a picnic, and sometimes they went to a party together. So maybe she should grieve him after all. He was better than nothing.

She decided she would grieve him for a little while. She didn't have anything black, but she could find a black rosette or a black armband, and wear that, and then people would know that she was pining for Singing Sean. She could grieve maybe a week, and then decide about a marriage. It wouldn't be to Mickey Metzger. She'd pick someone. She wasn't going to get shoved into anything. She'd take her time, too. Whoever wanted her could just show it a little, and buy her a ribbon or a hat, or take her to Helena on a holiday. With any kind of luck he'd be impotent, and she wouldn't have to worry about all that. But she'd been real unlucky on that count. Sean had wanted her about twice a day and three times on Holy Days.

That evening the racket from the mines seemed louder than usual. The stamp mills were thundering, ore dropped down chutes into ore cars, the whistles were howling. There wasn't much peace in an eventide in Butte, and twilight was never a vespers. She got into her nightdress and then invited her children into her bed.

"Come rest beside me, dearies," she said.

Eloise liked the idea, but Tim and Tom eyed her sternly, afraid that she'd get mushy or something. But they settled beside her, the girl on one side, the boys suspiciously waiting on the other.

"Your pa is gone and we've got to stick together," she said.

"I miss him," Eloise said. "I'm going to cry."

The boys didn't deign to surrender to this female sentiment.

"It seems like everyone's got notions in their

88

heads. Just because we've lost Sean, they all have schemes. The company doesn't want anything to do with us. They say, the accident didn't happen during his shift, and he shouldn't have hopped the ore car. They're right. They took his labor and paid him a wage and all is even. The union thinks I owe them something. They got your pa his job, good pay, and pushed for safety too. But I don't owe them anything. Your pa paid his dues so we're even. Your pa gave something and got something from them. But they're pushing on me to find a new man."

"I don't want a new daddy," said Tom.

She sighed. "I'll fight as long as I can. A woman doesn't have much say in it. But here's what I'm thinking about. There's always some work in the hotels. I can make beds and sweep rooms and do laundry. It gets me fifty cents a day. Your pa was getting three-fifty, but the union got some of it and there were others that had their fingers in his pocket now and then. Fifty cents maybe, it isn't enough. But Tom, you're old enough to sell newspapers. You get one cent for each paper sold. If you could sell a hundred papers, you'd earn a dollar a day."

The boy stared at her. This was the first time in his young life he'd even imagined he could earn money, like his pa did.

"Tim, you're almost old enough to be a messenger boy. You need to learn to read better so you know where to take messages. So you work hard on reading, and I'll see whether they'll take you to run messages. That might earn you fifty cents, and maybe a tip too.

"We can live if we all work. And I can sew and mend. I mended your pa's britches and things. Mines, they tear cloth apart, you know, and the miners are in rags. So I can do that, and maybe you can help me, Eloise."

She stared up at her mother, but didn't say anything.

"If we earn two dollars a day, we can live," Alice said. "Your pa soaked up some, and we don't have to feed him or keep him in boots. Oh, and don't forget we can find things that got tossed away. Firewood, anything of value. We'll get that. Timmy, until you're bigger, there's something for you to do every day. Tomorrow, get a sack and pick up coal that's fallen on the tracks. There's always some. Get us enough for next winter. We've got to keep the stove going."

The children stared uneasily, processing all of that. They had just discovered they would have to support themselves, at least in part, the rest of their lives. Whatever anyone felt like saying about Sean, he'd kept his family clothed and fed and sheltered.

"Maybe you should find a new pa," Eloise said.

"Now you mind your own business! I'll decide that! Now you all go to bed!"

She watched the children slide away. They'd had a hard three days, and she had just made the future harder.

She lay in the darkness, mad at Singing Sean Brophy.

Ten

At last. The messenger boy, Watermelon Jones, had delivered a note to John Fellowes Hall. It was from Clark, his employer.

"I'll catch you next time," Hall said to the messenger.

The boy in the stiff green uniform looked a little crestfallen, and retreated. Hall thought that such louts should not be overtipped, and limited himself to a nickel every third or fourth delivery.

Hall's presence was requested at the Clark bank in an hour. It was initialed by Clark. Good. That would give him time to get a shoeshine and spruce up. Newspaper plants had a way of grinding ink and grit into everything, and the *Mineral* was especially bad because nothing separated the editorial sanctum from the typesetting.

Finally, finally, the talents of the editor were about to be recognized. Maybe there would be a raise. He had discovered that he was not earning as much as Marcus Daly was paying Durston, the editor of the *Anaconda Standard*. That offended

Hall right down to his bone marrow. He thought the *Standard* wasn't worth the paper it was printed on.

He had not received a word of praise or encouragement from his employer. For weeks on end, Hall had brilliantly filled the columns of the *Mineral* with items that damaged Marcus Daly, or raised questions about what the Anaconda Company was up to.

There had been frequent editorials boosting Clark's effort to win a seat in the Senate. He had praised Clark's skills, let it be known that Clark was a friend of the workingman, announced that Clark, in the Senate, would checkmate efforts to repeal the Silver Purchase Act, which Butte relied upon for its prosperity.

He had lambasted the Republicans, supported the Democrat candidates for the Montana legislature, which in turn would elect a senator in 1893. He had warned against the rising Populist movement, with its hostility against malefactors of great wealth, and expressed outrage that Marcus Daly was making common cause with these rural bumpkins.

He knew himself to be a splendid newsman, maybe the only top flight one in Butte. Nothing escaped him. He despised his cubicle in the servant quarters of Clark's brick mansion, but also saw the utility of it. Good newsman that he was, he had befriended the servants, and found out most everything there was to know about Clark. Those political dinners, for example. Clark was carefully wooing the candidates at sumptuous meals, placing a costly favor at each place setting. Some of these were diamond stickpins for cravats. Sapphire brooches for the ladies, although Clark entertained few of them.

The only thing that truly annoyed Hall was that he hadn't been invited to these affairs. Surely he should have been at Clark's elbow, meeting the candidates, sharing philosophy, acquiring valuable insights that he could place in the news columns. He resented being confined to servant quarters, as if he were the equal of a chambermaid. Clark hadn't the faintest idea of the professional skills and experience that went into the making of a seasoned newspaper editor. He seemed to regard Hall as someone on a par with a pipe fitter or deliveryman. What did this idiot of a financier know about editing? What did he know about nuance? The meaning of words? The art of rhetoric? The things learned in schools and in the school of life?

Hall had sent clippings from the *Mineral* to his employer, intending by main force to call attention to his work. But all he received was cold silence. He deserved a raise, too, especially for his reports on Daly's railroad, but no raise was forthcoming. Each week the printers and reporters at the paper would receive their pay in a brown envelope, and that included Hall.

Each day, he had expected a summons to the bank office, where he would receive a word of praise or a little favor of his own. He could use a diamond stickpin for his own cravats. But nothing happened. That's when he decided, as long as he was stuck in the mansion, to learn more details about Clark. It didn't matter what: just details that might someday be useful. And so he collected information wholesale. Who made Clark's silk hats. How many pairs of cuff links the man had. Who bought Clark's expanding art collection. Who paid Clark's bills. And why were they sometimes not paid in a timely manner?

It became routine for Hall to know of every guest, and know the gist of every dinner conversation, and the names of all of Clark's household suppliers and outfitters. He also knew who visited in off hours, the furtive meetings, the names of men who slid into the mansion at odd hours, only to hasten into the dark soon after.

And still not a word of praise. Hall considered himself a loyal man, and knew that he would endure Clark's neglect because he must. But one of these moments, when he finally had a chance to talk with his employer, he'd let slip the fact that Marcus Daly might well want him as an editor at one of Daly's several papers. Maybe that would awaken some sense of Hall's true worth. If Daly wanted him, then Hall's value would go up.

Maybe there'd also be a fine Christmas bonus.

Meanwhile, he was busy turning his paper into the most brilliant sheet in Butte. He used a lot of two-dollar words to show his erudition. He wanted to reach the most influential people, not the hoi polloi, who could barely read anyway. So he used elegant words, just to show the world that the *Mineral* had arrived.

Clark had summoned him. So John Fellowes Hall swiftly wiped his hightop shoes, buttoned a fresh-starched collar on his shirt, and headed up the slope to the Clark and Bro. Bank, filled with excitement. On this breezy day he would receive a raise, or at least commendation, or maybe a privately voiced assignment that would propel Clark into the United States Senate.

Butte was a noisy place, and one lived in the midst of subdued roar. Steam boilers hissed, ore rattled down chutes and into hopper cars, whistles howled, trolley cars clamored along their rails. And for some odd reason, everyone shouted. Why couldn't the citizens of Butte address one another in muted tones?

Hall passed a corner where the boys from rival papers hawked their wares, usually by reciting the headlines, or jamming a paper into a passing man and waiting for their nickel. There were plenty of papers in town, so each busy corner was turf to be fought over by rowdy newsboys, and once in a while some poor little bugger got driven off, and

95

had to sell his sheet where there was less traffic.

"Hey! The copper king bought a smelter!" yelled one.

Hall ignored him.

"City faces doom!" yelled another, a red-haired punk. He was smirking. He knew how to sell, and was pushing copies onto people. Hall eyed the headline. "Silver Bill Advances," it said in large type.

"Doom! Three cents, pal," the little bohunk yelled. "Doom for Butte!"

Smart lad. But he wasn't selling the *Mineral*. He was a damned Republican. That was the *Butte Inter-Mountain* sailing out of his freckled paws. But if there was anything people of all parties in Butte agreed on, it was the menace of repealing the Sherman Silver Purchase Act which required the government to purchase a lot of silver each and every month.

Hall escaped, and plowed through the polished doors of the bank, and hastened up the creaking stairs to the sanctum sanctorum. This would be a great day, and he'd remember to write home about it.

Clark's shapely secretary, who wore tight pleats this summery day, nodded. She seemed to know who Hall was, because she vanished behind pebbled glass doors, and returned swiftly.

"Mr. Clark will see you now, Mr. Hall."

He wasn't forced to cool his heels, and that was

an excellent sign. He straightened his cravat, and plunged in. The great man was waiting. This warm day he wore a brown broadcloth suit of clothes, with tan silk lapels, and a cherry-colored cravat. This was as informal as the mining magnate ever got.

"Sit! Sit!" Clark said.

Hall did, but Clark remained upright in his patent leather shoes. It evened things up. They were eye to eye.

The paper's losing money," Clark said.

"But gaining influence," Hall said.

Clark looked annoyed. "Influence doesn't pay the bills. The fact is, advertising revenue has declined in every week since you took over. And the paper is selling fewer copies, too."

Hall didn't like the sound of that. "But we've got your campaign going. We're making you the next senator."

"The *Mineral* is not earning a profit. Everything I own earns a profit. If it doesn't earn a profit, I get rid of it. And that includes newspapers."

"Ah, we could put newsboys on more corners."

"Every mine, every smelter, every utility, every waterworks, every lumber company, every bank I own shows a profit."

Hall began to itch. "Well, sir, the *Mineral*'s real profit is influence. We are highly profitable if the paper's influence on voters is considered. We have won more votes to the Clark banner than anyone can count. And I'm proud to say that I've engineered a political shift in Butte."

"Advertising," said Clark. "Get more ads. A lot more. That'll be your task. Get ads and make a profit."

"But, sir, that's the province of an ad salesman."

"You are now appointed ad salesman. My good man, each week that you've been at my newspaper, revenue has declined. The paper is now earning five hundred seventy dollars less each week than when you started."

"But that's no responsibility of mine, sir."

Clark sighed gently, his bright gaze boring in. "I will need to instruct you in simple business economics. A newspaper is a product, like everything else. If the stories in the paper don't appeal, people buy other papers. Your news isn't what citizens wish to purchase. If people don't purchase papers, advertisers won't buy ads. Advertisers want circulation. So here is what you'll do. Write stories that people like, so the *Mineral* sells well. And then visit our advertisers and sell them ads."

"Well, fine, sir, but I don't have time for both."

"Then sell ads. That's where skill is needed."

"But someone must write and edit the paper."

"Leave it to your flunkies, Hall. There's no skill in it. Anyone can do it." He paused, bright-eyed. "And maybe the flunkies will bring back what's been lost."

"Sir, that's not the way to build circulation. We need to hire good cartoonists. We need a woodcut artist. We need more reporters. We need to sell issues in Anaconda and Helena and Bozeman. So we need to print more and ship them out."

"Profit, Mr. Hall. Give me a profit and I'll hire more lackeys for you. Reporters are a dime a dozen. Artists are a dime a gross. Plump cartoonists hang from every fruit tree. Editors, why I could hire twenty with the snap of my fingers. But ad salesmen, they're hard to find. Where can I find that sort of talent?"

Hall was certain he had no idea. A salesman was a salesman. A salesman could hardly string a sentence together, much less write a compelling editorial, or create a newspaper page that was compelling and balanced and beautiful.

"Ah, Mr. Clark, you must be aware that Marcus Daly's Anaconda paper loses money by the cartload. It's a rich man's toy. He's let Durston hire away the best men in the country."

"That's what'll sink him, Hall. The minute you put money into losers, you're acting on sentiment, not sound business principles. Nothing owned by Clark loses money for long."

It was becoming clear to John Fellowes Hall that his employer was, in a way, demoting him. Turning him into a drummer, a salesman, doomed to wander with an order book in hand, into every saloon, restaurant, greengrocery, butchershop, harness maker, barbershop, pharmacy, beer hall, clothier, and coal dealer in Butte.

"Mr. Clark, you're about to see a miracle," he said.

"I don't believe in them. I believe in hard work and a keen eye and canine teeth in the throat when necessary."

"A very good way to live, sir."

"We're done then, Hall. I will keep an eye out."

Clark turned away and peered out the window upon his fiefdom. Hall rose, fled, and headed for the paper, without a raise and without a promotion, and without a future.

Eleven

It was time to land on the widow. Big Johnny Boyle had run out of patience. Day after day, Alice Brophy had hidden from sight. She didn't answer her door. Johnny wanted to get this over with. He'd taken two sawbucks from Mickey Metzger to deliver the witch, and so far she hadn't been delivered. But this time he would deliver her, from hair to toes, if that's what it took.

He'd hardly made a dime on her. He'd collected a hundred and change from the brothers for Singing Sean's funeral, and that meant he kept only dimes for all his work. Plus the sawbucks. He never had enough money because the brothers didn't pay him much and didn't have half an idea what he did for them. Ingrates, that's what miners were. Maybe it had to do with working in a hole all day. It made them strange.

He'd change that, and quick. Butte was a town that begged him to get rich. Big Johnny headed for Dublin Gulch himself this time. He wouldn't leave it to the Pick. He'd drag her out by the ass. So when he got to Alice Brophy's weathered cottage, he didn't knock at all; he plowed in and found her rolling a pie crust. She took fright, and yelled at him, but he just stood smiling.

"Yell all you want, sweetheart, but now you're going to come with me and you're going to marry Mickey Metzger."

"I will not! Get out of my house!"

He moved to grab an arm and haul her off, and was surprised when she hit him with her rolling pin. She cracked him across the jaw, and caused him to bite his tongue.

"You'll be getting out, Big Johnny, leaving me alone."

He just grinned and spit blood. "Come along, sweetie. You've been promised, and I deliver."

"You'll drag me kicking and howling, is what. You'll have the coppers on you, and they'll be protecting a widow lady."

Big Johnny didn't relish that. He'd drag a man over the cobblestones, but not a woman.

"Deliver, is it?" she yelled. "You're delivering me? You sold my body, did you? A pimp, are you?

101

What was I worth? Twenty dollars, was it? Well, Big Johnny Boyle, I'll tell you something. I'm not for sale."

"I'll deliver you, Alice," wiping blood off his lips.

"You tell Mickey Metzger that he'll regret the day he took me. I'll be a witch. I'll make his every moment miserable. I'll get out my meat cleaver, I will."

"He paid, and I'll deliver," Big Johnny said, halfheartedly. He hated the very thought of refunding the sawbucks. "You got no way to live," he said.

"I'll chambermaid, I'll wash."

"No you won't. You won't get hired in this town. What I say goes with all the brotherhoods."

"That's what you think. Now you get out of here. This is my house."

"It won't be for long, sweetheart."

"Get out!"

He smiled and got out. Maybe he could find some chippy down on Mercury Street and hand her off to Mickey, and keep the sawbucks. That witch. She'd starve to death, and her brats with her. He'd make sure of it. And her from County Clare, too. They sure got uppity when they came across the sea. It wasn't over. He'd get her delivered one way or another.

It wasn't hard to think of some other way to rake in a few bucks. Pissing Yablonski's grave needed a headstone. Pissing was a charter member of the Butte union, and had died when a lift plunged to the bottom of the pit. Pissing was remembered for wetting everything—utility poles, fence posts, trees, cornerstones. If it was there, Pissing wet it. He could wet a bank in downtown Butte in broad daylight and no one would see him do it. Johnny himself had seen Pissing wet the numbers in a cornerstone, the piss dampening the Roman numerals. His widow, Minny, was pleased as punch to get herself remarried, so Big Johnny got her a new husband, Smelly Stuchen, in two days, and pocketed some change. But now Pissing's headstone had vanished from Mountain View. No one knew who desecrated the grave, but it was time for the brotherhood to honor its own. He'd have the Pick send out word. Let every brother ante up, and there'd be a new headstone on Pissing's grave. And more change in Big Johnny's britches.

Butte was so easy to work if one was content with penny ante. But Big Johnny had larger ambitions, and this here wrestling match of the bosses would surely be the way to get serious about a living.

There was a killing to be made from the fight of those copper kings. The union had votes. And that was worth plenty. The Butte Miners Union wanted two things in a big way: four dollars a day for everyone, and eight-hour days. It wanted some better working conditions too. Better air in the pits, more holiday time, pensions, help for the sick and old, and a dozen other items. It would all be on the table when them bosses showed up for little talks.

There were a few other items, maybe more important to Big Johnny than to the mining kings. Like who gets to work and who doesn't, and how the hiring was done, and whether the union could veto anyone it chose. The bosses didn't like it, because they wanted to hire the best men and not get stuck with lazy bums. But Big Johnny didn't see it that way. If he controlled who went down the shafts, he had something to sell. See Big Johnny about a job. Three dollars and fifty cents, a day's pay, in his pocket, and he'd give the word, and the man had a job. There were plenty of unemployed miners around, glad enough to give a little to Big Johnny out of their pay envelope. And there were more coming in from the immigrant boats and wicker-seat passenger cars every day, all of them wanting a job.

Even so, that was penny ante stuff. The best way to advance his fortunes, and keep his girlfriends on the street rolling in joy, was to own the votes. Not his vote, but every vote of the brotherhood. So long as he could keep that Australian ballot out of sight, and make every man's vote public, he could deliver easily. Anyone who voted the wrong way would get himself pounded until his bones broke. And that was worth a lot of money.

He owned a thousand votes and controlled another five hundred, and a word from him would influence several other brotherhoods. So maybe he had three thousand in all. That was a pretty good bunch of votes. That was enough to send some of Clark's favorites to the legislature. Maybe enough to elect Clark a senator. It sure was an interesting proposition. He had a product to sell. What would the buyers pay?

He found Eddie the Pick at Trelawney's and waited for Eddie to buy him an ale. It took only a moment. Eddie's raised finger, a bartender's glance. Big Johnny liked it that way.

"The brotherhood's about to get rich, Eddie," he said.

"Then we'll have to tax ourselves," Eddie said. He was in favor of a graduated income tax to soak the rich.

"Nah, the brothers won't even know it," Big Johnny said.

That raised Eddie's brow an inch or so.

"We got stuff for sale. Three thousand votes."

"Your arithmetic is a little wet," Eddie said. "But two more pints and it'll add up."

Big Johnny didn't want to explain to the knucklehead. "What we've got to do is hold the money in trust for the brothers," he said. "If we give it to them, they'll just spend it. So we've got to keep it safe."

Eddie didn't like that. "You need to trust

the common man," he said.

"I do! He'll vote exactly the way we want, or you'll break his arm and then he can't work."

"Yes, there's that. Common men need some guidance, at least until we throw out the captains of capital."

"Eddie, do you know what Clark's been giving the candidates? As table favors? Diamond stickpins for their cravats. Think of that. Those bozos sit down to a fancy feast at Clark's mansion, and right there on the table is a little white box at each place. And those guys aren't even elected yet. No one says a word. Clark ain't making any noises. No one demands or gives a thing, you see? If we got invited and got some diamond stickpins, that doesn't mean we've agreed to a thing, you see? And we'd keep the diamonds safe for the brotherhood. If the brotherhood needs the diamonds, we'd turn them right over."

Eddie the Pick sipped and weighed and sipped. "Why me?"

"Because you're my knee-capper. I gotta have that. What if someone don't vote like we want? If I promise three thousand votes and someone don't come through, I'd be a liar, and I don't want to be a liar. If I say I can deliver, then I'll deliver, and that's where you come in. Got it?"

"Solidarity," Eddie the Pick said. "You're right. We have to have solidarity. We have to speak with one voice."

"Now you're talking. I think what I'll do is go talk to Clark. I'll have him invite us to dinner. You and me, and whoever else he wants. No women. This is a brotherhood, not some sisterhood. So he'll have us to dinner, just like the pols, and we'll see what sort of table favors he's offering us. Not that we have to accept them, you know. If it's not a good favor, we'll just take the brotherhood somewhere else."

"Yeah, solidarity," Eddie the Pick said, and downed the rest of the pint.

"One carat, at least."

"You know something, Boyle? I never wore a cravat in all me days. Keepin' the diamond safe for the brotherhood wouldn't do me any good."

"You have a point, Eddie. I think we need some other kind of favor, one that would fit better."

"I don't need nothing. I just want all the brothers to be happy. Maybe we could get a statue made. How about a statue of you?"

"Me? What would I do with a statue? I'm too ugly for a statue. Now, double eagles, that would be different. We could keep double eagles safe."

"They sure are pretty, double eagles. Nothing destroys gold. It doesn't rust, it doesn't erode, it stays the way it stays. That's what the brothers need, something that won't let them down in the future."

"It would sure take a lot of them. Twenty

dollars, that wouldn't keep a brother happy for very long."

"We could give one to each miner's widow. I think every man who dies in the pit, the widow should get one," Eddie said.

"That's a noble idea, Eddie. And you and me, we'll be the stewards and keep the double eagles safe."

"How we gonna do this, Big Johnny?"

The truth of it was that Big Johnny didn't know. But there was always a way. He had votes to deliver, and there were buyers for votes. And he could deliver to the highest bidder. That got him to thinking about who wanted the entire vote of the Butte Miners Union. Clark, he sure wanted it. So did Marcus Daly. And maybe that Republican, Lee Mantle, wanted it. Or maybe one of them crazy Populists. It wasn't just Clark itching for whatever Big Johnny Boyle might have to offer. It was half the big shots in Montana.

Twelve

John Fellowes Hall concluded he was working for a very smart idiot. The man knew nothing about newspapers. Hall left the bank brimming with annoyance and toying with some sort of spectacular public resignation on his front page. Who cared about Butte? Ugliest and most barbaric city west of the Mississippi. Permanently proletarian. Every man born to fail. So ugly that it plunged people into melancholia. Who ever heard of a happy resident of Butte, Montana?

So Clark wanted a profit. The *Mineral* must make money. The *Mineral* must sell more ads and boost circulation. And it would be the editor's task to achieve that. An idiot. Hall stood on a busy corner, gagging on smoke, wondering how long to stay in town, and how he might fill his pockets before he stormed off.

Sell more papers! Sell more ads! Something was tickling his mind, but he wasn't quite able to pull it up. He hiked generally downhill, which was the direction his life had taken, away from the mines, away from wealth, and toward the tecming hinterlands. Butte was made that way. The mines, sources of fortunes, wcre highest up; the privileged a little lower; commercial life a bit lower; and below that were the losers, the depraved, the trash heaps, bawdy districts, and cemeteries. Butte put its cemeteries at the lowest level, the farthest away from God that they could be. It made sense.

Hall didn't return to the newspaper, but drifted a little farther, onto Mercury Street, the precinct of the bawds. There were plenty of those, and plenty of males on the loose ready to spend their change on a spasm of the muscles. Mercury was actually rather discreet, almost cloistered, compared to some of the districts he had seen, where the wild side was on display and the ladies sat in windows or on their front stoops, and the pianos rattled in open doorways.

The place was busy, even though it was not yet evening. Mercury Street's parlors were always open, and welcoming one shift after another. He spotted two of Clark's subalterns emerging from a parlor house. They saw him and nodded. He saw that union boss, Big Johnny somebody, wander into a house across the narrow street. The girls rarely turned anyone down. It amused John Fellowes Hall.

That's when the thing he was looking for came to mind. The name that somehow arose at last was Joseph Pulitzer, and the paper he was trying to recollect was the *New York World*. That was exactly the right medicine. The *World* scarcely needed to hunt down advertisers. They flocked to the paper, wanting to buy ads. The *World* scarcely needed to struggle with circulation. It outsold all its rivals, and some days its newsboys sold every copy that had been run off the big presses. Ah, that was it.

Hall knew at once he wouldn't need to go out begging for ads. He wouldn't need to begin desperate campaigns for more readers. He would lift a page from Joseph Pulitzer's *World*, and that would suffice. Cheerfully, he turned uphill, and soon plunged into the *Mineral*'s bleak sanctum.

The *Mineral* would never be the same.

He was feverish by the time he reached his writing table and grabbed some foolscap and a nib pen. The rich! Scandal! Sensation! The seamy side! Crime! Anything shocking! And one crusade after another, a great thundering noise that would rattle every windowpane in Butte! Did Clark want a profitable newspaper? He'd get one that would earn more than any of his mines!

Ah, but where to start? That was simple. Clark himself. The man would relish the glare of the lamps.

"William Andrews Clark has been holding gala entertainments that are the talk of Butte," he began. "Mr. Clark, who has announced his availability for a seat in the United States Senate, has been acquainting members of his party with festive dinners. Each of his guests discovers a table favor at his place at the great dining table, where twenty may be comfortably seated and served gourmet wines and dinners by a staff of discreet waiters.

"And what do these gents discover when they pull the ribbons and open the white pasteboard box at their seat? A diamond-studded tiepin, given as a gesture of Mr. Clark's ongoing interest in their well-being . . ."

On and on he wrote, describing the black-tie dress of all the swells, the menus—his room in the servants' quarters of the mansion was proving valuable after all—the French wines, the desserts, the Havanas freely passed around the table, and Mr. Clark's gracious welcome to the manse.

Ah, now Hall was cooking. On the police blotter that day was a murder of a whore by a customer of hers. Normally, he wouldn't have deigned to publish the story. But he was no longer the Hall he was the previous day; he was an acolyte of Pulitzer, and a story like that might be turned into the day's headline. He discovered his reporter, Grabbit Wolf, at work on an obituary.

"Forget that," Hall said. "We have a murdered whore. Her name is Lulu the Boiler. Her customer, Bloody Billy Bones, is in custody. That's going to be our lead story."

Grabbit looked startled. "Lead story?"

"Banner headline. Give it all you've got, and if you don't have enough, make it up."

Grabbit blinked, once, twice, and slowly exhaled. An eyebrow shot up. "We're talking lurid, right?"

"Right! I want every father in Butte to hide this edition from his daughters."

Grabbit sighed. "I've waited all my life for this," he said. "I've gone down to Mercury Street fifty times looking for a story I could publish. But until now there weren't any."

"Hurry up, man, and let me see the copy."

Ah, a start. He would make Joseph Pulitzer's *World* look sedate. He would make Pulitzer look like an amateur. And thanks to his genius, the

Mineral would grow fat. William Andrews Clark would smile.

What next? Ah, of course, a Pulitzer-style crusade. That was easy. He already knew what rankled his employer, and that was the town's Chinamen. That would be the crusade. Drive out the yellow heathen. Drive them out of Butte, out of Montana, out of the United States. Cut off their pigtails, stop their tong wars, send them packing. They were stealing jobs from real Americans. Deport them all.

They were, actually, doing valuable things around town, finding employment as launderers, street cleaners, noodle parlor operators, and operators of opium dens. But that made no difference. Clark would go for this. Clark wanted America for Americans.

And that was the name he gave his crusade. For the next month or so, there would be a crusade piece on the front page of the *Mineral*, and when he had worn that topic out, he would find another.

There were things to do. Scandal news required snitches. And that meant having some loose change around to give a chambermaid two bits, or a bootblack a spare dime, or a barkeep a dollar, if the stuff was juicy enough. He knew where to find snitches, and within a few days he would have fifty on his string, and the more enterprising ones would soon be making some real money, courtesy of the *Mineral*. And it didn't even matter how accurate they were.

He headed back to the printers.

"From now on, every lead story gets a headline in war type," he said.

They looked at him as if he was daft. War type was reserved for wars. It was the biggest type a newspaper owned.

"Grabbit's story. Give it war type," he insisted.

A toothless old compositor smirked. He knew the racket.

"Print an extra two hundred," he said.

The *Mineral* missed deadline by a half hour that afternoon, which made the newsboys snarly. They hung around the delivery door with empty canvas bags, making rude noises and misbehaving. Hall saw it as an opportunity.

"You there. Listen to me. This issue of the *Mineral* is going to sell like hotcakes if you know what to do. You can make money. We're printing extra copies. Now what you'll do is yell murder, murder, murder. Or Mercury Street murder. Hold up the front page. It'll say murder, and you'll say murder, and you'll sell every paper you've got and come back for more. Got it?"

"Who croaked?" asked one little punk.

"A whore."

"A whore's murdered," the punk said. "I got it."

"What's her name? She better be good looking," said another brat.

"She was the most beautiful one on Mercury Street."

"I bet," said the brat.

"We're printing extra. You sell out, you come back for more, got it?"

"Bullshit," said the punk.

The papers finally did come off the old flatbed press. Clark was too cheap to buy a modern rotary press, and it took so long to publish some afternoons that the news was out of date.

The little vultures scooped up their allotted papers and trotted off to every corner of town, including the mineheads. There were some, coming up to daylight, that wanted nothing more than a paper.

The press was still churning out the extra copies when Hall returned, and the only thing to do was wait. Most of the news and composing men had abandoned the place and wouldn't show up until dawn. But Hall waited. He wanted to know one thing: whether those extra papers would fly out the rear door.

An hour later he had his answer. They did. Every one of the two hundred spares.

He headed for the stinking washroom, feeling begrimed. He found some abrasive soap, the kind printers used to scrape ink away, and scrubbed furiously, his face, his hands, his wrists. He hated black ink.

Then he clamped his fedora on his well-groomed hair and headed out the door, the last man out of the shop. He headed uptown, looking for newsboys, but most of them were done for the night. One kid from the *Inter-Mountain* was still hawking his wares.

Hall didn't feel like heading for his monastic cell in the servants' floor of the mansion. He felt like a drink. He felt like some good whiskey. He felt like a bout in a good saloon, one patronized by merchants, so he wandered the streets until he came to the Gallows. It was hot in there, but rotating ceiling fans subdued the worst of the heat. These people were brokers, the sort who bought and sold shares in the mines and smelters. Some still wore green eyeshades.

Hall eyed the place for newspapers, and spotted an *Anaconda Standard* on the mahogany bar, and an *Inter-Mountain*. But no *Minerals*. He was faintly disappointed, but then he saw a couple of papers carefully folded with the headlines facing inward, poking from some suit coats. That was good. The gents were hiding the front page.

A saloonman with a walrus moustache served him a bourbon and branch, which he sipped quietly, just listening to the talk. But it was all stocks and bonds, up and down, bull and bear. He drank up and ordered another, and listened. But it was as if the *Mineral* didn't exist. Maybe this was a Republican saloon. Maybe this was a Daly bar.

The more he sipped the good whiskey, the less

116

happy he became. He didn't like his job and despised his employer. He was far away from Amber and the boys. He had always considered himself the finest newsman anywhere, but now he was churning out a scandal sheet. His employer was demanding a profit. Didn't Clark know that great papers never earned a dime? They were great because they didn't spare any expense tracking down the news and presenting it elegantly to intelligent readers.

But the *Mineral* was now a rag. A guttersnipe of a paper. It occurred to him that he was making a coffin out of this job. He'd have no credentials to take to the next position. He could not show copies of his paper to the next employer. He'd sold out. Everything he'd stood for in journalism had been pitched out the door.

He stared morosely at the men bellied up to the bar, men with their feet on the brass rail, men talking prices and politics. He signaled the barman for another shot, and he downed that and downed another, feeling worse and worse. If he had any sense he'd walk away from Butte. He'd take the next steam train back to civilization.

He had one final shot, wove his way out the door, couldn't remember where he was, and finally couldn't remember anything. So he went to sleep.

Some hours later he came to in a dowdy old cubicle with iron bars across his horizon.

"So, you're awake," said a copper. "I need your name. I have to book you."

Hall stared upward, aware that he lay on a stinking bunk.

"Of course you can donate two bucks to the policemen's retirement fund," the copper said.

Hall did, and wobbled back to the mansion of William Andrews Clark.

Thirteen

Royal Maxwell loathed the crone, and she loathed him, but that did not hamper the transaction. He was wondering what Agnes Healy, the famed seer, had in store for him. And she would receive her pittance for telling him.

"So you're wanting to see who's going to die, are you? You're looking for business, are you? You're maybe hoping for a wreck, so you can run the bodies through your place like sausages, are you?"

"I'm always interested in death, madam, whether from the mines or simply from old age or some mishap. God bless the departed."

"I'll bet you are. Each one puts the greenbacks in your pocket. Well, maybe I won't tell you what I see. Maybe you can just guess. Maybe you should be surprised. What if I see you're next, eh? What then?"

She did this monologue every time, and he didn't mind. His business was burying people, and he was all in favor of death. But he was looking for anything else of value, knowing that when her lightning struck, it was a valuable glimpse into the future.

"So what about politics?" he asked.

"Why should I know anything about politics, may I ask? I leave politics to crooks where it belongs. I don't listen for answers to politics."

"The elections, then. Who will be our next senator?"

She slid into a trance, rapt, and he knew she was connecting somehow with that other world.

"No one," she said. "There won't be a senator."

"That's absurd. There'll be a senator elected."

"No one. Montana will have one senator."

"Not Clark?"

"Who am I to say, eh? You asked; I listened."

This was certainly odd. "What about a Republican, then?" he asked. Royal Maxwell was ardently a Republican, and found the party soul-satisfying. He wished all people could be Republicans. That would help business. The Democrats were proposing mine safety legislation, and he was opposed because it was bad for business. The Populists were even worse. They were proposing all sorts of sanitation and pure food laws, which would cut into his business. There was only one thing any funeral director could be, and that was a true-blue Republican. With any luck, he could bury a lot of Democrats.

"Who'll win the elections this November?" he asked.

"How should I know? I don't prophesy; I just get hit by lightning once in a while, and then what's to come is clear. There's nothing about elections in my head."

"I want to know how the Republicans will do. I want to know if Marcus Daly's deserting the Democrats and joining the Republicans."

She sniffed. "You sure are a rotter," she said.

"I'd be pleased to bury every Democrat in Butte," he said. "I'd give them the best send-off they ever had."

She closed her eyes and seemed to vanish from the room, but then she awakened abruptly. "It's a mess," was all she said.

"Well? What?"

"I'm just a poor widow trying to bring a little something to people."

"Well, see about this. Where's the state capital going to be? In Anaconda?"

It had been left to the citizens to decide that. Helena was the temporary one, favored by Clark, and most other people around the new state. But Marcus Daly had his own design, a capital in his own carefully laid-out town of Anaconda at the foot of Mount Haggin, the dome dwarfed by the stack of his giant copper smelter. The very thought of a capital owned by the Anaconda Mining Company was as loathsome to Maxwell as putting the capital in Great Falls, which was the other serious contestant. He was a Helena man, but so were most Republicans.

She frowned, stared into space, and shrugged. "I don't know," she said.

There was no arguing with that. She saw or she didn't. She peered somehow through some lens of time, and sometimes the future was there in a glimpse as bright as heaven. But not now. He felt vaguely cheated and thought he'd leave a dime, not two bits. But he thought better of that.

He peered around the shabby kitchen. The woman got barely a life out of her gifts. There was no stored food; no tins of flour or beans or sugar. She looked so thin that he wondered if she was even feeding herself.

"Death," he said.

"That's what you came in for. You can't fool me. Politics, all that, you were just trying to hide why you're here. Death you want. Business you want. If I say twenty next week, you'll order twenty coffins."

"How can I fool someone who sees through veils?" he asked, not unreasonably.

She glared at him. "I hate this," she said. "You make a ghoul out of me."

"Think of it this way, madam. The more I know

what to expect, the more I can be of service to those who grieve."

"Oh, horsepucky," she said.

She closed her eyes, opened them, stared into space, and shook her head.

"I have good news," she said quietly. "No one will die in Butte for the next two weeks."

"Two weeks? That's unheard of. There's several poor souls passing to the nether shore almost daily."

"Two weeks," she said.

"Your crystal ball's cloudy today, madam."

"I'm not a seer. I've told you that. I don't commune with spirits. If something comes to me, it's out of the future, like something seen in the white light of lightning."

"Two weeks? Someone in Butte croaks every day."

She turned silent and stern, so he slipped her two bits and headed out the door. This was the worst-ever session with Agnes, and he swore he would not darken her door ever again. No senator in office! Two weeks with no one cashing in! What a lot of malarkey. He peered around, to make sure no one had registered his visit to the witch, and then slipped downhill, not wishing to reveal his presence in that neighborhood. He would have a good story or two to tell his Republican cronies running for various Butte city offices. Oh, Agnes would be good for something, if only a laugh.

But damn, when was she ever wrong? He'd go broke if he didn't have a miner or a bartender or a dead infant on his doorstep that long. She had it wrong. He didn't wish death upon anyone. He merely welcomed death in the abstract; in a statistical sense. He wished good health upon every mortal he had ever met, and those he hadn't. He wished good health upon himself, which he lacked because he had visited Mercury Street too often.

He had thought at one time of calling his establishment the Golden Rule Mortuary: Bury Others as You Wish to Be Buried. That might encourage people to spend more, and of course it was ethically beyond criticism. But too many people were cheapskates, and wanted to plant their loved ones without the dignity of the finest caskets and the most splendid send-offs. It saddened him that the world was so crass.

Two weeks. He could barely survive such a drought. He couldn't keep his pants buttoned that long. But even as he plunged toward his own place of business, a thought began tickling his fancy. A branch in Anaconda. The company was obliging him with accidents in Butte: good cave-ins, fires, runaway lifts, silicosis, rocks landing on people's heads. It could just as well oblige him with business in Anaconda, where the world's largest smelter burned workers to a crisp, polluted the air with arsenic fumes, crushed anyone who got caught in its giant machinery, and emitted pure copper, save for the occasional bits of flesh and bone caught in the furnaces. A branch in Marcus Daly's backyard! There would never again be a two-week drought. Now that Daly's little railroad was shuttling between Butte and Anaconda, there'd be no difficulty getting from one mortuary to the other. And with the telegraph alerting him to need, he could operate both. He could keep a lackey there, whose sole task would be to wire him when needed, and make comforting noises to the bereaved. Yes, he knew of a dozen brats who'd fill the bill, and not cost anything if he gave them a bed and an attic room over there.

The idea appealed to him so much that he spent the rest of the afternoon expanding on it, and kept coming to the thing he could no longer escape. Daly was right. The capitol building of Montana should be built in Anaconda, and then Royal Maxwell would get to bury tony politicians and powerful bureaucrats, and not just riffraff. Yes, with a branch he'd flourish, and he'd get the right sort of clients, the ones with folding money and big houses and estates.

He felt almost dizzy. Agnes Healy had led him to something grand. For the two bits he'd tossed her, he had received a brilliant expansion of his business to a lively new town that might become the state capital. He'd quickly drive out any

124

competition, with the finest funeral parlor in the Northwest, fluted white pillars in front, a fine electric-lit dias for viewing, and cemetery lots to sell. That reminded him he would need to start a cemetery over there. No point in leaving that to others when he could have all the plots to himself.

He was so taken with the whole idea that he checked schedules, found he could spend the whole afternoon over there, maybe put himself into business in very little time. If Agnes was right, he wouldn't be needed in Butte for a good while. He stuffed his check register into a briefcase, walked down to the Butte, Anaconda and Pacific depot, purchased a round-trip, and was soon rattling his way over to the future capital of Montana. He settled into the austere wicker seat of the passenger car, read the *Mineral* and then the *Butte Inter-Mountain*, and by the time he had sorted out the Democrats' lies in Clark's rag and absorbed the truths in the *Inter-Mountain*, the train was squealing to a halt at the foot of Mount Haggin. It was exhilarating. Anaconda was not a claptrap slum, but an orderly, new, well-planned company town. Good for business, he thought.

He perused the town, especially the blocks surrounding Marcus Daly's new luxury hotel on Park Street. He was a sensitive man, and thought it best not to locate next door, even though the hotel and the funeral parlor would fertilize each other's business. Where better to hold a wake than

Marcus Daly's great brick hostelry? But close. A few steps would work nicely. No further than Commercial Avenue, and closer if he could manage it. Surely, people died in hotels, and he wanted his parlor to be convenient.

There didn't seem to be the right sort of vacant structure in the new town, but he spotted a store that might do with a noble facade in front. It was narrow, but deep and had a rear room, which he would need. Yes, it would have to do. And only two blocks from the hotel. Even the rich could manage that. He loathed the rich; they were people who were always shifting their loyalties and looking for every advantage and betraying their former colleagues. That's how they got rich. Not like Royal Maxwell, who had an unwavering loyalty to the dead. He was proud of that. His loyalty to those who had passed by never wavered.

He spent the rest of the day arranging for a mahogany altar, a stained-glass window depicting shepherds, pine pews, a pulpit, zinc undertaking tables, a handsome cream pilaster facade for the building, advertising with Daly's paper, the *Anaconda Standard,* and scores of other details. He would need to find a flunkey and install him in the attic. And since there was only telegraph, not telephone, he would need to teach the flunkey to wire him when a customer showed up and then go fetch the departed with a black lacquered handcart.

He caught a late train back to Butte, satisfied with his coup. Within a few days he would be burying two or three a day, maybe more, and expanding his business as fast as the copper kings were expanding theirs. And he would need to formulate some plans to drive off competition, too. The copper kings were wrestling for the bonanza deep in the richest hill on earth, and Royal Maxwell knew he would wrestle for the richest mortician's paradise on earth. For a moment, as he sat in the rocking railroad coach, watching Butte's slope grow close, he felt a certain brotherhood toward William Andrews Clark and Marcus Daly. They were all looking for the pot of gold at rainbow's end. He was one of them, a businessman flexible enough to make a killing.

Fourteen

For the moment, Marcus Daly would set aside the weight of the Anaconda Copper Mining Company, and deal with a minor thing, but one that had acquired an odd importance to him for reasons he couldn't quite explain to himself. He summoned his assistant, Dell Ryan, and ordered his carriage.

Soon, he was trotting westward from the smelter complex into the serene town of Anaconda, which he had personally laid out, attending to every detail from the width of its grand boulevards to the perfection of its water and sewage systems. Anaconda was his Paris. It would be more than a city; it would be as close to paradise as anything on earth could be. It would be a place of perpetual innocence and charity, a place for his oppressed people to raise families and populate the virgin world.

As he drove westward he took note of every detail; not even a new storefront escaped him. He could not control everything that happened on the lots he had sold off, nor did he want to. But he did keep a shepherd's eye on his city, named for his company, and devoted entirely to the comfort and safety of his army of smeltermen and executives. He turned on Commercial and drew up at the new mortuary, the former store that was swiftly being transformed into a sort of churchly establishment. It was Maxwell's project. Daly knew the man all too well.

A funeral parlor was welcome in Anaconda. There had been none, and what few funerals the town had seen since its inception had involved an imported mortician. He studied the feverish activity, sensing that the proprietor wanted to get into business immediately and not miss a single death. He parked the carriage a little away, so the activity would not disturb his sleek trotter, and anchored everything with a carriage weight.

He entered, discovering as much activity within

as out front, as a horde of craftsmen converted the interior into a chapel, with two viewing rooms and a reception area. Those parts of the establishment not open to public view lay at the rear, and that was where Marcus Daly headed, hoping to find the proprietor.

He was in luck. Royal Maxwell, in shirtsleeves, was stacking coffins in a corner.

Daly's presence startled the mortician, who suddenly wiped his hands on a towel.

"Why, it's Mister Daly," he said, worry leaking from him.

"You chose carefully, Maxwell. A suitable distance from my hotel, a discreet walk from it. You're the first one in my city."

"Why, I'm honored by your visit, sir."

"That will depend," Daly said. He had a way of leaving things hanging, portents twisting in the silences.

"I take it for a welcome," Maxwell said.

"I created this. I laid it out. Named each street. Worried my way through the water supply, sewer system, and all else. I thought some about where it should lie, and chose this place because of its view. See Mount Haggin? It looks over us. It's the source of our water, but also our serenity. It rises up and up, and we can't see the top from here. I thought to myself, this is a good place. This is where my people can live in peace and get a good wage and see their children and grandchildren grow."

"Why, yes, sir, and now I'm glad to provide my services to them," Maxwell said, a smile building.

Daly ignored that. "It took a railroad to get it right, sir. A smelter as large as ours consumes more wood and coal than you can imagine. It burns through heavy equipment. It handles tons of ore that arrive each day in long strings of hopper cars. It will soon be much larger. The cemetery's small, but it'll fill soon. We're growing by several dozen people a day."

"I hope to be of service, sir," Maxwell said.

"This is the place for the state capital," Daly said. "Helena's fine, but doomed to be a small town. Its placer ores have run out, and it's living on nothing. The people of Montana will decide all that next year, and of course Helena wants to remain the seat of government. But we have other plans. Anaconda is the right place. I know exactly where the capitol building should rise, up that slope there, at the base of Mount Haggin, where its dome will overlook the whole state. It's a clean, new town, not one sullied by abandoned mines and graveyards—of equipment, of course. My company will proudly back this very place and donate the land to the state. That's why I'm pursuing this. There's not a top man in the company that doesn't want the capital right here. We want the best and brightest of the legislators and public servants right here. We want them to enjoy my hotel, the best in the state, and we want them to enjoy fine dining, every amenity, good transportation. We intend to make Anaconda as easy to get to as Helena, even if it's a little further to the southwest. Do you see?"

"Oh, Mr. Daly, count me among those who'll push for it. I'll support it."

"Will you?" Daly asked. "How?"

"I'll give politicians the fanciest send-off anywhere."

"I'm sure you will." Daly eyed the man. "We're working stiffs here, Mr. Maxwell. We're from the old country, and haven't got much put by. Now take Mrs. Brophy, in Butte. Mrs. Sean Brophy. All she needed was a dignified funeral, at the hour of her choosing. The Butte Miners Union paid you once, and I paid you again, and you got two fees for one funeral and still let her down, telling her when it would be."

"Oh, a sad mix-up."

"Maybe. Maybe not. But in Anaconda, there's going to be funerals that will honor the dead, no matter how poor they might be. And there'll be a modest fee, paid once. I don't give a fig about politicians, Mr. Maxwell. If you want to bill their widows six times for one funeral, go ahead. But I care for all my brothers, the ones who shovel coal all day, who empty the ore from the hopper cars, who pull cinders out of the furnaces. As I did. I care for them, sir, and you will too, because if you don't, I'll go into the funeral business, and I'll see to it that every man who works for me is honored the way he should be, and his widow comforted, and his remains put to rest. That's how my new city will be, sir. Anaconda's going to be a city on a hill, and when it becomes the capital of Montana, it's going to shine. Is that understood, Mr. Maxwell?"

The ferret-faced man nodded, offered a hasty smile and a puffy hand, which Daly accepted gingerly.

Maybe Anaconda was a company town, but it was going to be a good company town, he thought, as he lifted the carriage weight and steered his trotter away.

It wasn't far to the offices of the *Anaconda Standard*, where he would talk to Durston.

The paper had cost Marcus Daly a fortune, but he had not tried to cut back. He knew little about these things, but knowledgeable men told him it was one of the finest dailies in the country. He wanted it to be so, and had imported the newest equipment and best men to make it so. It was more paper than a town the size of Anaconda could support, and even with some sales in Butte, it was still costly compared to its circulation. But for the time being, that was fine. He could not expect to curb the ambitions of Clark, or win the votes of electors throughout Montana when it came to selecting the permanent capital with an ordinary rag. So a significant portion of the company's profits ended up in the pockets of some great political cartoonists, great reporters, and Durston himself, the resident genius, with a doctorate in philology, and a courtly manner, and a command of everything associated with publishing.

He found John Durston in his lair, scribbling another editorial, which he usually featured on the front page. The *Standard* was not shy about expressing its opinions, both with editorials and with elaborate cartoons.

"You, is it?" Durston asked. "Are we going to oppose capital punishment? Are we going to come out against the Church? Will we rail against Christmas?"

Daly smiled. The Republican Durston had transformed himself into a Democrat upon joining the Daly armada.

"Have we got Clark where we want him?"

"No. We bloviate and he bribes."

"What will stop him?"

"Woodcuts. Photographs. Images, Mr. Daly."

"That's as good a wrecker as any."

"Clark's a stuffed shirt. Black silk stovepipe hat. French cuffs. Elaborate chin whiskers. Spats. Shoes so shiny they reflect his face back to him. Remember, the average citizen of Montana wears bib overalls, brogans, and a battered felt hat."

"And you're working on it?"

"Every issue. You bought the most expensive cartoonists in the republic."

"Yes, and I mean to get my money's worth. Now, the easier task. What are you doing for my city?"

"Woodcuts. Streetlamps. Cobbled streets. Mount Haggin. Pure water. That's a big one, you know. Rail connections. And there's a little something for you to do soon. Host the Montana Press Association in your fancy hotel, everything on the house. You've got a rail connection now."

"Ah! You're worth your high pay now and then, Durston. Set it up. We'll have the whole Montana press here, and show off a bit."

Durston smiled. "Trinkets, favors, mementos. Ah . . . a quart of Kentucky's finest as a take-home."

"Draft a plan in one paragraph and I'll okay it."

"It should get you a capital," Durston said. "A hundred editorials, a hundred stories, a hundred woodcuts or photos. A dinner plate, ANACONDA, MONTANA, STATE CAPITAL in gothic gilt letters, the dome rising in front of Mount Haggin."

"Durston, what would I do without you?"

"Employ two semi-competent altar boys."

"Altar boys?"

"That's what I am, Daly, your altar boy."

"All right, now tell me where we're weakest."

"The *Mineral*'s game. Their man, Hall, has a certain genius at twisting the news. Does the company build a railroad? That's so it can gouge passengers. Does Mr. Daly desire that the capital of Montana be Anaconda? Then run a series of cartoons, each showing the very top of the dome of the state house below the stack, below your office. With the state flag flapping below the company flag. And then there's the one showing fat Anaconda executives toting bags of boodle out of the state capitol building."

"Well, that's not far off the mark, is it?"

"It doesn't play well in Great Falls."

"Can we checkmate the *Mineral*?"

"I know Hall. He has a past, though I don't know what. Shall I make some inquiries?"

"Cover all the news, Durston. Cover the *Mineral*."

"Mr. Daly, you're a man after my own heart."

"Only as long as I pay you top dollar, Mr. Durston."

"Very true, sir. Shall we accuse Mr. Clark of anything?"

"A man's private life is his own business, but his public life is public business."

"Would you regard unusual gifts to be public business?"

"Check every land transaction from now on. Anyone who makes a large purchase of land, or who is gifted with land, or who is suddenly an owner of any business. Yes, Mr. Durston, let us find out what politicians and what cronies are enjoying Mr. Clark's favor, eh? Not just Silver Bow County. Look into Deer Lodge, Great Falls,

Missoula, Bozeman. And see if any Republicans are sporting cuff links and real estate."

"I'll put two men and two cartoonists on it, Mr. Daly."

"Good. If Clark is handing out diamond cuff links and gold watch fobs, let's find out who the happy recipients are, eh?"

Duston eyed his own barrel cuffs sadly. "Nothing but a little ink on these, sir," he said.

Fifteen

The Silver Bow Club annoyed William Andrews Clark. It was entirely inadequate. He had founded it a decade ago, and now it was housed on the fourth floor of the Lewisohn Building on Granite Street, far too modest a place for men of substance. But there was little Clark could do about it until a proper clubhouse could be built, suitable for the accomplished men of Butte and their visitors. So these precincts simply irritated the copper magnate, and he fumed away his moments there and hoped not to see his rival Marcus Daly, who was a member but rarely visited the place. Clark wished the man would resign; he didn't belong among the city's elite, the men of vision and discernment, the men who had built and financed the mines and smelters and built up the city and its streetcars and waterworks.

But he especially wanted not to see Daly because the man had ruined the Democratic Party, and was making open alliances with Republicans, and was deliberately thwarting Clark's ambitions. The elections of 1892 had gone badly for the Democrats. The rising Populists had cut into the Democratic majorities and had elected three men to the legislature. The Democrats had lost the governorship and other offices. At least the elections had kept Daly from locating the state capital in Anaconda, and the state was still governed from the temporary capital at Helena. With his own party sundered into factions, and with the Republicans split into a liberal pro-silver wing and a conservative pro-gold wing, and the appearance of the fevered Populists, who had become power brokers because they held the votes that would turn any faction into a majority, the prospects for Clark were dim. But he was no quitter, and if it came to buying votes again, as he had in 1888, he would do it. He intended to become a United States senator, and nothing on earth would stop him. Except maybe the miserable traitor Daly.

"Fancy place," said Mark Bitters.

"Not a bit fancy; an embarrassment. I've had to entertain James J. Hill in here. It was like dining in a henhouse. Can you imagine what Hill must have thought?"

This was the first time he had permitted his

bagman, Bitters, to enter these guarded confines and he was not at peace about it. The Silver Bow Club was intended for the rich, not this sort of barbarian who sat in the wing chair across from Clark.

"Is there anything you wish?" Clark asked.

"I don't suppose there's any red-eye," Bitters said.

Clark summoned a white-jacketed attendant. "Bring him some whiskey." The attendant nodded.

Bitters had been joking. He knew what would be on the bar shelves here.

"You're going to repair the mess in Helena," Clark said. "And do it invisibly."

"When am I not invisible?"

Bitters had a point. He was a full-time retainer of Clark's, but not on any company payroll or connected with any firm doing business with Clark's numerous enterprises. Clark paid him in cash from his bank. He thought six hundred a month sufficed to steer Bitters away from all but the most extravagant bribes, and also keep Bitters from skimming cash off the top. He suspected he was wrong, but did not intend to pursue the matter too closely because boodlers had big mouths themselves. Suffice it to say that Bitters was receiving enough every two weeks to ensure his semi-loyalty.

Bitters was from Kansas City, where they knew

a thing or two about how the world worked. He was a cheerful sort, and almost handsome save for a pocked face and a swiftly growing paunch. He had graduated from a private high school, St. Elizabeth's, and had more education than Clark himself, which was useful. Clark was never quite sure how to pick up a fork or when to use a spoon or whether it was acceptable to dab his mouth and beard with a linen napkin. In fact, Clark secretly studied Bitters, whose manners were impeccable, looking for small, telling clues about breeding. Mark Bitters was well-bred, even if he had devoted himself to the life of a scalawag. Clark had no such inheritance. He came from a rural Pennsylvania family and had made his way West doing whatever shoveling and chopping and hoeing and sawing could feed and clothe him. So there was much to learn from Bitters.

"Be subtle," Clark was saying, eyeing the stately room for stray ears. "It goes against a man's conscience to receive gifts, but the same gent'll welcome a business partner, or a payment for services."

Bitters looked bored, as well he should. But Clark intended to make his points and establish his boundaries anyway. It was his privilege, and Bitters was his boodler, and subject to his instructions. Clark saw no wrong it it. Every man had his price; it was simply a matter to finding it. That was what business was about.

"I'll buy the whole state, if that's the deal," Bitters said. "I can buy anything except Mormons. I can buy Episcopalians and Catholics and Unitarians. I can buy Swedes, Finns, Frenchies, Italians, Bohemians, and Irish. I can buy New Englanders and Confederates, Abolitionists and slavers. I can buy farmers and dairymen and pickled pigs' feet bottlers. I can buy editors and conductors and teamsters."

"I don't want you to buy anything, Mark. Just make ordinary business arrangements. There's hardly a man in Montana who doesn't need a business partner."

Bitters was smirking. He sipped his amber spirits and eyed the world cheerfully. That somehow annoyed William Andrews Clark.

"The senators of Rome wore white togas, signifying citizenship and office. They were the most powerful and respected men in the republic. They debated each other on the most civilized terms, and so governed the world. You wouldn't know about that. I've made a study of it, Mark. Anyone with some diligence can make a fortune in this country. All it takes is a little rattlesnake juice and courage. Great businessmen are a dollar a dozen. But there aren't very many senators, and once that title attaches to the name, Bitters, the man has a reputation. He is senator. He is Senator Clark. Even after he's served his term, he is still Senator Clark. I have one thing left to conquer,

Bitters, and that is high public office. I don't aspire to the purple toga—you wouldn't know about that. The toga of magistrates, and eventually the toga of emperors. I have no wish to wear the purple. But get me the white toga, Bitters, not because I've earned it, but because I insist. This is something you surely will do, daily, hourly, at dawn and midnight, on Sundays, on holidays, on Sabbaths, on new moons and during burials and weddings. You will spend your time in Helena, and you will be on the floor of the legislature, and you will be meeting with every elected man in Helena, publicly and privately, and you will have two purposes before you at all times: I will wear the toga, and the capital will not be abducted by Marcus Daly and built in the shadow of his smelter smokestack."

Bitters sipped, smiled, nodded, and sighed.

"We have made the arrangements," Clark said. "I have a portmanteau filled with presidential portraits, mostly Grover Clevelands and William McKinleys. Do not waste a nickel. Do not pay for perfidy. The less you spend, the more will be your reward."

Bitters lifted his glass. "Cheers," he said.

Clark lifted the portmanteau from beside his armchair. It was no ordinary bag, but one with brass furniture at the corners, and knobby rhinoceros-hide sides and bottom, and an unusual brass lock. The black hide looked thick enough to turn a bullet, and the lock covered a large part of the top of the bag.

"Abercrombie and Fitch," Clark said. "A New York outfitter. Opened this year. I bought three in all, and should have bought a dozen, except Africa would have run out of rhinos. British artisans went to work on the hide, staining it black as sin, and rubbing that glow into it. Ebony and brass; it's not a bag one would ever forget, eh? Now you will find loosely attached an umbilical cord, attached to a wrist bracelet. The bag cannot be easily snatched from your limp hand by a footpad lurking under a gas lamp. Given your physical decrepitude, from an excess of ardent spirits, I thought to add a measure of safety."

"I'll squander it," Bitters said. "Should get me to Paris."

"Yes, and squander it well. The bag cannot be returned to me, not ever. Give it to a curio shop when it's empty. Don't keep it. There is no label in it. The source of the bag must remain entirely unknown."

"When I run out, what next?"

"A one-word telegram to me. The word is rhino."

"Ah, good. I hope not to wire you at all."

"Bitters, the serial numbers are all recorded."

"What's that supposed to mean?"

"It means I will have some idea whose businesses I am partnering."

Bitters lifted the bag. "This is heavy," he said.

"Lighter than gold, sir."

"I mean duty. Responsibility."

"That's a new idea to me, Bitters. Whatever could it mean?"

"I've never held a rhinoceros bag before, sir."

"Let's hope it's your last. Now, then, Bitters, you head for the legislature and get a bit in its mouth and tug."

Bitters eyed his drink, downed it, and set the glass on the end table. Within seconds, a white-coated attendant had whisked it away. Bitters stood, hefting the ebony bag, and winked.

That did not appeal to William Andrews Clark. He wished Bitters had noticed the workmanship that had gone into the bag; the riveted brass furniture, the glossy leather, the knobby exterior, the elaborate handles. But all that was too much for Bitters. Why did 99 percent of human beings lack the slightest aesthetic sensibility?

The greenbacks had arrived in the express car safe of Hill's Great Northern afternoon train to Butte, and had come from the Morgan bank in New York, discreetly wrapped in onionskin.

Bitters would lease rooms off of Last Chance Gulch, and begin to arrange amiable meetings with the legislators as they arrived ahead of the January session. They would know him only as a gentleman who represented substantial interests. His business card said only that he was a commission broker. There would be no talk of financial matters, not then. Bitters was an experienced boodler, and would make no mistakes. That's why Clark had trusted him to a degree. He didn't quite trust anyone who lacked aesthetic sensibility, and there wasn't a shred of evidence that Bitters had ever seen beauty or symmetry or grace in anything, except maybe a thousand-dollar note.

The Silver Bow Club was annoying him again.

He rose to leave, but even as the white-jacketed attendant rushed to get his chesterfield and top hat, Marcus Daly emerged from the vestibule. They saw each other, and Clark knew there would be no escape. He also knew he would be up to whatever affability was required, no matter what fires flared and boiled just behind the dam of civility.

"Why, it's you, Marcus," he said, instantly offering a manicured hand. Daly's hand would not be manicured, and might still bear the scars of hardrock mining. Daly didn't look a bit trapped, and shook the extended pale hand, as if it were a gentleman's club seal of peace for the moment. "Won't you join me for a libation?" Clark asked, hoping for the negative.

"Delighted," Daly said.

And there they were, opposed in matching brocaded wing chairs.

"Are you content with the elections, Mr. Daly?"

144

"No, not at all."

"I imagine you're distressed," Clark said. "I'm less distressed. I'm quite at ease about the elections. Good men in office, that's what lies at the heart of democracy. Now, this may be a legislature that gets things done."

"The wrong things done," Daly said.

Clark always had an advantage over Marcus Daly, who was slow-witted if not retarded. And now it was going to be fun. The Silver Bow Club seemed to blaze with light, as the copper titans collected all the sun around themselves.

"Well, as civilized men we can agree to promote differing visions of the public good," Clark said. "Now, I'll want a capitol building with a dome that rises higher than any other structure in Montana, and you'll settle for one with a lower dome."

"Why yes, and I want a United States senator who rises above all other men in the state, but not one of short stature," Daly retorted.

That was an insidious and cruel blow. William Andrews Clark drew himself up to his full five foot and seven inches, and smiled.

"Here's to the future," he said. "Nothing short, and nothing low."

Daly laughed.

Sixteen

The more John Fellowes Hall contemplated his first name, the more annoyed he became. John was simply not a suitable name for a man of genius. He seriously considered Jon, which seemed more modern and elegant, but he finally rejected that, too. Instead, he changed his signature to J. Fellowes Hall, quietly burying his first name. He knew a man whose first name was Sylvester and whose middle one was Lawrence, and who changed his name to S. Lawrence. It made sense. Who could possibly want to be named Sylvester?

So J. Fellowes Hall was how he signed his name, and how he was listed in the masthead of the *Mineral*. That had a nice ring to it. The paper, of course, had bloomed under his superb management, and now was the most lucrative in Butte. All he had done was move the daily police blotter to the front page. Grabbit Wolf interviewed drunks, murderers, thieves, confidence men, and a wide variety of doxies and punks, and out of it all came the perfect stew to capture readers and nab advertising. And J. Fellowes Hall had done it all without even selling a one-inch ad to anyone.

Of course William Andrews Clark wasn't thrilled, and tended to be a little stuffy when it came to the content of his paper, but the fat profits from the *Mineral* trumped any reservations he had, and he huffily let Hall have his way. The more readers, the more his campaign for office in the United States Senate would prosper. The more readers, the more he could keep Daly at bay.

And now, with the bitter winds of January, 1893, the legislature was collecting in Helena, there to decide several crucial matters, most importantly the naming of Montana's next senator. There were reformers who thought senators should be elected by the people, but they were lacking gravity. The proper way, the constitutional way, was for state legislatures to select them and send them off to Washington.

It was going to be a messy legislature, with the Democrats divided between the Daly and Clark factions, the Republicans divided between gold and silver factions, and there were a few Populists in there who could tilt the voting in any direction.

Hall decided to cover the shenanigans himself, and leave the coverage of Butte to Grabbit Wolf, who was an adept at writing blood, gore, mayhem, immorality, and any news at all rising from Mercury Street. The *Mineral* would not suffer from a brief absence of its guiding genius.

In truth, Hall itched to get out of town. He had not yet extracted himself from the servant quarters of Clark's mansion, and had no prospect of it until Clark headed off to Washington. Meanwhile,

J. Fellowes Hall was enjoying a respite from marriage, and regularly wrote Amber to be patient; Butte was an abominable place, cold and cruel, and no place for gentlefolk or children. That was true enough to satisfy Hall's integrity.

So one bitter day Hall climbed into his lamb's-wool chesterfield, wrapped a wool scarf around his neck, put on a formidable black fur cap with earflaps, and had a hack take him to the depot, where he caught the morning train to Helena. He had arranged for rooms, and planned to settle in for the duration of the session. Hot news he would wire to Butte, and damn the cost. Routine stories would go via special pouch on the trains.

The temporary capital was bustling, and there wasn't room for the legislators and everyone with axes to grind, but for a king's ransom lodging could be had at the great redbrick mansions on the west side, the homes of cattle barons and mining kings and railroad moguls, most of which had carriage houses that could be rented for a fancy price from the servants if not their masters. He was worth it. He would charge the cost to the *Mineral*, and Clark would swallow it without a whimper. It would be servants' quarters again, but Hall was used to it.

He knew how to operate; the axe-grinders and legislators would come to him. He was, after all, the editor of choice to approach, the editor who had turned the *Butte Mineral* into a powerful and widely read sheet. He liked Helena. It still had the aura of a gold-digging town, and some of its solid brick and stone buildings were reputed to sit on rich placer ground. Swift inquiry led him to the Georgian Chop House in Last Chance Gulch. That would be the watering hole of the Democrats; across the gulch was the Dreyer Arcade, which would be the club of the Republicans, while the Populists made a great show of being poor and would come only as guests.

At the Chop House he made an arrangement; a certain corner table, clad in white linen and suitable for four, would be his every afternoon and evening, for a price, of course. When the legislature met, Helena's prices and wages tripled, and tips quadrupled. But J. Fellowes Hall didn't mind. The paper would pay.

"And put my drinks on a tab," he said. "I'll settle at the end of the session."

"Very good, sir. Mr. Clark is a regular customer of ours. Mr. Daly, too."

"And if anyone asks, tell them I'm Hall, J. Fellowes Hall. That's all. They'll know."

"You're a mining man?"

"An editor, sir. Do I look like a miner?"

The majordomo hurried off.

It all would work out fine. There was no need to attend sessions or listen to the mumbling, when everything he needed to know would make itself plain right there at his table, and the people he

149

needed to see would appear, and the asides and jokes he required would slide into his ear.

By the end of the first evening he was on a first-name basis with most of the legislature. At his table was a bottle of good bourbon, glasses, and a bucket of ice straight off the peaks above town. By the end of the second eve he knew Daly's operatives on sight, and sometimes he saw one of Clark's men, a slippery fellow named Bitters that Hall suspected of being Clark's chief of staff here in Helena. Daly's men were all wearing Anaconda buttons. Clark's were wearing copper-colored ribbons with Clark's name gilded in silver on them, a thoughtful decoration.

The voting for a new Montana senator had begun, and it was deadlocked between several Democrats and a Republican or two. None of that was important. No one was close to a majority, and Clark himself was near the rear of the pack. Federal law required that the legislature vote daily in session until a United States senator was elected, and Hall expected it would be weeks before the dust settled. The winner would need some help from the Populists and in Clark's case, from some Republicans too. Daly's men were heading across the gulch more and more, looking in the opposing party for the votes they needed to stop Clark— and win the permanent state capital for Anaconda. As for Daly himself, if he was in Helena, he certainly wasn't dining in the Chop House.

Hall enjoyed the show. The boodlers were busy. No cash ever crossed a linen tablecloth, but it was plain there were deals done and bank accounts fattened. Now and then a calculating politico slid up to his table with some news, or accusations, or scheme, which Hall duly recorded and shipped off to his rag, usually on the morning train. He had a way of listening without taking notes, which usually made people more effusive and less guarded. A question here and there, a nod, a smile sufficed. He kept the *Mineral* well fed with gossip, with whatever was damaging to the Daly interests, and with insinuations of bribery which were carefully tailored to avoid libel but heavy with suspicions and hints. If a legislator suddenly seemed cheerful, that was grist for Hall's mill.

J. Fellowes Hall knew he was a master, and over the days and weeks of the session, he managed to portray the Daly men and the Republicans as rascals, bribe takers, and crooks. He made a specialty of implying that so and so was miraculously affluent, spending vast sums on dining and wine, and sporting new wardrobes gotten up by Helena's busy tailors. Hall never missed a trick, but neither did Daly's rag, the *Anaconda Standard*, whose black headlines and political cartoons depicted the Clark forces in much the same light.

One day a mysterious lady of indeterminate age appeared unescorted at the Chop House, and settled into a corner table opposite of Hall's. It was impossible to ignore her. She was slender and exotic, vaguely Mediterranean, with jet hair. She wore the most demure of woolen suits, gray with a pleated skirt, all buttoned tight from neck to toe, but at the neckline everything changed. Above was pale and ethereal flesh haloed by black, and soft brown lips always slightly open, with a slim nose and warm brown eyes completing the ensemble. If the demure gray dress suggested primness and propriety, everything from the neck up suggested wanton delight in the ways of the world.

Hall eyed her amiably, knowing he'd soon have her secret. The main thing was to see what male joined her. It was not proper for an unescorted woman to remain for long in a reputable restaurant. But no male showed up, and she proceeded to order wine and a salad and with these before her, mostly as a barrier to unwanted male attention, she continued to eye the politicians. She scarcely ate, but did consume some red wine, and then another glass.

That somehow annoyed J. Fellowes Hall, and he toyed with the idea of introducing himself, but counseled patience. He'd soon enough know her designs. But that evening passed without another clue. The lady gazed, sipped wine, eyed the hurly-burly crowd, even as every male in the Chop House eyed her.

Hall sensed she was about to depart, and decided to break with his own habit, and summoned a waiter. "Invite the lady to my table. Tell her I'm J. Fellowes Hall, editor of the *Butte Mineral*, and I will record her every word for posterity."

The waiter delivered, and Hall found himself being scrutinized, one female eyebrow raised, while two brown eyes took him in. She nodded. The waiter returned. "She accepts and will join you presently," he said.

She appeared shortly, and settled in across from him. "You're Mister Hall, and I'm Miss Anonymous," she said.

He discovered no ring on her left hand. "Anonymous?"

"That's how it will be, but you may call me whatever name you think might fit."

"I will call you Queen," Hall said, "because that is your station in life."

She laughed. "The Virgin Queen, like Elizabeth of England?"

For once, Hall was tongue-tied.

"I am here unescorted, which raises questions about my reputation, which you have probably already resolved," she said.

"I, ah, was merely speculating. I believe you are here because of the session."

"No, I'm looking for a man. My intention is semi-honorable."

"You, ah, I am lost, Queen."

"I wish to be kept by an appropriate man. One with adequate funds to make a beautiful lady very happy. This is entirely the proper spot for that, so you could say I am surveying the terrain."

Hall was entirely flummoxed. In all his years of toil in the news profession, he had never encountered such candidness.

"Have you any prospects?" he asked, delicately.

"Not you," she said.

That was among the most deflating moments of his life. It made him wish he had not been stuck with parents who misnamed him.

"Well, Queen, politicians are an impoverished lot. No one with means ever indulges in this hurly-burly. I'd suggest that you come to Butte, where mining men are making more money in a week than beautiful women can spend in a lifetime."

"I'll probably take you up on it," she said. "Thanks for the wine."

With that, barely two minutes into an interview, she abandoned him and returned to her own table, there to review the prospects.

It annoyed him. He planned to treat her badly in a story about Helena's morals, but it would take a few days to figure out how to do it.

Meanwhile, there was the annoying struggle filling the columns of every paper in Montana.

The Democrats had a thin majority with the help

of the Populists, but the stiff old Republican vigilante Wilbur Sanders came close to carrying the legislature. Most of the Democrats favored Clark, but Daly's faction supported William Dixon, who was Daly's attorney. Then the Republicans ditched Sanders and supported Lee Mantle, editor of the *Butte Inter-Mountain*, who might get the votes of the Daly Democrats, except that the Daly contingent continued to back Dixon. And it was plain that both Daly and Clark boodlers were attempting to break the deadlock with thousand-dollar bills.

By early March, Clark had 32 votes, Mantle 25, Dixon 11, and old Tom Carter 1. Clark needed 35 for the majority, and waited in Helena with his acceptance speech in hand, only to fail. A Daly ally, Senator Matts of Missoula County, made it plain: he said that Clark's tombstone would someday read, "Here lies the man who thought he could buy up the legislature of sovereign Montana and got fooled."

The Daly Democrats then joined the Republicans to force adjournment. The legislature had elected no man senator, which meant that Governor John Rickards, a Republican, could call a special session, or appoint someone to fill the vacancy. He chose to appoint the Butte editor Lee Mantle, but the United States Senate wanted no part of it. Montana was without a second senator, and Rickards continued to refuse to call a special session, knowing it would result in a Democrat being elected, so the state drifted along without two senators.

Daly didn't get his capital. Clark didn't get his seat in the Senate. But a lot of Montana's politicians were suddenly affluent.

Seventeen

The snazzy young man stepping off the railroad coach was no stranger to Butte. He'd been in town twice, but this time he intended to stay. In his portmanteau he had a miraculous money machine. It would take a while to crank it up, but soon it would make him, his brothers, and his backers, rich. He had no large ambition other than to make a fortune for the fun of it, and then squander it in bedrooms and restaurants. If he could rattle a few financiers along the way, that would be entertaining too.

The city was cold that March day of 1893; but when was Butte ever warm? It hugged the Continental Divide. Minerals were wherever they had been laid down long ago, and in this case, the richest hill on earth was perched on a high western slope of the northern Rockies.

He got a hack and directed the driver, Fat Jack, to find him some excellent rooms preferably in the downtown area. He was used to great comfort back East, and knew he would soon enjoy such comforts in Butte, but not just yet. The driver, it turned out, knew just the place, and deposited him at the Butte Hotel, in the heart of town, surrounded by saloons and eateries.

F. Augustus Heinze gave the gent a generous tip, asked him to pick up his black leather trunk from the express car, and bring it also. He rented a suite by the month, deposited his portmanteau, and set out afoot for the eastern reaches of the hill, Meaderville in particular, to take a close look at the site of his new smelter, which would be called the Montana Ore Purchasing Company. The smelter was the culmination of years of planning, education, capitalization, and evaluation of the many independent mines operating on the hill, mines that shipped their ore to the great mills and smelters of the Anaconda combine, or the Boston and Montana Company's reduction works in Great Falls—and paid more than they should.

F. Augustus Heinze was not inclined to work any harder than he had to, and would have taken a hack to Meaderville but for his wish to pace every foot of Butte once again, letting the city settle itself in his mind. He had ventured West while still in his teens, with degrees from Brooklyn Polytechnic and the Columbia School of Mines, intending to make a princely living at mining. When he had arrived in Butte the first time, he was swiftly hired as a mining engineer, and spent his days deep underground, reading the way the veins went, mapping copper and silver veins indelibly in his mind. He had an uncanny grasp of what lay under the surface of Butte, and he knew it. In time he returned East, wrote for a mining journal, took additional courses in geology and mining in Europe, and returned well schooled to begin his adventure.

His father, an importer who had created a modest family fortune, had resisted.

But now his father was dead. And his brothers, Otto Charles and Arthur, were willing to venture the family's modest capital in this big plunge. Fritz Heinze—he hated the name Fritz, avoided it and asked others not to use it, but it stuck anyway—owned 51 percent of the new company, which would reduce ore cheaply for the dozen or so independent mines on the hill, thus saving their owners large sums. It was all there in his portmanteau. He had much the sense about mills and smelters that the Guggenheims did: lodes come and go, mines give out, but a smelter remains profitable for long periods, drawing upon one or another mine in the surrounding mineral belt for its sustenance. But Fritz had a larger vision than the Guggenheims: he knew where the veins lay thick and fat and rich, and he planned to claim them, and feed his own ore into his smelter. Somehow, in his head, he had a map of the richest veins on the hill, and he intended to use his knowledge to get very rich.

Meaderville lay upslope and east, and was a favorite recreational quarter of Butte, known for its choice restaurants, cheerful nightlife, and sedate Italian neighborhoods. That was perfect. Fritz would mine the ore, smelt it, and mine the saloons and eateries all at once. Fritz stood five feet ten inches, and weighed two hundred pounds, and was lithe and thick and muscled. He was not handsome but made up for it with a lively eye for a curve, and a great deal of suave cheer. He wore a bowler and well-cut coat, in accordance with his class. His mother was a Lacy, from a family both Irish and Episcopalian, while his father Otto was a German immigrant who had prospered at once in the New World. Fritz Heinze had not known a day of hardship and intended never to know one.

He had been born in December of 1869, which made him twenty-four on this cold day in Butte. In his portmanteau he had the incorporation papers, the deed for Meaderville land, the blueprints, and the contract with a Butte construction company to begin work on the smelter. He hiked to the site, noted that the contractor had staked the ground and was ready to go. Within sight were various independent mines, whose owners would relish the chance to turn their ore into copper and silver and maybe some gold for a tariff well below what the giants were charging, and he'd do it right there on the hill, too, saving them the cost of hauling.

He eyed the city below him, bustling and busy now, dominated by Clark and Anaconda but with a dozen or so powerful independents, such as the Boston and Montana Consolidated Copper and Silver Mining Company, and the various mines operated by the Lewisohn brothers. These men owned the Leonard and Colusa mines, the Mountain View, West Colusa, Pennsylvania, Liquidator, Comanche, and Badger State, while the Butte and Boston Company operated the Mountain Chief, Silver Bow, Grey Cliff, LaPlata, Blue Jay, and the Belle of Butte. Most of these mines were shipping ore clear to Great Falls, but F. Augustus Heinze had other plans in mind for that ore, hauled at such cost so far away.

Everywhere he looked, he saw the shine. The hill glittered. The money trees were growing fruit. He wasn't one to toil, and didn't intend to. Hire others to do that. Hire good men to run his smelter the way he intended, using the best fluxing and milling processes in the world. Hire good men to wrestle the raw ore from deep down, and crush it and bleed it and heat it until it yielded treasure. There was the itch in him to apply his unique knowledge, hard-won at American and European universities. There was every need to examine prospective mining properties himself; his knowledge of geology and mineralogy would suffice. There was no particular need for him to bother with the rest.

His late father would not approve; his mother's wish that he would pursue the arts or a profession didn't matter. He doubted that his two brothers entirely approved, but they had reluctantly anted up the family inheritance. He studied the Meaderville site, satisfied with it, and then hiked back to the central city, having had enough of cold and thin air and smoke.

There were more important things to occupy his time.

He attended to his grooming, washing up, combing his somewhat rowdy hair, and then descended to the street, in search of a good chop house. He was ready for a tender steak, some roulette, and a few ladies, preferably of the demimonde. He could always find such establishments in Meaderville, but his purpose this eve was to find cheerful establishments near his hotel. That proved to be easy. He had a way of knowing instantly whether a hostelry suited one of his several moods.

Park Street proved to be a cornucopia of such places, so he ducked into one, found it amiable, and settled himself at the mahogany bar. A barman in a white shirt and bow tie soon supplied him with some good Glenlivet on ice, and he sipped gratefully while surveying the clientele. There were several accountant types on the bar rail, which was fine. Fritz liked accountants. Yonder, pushed against the flocked green wallpaper were couples, one probably married, another consisting of a bewhiskered and portly old gent with a thin blond lady who looked nervous and kept fingering a keepsake at her breast; and a third couple who looked bored with themselves and their world. None appeared to be hurting for money, and all were dressed to the nines for an evening on the town.

"I wish to send drinks and compliments to those couples," he said, pointing them out to the barman. "Tell them, courtesy of Augustus Heinze."

The barman was skilled, or else a quack, because he set to work on the libations without further inquiry, and a waiter soon delivered the goods. The couples craned around, nodded and smiled, and lifted their glasses in salute.

It didn't take long. Before the evening was well mellowed, he had met portly old Agamemnon Bulwer and his young vamp Alice Cronsnoble. He was a private banker capitalizing mines, and she was, well, the object of his attentions. The married couple proved to be Salmon and Tootsie Hogarth, he a mining engineer with the Clark group, she a drunk who made eyes at Fritz. And the bored couple proved to be a hotel owner named Higgins, celebrating his birthday, along with his lady friend Esmeralda, who was hoping the evening wouldn't last long.

"I say, fellow, come tell us about yourself," said Bulwer.

"A new man in town, sir. F. Augustus Heinze, from various quarters of Europe and the East Coast."

"Ah, so? You have a specialty?"

"Why, women are my specialty, sir. I have a graduate degree in women, and I am a doctor of female philosophy."

The old boy's eyes lit up. "I'll want to read your dissertation."

"It involved a great deal of research," he said. "Paris, New York, Istanbul, Buenos Aires, Sumatra."

"What does the F stand for?" Alice asked.

He sighed. "A name I got stuck with, and which I wish to bury in the bottom of the shaft."

"Fess up now, Heinze."

"Fritz, sir. It is painful to me."

"Well from now on, Heinze, you're Fritz."

Heinze sighed. This was not new to him. But he would suffer what he must to make the acquaintance of an investment banker.

"Your trade? Your trade, sir?" Bulwer asked.

"Predator, sir. Shark. Barracuda. I plan to eat a mine a day."

"By Gawd, Butte's the place of destiny," the old goat said. "Well, Alice, shall we go start an earthquake?"

"I have a headache," she said.

"My pleasure," Fritz said. He rose, and soon was making other friends at other tables.

Heinze enjoyed them. Esmeralda was making eyes at him and Tootsie was pushing her knee into Augustus's thigh. He was off to a good start and the evening flew by amiably. From Salmon—they got onto a good professional basis swiftly—he learned that the Rarus mine had some timbering problems, and water trouble on the seventh level; from the hotelier he discovered that Butte's city water supply was precarious and tainted, and the Clark interests were not inclined to improve it. But it was old Bulwer who intrigued him the most. Give a banker a drink or two, and suddenly the world opens up. He learned the names of half a dozen mines seeking development capital, and why Bulwer wasn't going to accommodate four of them, and why he called the vamp his secretary and installed her in her own suite.

Heinze picked up another round of drinks, conferred his best wishes upon his new friends, gave them his business card, and drifted to the green baize tables in an adjoining room, where a thin, tubercular croupier was operating a clattering roulette wheel and another fat one was operating a faro game. Heinze studied the lacquered wheel a bit, spotting a slight wobble and a halting conclusion to each spin, and decided not to waste his money there. Instead, he bought into a faro game, bucked the tiger, lost a few dollars, and abandoned the parlor.

He dined on filet mignon and mashed potatoes

plentifully smothered in gravy, and then headed over to his hotel, content with the evening. He had six new friends, a heap of valuable and confidential information, three women who were inclined to be accommodating, and several new business connections, most particularly an investment banker.

He entered the lobby, cast aside an impulse to hike down to Mercury Street, and headed toward his suite. Business was always fun. He did his best work evenings, and this evening had been just capital.

Eighteen

Alice Brophy found employment as a laundress for a dollar a day, which was more than she expected. Her employer was the Florence Hotel, which was a vast rooming house rather than a hotel, close to the Anaconda Company mines. Marcus Daly had built it to accommodate his miners. It was a rambling structure, with rooms containing two iron cots, and it was home to over six hundred, mostly off the immigrant boats from Ireland.

Her task was to give each miner a pair of fresh sheets once a month, take in the old, wash and mangle them in the steamy and miserable basement, in an endless cycle. Some of the women who had been in service longer were chambermaids, looking after the lobby, billiard room, library, and the toilets. There were eight porcelain stools and a trough in the basement, always foul, and all overused. Residents didn't stay long: the Florence served as a way station for the flood of men arriving in town daily. As usual, Marcus Daly had seen the need, and built the edifice. It was called the Big Ship, after someone noted that enough whiskey was consumed there to float a big ship.

A dollar a day was good money; most hotels paid seventy-five cents a shift, so Alice took it gratefully. And it was only a short walk to her cottage, so she was never far from her children. The boarders were young, single, and poor. They paid thirty-five dollars a month and got big breakfasts of oatmeal gruel, stirred in giant pots, which nourished them during their long stints in the pits. Alice considered being a cook, but decided instead to wash sheets. She liked the faintly burnt smell of sheets as they emerged from the mangle, and she liked to carry them up to whatever floor was being serviced.

She felt relatively safe there, mostly because these men were Irish, and they would treat a colleen good and proper. But not always, and especially not when their brains had been loosened by a little whiskey. So it was always a risky thing, taking sheets up and bringing sheets

166

down, and sometimes she had slapped a galoot or howled for help. But so far it was working out.

She worked harder than the miners, who took home three dollars and fifty cents for a nine-hour day, and that annoyed her. In fact, the more she thought about it, the more she steamed at the very thought. It was bad enough being a woman and getting bounced upon by a randy man when all she wanted was to sleep. But they were getting much more money. She lifted tons of sheets each day. Wet sheets, stinking sheets, dry sheets. Sheets that made her want to puke. She lifted more weight each day than any mucker in the pits. What she could do for three dollars and fifty cents a day! The things she could have! The comforts she could give her children! The world lacked rightness.

Maybe she would tell Marcus Daly about it. This was his ramshackle hotel; this was his way of keeping labor coming to Butte. But he was treating men a lot better than women. Not that this was much of a hotel. It stank. No one cleaned it regularly. There wasn't much air. It just hung in the rooms, wet and stinking and without any oxygen in it. She swore there wasn't a vent in the building. The place had a "dry" room where miners could doff their sweat-soaked mine britches and put on some dry clothing. But that changing room was airless and stank too, and it was said half the miners of Butte either had miner's lung or consumption, and none more so than in Dublin Gulch, sprawling close to the great Anaconda mines of Marcus Daly. Maybe she'd get it, and then her lungs would quit, and she'd cough red into the sheets, and quit working, and die in her cottage, and she'd leave orphans behind, who'd run on the streets and probably die of consumption too.

This Florence was just a big warehouse for men who drank and puked and went somewhere else. So what if Marcus Daly thought he was doing the Irish a favor. He wasn't. He was sending them to an early grave.

The more the widow Brophy toiled, the hotter she got, and as she trudged the stinking dark halls of the stinking building, she built up a head of anger as strong as the steam in a boiler. Her brats were running loose, and when could she see them? No school for them; just out in the smoky cold air, doing whatever they did out in the city. That was a woman's lot to have to break her back scrubbing sheets and stirring the tubs and abandoning her babies.

At least she didn't have to get married and have a miner bounce on her every night. At least she didn't have to fend off Big Johnny Boyle who thought she was some sort of cow he'd sell for a price. Those union bosses, they were something, full of talk about making the world better for men—which was only half the human race.

Alice Brophy, widow of Singing Sean, discovered Feminism and Socialism at the same time, and knew she had found the stairway to heaven.

One winter's day she was straightening the library at the Florence and came upon a tract, in the form of a folded sheet of newsprint, lying on a table. It was called *Justice*. It also said "free." So she took it. She could read some; her ma had insisted, and she had gotten a little more in church schools and rude Butte public schools. A woman needed to read. She couldn't be seen wasting time, so she hid the tract in her bosom and continued through the day's chores, all ten hours of them, and didn't read her free tract until she got home and lit the coal oil lamp. Even then she had to feed her clamoring yowlers, who were turning into little outlaws she had to yell at.

But at last she read the pamphlet, which sounded a lot like the Bible, full of things like "Oh, my brethren, we must fight for justice, so that every man can partake of the fruits of his labor equally with the others, and so the poor and humble will be rewarded, and the rich shall have their ill-gotten gains plucked away from them."

There was a program in it. Let the means of production be owned by the government, and let workers receive the fruits of their labor according to their need and contribute their labor according to their ability. She settled deep in her sprung-cushion chair, a vision upon her. These people didn't say anything about women, and how women worked and didn't get paid much, but at least this was on the right track. She liked the idea. Maybe these good people would extend their thoughts and programs to women someday. But maybe not.

She studied the sheet, looking for its source. It was produced by the Socialist Labor Party, and seemed a lot like the union literature she was familiar with. It talked about a lecturer named Daniel DeLeon, who would visit Butte soon. There were other names in a masthead, people who sure had odd names, like Eugene Debs. That sure was no Hibernian as far as she could tell. And Samuel Gompers. Now what sort of name was that? This was all the work of foreigners. But maybe it didn't matter. The Butte Miners Union was Irish. So was almost everyone in the Florence Hotel. So were most of the people in the Anaconda, Neversweat, and St. Lawrence mines.

She thought and thought about what she had read, and the more she thought, the better she liked the whole idea. If the government owned everything, and paid equal wages to everyone, the rich wouldn't get rich and the poor wouldn't be poor. And the poor wouldn't have to work such long hours, or get so tired, or get so sick and broken on the job, because the government would make sure that everyone was treated right. Maybe it wouldn't work out perfectly, but it surely would be an improvement on what existed there, on the raw hill, where she was surrounded by thousands of desperate people barely hanging on, and a few fit men with gold watch fobs and silk top hats riding around in carriages.

She couldn't find out any more. She scoured the Florence library. During the rare moments when she had some freedom, she hunted for reading rooms or rental libraries. But the Socialist Labor Party had been nothing but a chimera. Then one day she decided to ask Big Johnny Boyle. He'd know. And she wasn't afraid of him, either. She'd defeated his designs, and found means to support herself.

Getting to see Big Johnny wasn't easy. She needed to trade hours with another laundress, and get their boss to approve. That was Mrs. Murphy, and she was the head laundress, and she was beholden to the hotel not to let any working woman feign so much as a headache, much less the vapors. But Alice got it arranged. She traded hours with Agnes Boxleiter, and Mrs. Murphy reluctantly agreed, even if she sniffed something wrong with it.

So the widow Alice Brophy walked the long way over to central Butte, and headed for the Butte Miners Union, which was Local Number One of something, but who cared?

Sure enough, there was Big Johnny parked in a chair, with Eddie the Pick, like always.

"Do I know you?" Boyle said.

"Not if I can help it," she retorted.

"I think you're Brophy's widow lady," Eddie said.

"Oh, yah, you want a husband now? Quit work?"

"No, it'd be more work, marrying. Now I get off after ten hours."

"In a house, it ain't work. What's work about it? You want a husband?"

"No, I want you to tell me about something. What's the Socialist Labor Party?"

"Oh, them. They're horning in on the unions. Piece of trouble, keeping everyone unhappy."

"I read their program. They're going to make my life better."

Eddie the Pick grinned. "Everyone's got a program. I can make your life better."

"I get enough of that at the Big Ship," she said. "And I also have a hat pin and I know where to stick it."

"What do you want to know about the Socialists?" Eddie asked.

"Where I can join, and where I can read up."

"Why? They don't care about laundresses," Eddie said. "They might care about your husband and his wage and his hours, and who hires him. But not a woman."

At least Eddie had a sense of her mission, which was more than she could say for Big Johnny Boyle, who was sitting there grinning.

"How much you making?" Eddie asked.

"A dollar a shift."

"What do you want to join for? That's as good as it gets for a woman."

"A mucker shovels twenty tons of rock a shift and gets three-fifty. I wash more tons of wet sheets, and carry them up, and bring the dirty ones down, and I work harder than a mucker and no one pays me the same."

"Yeah, well, that's tough," Big Johnny said. "Wish we could help."

But Eddie motioned her over to the window. "That's the hill up there. That's how it is. No one's gonna change anything. No United States government's gonna take over them mines. No bureaucrat's gonna pay you the same as a mucker down in the pits."

"I have to start somewhere," she said.

"Fly the red flag?" Eddie asked.

"Is that the color?"

"Socialist color." Eddie headed for a table groaning with stuff no one wanted to read, and shuffled through some of it. "Here's some talks by DeLeon; he's their current hot shot. And Debs. Here's all about Debs, good union man until he turned red on us. And Gompers. I never had much use for Gompers. But here, dig around in here."

173

"I'll return it."

"Keep it. It just gets us into trouble. When they see red, they send in the National Guard."

"Any of this going to help women?" she asked.

"Just get married, sweetheart," said Big Johnny. "I'll fix you up so you never have to work a day in your life."

"Bullshit, Johnny Boyle," she said.

That stopped him cold.

"I'd work twenty hours a day and not get a dime, and have nothing but babies out of it."

It turned oddly quiet in there.

"You'll want to read everything that Susan B. Anthony has written, and maybe join the Woman Suffrage Movement," Eddie said.

"Suffer what?"

"Get the right to vote."

"What good would that do?"

"Oh, maybe vote for better wages. Maybe vote for better hours. Maybe vote so women can hold property. Maybe vote so women get equal pay."

"Are they Socialists?"

"Beats me," said Eddie.

But then he produced a miracle. There was some suffrage stuff in that unkempt pile, tracts, a booklet about the Feminist movement, a portrait of Susan B. Anthony, and other stuff.

"Thank you," Alice said.

"Good to get that stuff out of here," Boyle said. "Goddamn biddies."

Alice hauled all of it in her apron, since she didn't have a bag, and after that she studied everything she could find, and read by the light of her kerosene lamp, and ignored her brats, and kept on reading. Now that she knew where to order the tracts, she spent money on postage and let her lousy brats starve, and when they whined she told them to boil their own potatoes, which they did, and when they complained that she didn't join them, she told them to go out and make their own living; she was tired of them.

And somewhere along in there, someone started calling her Red Alice.

Nineteen

Slanting Agnes sure didn't like the man. But he had become a regular, and he left amazing tips, and those tips kept her going and got her a knit shawl for Christmas, so she tolerated him. Sort of. She always let him know it. He was a rotter, that's what he was. But at least he showed up very early in the morning, and not when she had a dozen others waiting to see her. He came early because he didn't want to be seen by anyone.

J. Fellowes Hall was his three-button name. Definitely not Hibernian, which she held against him. He ran that paper, but it took her a while to figure it out. He came every few days to sit at her table, sip her tea, and ask questions. He hardly ever asked about himself or his future, and she was grateful for that. She hoped he'd stumble into a mineshaft someday. He peppered her with all sorts of questions, sometimes things she knew nothing about, and that made her grouchy.

She didn't know he ran the *Mineral* until she saw her own words on its front page. He had asked her if there would be a mine accident the next day, and she said yes, two Boston and Montana men would die when they fell into a smelter furnace. He had stared at her greedily while she closed her eyes and summoned word from beyond the present, and then the future arrived like a flash of lightning, and that's what she saw, and she mumbled it to him. He had hurried away and written her words in his newspaper, so the paper was predicting that there would be an accident at the smelter, and the *Mineral* published that, and then it happened. And after that, Clark's rag sold twice as many papers as before.

She felt bad, like she had exposed those grieving families to the glare of words on paper, so everyone knew that the deaths had been foreseen.

She had made one demand of J. Fellowes Hall, and that was to keep her name out of it. If he published her name, he would never sit at her kitchen table and get the future from her again. He had agreed, but she distrusted him. One of these days he would betray her, and then she would have hundreds of angry and bitter people at her door. Not that she was such a big secret. She had put her card into several papers over the years, and most people knew she had been given powers.

She still saw Andrew Penrose, for example, and he was still looking for mine disasters, and still trying to find some way to keep them from happening. But most of the bills and coin that filled her little jar on the table came from J. Fellowes Hall, so it didn't do much good to despise the man. Since that first vision of the smelter accident, he had published a dozen more visions. But sometimes when he was urging her the most, she went blank or some little tendril of contempt rose up, and she told him it wasn't his business, and she'd seen enough of him. She didn't care whether she was polite or not. You couldn't be polite to someone like J. Fellowes Hall all the time and keep your head on straight.

The *Mineral* was full of sensations, publishing things before they occurred, and it was the best-read paper anywhere around there. That man liked to know whether there would be something bad on Mercury Street, like a murder or a suicide, and once she had a terrible white vision of a girl being knifed by her pimp, and she had told Hall about it, and he had run the story before it happened, and the Butte police wanted to know how that could be. The rag sold an extra five hundred papers that time.

Now, J. Fellowes Hall was perched on her rickety chair sipping her good tea, and he wanted her to look ahead and say where the state capital would be. Helena? Butte? Great Falls? Somewhere else?

"How should I know? And who cares?" she snapped.

He pulled out a five dollar bill and laid it on the table.

She hated that. It was a bribe. "I won't," she said.

"Will Tammany win?" he asked.

She liked that. Everyone in Butte knew about Marcus Daly's great horse. Tammany was the pride of Daly's stock farm. A portrait of Tammany was enshrined in the parquet floor of Daly's Montana Hotel in Anaconda, and anyone who stepped on the large image of the revered horse had to buy the house a drink. Tammany ran in all the great stakes races back East, and made a lot of money for Marcus Daly. And Tammany was just one of several great Thoroughbreds raised right there in Montana.

"I don't know and I won't try," she said. "You'd just go bet on it. I won't abuse what's come to me. It wouldn't be a proper bet."

"I wouldn't bet; I want to say it before the race, so the *Mineral* sells a lot of papers."

"I won't try," she said.

He seemed faintly annoyed. Twice she'd refused him this early morning. That suited her just fine. There was something about the man that made her want to stick a hat pin into him. He sat there, plainly disappointed because he didn't have any fancy item to put on his front page. He eyed her door, as if thinking to go.

"Who's going to win Butte?" he asked. "Daly and his Anaconda Company, or Clark? They've been wrestling with each other for years. So, look and see."

"I don't know if I feel like it."

"There's unending wealth down there, beneath our feet. Copper and silver and gold. Enough to make someone the wealthiest man in the world. Someone's going to get it. Who?"

She eyed him, guessing at his motives. What could he put on his front page? "All right," she said.

She closed her eyes, hoping nothing would happen, hoping no white light would fill her vision, hoping she wouldn't be transported to some place in the world to come. But her hopes failed her. She saw a man she had never seen before, and he was well dressed, too. And he was here, right now, and a name came to her. She didn't like the name. What kind of man was that? He wasn't a Hibernian, and he wasn't even Catholic. But he was holding the richest hill on earth in his soft hand. And laughing at the world.

J. Fellowes Hall was watching hawkishly.

"So?" he said.

"No one you know," she said.

"Of course it's someone I know. Did Daly sell to someone else? Clark, he's the king of the hill, right?"

She shook her head.

"No, this one is a newcomer, sort of. He sees the way the veins go. It's like he has magical vision. He knows how the ore got laid down."

"A geologist."

"I wouldn't know that. He's got a lot of learning in him, I know that. And he's not like me, not like people who've been born dirt poor. His pa, his pa sent this man off to schools, lots of schools. And now he's got it all in his head."

"Are you just making him up?"

"You can leave this instant."

"I'm sorry; that was uncalled for. Who is this man?"

"I can't pronounce it. But he's half your age. He's barely out of school."

"There's no boy genius in Butte."

"Fritz, that's his name. Heinze, or something like that, his last name."

"I've heard of him. He's building a smelter in Meaderville. Sorry, madam, but he's not about to take over the richest hill on earth."

She sighed, tired of all this, and wished the man

would leave. She had dishes to scrub. "All right then," she said. "You asked. I told you." She rose, wiping her hands on her apron.

"No, wait. How will he take over Butte from two of the most powerful men in the United States?"

"He's smarter. He doesn't need to work. That F, it could stand for Fast instead of Fritz."

Hall lit up, and she knew why. Anything scandalous in Butte ended up on the front page of his rotten paper.

"Is he the playboy of the western world?"

"How should I know? I'm fey, I see things. That doesn't mean I know anything."

"Will he start his own paper?"

"You would ask it, wouldn't you? You'd sell yourself to him if you thought it might get you something."

"Madam, you do carry on. I'm a faithful man. I'm under obligation to Mr. Clark, who hired me, and I have no other plans."

"Except ditching him at the first opportunity."

She didn't know how she knew it, but she was certain of it. He looked uncomfortable.

"He doesn't like your paper and you don't like him. He never gave you a raise. He blames you for not being made a senator. He thinks your paper's not up to Daly's paper, right?"

"I don't know where you got such absurd ideas," he said.

"Because I saw it."

Hall didn't run, but neither was he asking more questions. "I want you to know," he said quietly, "that I esteem William Andrews Clark as if he were my father. I have built his paper into a fine, well-read daily greatly admired by all newspapermen in Montana. The loss of the Senate seat was not my doing. He was a little careless. I have no plan to depart from Mr. Clark's hospitality, or employment, nor would I ever permit myself to be disloyal."

"We'll see," she said, relentlessly. The man probably would be working for F. Augustus Heinze as soon as that dapper little porker started looking for an editor.

"You misread me. In fact, you're not fey, you're just scrounging a living from guesswork. I ought to be more careful about my news sources."

"You'll be taking Heinze's coin soon enough," she replied.

He eyed the five-dollar bill on the table, plainly itching to pocket it, but then changed his mind at the last, and left it there. It had the look and feel of dirty money.

"Take it back if you're not happy with me," she said.

He let it sit. "I don't think I will permit my paper to ventilate your random thoughts. A mistake on my part," he said. He dropped a soft hat over his locks and departed, shedding ice and disdain like a calving glacier.

The poor dearie, she thought. He doesn't know what he's in for.

It was turning into a rare spring morning. The boys had been off at dawn to fish in Silver Bow Creek. No one caught any fish there, but that didn't deter the boys. That's what spring Saturdays were for.

The five dollars on the kitchen table disturbed her. Hall had disturbed her. He made her feel like she wasn't fey at all, just an old biddy with an imagination. She untied her apron, got into her old cloth coat because it was still chill, and in spring Butte could be anything from bitter to sweet. She headed toward Meaderville, which was a goodly hike, but she needed the air. Phantasms! Is that what he thought? It was an uphill walk, but she never slowed. She knew intuitively where to go, a stretch of level ground that was all torn up. A building was rising there, and laboring men were swarming over it, as if its owner wanted it in operation tomorrow. But it was a long way from being done. Even though the building was just walls, some black iron equipment was being anchored inside, and she knew those would crush ore and mix it with fluxes and then fire it in big furnaces being built there. This is what she had seen, this place.

He was there, medium high, dapper, in a loose black suit coat, an open collarless shirt, and a black bowler, looking rather out of place among the workmen in their dungarees and brogans. She stood watching this man she had seen earlier, in one of those sudden, shocking transports into another time. The sight of Fritz Heinze assured her. He was the very one she had seen. If she asked him his name, it would be that name. There was something assuring about all this. It made her mad at J. Fellowes Hall, who had questioned her gifts. She peered a while more at the young man, barely old enough to shave, she thought, and then walked back to her cottage in triumph.

Twenty

Royal Maxwell felt the world was passing him by. The rich got richer and people like himself, honest and circumspect tradesmen, struggled. Here he was, surrounded by wealth. It lay beneath his feet, incalculable and endless, enriching only a handful. The Maxwell Funeral Parlors were not profiting from it. That was the trouble with death. You had to wait for it. You couldn't hurry it along, except now and then. You couldn't have a big sale or a closeout or a special. There were dry stretches when the world seemed to stay alive and defy the inevitable.

What annoyed him most about Marcus Daly and his Anaconda Copper Mining Company was that it was taking over the entire economy. It wasn't just mining copper and silver; it was running a railroad, operating sawmills and lumber companies, mining coal, running utilities and water companies, generating heat and electricity, and operating hotels and rooming houses. Marcus Daly and his henchmen were making a killing, but undertakers weren't.

That was his frame of mind as he hiked up Galena to the Butte Miners Union for a little talk with the bosses. He found Big Johnny Boyle there, but not Eddie the Pick. Johnny was reaming earwax with a paper clip.

"Who died?" Boyle asked.

"Not you, I see," Maxwell replied. "A big pity. I'd have to charge extra to have a long box made. You'd earn me a little more than typical."

"You're here for something bad."

Maxwell drew himself up to funereal dignity. "Well, if you call making some money for the union bad, or burying your members and their families with dignity and peace of mind, then maybe you're right."

Big Johnny grinned. "Like I say, here for something bad."

"That's the way people think about death," Maxwell said. "I think about comfort and peace. I think there's something the union can do for its members. Provide a funeral benefit for every member and every family member."

"I knew it," Boyle said. "I just knew it."

"Twenty-five cents out of every pay envelope. Just two bits. You keep a nickel for the bother of it all, I keep twenty cents. For that, every member gets a good burial, and so does his wife and children. It won't cost them a thing, except for flowers and the wake. The union makes a nickel more each week. I take the twenty cents, times your eight hundred members, and I'll be ready day or night, weekdays, Sundays, holidays, to be of service, all paid for."

"I just knew it," Boyle said.

"That way, when the time comes, the widows and children will be protected. No unexpected bills. And you won't have to pass the hat anymore. A member dies, and it's all covered. Guaranteed wooden casket, best pine in Montana, fresh varnished, and everything arranged."

"So, twenty cents times eight hundred times fifty-two weeks, right, Maxwell?"

"Yes, and twenty, thirty, forty, fifty dignified funerals all taken care of; no heartbreaking bills sent to the widow."

"And the union gets a nickel a week per member, right?"

"Well, of course, that would be up to you. Perhaps you'll wish to forgo that, and just charge your members twenty cents a week."

"We usually pass the hat to give the widow a start somewhere," Boyle said.

"Well, you could make it fifty cents a week

and begin a widow's fund."

"What party are you, Maxwell?"

"Oh, why, I lean this way and that."

"Just tell me yes or no. You ain't a Democrat."

"I'm with the Democrats on silver, you know. I'm a true-blue silver man."

Boyle grinned. "Yeah, if the silver bill passes, Butte maybe shuts down."

"I'm against corruption."

"Yeah, aren't we all. Look, Maxwell, there's a lotta stiffs trying to make a buck off of working-men's backs. Including me. I live on their dues, right? But they get three and a half a day if they're lucky, and there's not a nickel left over, you get me? Not a nickel. Two bits out of each paycheck, that's taking food out of mouths. That's how tight it is."

"Sure, one less mug of ale," Maxwell said.

Boyle stared at him. "It figures," he said. "Here's the scoop, Maxwell. I'll talk to Eddie. I'll talk to my men. And we'll do some arithmetic. But offhand, I'd say forget it. The owners got a piece of each man; they get rich and no one else does. You want to do some good? Get the owners to foot the funeral bill. Go talk to the whole lot. Maybe start with Clark; he's running for Senate again and maybe he'd make a gesture or two."

That was about what Royal Maxwell supposed.

"Well, sure, Johnny. I'll check back."

But Johnny was leering at him.

Clark, then. Royal Maxwell headed for the Clark bank, hoping to corral the man himself. This would be an easier sell, with the 1894 elections looming.

The strange thing was, Clark's svelte secretary herded Maxwell straight in, and there was the dapper man himself, not a hair out of place, his bold, intelligent eyes raking Maxwell.

It was easy for Maxwell to make his case: Clark wanted votes and here was a cheap way to get a lot of them from workingmen.

Clark listened intently, those blue eyes unblinking.

"I operate for a profit," he said. "You'd have me buying a sort of funeral insurance for my thousand-some employees. That would be another expense against my income from the mines and smelters and other businesses."

"It would win you a lot of votes, sir. Death benefits for all workers."

"Would it? Might it not imply that people perish in my employ? That it's a way of solacing my workers for unsafe conditions? Buying them off perhaps?"

"I think they'd rejoice, sir."

"I can scarcely imagine a miner voting for me because I've promised his widow I'd foot the funeral bill, Mr. Maxwell. Good day."

That didn't take long. There were many other, lesser mines and smelters to see about. He hiked toward Meaderville. The new smelter was well along. Maybe the new firm would want a funeral benefit. The fellow's name was F. Augustus Heinze, and he was so young he probably hadn't thought about death, which might be good.

Sure enough, there was the fellow in a black cape and hat, braving the cruel Butte winds, immersed in some talk over some blueprints. Maxwell waited discreetly until he could approach the new man.

"Maxwell here, Maxwell's Funeral Home," he said.

"I'm not planning on it," Heinze said. "Come back when I'm seventy."

"A benefit for your employees, sir. It will help retain loyal workers."

"A free pint of beer would do it better," Heinze said. Nonetheless he let Maxwell spell it out.

"I've never met a mortician," Heinze said. "Meet me for a drink at the Chequamegon. My treat. You can tell me your business plan and I'll tell you whether I want a share."

Sure enough, when Maxwell penetrated the watering hole later that day, Heinze was waiting for him and promptly bought drinks.

"Now, Maxwell, tell me about your business operation," Heinze said.

"Well, the whole secret of it is to get people to pay in advance," Maxwell said. "It costs almost nothing to stage a funeral and burial, save for the cost of some grave diggers and a preacher. I have boxes galore. I can get a carpenter to make me a utility coffin for five dollars. A little stain turns pine into hardwood, sort of. So the trick is to get people paid up beforehand, and then wait it out. Here's the thing. People move away and forget they're paid up. I bury only about two-thirds of the paid-up people. The rest I never see, so I profit from it far more than you might expect. If I got the mine owners or the mining union to provide free burial, I'd be almost as rich as the copper kings."

"You're a man after my own heart, Maxwell. But I can't do it. I can't offer my employees paid-up funerals. I'd get old men, and I don't want them. What I have to offer to get the men I want is safe working conditions. So we're at cross purposes here. We're on opposite sides of croaking. You're for it, and I'm against it. But here's what I'll do. If one of my employees is a hardship case and he departs from this world, let me know. It's always good business to treat a widow well. It makes hiring easier."

"I think we're kindred souls, Heinze," Maxwell said. "Now you tell me your business plans."

Heinze shrugged. "It's perfectly simple. I'm building the best smelter in the area. It employs the latest reduction techniques gotten from the University of Freiburg. It's close to a dozen independent mines which ship their ores to costly smelters run by Clark or Daly. I'll earn them a

190

much larger profit by milling or smelting at lower cost. And I'll plow my profits into the best mines that will feed my smelter. I'm a geologist, Maxwell, and I spent a goodly time in the pits here, and I know where the ore is and how to stay a few jumps ahead of the owners."

"You think you can tackle Daly and Clark head-on?"

"Not at all. My plan is to ignore them entirely. There's a bonanza here, and I'll have it before long. I know where the veins go, which is more than most of the owners do. They've hardly been in the pits, but I spent a year down there. Making a fortune here is almost child's play, don't you know?"

"I suppose there's more money in copper than in funerals," Maxwell said.

"There's money in anything, bodies or bodies of ore."

The pub seemed empty that night, and Maxwell was contemplating dinner, drinks, and who knows what? It was cold outside, and he dreaded the long walk to his funeral home and its suite at one side. But there was no escaping Butte's brutal weather.

"Say, Maxwell, you up to a lively evening?"

"I really should check at the mortuary; who knows what happens and when it happens?"

"You know of some club or saloon where a man can have a fine old time?"

"Not here?"

"Oh, I have a fine time here; I've met half of Butte's upper crust here. I've already cut deals with seven independent mines to reduce their ore. And I've entertained the wives, too. Nothing like a bottle of cologne for a lady. But Maxwell, I'm not resolutely single."

Illumination lighted Maxwell's cranium. "Well, I know of a fine place, amply stocked with wine, women, and song."

"Ah, now you're talking. Lead the way, Maxwell, and I'll be the dog at your side."

They bundled up against the bitter wind, and Royal Maxwell led his new protégé to the edge of the famed district where miners squandered their payday cash. He headed for the Clipper Shades, on Wyoming and Park, a saloon and dance hall, with a bevy of ladies at hand, and a trade that never ceased night and day.

That was all that F. Augustus Heinze needed. He surveyed the motley crowd as if he knew the secrets of them all. A gent with a sleeve garter was selling dance cards. A rude combo with an accordian and fiddle was generating some sour music now and then. The barkeeps in grimy aprons were peddling rotgut at fifteen cents. The ladies were either dumb Doras off the farms or worn-out hussies with faces of India rubber, blue varicose veins mottling their calves, just visible under bedraggled flounces. A rude oil painting of a lusty nude hung over the bar.

The laughter was an artifice. The music was a bandage. The smoke in the air barely concealed the sweat of the miners, and the perfume of the dancing girls scarcely hid the stink of desperation.

But none of that fazed Fritz Heinze. He bought a two-dollar card, good for twenty dances.

"Looks just fine, Maxwell. I'll have a whirl," he said.

"I'll drink," Maxwell said.

"I always tell the ladies I can't dance, and they love to teach me. I'm a very good student," Heinze said.

"Yes, well, I'll see you down the road," Maxwell said. He had a rendezvous on Wyoming Street, and he hoped it wouldn't lead to another round of mercury pills.

Twenty-one

The election of 1894 was looming, and J. Fellowes Hall girded himself for the annoying task of interviewing his annoying employer, William Andrews Clark. The man was loathsome. His grotesque whiskers and cold blue stare raised Hall's bile. Hall had thought a hundred times about quitting, but in fact he rather liked editing his yellow rag, and liked the long vacation he was taking from his family. He dutifully sent Amber a hundred dollars a month and advised her to stay in the East because Butte was not suitable. Hall continued to live in the servants' quarter of the Clark mansion, which he accessed by a rear stair, and thus enjoyed free rent in the house of the man who made his flesh crawl. He thought that was entertaining, living up there for nothing while loathing his host.

The feeling was mutual, of course. Clark loathed him, and made no bones about it, but kept him on because the *Mineral* was solidly in the black, which no other editor had succeeded in doing, and it dominated Butte. Profit trumped scruple. But the outwardly pious Clark squirmed at the thought of owning a paper whose front pages were devoted to scandals and Mercury Street murders.

Hall approached the Clark bank with some amusement. This would be entertaining. Clark made him wait a half hour, staring at a Tiffany electric lamp, before deigning to see his own editor, but at last Clark's shapely brunette receptionist bade him enter, and Hall discovered Clark armored behind his desk, and unwelcoming.

"Time to do an election story," Hall said. "We need your platform."

"My platform is to elect every Democrat on the ticket."

"I mean, your program. What you stand for."

"My program is to elect every Democrat who will elect me to the Senate."

"No, I mean, what improvements do you have in

mind for Butte and Montana?"

"That's nothing I would share in advance, Hall. They'll all see it soon enough."

"Well, sir, getting elected to the Senate requires legislators who are favorable to you. So the public needs to know what you're thinking."

"You think I don't know that, Hall? You have no grasp of politics. I am running entirely on my virtue, and on my loyalty to the Democrat Party, unlike Daly, who spends his every waking hour making alliances with Republicans."

"Ah, Mr. Clark, what about taxes?"

"I'm against them."

"Ah, what about President Cleveland's silver bill in Congress?"

"I'm against it."

"Where do you want the state capital?"

"Helena. Anywhere but Anaconda."

"But Anaconda's convenient."

"Hall, you go back to your rag and make no mention of me. You just attack Daly and the people tearing apart everything we've built here."

"I really need to publicize your program, Mr. Clark."

"You'll soon call me senator. Refer to me as the prospective senator in the news. Never again call me mister. You may also call me the owner and proprietor of any of my businesses. Or president or chief executive. You may not refer to my origins. I don't want them known. Daly, he imagines being an immigrant off a boat gives him virtue, but it doesn't. It only makes him presumptuous. He's too big for his britches. You may say that I am from a good family."

The interview limped along in that fashion, with Hall getting little to work with, and Clark being as cagey and uncommitted as he could be. And all the while, Clark glared at him, dared him to object. Hall came away, after a brief while, feeling that Clark had no program and didn't want a program, and didn't want to be pinned down to anything except that he was the man for the Senate.

It was odd, what Butte did to people. Maybe it was in the air. Here was a man of boundless ambition and achievement, but he wanted only one thing: the title of Senator in front of his name. Senator Clark of Montana. Senator Clark! Nothing more. Of course he had self-interests in mind. A Senate seat would enable him to oppose legislation he thought might damage him, and push bills that might improve his business. But nowhere in all of this was a program for a commonwealth, a vision, a dream of Montana or the nation beyond his small life in Butte, Montana.

Not that Daly was any better. His two political objectives were to defeat Clark and put the state capital in his backyard. That was it. Toward that end he bought costly newspapers, hired costly editors and reporters and cartoonists, gave extravagant gifts to politicians and newsmen, and curried the favors of powerful men in other parts of the state. When it came to ambition, or achievement, Daly's greatest ambition was to see his racing horse Tammany enter one winner's circle after another. Not even defeating Clark or snatching the capital from Helena was so great a prize as a victorious racing stable. The man had no more political vision than Clark, and maybe less. So there they were, two titans locking horns.

Was it something about Butte? The endless bone-numbing cold? The arsenic in the air? What was it about the richest hill on earth that turned titans into squabbling boys? Yet, Hall thought, that wasn't quite fair. Daly had a vision of sorts: an Irish Valhalla, a place of refuge and prosperity for his fellow Hibernians. That was more of a public vision than Clark had in his well-groomed noggin.

Yet, at bottom, Hall admired Daly far more than Clark. Daly was the more honest and earthy man who was incapable of snobbery, who would never conceal his origins, who mixed with people of all stations, who had a keen vision of a world that welcomed and nurtured those who struggled to gain even the smallest comfort and security. Yes, Daly was a better man. And Hall's task was to assail him for it. He laughed. The world was an odd place. By day he would write scathing editorials about Daly; by night he would salute him in the nearest pub. By day he would support the campaign of Clark for the Senate; by night he'd laugh at his boss, and find out anything damaging that he could worm out of Clark's domestic servants, and gossip about it. It was fun, this life in the worst, cruelest, most generous, and amusing city in the United States.

It had been an odd interview, about what one might expect from William Andrews Clark. The strange thing about it was that it was forcing Hall to think about himself; who he was, what he aspired to be, what he believed. He had not walked far into the bitter day, with Butte's smoke choking the streets, when he came to a decision. It was purely impulsive. He had not given it any thought. He turned westward, into the wind, and began looking at window signs. What he wanted was one that said FOR RENT. Housing was tight in Butte, even though the city had recklessly risen on every spare lot developers could snatch up. Housing for the poor was shortest, which was why Anaconda Copper Company had built vast dormitories, amusingly called hotels, for all the drones in the mines. The miners got decent wages, but the costly city snatched them away, and they were no better off than poorly paid common laborers back East.

He found a promising rental sign in a promising three-story apartment on West Park, and swiftly negotiated the eighty-dollars-a-month rental from a harridan with a distrusting look in her face.

"What's your line?" she asked.

"Newspaper."

"Which?"

"The *Mineral*."

"Oh, shame on you. Gossip and things no one should ever see. I never miss an issue." She eyed him. "You work for Clark, right?"

He shrugged.

"He's a piece of work. I could tell you a few things. Next door, he's got a little blonde stashed away."

"How do you know that?"

"Aren't you the nosy one. I don't think I'll rent to you." She eyed him.

"I'll take it anyway. Here's my eighty. I'll move in this afternoon."

She counted the cash and nodded. "What are you gonna stash in yours?" she asked.

"Just myself."

She looked disappointed.

It took a while to get a cartage man to meet him at the Clark mansion, and to get his few items together, but by evening he was settled. He didn't plan to tell Amber about it, and he'd just let her write him at the paper, as always.

He had just increased the cost of living by the price of rent, and yet he didn't mind. For two years he had worn Clark's collar, living there in the big redbrick mansion. He felt almost giddy, his own two-room suite enfolding him now. He had no kitchen; just a parlor and bedroom and a water closet. It was all he wanted. He couldn't boil an egg, but there were plenty of all-hours eateries in Butte, catering to each shift. The landlady furnished sheets and a weekly maid, but he had to buy his own bagged coal for the parlor stove.

He sat on the edge of his bed, relishing all this. He hadn't realized what life in Clark's servant quarters was doing to him. He had been turned into Clark's dog, and had a dog collar on him, but now he was J. Fellowes Hall once again, the crème de la crème of his profession. He had thought he was keeping an eye on Clark, back there, but just the opposite was true; Clark's staff had been keeping an eye on him. All his comings and goings had reached Clark's ears. Maybe Clark's uncanny ability to recite everything someone else was thinking had more to do with his staff, and less to do with any occult skills.

The windows faced west, squarely into the blank wall of the next apartment building, with no view at all of Butte or the distant snow-wrapped peaks or the sprawling valley. Well, at least he would have whatever entertainment lay in those blank windows across a twenty-foot alley.

He knew suddenly that he would take the *Mineral* in whatever direction he wanted to take it, without paying heed to Clark. He didn't worry about being fired; getting axed by Clark would be an honor, not a crisis.

He wrapped a scarf about his neck and dove into his topcoat and made sure his new skeleton key was in his pants, and then set out for the paper. He was actually two blocks closer to it than he had been, which would be valuable as winter set in. But it was only September. In Butte, September could be wintry, as it was now, with snow collecting on the surrounding peaks. He found no one in the newspaper, and that suited him fine. He lit the lamps and stirred up the stove. Then he collected some foolscap and set to work.

"The *Mineral*," he began, "is pleased to record an exclusive interview with Butte's premiere citizen, William Andrews Clark, who is seeking to represent Montana in the United States Senate. Mister Clark's program is to elect true-blue Democrats to office, his definition of a true Democrat meaning not the weaseling Daly variety, which he regards as renegades who have sold their souls to rival factions. Mr. Clark's great ambition is to elect Democrats of the true-blue variety to every office in Silver Bow County and Deer Lodge County and the government of Montana. He proclaimed his support for this program, and his willingness to back it with all his resources. If elected to the Senate, he promises to work for the benefit of Montana's business. He has declined to name the planks of his platform, but is desirous of being understood to be a man devoted to his party, his good reputation, his integrity, and his acumen.

"Mr. Clark is desirous of establishing the state capital in Helena, and is unalterably opposed to settling it elsewhere or allowing the state to come under the thumb of any entity or organization or person who does not have the interests of the entire state at heart.

"Toward these ends, Mr. Clark has opened his purse, supporting the election campaigns of those who favor his program. His door is open always; let any man who supports him stop by and make his acquaintance, and hear in Mr. Clark's own words what lies in store if he is elevated to high office."

Hall smiled. The next issue of the paper would make some entertaining reading.

Twenty-two

They mobbed him in Helena. No sooner did William Andrews Clark alight from the parlor car than they hoisted him into an open carriage and started to haul him through town. Then they unhooked the draft horses and pulled the carriage themselves, these roistering citizens of Helena. Clark smiled, settled into the quilted leather seat, drew his cape tight, and settled his silk stovepipe tighter, against the November cold.

Helena would be the state capital. Clark and his powerful allies across the state had whipped Daly's forces by a narrow margin, even though Daly had spent extravagantly on cigars, five-dollar gold pieces, rallies, advertisements, and bottles of good whiskey. It was said he had squandered over two million dollars of his own cash on the Anaconda campaign. But it wasn't enough.

Clark was mildly pleased. The 1894 elections had actually gone to the Republicans, largely because Clark's and Daly's campaigns had torn the Democrats apart. So Montana would have two Republican senators, Lee Mantle and Tom Carter. And Clark would not have the title in front of his name. It annoyed him to spend so much and get such poor results.

Still, he was being drawn through Last Chance Gulch by a mob of cheering citizens who would be grateful to him always. There were plenty of people in the state who preferred Helena, which was more central, and wasn't in the shadow of the Anaconda company, and Clark had welded them together, in all their diversity, on this issue—and won.

He turned to his man, Bitters. "Drinks on Clark tonight. Tell the saloon men to send me the tab."

With that, the crowd whooped its way to the

203

nearest watering holes, where the bartenders were instantly overwhelmed and took to tossing full bottles into the crowd rather than pouring. Clark knew he would foot a formidable bill, but what was victory for, if not a little celebration? And in the process, he would gain a few thousand votes next time he placed his name in the Senate race.

Oh, it was a fine eve, even if it chilled him. They pulled and hauled him everywhere, and from every alley more Helenans erupted to cheer him, even children who escaped their beds. Clark didn't much care for children, and preferred that they stay out of sight and not crawl all over him with their sticky hands. Children were an annoyance.

It was an odd thing, though. He felt no great elation. Whipping Daly wasn't as much fun as buying a splendid new mine or building a smelter. It wasn't on a par with outsmarting half the financiers in New York. But even if he lacked much feeling, his mind was busy every second calculating the effect of his great triumph. Daly was through. Clark knew the man well enough to know it for a fact. Daly's heart had been focused on the capital fight, and he'd lost in spite of his open purse, and that was the end of it for the Irishman. Clark knew exactly what Daly would do next. He'd retire to his Bitterroot Valley stock farm and raise great racehorses and win a great many of the races in which he entered one of his

Thoroughbreds. Clark knew such things. He'd always had an uncanny way of reading people. Daly's defeat was, in a way, mortal. From this day forward, Daly's spirit would wander, his body would slow and sink, and his interests would scatter. Clark supposed he should be exultant about it, but he wasn't. He didn't see how this great victory would change his own plans much.

In the morning he took the train back to Butte, feeling oddly hollow. He had won, hadn't he? He was the king of the hill. He had defeated the octopus. He had preserved Montana from a terrible fate, a state in the thrall of a private corporation. Maybc hc was feeling low because there were no more battles to wage. He sat in the parlor car attached at the rear of the train for him, all alone, the whole luxurious car his for the short ride. The rails carried him south, through a winding foothill country, and finally across a high plateau that was already wintry. The cattle that grazed on those pastures in summer had long since fled, and Montana had returned to its primal estatc, which was wilderness.

Butte was an odd island of city life high in the emptiness. He thought it was the emptiness of the state that was eroding his spirits now. He would do better among his colleagues in Butte. He enjoyed the city life there, the club, the dining, the deals, the politics. He thought of his late wife, Kate, who had fled Butte for warmer and more

205

civilized climes. She had died in 1893 in New York. She hovered at the back of his mind, a ghostly figure, along with his living children, Mary Joaquina, Charles Walker, William Andrew, Jr., and Paul Francis, who seemed as distant as strangers and usually living as far from Butte as they could manage. He didn't blame them.

The scenery was majestic, yet it made no imprint on him. He puzzled at those who said they were lifted upward by natural beauty. There were great peaks in sight, and alpine meadows, and black pine forests, and crystal creeks, and yet it meant nothing. Nature was hollow. A good painter might produce something interesting, but there was nothing in the natural world except lumber and copper. Maybe water. That was a resource too.

Getting and spending. Was that it? No, respect was the thing. Millionaire Clark, the richest man on earth was less important than Senator Clark, the most respected man on earth.

He stepped off of his parlor car two hours later, and instructed his coachman to take him directly to his newspaper. He hadn't set foot in the place for a year or two. As long as Hall was making it pay, there was no need. And Hall was doing that. It was the best-read paper in Butte, with the most ads and the most street sales. Nothing else mattered, not Hall's obvious animosity, not Hall's sensationalism. If Hearst did it and Pulitzer did it, then a paper belonging to William Andrews Clark could do it.

The horses' breaths were steaming from the uphill climb when Clark emerged from his black cabriolet and pierced the ink-stained interior of his paper. He found Hall, eyeglass perched on his nose, in his little cubbyhole at the rear.

Hall looked up, startled.

"We beat Daly. It's over. From now on, not a word about him, not a word about the Anaconda company, not a cartoon, not a sharp editorial, not an innuendo. He's done. I know the man. He'll spend the rest of his life at his stock farm raising racehorses. You get that?"

"Have you reconciled with him?"

"What's there to reconcile? There's nothing left of Daly. His heart got cut out of him."

Hall stared.

"You aren't accepting my instruction, Mr. Hall. Are you sure you wish to continue in my employ?"

"I'm only trying to understand. Yesterday we were opposed to Marcus Daly and the company; today we're silent."

"Exactly, Hall. And keep me out of the paper too. Not a word."

"Have you given up the Senate?"

"Let people think so if they wish. It'll be real politics now, Hall."

"What do you mean, real politics?"

"That which is never seen, never heard, never felt."

"Are you running for the Senate or not?"

Clark sighed. "When have I stopped?" Hall looked bewildered. "There are public politics and private politics," he said. "There are public campaigns and there are private agreements between people of like mind. I am switching from one mode to another, and abandoning nothing."

That, at last, seemed to penetrate the thick-skulled editor. And it was also a veiled threat. If Hall didn't keep Clark out of the spotlight, Hall would be looking for work.

"The *Mineral* is now a pussycat," Hall said.

That annoyed Clark. "It is nothing of the sort. You will be vigilant to protect the interests of the company. Or companies. You know exactly where to stand on radicalism, wage increases, unions, strikes, taxes, regulation, and anything else that comes between the right of a company to make the best of its resources."

Hall stared, comprehension at last in him. Clark could read the man perfectly. He knew all about Hall's loathing for him. All about Hall's vanity, his imagined reputation as a fine newsman, his itch to operate a paper without the control of its owners. He knew why Hall had fled the coop, taken an apartment. He knew that Hall would have trouble finding another position. He knew that Hall was making no provision to bring his wife and children to Butte, and it wasn't hard to imagine why. The man had gone from John Frank Hall to John Fellowes Hall to J. Fellowes Hall, as if each new name was a step up the ladder.

Clark smiled. "See to it, Mr. Hall."

He wheeled away, dodging the inky chases and forms, keeping his white cuffs well away from the Linotypes and pots of sticky black ink, and finally made it to his cabriolet unscathed. He wouldn't need to charge the *Mineral* for ruining his French cuffs.

Newspapers were worth a lot less than he had imagined. Poor Daly had sunk a fortune into the *Anaconda Standard*, brought in first-rate reporters, cartoonists, printers, and a fine editor, Durston. And what did a million dollars get Daly? A death blow. It would have gone better for Daly if he had no noisy paper at all, especially one that was brilliantly edited. It would go better, Clark thought, to keep the *Mineral* bland, keep his name out of the news, keep his dealings private, and line up the legislators who would send him to Washington with cigars and claret and quiet dinners rather than public pronouncements. Let all the papers howl and opinionize; it all came to nothing. He only wished he had realized it sooner. He could have saved the investment. He was stuck now, and the rag was earning a good profit, so there was no point in selling it off. But the Clark press would never again trumpet and bellow.

In two years he would have another crack at the Senate. Meanwhile there was money to be made, and pleasures to be bought. His brain teemed with schemes. He had an eye on California, and a killing in Los Angeles real estate or California sugar beets or maybe orange groves. He thought to have himself a plantation in South America, and there were always mines to buy, smelters to build, and maybe a railroad or two.

It was grand to spend everything he could. He fancied himself a connoisseur of art, and planned to buy Rembrandts wholesale. He had a New York mansion in mind, one that would tell the world who he was, and the more gargoyles the better.

He was young and lusty, and well formed, and rich enough to have whatever he wanted, and just now he thought a lovely lady would fill the bill. There were always ways, especially a trip to Europe. He had lost a fine cultivated wife. He would have more. And not just anyone, either. He knew his prowess. He had always been drawn to brunettes. No, that's not what he meant. Brunettes had always been drawn to him. Yes, that parsed it better. And France. The worldly dark-haired women of France made him weak at the knees. And so did his young American ward, Anna Eugenia La Chapelle, who was studying art in Paris. He would go to France, enjoy women and art and fine wine and look in on Eugenia. He could have anyone or anything he wanted. There were a few in Butte who turned his eye, but he had mostly evaded all that. Not anymore. It all was so easy. A lady could be had for a pearl or a sapphire.

The first step would be to fire all of his political operatives. The less people knew about William Andrews Clark, the better. Mark Bitters, who knew him best and conveyed mountains of greenbacks here and there, would be the first. There would be others departing, and when he was done, William Andrews Clark would enjoy a life of such obscurity and mystery that he would live in perfect liberty. This election had taught him a few things, and one of them was to disappear from public view, except under circumstances he would control. The thought elated him.

Twenty-three

F. Augustus Heinze was having a fine time day and night. Fritz, as he was known in Butte to his displeasure, had his Montana Ore Purchasing Company smelter up and running, coining money from the start. The smaller independent mines swiftly found out he could process their ore faster, at less cost, and with greater efficiency than the major smelters. Heinze's education at Columbia University and in Freiburg, Germany, was paying off. The investment of the limited inheritance originally opposed by his brother was returning a fine profit month by month.

And so far, the big operators scarcely noticed. They were good businessmen, aggressive operators with a sharp eye on costs and opportunities, and he respected them. But they also amused him. Imagine wasting millions of dollars trying to get into the Senate or move the state capital. That, to Augustus, the name he gave himself, was entertainment. And so was Butte. He began collecting copies of all the mining claims and patents on the hill, legal descriptions, boundaries, the names of those who filed the claims. The boundaries fascinated him. He had never seen such a hodgepodge of borders careening this way and that, turning claims into trapezoids, rectangles, notched squares, angled pieces, and forms beyond classification. How could anyone belowground know exactly where a property ended and a neighbor's began? Of course no one knew, and few were paying close attention to boundaries. He arranged to have a look himself, and soon found ample evidence of skulduggery deep below the grass.

He found himself in a dizzying world of data. There were the veins themselves to consider, and the directions they lay at various levels. He wished he could build a three-dimensional model of Butte's hill, with copper rivers running this way and that. Then there were all the lawsuits about claims, the piracy of ores, the exact boundaries of

212

various mines, as well as stockholder suits, and indeed, who owned what. He was a quick read, and somehow examined all these cases and filed them away in his copious brain.

The boundaries were a mess. The law was a jumble and the courts jammed up. The surface rights were a mess. It was all just the sort of milieu that F. Augustus Heinze thought was delightful. He loved a good tangle. What enchanted him most of all was the federal 1872 mining law, with its famous apex rule. If a vein apexed, or reached the surface, on one claim, its owner could pursue the vein into neighboring claims. He had a right to the whole vein. That so enchanted Heinze that he thought it was a gift from heaven.

His evenings were just as devoted as his daylight adventures into the dusty warrens of clerks and courts and real estate offices and surveying companies. By lamplight, he was planning to meet and enjoy the entire population of Butte, and set about it with great gusto. One could scarcely get ahead in a rowdy place like Butte without knowing everything from mistresses to ambitions.

It was a peculiar old gent's ambition that fascinated F. Augustus Heinze. For one evening he became a brass-rail companion of a certain slovenly gentleman who was downing whiskeys at a regular clip. The man had an untrimmed gray beard to match his untrimmed hair, along with a soup-strainer mustache. There appeared to be as much food as hair in the man's beard, and still more caked across the gent's suitcoat and pants.

He was explicating a Populist view to anyone who might listen, and no one was. Heinze, always looking for fresh zoo animals, lent the man an ear.

"Augustus Heinze here. And you, sir?"

"William Clancy by birth name, son of a bitch by any other."

"You're a man after my own fashion," Fritz said. "A Populist, are you?"

"A man of the people, sir. A man opposed to the great powers, the high and mighty, the moguls and their mistresses, the nefarious and crooked banks, all politicians, and any capitalist who owns a utility or monopoly."

"I guess that leaves me out."

"Not if you quench my thirst, sir."

Heinze swiftly ordered another whiskey and branch for the man. When the barkeep set it next to Clancy, the old man didn't deign to notice it. But somehow he knew it had arrived, and Heinze surmised that pretty soon a gnarled hand would snap it up and pour its contents through the soup-strainer that entirely hid the man's mouth.

"I'm opposed to the whole lot, Mr. Clancy, but I confess to owning a little smelter in Meaderville."

"Well, we see alike then; the little fellows against the big bastards."

"What have you against the big outfits?"

"They are slavers, sir. They enslave us. They rob the honest yeoman of his rewards. They buy entire legislatures. They connive to steal a fair wage from labor. I ally myself with any mortal who is a friend of the poor and oppressed."

"Are you running for office, Mr. Clancy?"

"You insult me, sir. I am not a politician feeding at the trough. I am running for district judge. I will be the first Populist judge in Montana, and strike out for liberty, justice, fairness, and an even distribution of wealth."

"Judge! You're a lawyer, then."

"Don't insult me, you whelp. I am no more a lawyer than I am a barber. And barbering is the more noble profession."

Given the condition of the man's locks, the statement had force.

"If I succeed to office in eighteen and ninety-six, I will bring the malefactors of great wealth to heel."

"How would you do that?"

Clancy strained an entire tumbler through his soup-strainer, and eyed Heinze malevolently. "The law is an ass, sir. I will ignore it as much as possible. My goal is justice, sir. I will restore equity, punish the greedy, slap the fingers of the avaricious."

"What do you do now, sir?"

"Not a thing. I am reduced to cadging drinks from suckers. On good days I enjoy the luxury of a union hall, where I read papers and sign petitions. On bad days, I freeze half to death. But I am also a participant in a great cause, sir. The Populists are the light of the world, and we will illuminate the city on the hill."

That was a little too much metaphor for Heinze, but he was struck by something. Clancy was a man of passion, and however he looked at the world around him, he intended to do something about it.

"You are what I call a justice man, then," Heinze said.

Clancy's eyes burned like coals. "I will manufacture it. I will invent it. I will impose it. I will spread it. I will divide it up and give each humble person a piece of it."

"This is when you become a district court judge?"

"There is a slight filing fee and paperwork, Heinze. Maybe you could look after it for me."

"I will do that," Heinze said. He pulled out his fountain pen and made a note of it, while Clancy filtered another bourbon through his mustache.

"And don't confuse me with Big Mutt Clancy; we are no relation."

"Who's that?"

"I wouldn't know, sir."

"Consider yourself elected, Mr. Clancy."

The old man eyed the younger one. "That in itself would be an act of supreme justice, young fellow. In the blink of an eye, a man felled by injustice would be restored to justice. Coin of the realm would flow into his empty pockets. A regular guaranteed salary commensurate with my faithfulness and ability, sir, is something the titans of Butte haven't seen fit to offer me, no matter how fine the services I offer. Yes, arranging that for me would be justice so profound and bright that your light would illuminate the heavens."

More metaphor, Heinze thought. The man was a metaphor machine.

It wouldn't hurt to have a friend on the bench. Especially that district court bench, where mining cases were heard all day, every day. All those companies with mines cheek by jowl were at each other's throats, and those cases were stacking up in Butte's district courts.

"Judge Clancy, I see your tumbler is empty, and it is my pleasure to refill it," Heinze said.

"I believe in progress," Clancy said. "We move from the dark past to the bright future. We move from aches and pains to euphoria. We move from the pain of bad luck to the highlands of joy. Why, yes, that is a gracious gesture on your part. Now what was your name again?"

"Augustus. Call me Gus. Augustus Heinze, a man of modest means and a bright future."

"Then we are brethren," Clancy said. "Indeed, I'll match you drink for drink."

"You've already outdone me, Your Honor, but I

will make sure you are well supplied."

"You are a daisy, sir."

"Your Honor, I'll arrange matters with the barman, and henceforth, you may expect a libation at any time, courtesy of Augustus Heinze."

"Ah, you are a Progressive, a Populist, with a great sympathy for the oppressed."

Clancy's breath was rank, and Heinze thought to escape, but considered the hour well spent. He made certain arrangements with the proprietor, and departed. The air outside carried more than the usual burden of sharp-edged smoke. Was there no fresh air in Butte, a city surrounded by wilderness and mountains?

It might be a trick to get Clancy installed in office, but if that could be managed, everything would be in place. An ambitious man in Butte needed a sympathetic judge. Heinze resolved to work on it. Meanwhile, there were things to do.

There were a couple of lackluster mines that had interested him, the Glengarry and Estella. He had prowled them carefully, applying every bit of geology he had mastered at the University of Freiburg, seeing which way the veins ran, and seeing also how the managers obtusely ignored the obvious. He planned to lease them if he could. His Montana Ore Purchasing Company smelter was on precarious footing, depending on ore from the independent mines. He wanted some ore of his own, a guaranteed flow for his smelter. He owned

51 percent of his company; his brothers the rest, and it was up to Fritz to make it pay. His mind wrestled with that ceaselessly.

He had leased the Estella from a savvy old mining man, James Murray, who had been in Butte from its early days. It was a simple enough deal. As long as the copper ore was low grade, Heinze would retain most of the profit; but if high grade, Murray would get a much larger share of the profit. Heinze knew exactly where to go for the high grade, and sent his foremen into the pit with certain instructions: add waste rock to the high-grade ore so the resulting mix going into the smelter would be low grade. There it was in the official reports: so many tons from the Estella, so many pounds of copper gotten from it, and the Heinze brothers kept nearly all the profit. The mine proved to be a dandy, and Heinze had been coining money from it. Even Murray ruefully joked about how he had gotten suckered. Heinze's company was now in the mining as well as smelting business, and the cunning Fritz was enjoying a few winks and smiles. If Fritz was enjoying the con, Butte was enjoying it even more.

And there were more prizes awaiting Heinze's attention, not least of which was the splendid Rarus, just east of the Anaconda company's great Anaconda and St. Lawrence mines. Heinze laid out three hundred thousand cash for it, and was soon running high-grade copper ore into his smelter, simply because he knew where to pry it out. All of his earlier years working as a geologist were now paying off. With the flood of cash from the smelter, he bought a half interest in the Snohomish mine, and large interests in the Glengarry and Johnstown mines. His smelter was soon turning out over twenty million pounds of copper a year, and earning the family a dividend of over 30 percent a year. In two years, he had converted the family's original investment of a million and a half dollars into twenty million. And he was just beginning. The 1896 elections were looming, and it was time to help his bibulous friend Clancy into office. A friendly judge would help the Heinze brothers even more than Augustus Heinze's skills in geology ever would.

Twenty-four

Red Alice knew she was in the right place at the right time, doing the right thing. There she was, in a giant Anaconda boarding house for new miners, slaving away for one dollar a day. But all that toil didn't matter. Dragging grimy sheets off beds and putting new ones on didn't matter. Stirring sheets into cauldrons of boiling water, and then pulling them out didn't matter.

What mattered was that she was among the

poorest, sickest, weakest, and most hopeless men on earth, and that was what she liked. They were mostly immigrants from the old country, who'd come steerage class and got sent west by Marcus Daly's recruiters who were offering a miracle: steady work, three and a half dollars each day, six days a week. There would be a boarding house, two meals a day included. Money enough for room and board, money for a little whiskey, money to send back across the seas for the rest of the clan. Money enough to laugh a little, and money enough not to feel a hollow in one's belly. But not more than just enough.

She got some help from Eddie the Pick, who drafted a letter for her to mail to the Socialist Labor Party. Please send pamphlets. Send literature. She'd take great care to get it to the right people. Send it to the Butte Miners Union and she would pick it up there. She enclosed a dollar to help them with the cost. Much to her surprise, a bundle arrived, and Eddie the Pick even delivered it to her cottage, and she snatched it before her brats burned it all in the parlor stove to make some heat.

"Workers of the world," it said. "There is a bright promise awaiting you. Better times are coming. You don't need to suffer and starve. You can prevent men from stealing your valuable labor. You can stop the rich from using you, squeezing life out of you, exhausting and sickening you until you die, so the rich can drive around in carriages and butlers can open their doors."

She sure liked that stuff. She pored over the tracts until light failed, ignoring the brats who wanted food. She gave them the evil eye. They were Singing Sean's brats, not hers. He made them, and she was nothing but Singing Sean's cow. Let them fix their own food; let them earn their own keep. But sometimes she relented, and drew them to her and smoothed their hair and cried, and then got mad at them for wasting her time.

So this was it! She counted three hundred twenty. The brats had burned some, but she had a lot. One apiece for most rooms. Some of the workers off the boat couldn't read. The Finns and Bohunks and Italians went to their own boarding houses, but the Florence was Irish and Mr. Daly made it so. She remembered him kindly. He had personally got Sean buried proper. Maybe he'd become a Socialist someday. She'd get a pamphlet to him if she could.

The next day she took the first hundred with her, and when the time came for her to take hot, dry sheets up to the top floor, she added some Socialist Labor Party pamphlets, and whenever she left sheets in a room, two for each iron cot, she also put a pamphlet on the dresser. Let them see it. Let them think about whether they wanted to be slaves all their lives. Let them know there might be a better way!

That afternoon she delivered sheets to fifty rooms, and left Socialist pamphlets in each. The next day she spent scrubbing and mangling, and didn't get into rooms. The day after that she collected used sheets, and carried tons of them down to the laundry. But the day after that, she delivered clean sheets to the second floor, letting herself into each smelly room with a passkey, and leaving a Socialist Labor Party pamphlet wherever she went.

That's how it went for a while, so she wrote the party and sent them another dollar, and asked for more tracts, preferably something new. No one talked with her about them. The men came and went, and she wondered if anyone read them. She didn't see any lying around. There were none in the library. None in the toilets. They sort of disappeared. Maybe some men couldn't read, but others could, and maybe they talked about what they had read when they were in the pit, or lunching down there. Or maybe they talked about all that in the saloons, where some of them went for a double drink of ale and whiskey commonly called a Shawn O'Farrell.

She wished she had fierce pamphlets to give the worn women in the laundry room, but she only had pamphlets for men, for those who could vote, for those who lifted rock all day. But at least she could talk to the women as she stirred the great kettles and pushed the sheets around in the steaming water.

She couldn't say much because Mrs. Murphy was always watching, ready to dismiss anyone who slacked off or caused trouble. Mrs. Murphy wanted sheets to be brought in on schedule, cleaned and mangled on schedule, and carried up to the hundreds of rooms on schedule. And to achieve that, Mrs. Murphy simply handed a pink slip to any woman who failed to do her work.

So Alice Brophy kept quiet, worked a little harder than most, smiled at anyone she thought might be eyeing her, and laundered hundreds of sheets each day.

One day when she was hurrying to the top floor, a coughing man in the little library waylaid her. She eyed him warily; half the newcomers had consumption, and half the ones leaving the Florence had silicosis, miner's lung. This one was gaunt, had wire-rimmed spectacles, and was wrapped in an ancient khaki army blanket.

"You're the one putting out the tracts," he said.

She refused to acknowledge it. She wasn't going to buy trouble if she could help it.

He coughed gently, his fist against his mouth. "It goes against God, you know."

She couldn't identify his accent. Was it Irish? English?

He smiled. "Belfast. Irish father, English mother. Church of England."

"Bloody rat, then."

"No, I'm curious what you know about Socialism. Do you really believe a government should steal everyone's wealth and then hand it back according to its own politics?"

"It's in the Holy Bible," she said. "Everyone possessed everything in common in the early church. It says so."

"Voluntarily," he said, "and it didn't last. What you do voluntarily, in a commune, is different from a government confiscating everything by force."

"I don't know about that, but it makes no difference who does it. Everything's got to be evened out."

He coughed again. "Only that's not what happens."

"I've got to work," she said. "Wake up and help other workers."

He wheezed horribly. "Thank you for the visit," he said. "I'll be here tomorrow, same time. You intrigue me. Tell me your story. How'd you end up doing this?"

She started to tell him she didn't have time for a heretic, but she simply lifted her load of clean sheets and fled. Church of England was he? Marcus Daly must be daft, letting the likes of him in, him that bled Ireland white, him that let everyone starve in the famine. He'd have an Irish name, and who'd know the difference?

She had a new tract they had sent her, this one calling for a general strike, a big strike everywhere, in every county and every state, until the capitalists caved in and treated working people better. Labor would flex its muscle. The rest of the tract was devoted to the Socialist Labor Party, its leaders and its platform. She left one in each room, on the dresser next to the sheets.

He was there the next day, huddled in that worn chair, a blanket around him, coughing and pale.

"So, you want to talk a little?" he asked.

It seemed an effort for him to talk at all, and he wheezed horribly. "You should be in bed," she said.

"It doesn't matter. This is my last day here."

"Last day?"

"Rent costs money."

"Where are you going?" she asked.

He ignored her question. "What do you earn?" he asked.

"What business is it of yours?"

"Seventy-five cents?"

She shook her head. "More."

"How many tons of sheets do you carry each day?"

She stopped, and set down her load of sheets. "You don't know what it's like to be a woman," she said.

"That should be your cause. Not Socialism."

"What do you know about it?"

"I have a wife in Belfast. I won't ever see her again."

"Have a wife, do you? That makes it worse. Wives are for your pleasure and bringing up babies for free."

"Exactly. It needs changing."

She stared at him.

"You're a Feminist too?" he asked.

"I've been reading Susan B. Anthony."

"Tame," he said. "Much too tame. Try Victoria Woodhull. Free love. Try Elizabeth Cady Stanton."

"Free love is it? Now I know what you're after. I should charge for it."

"Free, I mean unfettered."

"I don't want anything to do with you," she said, plucking up her sheets.

He coughed and grinned. She wondered what he was reading.

"I'm William Ward," he said. "And you're Red Alice."

She ignored him and started up the long mean stairwell that would take her to the top floor. Every step was a burden, with fifty pounds of sheets in her basket. Her heart was pounding by the time she got there, so she set the load down and got her breath. The narrow corridor stank. Men stank. Their rooms stank. She wondered why the Florence bothered to change their sheets.

She opened one room with her passkey, left two sets of sheets and one pamphlet on the dresser, and locked. She did the same with the next three rooms. In the fifth room she left the sheets, spotted two quarters on the dresser, and ignored them. That was a lot of money; half a day's pay. The room stank like all the rest. The men would change their own sheets and leave the dirty outside their door to be picked up. She left a Socialist Workers Party tract and locked.

When she got back down to the basement, Mrs. Murphy was waiting for her. Mrs. Murphy was a big woman, almost six feet and gray haired and heavy.

"Out," she said. "You're done here."

"I do a good job!"

"No you don't. You steal."

"I do not! Search me!"

"Out."

"I want my pay."

"Out."

"It's not stealing. It's something else," she said. "Why are you doing this?"

Mrs. Murphy paused, if only for a second. "Leave, right now, and don't come in, and don't ask for a recommendation."

"It's because I'm Red Alice."

"It ain't anything the company wants in its rooming house."

"How'm I gonna feed my babies?"

Mrs. Murphy thrust an arm out and pointed at the door.

"You owe me," Alice snapped.

The boss lady grabbed Alice and propelled her out, and up the basement stairs, and out the side door of the Florence. She spotted Big Benny Brice, the flatfoot who usually kept the peace in the Dublin Gulch area, and headed his way.

"They just fired me," she said.

"What for, Alice?"

"They said I was stealing."

"Nah, they fired you for the pamphlets. They were going to have me pinch you for stealing, but I just laughed."

"I'm about ready to steal. Not from the boarders but from the hotel. They owe me two and a half days."

"Alice, don't. You can't beat the company. They own the politicians and judges and me. I'm a company man even if no one says it."

"How'm I going to live?"

Big Benny turned real quiet. "You could get married," he said. "I know two cops looking for a woman."

"I'd rather sell it," she said. "At least I could quit."

"Stay outta trouble, Alice," he said.

"I'd go from a dollar a day to nothing a day if I got married."

"Your choice," he said. "But don't come whining."

"Big Benny, you're a shit," she said.

She was thinking about her empty stomach, and the brats and what her options were.

Twenty-five

William Ward wasn't in the Florence. She hunted for him, dodging the laundresses and Mrs. Murphy, but he wasn't there.

"Where did he go?" she asked the desk clerk.

"No idea."

"Well he had to go somewhere."

"Try the hospital. Try the cops."

"Is there a poor farm, an asylum?"

"Not as far as I know, Alice."

"It's cold outside."

"Yes, freezing, ma'am. He can't live outside."

She gave up, angry at the world, angry at herself. Why did she care? A Belfast Orange Irish with consumption. To hell with William Ward. She headed into the bitter air, choked on smoke, and headed for the union hall. A cruel wind whipped her skirts, and icy air pierced her thin coat.

The miners' hall was well heated, with a coal stove radiating warmth. Big Johnny Boyle was sleeping on a bench. She stabbed him with a finger, and he erupted.

"What are you doing here?" he asked.

"Where do sick broke miners go? Like consumption?"

"Beats me. Try the saloons."

"He hasn't got a dime. William Ward."

"We've got a sick fund," Boyle said. He studied a list. "Not on it. What's it to you?"

"He's got a wife in Belfast and he's dying."

"That's not our kind."

"Does anyone take care of them?"

Boyle hesitated, and came to some sort of decision. "They go into the pits and die. It's warm down there. Abandoned drifts, worked-out places. Some are seventy, eighty degrees."

"Without help?"

"They get help. The brothers bring in food and water."

"And when they die?"

Boyle shrugged. "Mostly buried back in there, rubble over them."

"Is he comfortable in there?"

"Bad air, filthy water, piles of crap, rats and vermin, typhoid, and dark except when someone comes to help. Dark, black, inky, stinking."

"Can you get him out? I'll keep him at my house until he's gone."

"What do you want him for?"

"Because no one else does."

"You've been fired, so how are you gonna feed him?"

"A little gruel, if he can get it down, isn't going to sink me."

Boyle stared out a grimy window. "Yeah, I know where he is. The St. Lawrence, in a worked-out area. I heard it this morning."

"Have them bring him to me."

"You don't want him. He's sick, your children—they'll catch it."

"Everyone in Dublin Gulch has con or miner's con already."

The hardness in his face seemed to soften. "All right, all right. We'll get him."

"And put him on your dole."

"We don't have anything for him. Half the miners in Butte are on the sick dole."

She headed into the bitter air and coughed. At home she found all three of her babies, waiting for her. "Eloise, make some oat gruel. Timmy get a fire going. Tommy, sweep this place."

"There's no coal," Timmy said.

"Go down to the tracks and get some."

"It's cold out."

But he slid into a worn coat and got a burlap bag and left.

"We've got a sick man coming. His name is William Ward, and he's dying. He'll be in my bed."

"It's about time you got slept with," Tommy said, smirky.

"Go wash your ugly mouth."

She wrapped herself in a scarf and coat and felt hat and plunged outside, under an overcast sky. The only good thing about cold wind was that it took the smell away. On a summer's day Dublin Gulch stank. That's when every privy behind every house stank. When the slop dumped in the mucky streets stank. When the hogs and dogs and hens and rats and cats that ate the slop stank. When the sweaty miners and worn women and little thugs who filled the streets stank. She thought the cold smoky air was better than foul summer air.

Dublin Gulch was jammed, four or five or six souls in two-room shacks, the winding street seething with life night and day. Red Alice turned in at Baldwin's grocery, begged some pasteboard from an old box, and a crayon, and made a sign: HELP A SICK MINER EAT.

That was all she needed. She toted the ragged cardboard up the gulch, got a chipped crockery bowl, and headed toward the St. Lawrence. If she hurried, she'd get there just when the shift got out. They'd know. They'd all know about William Ward down there, expiring in the foul air, the toilet smells, and the heat.

She arrived just in time, half frozen because the wind never quit sucking heat out of her. The miners poured out of the triple cages, their dungarees soaked with sweat, steaming suddenly in the bitter air. Some mines had changing rooms.

The dry rooms, as they were called, helped miners avoid pneumonia. The union was working on it. The miners eyed her sign, mostly ignoring her, and hurried toward their cottages or a pub and some ale, wanting warm before their soaked duds froze stiff.

"It's for Ward," said one.

"Yes, for him," she said.

He dug into his britches and dropped two bits into her bowl. She gave him a Socialist Workers Party tract, which he stuffed into his pocket unread. That's how it went for half an hour, until the last man reached grass, as they called the surface even if there wasn't a blade of it. She didn't see Ward. They didn't bring him up. Maybe Big Johnny Boyle was full of beans again. But she had given out twenty tracts and gotten two dollars and forty-five cents. She would keep it all for Ward, and feed him until he died and went to hell.

The icy wind drove her off Anaconda Hill, and she hurried down to Dublin Gulch, glad she had handed out all those tracts. No one had chased her off.

She entered her cottage, and it still was cold. Timmy hadn't gotten anything to burn. Eloise and Tommy stared at her, half afraid. In her bed was a man, ashen cold, shaking under his khaki army blanket.

"It's you, is it?" she said.

"You should have left me alone. It's cold here."

"It's also better air. I got enough to buy some coal, and you'll be warmed up."

"You're kind, madam, but misguided."

"What I do is my business, and I'm keeping you until you go to hell."

She found some ragged blankets on her children's cots, and heaped them over the sick man. He looked awful in the autumnal twilight, pale and yellow. His lungs rumbled. His eyes had sunk into their sockets, and his face had not been scraped for days.

"I'm obliged," he said, suddenly clouding up. For all his bravado, he was living out a horror. She dipped a rag into a pail, and sat down beside him.

"This'll be cold," she said.

She washed his face, cleaning away mucus, dried tears, the cake of silica dust and ash, and fear. She gently washed his forehead, and his cheeks and neck, his ears, his shoulders, and his forearms and arms, and then rinsed the grimy rag and smoothed his hair with it. His eyes followed her, and once in a while he wheezed, his lungs convulsing against the cruel disease eating them away hour by hour.

Timmy returned with a few sticks and two small lumps of coal. It would start a fire. She handed him fifty cents. "Go buy a bag of coal, fast, or I'll fix you good."

He eyed the quarters, eyed the strange gaunt

man in the bed, and scooted out the door. Tommy built a niggardly and heatless fire in the stove, while Eloise mindlessly stirred rolled oats in some water. The house didn't warm much. Alice fussed around too much.

"It doesn't matter whether it's voluntary or the government takes it from rich and gives it out equally," she said. "It's all the same to the poor."

William Ward tried to laugh, but all he did was convulse horribly.

"People are too cheap to share it without a shove," she added.

Timmy returned with a burlap sack of coal, and this caught swiftly, sending acrid fumes through the cottage but some heat too. The open stove door allowed flickering orange light to wobble across walls and the floor and ceiling.

"Where are you gonna do it with him?" Tommy asked, and snickered.

"Get your skinny ass outside," she said. He ignored her.

Eloise had the gruel heating, and was stirring it occasionally, her eye on the strange man in her ma's little bed.

Ward stopped quaking as the warmth reached him. His gaze followed the children and her as she busied herself.

"I suppose you'll tell me I remind you of your wife in Belfast," Alice said.

"Not a bit," he replied hoarsely.

"What is she like?"

"I don't know anymore," he said.

"Do you have children?"

"I haven't seen them in two years, and never will again." He coughed cruelly. Even a few words were too much.

She ladled some thin gruel into a bowl. "I'll spoon this into you," she said.

"I'm not sure I can swallow it."

She sat on the edge of the worn-out bed, and gave him a tiny sip, which he downed with difficulty. She fed more, and he had to dare himself to swallow it, working up courage each time he faced the howl of his ravaged throat. The children stared.

She turned to see them gawking. "You'll die of it too," she said. "The Irish all die of it."

It was true. For some reason, most of the denizens of Dublin Gulch were perishing of consumption, while other groups, in other places, weren't stricken so much by it. No one could explain it. The priests said it was because of sin.

"It's not sin," she said. "The priests, they don't know anything."

"It's caused by a germ, a microbe, Mrs.—Red Alice."

"It's caused by selfishness," she said. "If we had equal incomes, hardly anyone would get sick like this."

No one argued with her. She didn't really

believe it. But she wasn't going to let William Ward die without turning him into a Socialist, so she thought to start early and keep right on until he died. He'd end up in Socialist heaven. What she wanted was a deathbed confession. I have sinned, please forgive me, because I was not a good Socialist, but now I am.

Boy, would she like to get Big Johnny Boyle to hear that with his own ears.

He pushed her hand away. "I can't manage," he said.

"You hardly ate."

"What does a dying man need to eat?"

"I buried Singing Sean a few years ago. He got hit by an ore train on the street. No, that's not right. He tried to jump a car for a ride, and fell and got his legs cut off."

"Were there benefits?"

"Mr. Daly buried him, and they gave me a little."

"You've held things together," he said, coughing again.

"Don't talk about it," she said.

He didn't. The warmth and gruel seemed to subdue his restlessness, and even as she watched, he slid toward oblivion.

She didn't know where she would sleep. Share Eloise's trundle bed, she thought. It was a sin to have a strange man in her house, and him married, but she was tired of sin. She was tired of all the old rules and understandings.

She watched William Ward slide into sleep, and was glad that his color seemed a little better. He was gray or yellow when they brought him out of the worked-out part of the St. Lawrence copper mine. She never saw who brought him here but Big Johnny had made it happen. Somewhere, some of the brotherhood had cared, and brought him out. She found a stool and sat beside him, while her children watched her, half afraid to talk, puzzled by this intrusion. The house turned dark as twilight faded, and the stove cooled down, and the night sounds of the rowdy gulch amplified as the small tight world of the immigrants from the old country ignited into good humor.

She sat on her stool, watching the shadowed face in her bed, listening to his hoarse breathing, listening for the failure she knew would come soon, the moment when the con had eaten up the rest of him. She heard shuffling behind, as her babies found nooks for themselves, but she sat quietly, almost as if she were sleeping instead of keeping a vigil. She would vigil all night every night until the end. And it would be a vigil against the world, the system, the beliefs, the arrangements that had torn him from his wife and family, brought him here, and killed him. After he died, Red Alice planned to tell it to the world.

Twenty-six

It was the best of times and the worst of times for Marcus Daly. The Anaconda Copper Mining Company, newly incorporated, was earning fabulous wealth for its shareholders, paying fabulous dividends, and reinvesting its fat profits in new ventures. It owned a goodly portion of the richest hill on earth. Daly lived quietly in Anaconda, driving his handsome carriage from his Sixth Street home to his offices in the largest smelter on earth each day. He and the company's president, James Ali Ben Haggin, effectively controlled the company. After George Hearst had died, his wife, Phoebe, had sold her shares to the Rothschilds, who soon sold out their shares, which were now divided among many stockholders.

There were few crises. The fabulous Anaconda, Neversweat, and St. Lawrence mines poured out copper, a little silver, and a bit of gold. So did the adjacent Rob Roy and Nipper mines, in which the company had an interest. Daly's railroad hauled the ore twenty-five miles to the smelter. The company owned whole forests for mine timbers and fuel, Anaconda coal mines to fire boilers, an Anaconda foundry supplied by Anaconda iron and Anaconda quarries, the Anaconda water

240

works and electrical plant, one of the best newspapers in the country, banks in Anaconda and Butte, the Florence Hotel for the single men pouring into his works. He had built the Montana Hotel, the best in the West, with a splendid kitchen and saloon. And over in the Bitterroot Valley he had acquired twenty-two-thousand acres of lush, well-watered meadowland, and had built his handsome stock farm there to raise Thoroughbred racehorses. It had become the best stock farm in the country. It had miles of fence without a wire in it, rows of poplar trees lining the graveled roads. It had lush emerald paddocks. His horses trained in the thin mountain air, and did all the better running at or near sea level.

His great horse Tammany had won and won, and now was memorialized in the floor of the Montana Hotel saloon. Tammany's noble head and neck were rendered with pieces of hardwood, variously colored, all within a yard-square frame in the floor. Daly thought it was a suitable memorial for a horse that had won nine firsts, one second, and one third in fourteen races, and had won a legendary match race against Lamplighter, with forty thousand dollars riding on the outcome. People stared at that wooden rendering with respect, if not awe.

Marcus Daly stayed close to his wife, Margaret, and his four children, Margaret, Hattie, Mary, and Marcus II, finding time for them and for his church. They were quiet young people, not given to excess, and they pleased him. His rival in Butte, Clark, had taken to shipping his wife and children to Europe for long sojourns there, and then to California's orange groves, so that Clark lived largely alone, pursuing whatever were his fancies in deep secrecy. Those fancies were another reason why Daly was repelled by his rival. It was no secret that Clark had an eye for the women. But there seemed to be a peace between them now; Clark's gaudy paper, the *Mineral*, barely mentioned Daly or the Anaconda Company, and all its nefarious practices; and Daly's own *Anaconda Standard* was content to agitate for the silver standard, and ignore Clark.

Superintendent Daly found time to sit and visit with his smeltermen and miner. They were his people, and even though fortune had favored him, they were still of his blood and bone and heart, and he would lunch with them in cafeterias, drink with them in saloons, stop to talk with them as they rested on their shovels and picks, look after widows, contribute to their charities, see to their comforts. For anyone in the sprawling company, it was never a surprise to have Marcus Daly stop and visit. He knew many by name, not because he was currying favor, but because he actually enjoyed them, called them friends, and shared their joys and sorrows.

He was well into his fifties, and feeling his

years, but life was so good that he barely noticed the weakening of his body. He loved horseflesh, and racing became his passion. He built racetracks in Butte and Anaconda, and sponsored festive racing meets, which were often dominated by stock from his own stables. That summer of 1896 another of his great horses, Ogden, won the Futurity back East, and a purse totaling $43,970. That tickled Daly; his trainers had said the horse wasn't mature enough to run, but Daly had overridden them and sent him East anyway.

Could life be any better? Well, yes. Politics were intruding on it once again. Silver and gold were tearing political parties apart, and pitting the creditors in the East against the debtors in the West. The Sherman Silver Purchase Act had not survived, and the value of silver was in free fall. That was affecting most of the mines of Butte; the silver mines high up the slope suffered the most, but the rest of the mines, where silver was an important by-product, suffered as well. The Populists were becoming a major force, a third party capable of defeating either of the traditional ones. An alliance with the Populists was the only way for either party to win in Montana.

Daly openly supported the Populists and wrote checks. Their candidate, William Jennings Bryan, was eloquent and tireless, and framed the issues in terms of fairness; the poor needed help against the rapacious rich. He was a good candidate, well attuned to his rural auditors, able and charismatic. Marcus Daly liked him, and his appreciation for Bryan went far beyond looking after the price of silver. Bryan and his party wanted the free and unlimited coinage of silver at a ratio to gold of sixteen to one. He wanted to increase the money supply by fifty dollars per capita, which meant cheap and abundant money, some inflation, and opportunity for debt-ridden Westerners to set their economies moving.

Daly was wary of some of the Populists' program, with Socialist planks. But that didn't stop him. He saw in the Populists, and Bryan, a chance to unyoke the West from its Eastern masters, and he applied his resources to the task. The Republicans were running William McKinley, a gold man, and they had a lot of cash in the till for their campaign.

The Populists wanted government ownership of all transportation and communication companies, a national currency, a graduated income tax, direct election of United States senators, the secret ballot, a postal savings system, and a shorter work day for laborers. Some of that was welcomed by Daly and his wing of the state Democrats; some not. He knew that Clark was a silver Democrat also, and might be open to a fusion ticket with the Populists. For a change, they were both on the same side.

So Daly wrote large checks, sent his emissaries

to the conventions, and out of it all came the fusionist ticket he had hoped for. If victorious, the Democrats would send two electors and the Populists one elector to Washington to select the next president. Bryan campaigned mightily, and made a speech that resonated in every rural corner of the republic. "You shall not press down upon the brow of labor this crown of thorns, you shall not crucify mankind upon a cross of gold," he said. And many heard him.

That hot political summer paid off. The Democrat-Fusionist ticket, garnering support from rural ranchers and industrial magnates and miners and businessmen swamped the divided Republican party, and gave William Jennings Bryan three electoral votes. But nationally, the Republicans did much better. McKinley won easily.

That meant Butte would face austere times, Daly thought. Less expansion, fewer jobs, maybe the demise of some of the older silver mines, which were played out anyway. And there would be less credit, costlier money, making it tougher to start up new businesses. The Eastern moneybags with their sacks of double eagles had won.

What was there to do but return to his tasks? His mines probed deeper and deeper, and the ore was there. Two thousand feet, three thousand feet under the surface there was still good copper ore everywhere. The nation was electrifying itself, and the demand for copper for wires never slackened. Copper prices edged higher, and copper became the most-sought-for metal, its price inspiring a global hunt for new deposits.

Daly turned to his stock farm, buying the great sire Hamburg, and the dam Lady Reel, and soon had another bonanza, this one of sleek, young, well-bred horseflesh that conquered the whole world. This, then, was the dream. Copper was the means; the stock farm was the dream that pierced back to his youth and the horses he knew as a boy in Ireland. He shared his joy with his employees, who enjoyed days off to see the races at the racetrack on the flat below Butte, or in Anaconda.

Still, he worried, though it was not in his nature to worry. He was not an anxious man, and his bouts of anxiety surprised him. By design, the Anaconda Company was Irish. His successor, when the time came, would be William Scallon. There were others waiting in the wings, including John Ryan and Cornelius Kelley. Its hiring officers, shift bosses, and foremen included James Higgins, "Rimmer" Con, Dan O'Neill, Mike Carroll, John Crowley, James and Pat Kane, John McCarthy, "Fat Jack" Sullivan, and on and on, in every department. They gave preference to Irishmen like themselves, promoted men like themselves, made sure that the company remained Irish to its core, to its soul, if a company had such a thing. It was more than a corporation; it was a fraternity and a refuge for all the refugees from the emerald isle. Butte was New Ireland, its Irish population outnumbering all the other groups combined.

His lawyers were Irish. His accounting men were Irish. The company's friends and associates in Butte, such as Dan Hennessy, saw to the food and clothing and fuel consumed there. Most of the men in the pits were first-generation Irish. They were doing a good job, and the Irish Anaconda Company was minting money for its stockholders. It was paying enormous dividends, and still had ample cash to reinvest, expand, improve operations, so the company was growing, acquiring new properties, discovering still more copper and other minerals. It was also creating new markets for itself, supplying copper for brass, copper for plumbing, copper for anything electric. That was steadily raising the price of copper, and also raising the price of Anaconda stock. Owners of Anaconda shares not only reaped amazing profits, they enjoyed the appreciation of their investments.

It was a prize as glittering as John D. Rockefeller's Standard Oil, and that was what gnawed at Marcus Daly's heart. Ever since Phoebe Hearst had sold George's shares, nearly half the stock of the company was in other hands, in the open market, available to pirates and raiders and scavengers and get-rich-quick hustlers.

And that's what troubled Superintendent Daly. There were rumblings in the bourses of New York. There were adventurers quietly buying shares, working their way in, threatening upheavals. And some of those adventurers were Rockefeller men. There wasn't much Daly could do, and it troubled him.

The lawsuits were chafing him too. The richest hill on earth had generated scores of lawsuits, as corporations wrestled with one another for the incredible prizes that lay under the surface. The company had the best of the copper mines, but there were other mines, some of them silver outfits, clawing wealth from the rock. Clark had widespread interests. So did young Heinze, who was buying shares in independents. So did the Boston financiers, like the Bigelows and Quincy Adams Shaw who owned Calumet and Hecla. So did the Walker brothers, and the Lewisohn brothers, Sam Hauser, and A. J. Davis. There were the Butte and Boston Company, and the Boston and Montana, and the Montana Copper Company. And they were heaping up lawsuits against one another, suits that would be decided in Butte's overworked district court, presided over by an eccentric judge named Clancy.

Daly and Hearst and Haggin knew what lawsuits could do to fabulously wealthy mines.

They had been on the Comstock, in Nevada, the biggest silver strike ever known, and had watched the Nevada courtroom wars bleed powerful companies white, while aggressive litigators pocketed the silver fortunes that lay there. The trouble lay in United States mining law, which permitted the owner of a vein that apexed, or surfaced, on his claim to pursue the vein beyond the boundaries of his claim. That guaranteed fortunes for Nevada and California lawyers. Geology is not an orderly world. Faults move veins. The deposit of minerals is complex. Acidic groundwater shifts minerals from one site to another. That gave experts all the leeway they needed to testify in Nevada courts. They built models, opined about faults, guaranteed that such and such a vein did not really vanish; it simply had been moved eighty yards to the left and up forty yards as well. The courtroom dramas in Carson City and San Francisco were all that counted. Men who had found bonanzas and developed great mines ended up with empty pockets. Clever men got rich in the courtrooms.

From the onset, Daly and Hearst and Haggin determined to avoid lawsuits at all costs, and that meant buying every mine that neighbored their bonanza mines, or at least purchasing as much stock as they could in the neighbors', which would give them some control over what the other managements did. But now Daly wondered whether buying the neighboring mines was enough. That unkempt, garrulous clown named Clancy on the district court bench in Butte seemed to favor anyone who wanted to share the wealth. Other men's wealth.

Twenty-seven

Business was drying up. Royal Maxwell was in dire straits. A rival mortuary, Sullivan, had opened in Meaderville, and another rival, O'Fallon Brothers, had opened in Anaconda. Butte was expanding daily, hiring newcomers daily, yet no grieving person entered Maxwell's black-enameled double front door seeking his services.

He wasn't earning enough to keep his doors open, much less to support his habitual forays to Mercury Street, or occasionally to darker and meaner Galena Street when he was in a reckless mood. He felt as though he were an outsider in a town he had lived in for a dozen years. Maxwell's Mortuary had been there when Butte was small and rough. Maxwell had buried more miners than he could remember, and the carriage trade, too. He'd planted financiers, moguls, mining engineers, rich widows, rich mistresses, and the sickly children who imbibed too much arsenic from the smoke.

While he had rivals now, the plain reality was

that people weren't dying fast enough, and he could do nothing to encourage them to die sooner. He was faithful to his Republican party, which opposed regulation of business, which probably helped him a little, but not as much as he hoped. He was secretly a gold Republican, favoring sound money, but that was anathema in Butte, so he made all the noises of being pro-silver, pro-inflation, pro-easy borrowing. But it didn't get him any more business. A little more arsenic in the air would help, or a little more rock dust in the mines, but everything was going the other direction. The companies were inspecting the cables on their lifts. They were settling the dust in the pits, and building higher stacks to carry the smoke away from town. They were adding changing rooms to cut down pneumonia. The denizens of the most pestilential streets in town, in Dublin Gulch, all went to Sullivan, which was costing Maxwell a body a week. Well, it wasn't much of a loss. Who over there could afford a fine, first-class, dignified funeral, a parade, and burial in Mountain View, with a crypt and a headstone?

One day a story he chanced to read in the *Mineral* started him thinking about other prospects. Two frails had died the same day, one of suicide—she imbibed carbolic acid, which was the poison du jour—and the other had been killed by her pimp supposedly for keeping more cash than she was entitled to. Of course the *Mineral* made a front-page item of it, but that was the yellow press for you. Both of the ladies had been buried in a potter's field, by Silver Bow County, because no one had volunteered to pay for a burial.

Maxwell studied the report, and thought there might be opportunity in it. Virtually all of the ladies in the restricted district were being dumped in unmarked graves at the back of the cemeteries, alone and unremembered, with no one picking up the tab. They had become the county's burden and responsibility. They died frequently and young. They perished from syphilis and other diseases, especially consumption. They died of heartbreak. They died of loneliness. They died from wear and tear after losing their attractiveness and their income. They died when they had varicose veins marring their legs. They died of violence by all sorts of men. Some were beaten to death. Some perished after their faces had been slashed to bits with broken bottles wielded by males. Some died of opium or heroin or anything else that numbed their bodies. They flocked to town, joined their hundreds of sisters, and did not lack trade from thousands of bachelor miners. A few got married and escaped.

All of that intrigued Maxwell. There might be a fortune in it. He might also enjoy any lady's favors in return for the promise of a good burial.

He could become the one to bury all the frails and sports. They had money; they just didn't care enough about one another to blow any of it on a fine, bright funeral with a parade and drummers and a good crowd of spectators. But he didn't quite know how to approach anyone. And he didn't know how to get himself reimbursed for a good gaudy funeral. He could propose monthly payments in advance, but he knew how that would work out. He could approach the madams and try to get them to pay in advance. Or the pimps. But the more he puzzled it, the more difficult it seemed. And yet he had to try. Funerals for the demimonde might yet be bonanza ore for Royal Maxwell.

He scarcely knew where to begin. But he thought he could make progress. He was naturally unctuous, and had a dripping and buttery sympathy he could call up for all occasions. He preferred the tony parlor houses when he could afford them, so that seemed the place to begin.

And where better than Chicago Marlene's Parlor? He rehearsed his little talk, while trotting down there one afternoon—he wanted to make his pitch before business heated up—and soon opened the red-enameled door that let him into a tiny reception hall. No one wasted a square foot in the district. Chicago herself met him with an oozy smile.

"A word about business, Chicago," he said.

"Everything's for sale," she said. "At a good price."

"Well, if you have five minutes, I want to make a proposal."

She puckered up, and then eyed him warily. He followed her into a tiny side room.

"I charge twice as much as my girls, Royal," she said. "But if your tastes run toward sagging knockers, I'm here."

"Actually, I want to talk about the unmentionable that happens to us all," he said.

"I take sulphate of mercury," she said.

"I mean passing away, Chicago. The ladies here—well, they don't last long, and almost in the springtime of their lives they end up in a potter's field, planted there by Silver Bow County, forgotten. They don't even have markers. Just a little lonely patch of earth."

She looked ready to explode, so he hurried along. "You know, I feel such a great sorrow when I see those lonely mounds of earth at the back row of the cemeteries. I think, there was a life lost. No one cared enough to bury them properly. No family came to collect the remains or buy a coffin."

She was smiling. "You've come to sell funerals."

"Well, no, I have a better idea. Most of the ladies don't have a nickel to their name. It all goes to the Chinamen. I thought to myself, here's a public service I can do. I can offer free funerals to the suffering people in the district. Of course, if people wish to pass the hat and pay me what they can, that would be fine. But even if I don't receive a thin dime, I would be pleased to give all the people here a proper send-off."

She eyed him. "And meanwhile you want a free screw."

"Well, that too. I was thinking, a two-hundred-dollar funeral ought to be worth a hundred little moments with your nymphs. The bookkeeping should be easy."

She held out her hand. "Two dollars right now, or get your ass out."

"I don't have—ah, if the girls will service me, I'll service them at the appropriate time, in a gentle and dignified and entirely appropriate manner."

She didn't speak. She just stared, faintly amused. Then she thumbed him toward the door.

"Think about it," he said.

"I already have." She jerked her thumb.

That didn't bode well. The next parlor house, Twice Around Mary's, featured fat women, and he tried that. Twice Around listened silently, sighed, and said "No one here croaks."

He tried an obscure, dark place called Sam's next. No one knew whether Sam was a man or a woman, but she wore skirts.

"Don't you feel pity for the girls who perish by their own hand?" he asked.

"What are you, a preacher?" Sam asked.

"No, I am a man who cares about the lost. They drink carbolic acid, burn out their insides, and die in anguish. Then what? The county comes for them because no one else will. Not even the other girls will. And thus they end up alone, unlamented. Isn't it sad? Here I am, in the business, and no one ever calls on me. I'd gladly offer my services free if only to make the world a little kinder."

"What's your angle, Maxwell?"

"Well, I thought maybe I could exchange a few delights for the solemn promise to bury them well . . ."

Sam smirked. "I knew it."

"But really, the funerals would be free. All I'd ask is that you all pass the hat, and whatever comes my way, why, I'd be able to keep my doors open, pay for the hearse, serve the public."

"You sound like a carbolic salesman," Sam said.

Carbolic acid was the poison that the ladies of the night seemed to favor because it produced more agony than anything else they could drink. Who could explain it?

"I assure you, Sam, I am earnestly trying to uplift the spirits of those caught in the sporting life."

Sam giggled.

Next was Galena Street, a place loaded with cribs. His first stop was Cockeyed Louis, a famed pimp, who sometimes forced a customer into his joint at knifepoint. But Louis just grinned. "You pass the hat and I get fifty percent," he said. "Me, I'd just as soon knife a girl as pay for a funeral. They ain't worth it."

Royal Maxwell toured the district, mostly meeting silence and bleary stares. But wherever he went, he promised a fine, free funeral for the sports, with the hope they'd pass the hat.

The next day Cockeyed Louis croaked. An irate person unknown sliced his throat from ear to ear and left him in the gutter. Maxwell read all about it on the front page of the *Mineral*, which never varied from its sensationalism.

Ah, what a dilemma. He had promised a free funeral to the sports, and now one was thrust upon him. Not a girl, but a mean pimp, well known throughout town. He decided that his whole enterprise was on the line, so he volunteered. He headed for the Silver Bow sheriff's office, claimed what was left of Cockeyed Louis, who was lying in a cell until he could be planted, and took the deceased to his mortuary.

The first thing was to send word to the district, so he hired Watermelon Jones, the messenger, to stop at every parlor house in town with the word. There would be a parade and a planting at Mountain View on Thursday at three. That would be a good hour. He needed to be sure the sports were up, but wanted the ceremonies to be over before business picked up. He tipped Watermelon an extra dime for his hard work, and then set to work. He cleaned up Cockeyed, put him in a fine oaken box with satin lining, polished up the black hearse with the glass sides so all the world could see the fine coffin within, got some fall flowers, put on the black pompoms, and got the black horses he regularly rented from Willis's Livery, and then he was as ready as he could get. He would make a small, kind graveside oration in lieu of a cleric. He also hired a couple of drummers, one with a bass drum and the other with a snare drum, and a bugler to play taps.

He felt mighty fine about it. No one would show up to bury Cockeyed. But surely the whole sporting district would enjoy the show and pass the hat. Just to make sure, he brought a spare hat along to start the coins rolling.

Promptly at three on Thursday, Maxwell drove his shining ebony hearse from his establishment toward the district. The casket was heaped with flowers. There were black pompons; the horses were in nickelplate harness. A small black sign next to the casket announced the presence of Cockeyed Louis. And just ahead of his hearse the drummers tolled the hour, snare drum and bass drum in measured cadence. All in all, Cockeyed would get himself a fine send-off. Royal drove straight down Galena Street, and was rewarded to see eyes peeking through curtained windows even if there were few people on the street. Then came

Mercury, and finally Silver, a fine display for all to see. Miners in boots and worn britches stared. He thought maybe the miners might pass the hat, so he paused, handed a black silk top hat to them, and whispered that he would be grateful if they would collect on behalf of the much admired Cockeyed Louis.

"Jesus Christ," said one of them.

"Yes, yes, just right. Collect a little to bury the dead," Maxwell whispered, and set his hearse in motion again. Just to sweeten the odds, he drove Mercury, Galena, and Silver Streets once again, but the miners were lost to view. He finally headed south on Main Street, drawing lots of stares and even stopping traffic. What a fine funeral! Well worthy of a swell. But no one followed. It would be a long ride down to the cemetery, but his drummers marched resolutely, and at last he turned in, past the graves and trees, to the rear row, where an empty grave awaited. The crowd he had hoped for didn't materialize, and he finally recruited the drummers to settle Cockeyed in his grave. There was no one about; only the cold November air shivering his horses and the men.

He looked for the miners on the way back, thinking they would dump a handful of coins into his lap, but no one showed up, and he finally realized he had no coins and no hat. Well, it had been a fine trip; everyone in the district had seen

Louis pass by. They might not have liked Cockeyed—no one had ever said a good word about him—but that didn't matter. The whole district knew he meant it; he would give them free funerals, and keep only what was in the hat.

That evening, he discovered he was on the front page of the *Mineral*. "Notorious Citizen Gets Fancy Send-off," read the headline. "Our fair city witnessed a strange sight this morning. An elaborate funeral cortege rolled through town without a single mourner present. The two-hundred-dollar planting party for a certain scoundrel was rumored to be given for free by Maxwell's Mortuary, and it was also rumored that Maxwell was paying off a debt."

Twenty-eight

No matter how Katarina Costa dressed, it was never enough to conceal the heat inside of her. In fact, the more demure her attire, the more it seemed to advertise something within her that stirred long glances. She understood that perfectly. On this evening she occupied her usual corner seat at the Chequamegon, the rare unescorted woman who seemed to understand she was welcome if she adhered to certain clear standards.

This evening she wore a dignified gray

gabardine suit with a frilly blouse buttoned tight up to her neck, with a string of pearls. This contrasted somehow with her unruly jet hair and high cheekbones and Latinate features, and ember eyes whose gaze burned whatever it touched, which was usually men of substance. The heat of her face combined with the schoolteacherish clothing was what made her so fascinating to men, which is why she dressed as she did. In spite of her demure clothing, the lush shape of her figure was somehow invisibly present. She couldn't help it and didn't want to help it.

She didn't lack money, and spent it casually. A brief marriage to a mining engineer had left her in comfortable circumstances. What interested her far more was conquest. She met plenty of gents who turned weak at the knees the moment she addressed them, but they weren't copper kings, and barely interested her. Butte certainly had its rich men, most of them newly minted, but the rich were as common as hen's eggs as far as she was concerned. Butte did not have many powerful men, men whose wave of the hand or signature or command changed the course of stars and destinies.

There were only three now, though she had looked at various powerful gents like the Lewisohn brothers and Albert Bigelow and found them wanting. Marcus Daly was beyond reach, happily immersed in a good marriage and oblivious of other possibilities. William Andrews Clark was a more entertaining prospect, in spite of a cruel beard that surrounded a pursed little mouth. She could scarcely imagine kissing the man. All the other signals were just right. Clark was a widower, and in recent times he had sojourned in California, avoiding cruel Butte winters. Indeed, Clark's children were rarely to be seen at his redbrick mansion, where he entertained steadily. He was a dandy, getting himself up in luxurious clothing intended to wallpaper his humble origins. He had started to collect bad art and put on all the airs of old wealth, even if his was desperately new.

That all seemed perfect, and Katarina had discovered where the man dined and wined. That was mostly at the Silver Bow Club where she was not welcome, but the Chequamegon saw him occasionally, sometimes with two or three mysterious women. He never came with a single woman, never as a couple. He seemed utterly loathsome, which delighted her. She enjoyed her triumph over herself. The more she recoiled from some man, the more she was drawn to the gent. And Clark was the sort who set her teeth on edge and made her itch to head for the nearest exit.

She contrived to meet Clark by sending a waiter to him with a bottle of wine she had purchased for him. It was a gesture so unusual that it immediately attracted his attention, and he had excused himself and came over to meet her.

He had eyed her carefully, missing nothing. "You have sent a gift to a man who needs none. Is there a sentiment in this? Something on your mind?" he asked.

"You," she had said.

"Then I'm afraid you'll find yourself adrift," he had replied.

Nonetheless, he sat with her, ignoring his own table for half an hour, the conversation almost entirely his questions about her and her background and her demure replies.

He seemed more stimulated trying to guess her intent than attracted to her plentiful charms. Still, a man with a living brain and dead private parts might be entertaining so she had retained hope that the encounter would lead somewhere. But it hadn't. They encountered each other a dozen more times at the Chequamegon, and whenever he had women in tow, they were very different from Katarina. He always stopped at her table, exchanged a word or two, but it became plain that he wasn't examining her with bedroom eyes.

She understood it gradually. To him, the rural Pennsylvanian with English roots, she was the Latin firebrand. The ladies in his various parties were drawn from the same stock as himself. If any of them were his mistresses, enduring the scrape and tickle of that dreadful shrubbery around his lips, they were English or Welsh or Scots or perhaps Scandinavians. She thought the man might go for a French woman, but that would be as exotic as he got. Meanwhile, he shuffled his family from the Pacific to the Atlantic—anywhere but Butte. There was one woman who looked to be more daughter than mate, and she had a sneaking hunch that William Andrews Clark had a lust for seventeen-year-olds.

Katarina had trouble one night being seated. A new waiter refused to serve an unescorted woman, especially one with smouldering eyes. But he was swiftly overruled by Barney Scallon, the proprietor, who knew that most evenings Mrs. Costa ordered from the top of his menu. He had even set aside some wine for her. Butte was a whiskey and beer town, and wine drinkers were scarce, but he found a way to accommodate her, charging a fancy price for the small stock he kept on hand for her.

But soon she was settled in her usual corner, quietly waiting for whatever happened that evening to happen. She was always alone when she arrived, but not always alone for long. Women in the Chequamegon avoided her, sensing a plague upon their evenings. Men eyed her contemplatively, and she regarded each gaze as a triumph.

She had heard of F. Augustus Heinze and regarded him as a sort of young beaver, not in the same class as Daly or Clark. The gent was younger than herself by several years; somehow living life broadly while still in his twenties, and getting moderately rich. He had eyed her on several occasions, but this particular night she seemed to capture him, and he sat at his own table with half a dozen others, a mixed group of swells and ladies, maybe some of them a little racier than most. But he kept turning to glance at her, and she met his gaze.

He wasn't the most attractive of males, but was solid and cheerful. She didn't much care for him; she had higher standards than meaty twenty-nine-year-olds trying to build copper empires. She watched the party at that table, all of them lively and reordering whiskeys from the ubiquitous waiters. She mostly ignored them, and toyed with her own filet mignon, which she sawed into slivers and ate delicately. She enjoyed well-done meat, which she thought had something erotic about it.

Heinze was trying to follow the conversation at his table; but he looked bored. They were talking about the mines. That's what people did in Butte. He had bought the Rarus mine, a flagging producer that wasn't showing much promise until he steered his crews straight into spectacular ore. It lay east of the great Anaconda and St. Lawrence lode, and Heinze had discerned just where that mighty ore burst into the Rarus, and how it might be mined at a huge profit. He had bought interests in other mines, and seemed en route to becoming more of a mine operator than the manager of an independent smelter. A well-trained geologist, but not good for much else, she thought.

Katarina listened carefully. Most of what she knew of matters in Butte she had gotten by listening to table talk at the Chequamegon. On this particular night, though, Heinze wasn't interested in all that. Then he glanced at her again, and this time the look was so starkly and nakedly purposeful that she smiled. She didn't know where the heat in her came from but it infused her, and radiated outward, and once a man was caught in it, he was the prisoner of his loins. As young Augustus was.

He arose and approached.

"I noticed you're alone, and that's no way to enjoy an evening eating out. Would you join us?" he asked.

"Oh, I think not, but it's lovely of you to inquire," she said.

"I'm Augustus Heinze."

"I'm Mrs. Costa. Katarina Costa."

He was too much the prisoner to pay much attention. "Perhaps some other time?" he asked.

"Perhaps," she said. "I'm here most evenings."

That was invitation enough. He would be back, and alone.

"So I have seen," he said.

"I will send a dessert your way," she said.

He gazed, startled, and smoothly nodded. "I enjoy gallantry," he said.

He passed her tests. Maybe he would be worth an adventure even if it was demeaning to arrange something with a fledgling copper king rather than a lord of Butte. He certainly was a pleasant young man, well spoken, civil and polite, and endlessly cheerful. She might enjoy a minor conquest, though he wasn't half what Marcus Daly or William Clark were. She was opposed to nothing much; it would be easy to put the foundling on the doorstep of the love orphanage if it came to that.

Sure enough, he appeared at the Chequamegon at just the same hour the next night, and didn't hesitate a moment.

"I would be honored to have your company for dinner," he said gallantly. "If your husband wouldn't mind."

"My husband vanished years ago, and has not been seen since. Poor dear. He may be in Argentina, but I'm never sure. Last I heard, he was taking the waters at Marienbad."

"Ah, then we have much in common."

She waited for him to say what they had in common, but he didn't pursue it, and in fact he was referring simply to the reality that both were unfettered.

"What are your designs?" she asked.

"Copper is a handsome metal. It shines red. Its salts are lovely shades of blue and green. It is malleable. It conducts electricity better than anything else that doesn't cost much. It is fashionable to make roofs out of it now because it doesn't rust. It is the perfect utility metal, good for most everything. I should like to become a utility investor, good for whatever is required. And now, what are yours?"

"I am Diana the hunter," she said. "I like trophies."

He waited for more, but she had said as much as she chose to. He directed the waiter to bring whatever the chef thought was suitable, and they turned to banter, each testing the other, which sent the evening by in a rush.

His heat was upon him, but she thought to resist. "I will take you to dinner tomorrow night," she said.

"But I have plans."

"Break them."

He smiled, nodded, and that was that.

It was too easy; she was already bored with Heinze, and resolved to call him Fritz, the name he despised. He was virile and adroit, and she would enjoy all that when the time came, but she really wanted to pocket Clark, who it was whispered was overtaking John D. Rockefeller as the richest man in America. Now that would be something to set her cap on. This one, across from her, was still a boy.

The next evening he showed up promptly, this time in black tie; a dinner jacket with a black satin shawl collar embracing his ample frame. He carried a bouquet, and the waiters swiftly produced a vase for the table. She might be buying, but he was doing the romancing. The formal attire surprised her. He was an engineer and geologist, after all. Scarcely the background to put him in a dinner jacket. Still, it oddly matched her own dress. Perhaps they were both putting on the dog a bit.

She wore something less schoolmarmish this evening, a silky pearl gray dress with tiny cloth-covered buttons down her front, buttons he would wrestle with when the moment came. She read him instantly, and knew where this evening would head, and it amused her. As much heat radiated from Augustus Heinze as did from herself. Much too easy, she thought. But the bouquet was lovely.

Twenty-nine

William Andrews Clark sat in a mauve velvet wing chair in a small white parlor, waiting. Sometimes his cheeks itched, but they were so encrusted with wiry hair that he simply had to endure the itch. That was the price paid by men of substance.

The Silver Bow Club, on the fourth floor of the Lewisohn Building, annoyed him. It was not suitable for a man of his stature. Butte deserved better, but so far the club's directors had not seen fit to build an edifice suited to the eminence of its members. The one thing about the club that still won Clark's allegiance was all its quiet parlors, where substantial men could do substantial business in private. That was exactly what Clark wanted, and the club was better than his dining room, with all its snoopy servants, or his bank, where his desk was on a dais that placed Clark several inches above anyone on the other side of it.

So it had to be the Silver Bow Club, seedy by Clark's increasingly grand tastes, in spite of its quiet elegance. No one else seemed to mind, but Clark was always a man for appearances, and the club didn't measure up.

He could build a suitable clubhouse fifty times over, but then it would be his, not the club's, and that wouldn't do. He wasn't quite sure whether he was the richest man in the United States. There was always John D. Rockefeller to consider. But a single Clark mine, the United Verde, in Jerome, Arizona, was netting him four hundred thousand dollars a month. That mine was even more fabulous than his holdings in Butte, and appeared to be almost inexhaustible. He owned dozens of other mines, a Mexican plantation, and real estate in Los Angeles and Santa Barbara. He was making a killing in sugar beets. If he wasn't yet the equal of Rockefeller, he was a close second and catching up by the minute. It all amused him. Rockefeller lived in the East, and his every move was noted in the press. Clark lived obscurely in the West, unknown, and about to become the richest American.

That's why the Silver Bow Club annoyed him.

John B. Wellcome materialized, shed his gloves, topcoat, scarf, and hat, and sat in the other mauve wing chair, a faint smile on his lips. The man was Clark's chief lawyer, accomplished and genial, and a shrewd judge of character. The amusing thing was that most everyone liked Wellcome even when Wellcome was skinning their hide off.

"Cold," he said.

A steward appeared with a bourbon sour, unbidden. Wellcome nodded and sipped. Clark rarely touched spirits when he was dealing with weighty items because they clouded his mind, which was the worst thing that could happen to him.

"It'll be worse in January," Clark said. "I have the first endowment here." He motioned toward a black pigskin satchel. "There will be more endowments, as needed."

"Have much more ready."

271

"The session will be unruly," Clark said.

The Democrats had a large majority in the Assembly, but most of them were Daly Democrats, not unalloyed Clark Democrats. The Daly Democrats were little more than weasels, allying with Populists and silver Republicans to control the state. Clark would have trouble getting any votes from them, unless . . .

"Who can we get and what will we need?" Clark asked.

"I haven't the faintest idea," Wellcome said. "But most men have a dream."

"Don't speak of such things," Clark said. "Spend it all on virtuous Democrats. I will say it for the record. Let it never be said that I sought less than to reward loyal Democrats."

In Clark's eyes, Daly's brand of Democrat was worse than Republicans. The Senate term of Republican Lee Mantle was expiring, and it would be up to the legislature to elect a new man. And the Democratic legislature would elect a Democrat. But there were real ones, like Clark, and bogus ones who compromised and weaseled, like the whole Daly battalion.

Clark hadn't intended to run, having taken his lickings in the past, but in August, just ahead of the November elections, Wellcome and others had persuaded him to give it a try, especially with Daly's Anaconda juggernaut threatening to swallow the whole state. Daly had been operating quietly far from Silver Bow County, buying distant papers, forging alliances with businessmen, funding the campaigns of local politicians, yet almost invisibly. The old feud wasn't in its grave after all. Clark had swiftly produced a hundred thousand dollars, and his minions had also been out buying newspapers, and the result was that political democracy was going to Helena for the 1899 session.

All of which had revived old man Clark's feelings. The lust uncoiled in him once again. The prefix, Senator, ahead of his name mesmerized him. He would be more than a businessman, more than an entrepreneur, more than the richest of Americans. He would be the most influential and honored and powerful man of all. He was a reflective man, constantly questioning his own motivation and belief and understandings, and he had asked himself whether being a senator was what mattered, and whether life in Washington, and on the floor of the Senate suited him, and whether it would add anything to his happiness. He concluded that it wouldn't but he would do it anyway.

The title would soon bore him. The deliberations would soon bore him. The company of the powerful would soon annoy him. The business of fending off seekers and pleaders and lobbyists and logrollers would irk him. His time could be better spent in Europe, Paris in particular, where life was

273

lived with panache, than in steamy and sordid Washington. But he would do it anyway. He would enter the sordid world of politics. He would suffer the abuses of rivals and editorialists. He would endure the calumnies. It wasn't anything he wanted, which was why he would proceed. The day would come when he could tell people he was elected in spite of his contempt and revulsion of politics and politicians, who were all worms. Ah, yes, he would do it because he had not the slightest interest in it, and would enjoy his secret.

The meeting with Wellcome went quite simply. They hadn't spoken another word about politics or money or whose vote might be required, or what the Daly men might do. It was all beneath Clark, and boring too. When he won the Senate seat he'd celebrate, of course. There was nothing like a victory to get his juices flowing. But even a Senate victory would be nothing compared to one month's profit from the mines.

And it would likely bury old Marcus Daly. That's what he'd celebrate, when the time came. The old man wasn't well, but he was still the bulldog of Anaconda, and needed a final lesson. In fact, that was the whole of it. If Daly weren't on the other side, Clark wouldn't care about the Senate one way or another.

Wellcome vanished into the bitter December night, toting a black bag filled with green paper bearing the image of Grover Cleveland, and Clark permitted himself a glass of spirits now that business was complete. There would be two or three agents working the legislature, including Clark's own spindly son Charlie, a young boodler making his way in a hard world.

Clark waited some more; another guest was coming. Clark had debated whether to let this one through the front door, but decided there was some advantage in it. The man should have stayed in the servant quarters in the Clark mansion. He ordered a sherry and settled into his wing chair, knowing the loathsome man would be late. Being late was J. Fellowes Hall's leverage over people; it delighted the man to keep busy people waiting.

All of which was exactly what one would expect of a man of Hall's vanity. Clark had seen a lot of vanity in his day, and none more blatant than Hall's, which was written all over him, from his gaze to his posture. Clark had been so repelled at first he thought to fire the man, but on consideration he thought he could put such a vast buggy-load of vanity to work. Vain people could be valuable on occasion, such as now.

So he sipped his sweet sherry, smiled at the oil portraits of members on the parlor walls, and waited until the editor blew in, his coat flapping.

"I fear I'm a bit tardy," Hall said, without apology.

"It is the way you deal with people," Clark said.

A steward accepted Hall's flap-eared hat,

greatcoat, gloves, and scarf. Beneath all that was a tidy gray suit and a florid bow tie of a sort that was offensive on sight to Clark, which was exactly the intended impression. Like most toadies, Hall had contrived a list of items Clark liked and despised, and used it as needed. This wintry eve, Hall was running through his list of capital offenses.

"A drink?" Clark asked.

"Bourbon and branch," Hall said, settling in the opposing wing chair.

"You've kept me here past my bedtime," Clark said, "so I'll compress it all into a few words. I've kept quiet about it, but if the Democrats should decide to pack me off to the Senate, I wouldn't object. Politics have little interest to me, but I wouldn't resist the charge if it were laid upon my shoulders. As you know, I've strongly supported real democracy, and not the mongrel variety Marcus Daly has been promoting. Some people will do anything to hold office, but I'm not among them. I have my scruples, as you know."

Hall was smirking, which is exactly what Clark expected. There was nothing about Hall that Clark could not anticipate. The steward returned with Hall's drink, and Hall lifted it in a gesture of good fellowship.

"Cheers," Hall said.

Clark grunted. Toasts didn't come more banal. "Well, now, Hall, you've followed my instruction to keep me out of the spotlight, and that makes my life much easier. You are to continue with that, excepting only to say that I am a reluctant candidate for the United States Senate, and if a better man is selected, I shall be all in favor of it, so long as he is a true member of the party. Do you have that clear?"

Hall sipped and nodded.

"Now, Hall, I have it on good authority that Marcus Daly intends to influence this selection by any means, fair or foul. He and his powerful company have their own candidates, and would accept even a silver Republican. That's how unprincipled they are."

"Yes, sir, pragmatism is all that runs in Mr. Daly's head."

Clark wasn't sure what pragmatism meant, but it sounded like consumption or syphilis or dementia, so he nodded. "There are good men in Daly's company who see the folly of smothering Montana under Anaconda's corporate influence," he continued. "There are sage men, whose views reach my ears in a steady drumbeat now, whispering that this time, Daly will go too far, and will seek to influence the legislators with illicit offers. These will take all sorts of shapes and forms. It might be cash. It might be a financial partnership. It might be a sudden opportunity to purchase land, enlarge the ranch. It might be a contract to buy all of a man's cattle or produce or lumber. Boodle, Mr. Hall, comes in all shapes and conditions, and you spot it by noting a legislator's sudden prosperity. Is the man in the worn suit now sporting a new one? Is the fellow with a small farm now tripling his acres on the county tax rolls?"

"Boodling can't go undetected, Mr. Clark. It is always found out by an alert press."

"Ah, now you have the general idea, Hall. There will be an invisible link between every burst of prosperity one discovers among legislators and the bottomless pockets of Marcus Daly's company. Your task, sir, is to focus a ruthless eye on this crime against the commonwealth of Montana, to trace the threads back to their source, which will be the Anaconda offices of Marcus Daly. And when you have the evidence, you will shout it from the rooftops. Do you know what I mean? The headline, the front page, sir. The *Mineral* will devote itself to exposing every misdeed and foul bribe flowing out of Marcus Daly's pockets."

"I have it exactly, sir."

"See to it. Say little about me, other than that I remain on the sidelines, willing to serve if asked, but otherwise busy with my operations. If those truly loyal to the party want a true loyalist, they know where to find me. I won't be in any rush to travel to Helena when the session opens. I'll simply stay here, avoiding the circus, my reputation untarnished and without the slightest blemish. Got that?"

"Got it, Mr. Clark."

"Well, good, finish your drink then. I'm going home."

Hall looked amused, just as Clark supposed he would.

Thirty

J. Fellowes Hall was having the time of his life. Who would have thought it? The 1899 legislature was vaudeville. Never in all his career had news been so amusing and bizarre and ludicrous. And never in all his years as an editor and senior editorialist had Hall engaged in more buncombe, more hokum, more yowling and howling. He had become the most avid bunco steerer in the state. He surpassed every confidence man operating out of every saloon. The *Mineral* was not simply sensational; it was the most unreliable and mendacious in the nation, daily printing a sober-sounding account of what wasn't happening in Helena, while exaggerating or twisting what was happening. And of course the paper's finger wagged only one direction—straight toward Marcus Daly.

Hall didn't know it would be so rich. The legislature met in dark January, divided several ways. The Republicans were the minority, and divided between the silver and gold factions. The Democrats had a large majority, divided between Daly and Clark forces. And then there were the Populists, leaning toward the Democrats, but not anchored anywhere. The task was to elect a United States senator to replace Lee Mantle, whose term was expiring. The law required the legislature to meet and vote daily until a senator was elected and sent packing off to Washington. Each day's ballot differed from the previous ones. Favorite sons garnered courtesy votes and sank away. Coalitions bloomed and faded. The reluctant candidate William Andrews Clark ran nearly last, but gained a little ground week by week. He kept his silence. It served him to be the wallflower this time. The legislators met officially in session, and in hotel saloons, and behind doors, and in caucuses, and in the black of the night, and nothing much changed except that Helena was fattening from the sale of food and drink and hotel rooms and loyalties.

January faded into bleak, dark February without much progress, and it looked as though the state might once again fail to elect someone to send to Washington. The Republicans blamed the Democrats, and the Democrats blamed each other and the Republicans, and the Populists played hard to get and professed their virginity. And in the midst of the clamor, there were whispers of wealth changing hands, boodlers handing out stuffed envelopes, thousand-dollar Grover Cleveland bills being pocketed. There were rumors of mortgages being paid off, new business partners, farms with vast new additions, silent partners, fancier homes, fattening bank accounts. But still the diehards didn't budge, and the voting scarcely advanced in any direction.

Of course the editor of the *Mineral* had a fine explanation for all this: the company—no other name was necessary—was playing its own powerful game. Marcus Daly's minions, with satchels full of bills, were cutting deals everywhere. That's how Hall's paper saw it, at any rate. Marcus Daly was the spider, and he was spinning a web around the government of the state. As for the *Mineral*'s owner, he was sitting aside in quiet dignity, keeping his manicured hands clean, awaiting the solemn hour of his calling, if it came.

Daly's own editor, John Durston, was spinning other tales, and the *Anaconda Standard* was broadly hinting in cartoons and editorials that Clark was bribing the entire legislature. That was fine with Hall, who ridiculed his rivals in print. A good newspaper fight would only increase circulation. The entertaining thing about it was that Durston and his Anaconda paper were right: they had Clark pegged, and knew how to portray him. Their cartoons depicted Clark as an odious tycoon and swine, which pretty well fit. They had

Clark pitching bundles of greenbacks through hotel transoms. Every issue of the *Standard* that hit the streets of Butte was a delight to Hall, and he drew inspiration from the rival paper. There was nothing good to be said about William Andrews Clark. That added a certain spice to his task. How best to defend and promote the indefensible? They should give him a journalism prize. It was like being a Confederate writing editorials for a Union paper during the recent war. That took skill and patience and a sense of the absurd. He was very good at it, and did not underestimate his skills.

Day after day, the tally in the state legislature teetered this way and that, and it was getting tiresome. Clark continued to obscure himself, an invisible wraith minding his business in Butte. But slowly, he accumulated votes until he had collected most of those in his party. But that wasn't enough. The Daly holdouts didn't budge, and it was beginning to look like this legislature wouldn't elect anyone before adjournment. But then things shifted once more, and a few Republicans began to show up in Clark's ménage, which seemed most unusual, given the insults and calumnies each party had visited upon the other. But there they were, a few Republicans who had seen the light, reached for the holy grail, and were about to elect William Andrews Clark to the Senate.

Until a Republican from Missoula cried foul, and waved an envelope with ten one-thousand-dollar bills in it. The envelope bore the initials W. A. C. on its flap. Fred Whiteside, the archfiend, also added that two of his Republican colleagues had been bribed.

Nothing could have delighted J. Fellowes Hall more. The whole show was idiotic. What boodler would put the evidence on the envelope? W. A. C.! Right there, in script, for cops and prosecutors to pick up! Proof of guilt. Except that it was a good joke. A Daly joke. Even the most stupid boodler in Helena would not put thousand-dollar bills into an envelope marked with anyone's initials on it, especially those of Clark. So Hall set to work, as he always did. Another Anaconda trick. Marcus Daly's machinations. Anaconda, the crookedest corporation in the state. This time, Hall had something he believed in. Not for an instant did he think Clark would pen his initials on a ten-thousand-dollar bribe of the sort that could put Clark in the Deer Lodge prison for a few years.

But the funny thing was, everyone else believed it. Here was the proof! Clark had corrupted everyone and everything in Helena. Legislative committees set to work. Prosecutors set to work. Witnesses were paraded. Lawyers pled. Editors ranted. The nation's press was titillated. Reformers insisted on the direct election of senators. But nothing came of it. The evidence was lacking, just as Hall knew it would be. It didn't matter that some legislators' bank accounts waxed fat, and property expanded, and new homes were purchased, and some got shares in new businesses, or sweetheart contracts. It might be that some legislator inherited something from his deceased aunt, and another legislator had won a startling jackpot at poker. No one could prove a thing. But that was only fodder for every cartoonist in the state, including those of Hall's, who busily laid it all on Marcus Daly. It didn't really matter who bribed whom. The reluctant candidate was going to Washington, on the tide of Democratic, Populist, and a few Republican votes.

But that wasn't the end of it. The Senate Committee on Privileges and Elections began hearings as to whether it should admit Senator Clark to full-term membership, and once again the lawyers declaimed, witnesses testified, accusations swirled this way and that, and the stench of Helena soon threatened to engulf the Senate of the United States. Marcus Daly, then fatally ill, was not a good witness while Clark, still vigorous, was impressive. But the evidence ran against him. When it became plain that Clark would not be accepted, in May of 1900, he withdrew his name from contention, saying he didn't want his honor besmirched. Clark would not remain a senator this time around. The whole debacle had played out on a national stage, keeping editorialists occupied coast to coast.

But it wasn't over. Even as Clark resigned, his pals were hard at work. In Helena, they concocted a scheme that would put Clark back in the Senate, this time as an appointee of the governor, who would be filling the vacant Senate seat. But Montana's governor Robert Smith was a Daly man, and had to be drawn out of state so the lieutenant governor, A. E. Spriggs, a Clark man, could make the appointment. Smith was enticed to California to examine a mining property for Miles Finlen, the Butte mining entrepreneur, to whom Smith owed some money that could be repaid by performing this expert service. No sooner was Governor Smith in California and incommunicado, being miles from any telegraph, than Spriggs hurried to the capital and announced that the people's choice for senator should be allowed to stand, and appointed Clark senator from Montana, which at least on the surface seemed a legal appointment. But Smith hurried back, revoked the appointment, and appointed Martin Maginnis Montana's next senator, while all the world howled. It would be up to the Senate to choose between Maginnis, whose appointment was legally valid, and Clark. In the end, it did nothing. The session ended without a decision, which in effect kept Clark out of the Senate.

J. Fellowes Hall sighed, sorry to see the

vaudeville come to an end. It had all been so entertaining. It had filled his news columns for months, kept his cartoonists busy, sold papers, and stirred Butte as nothing else ever had. Clark complained publicly that he had been persecuted and besmirched, which Hall dutifully printed word for word, but it was over. Clark had lost the election and his reputation. The copper town slid back to quietness, which meant that Hall would have to draw his news from the police dockets again. He hardly knew what to put on his pages, now that the show was over.

The integrity of the state's entire government lay in ruins. The integrity of its legislators was wrecked. The editorial independence of nearly every paper in the state was compromised. Both Clark and Daly had bought any papers they could get their hands on, and attempted to influence those they couldn't buy, often by lending them money, or making political alliances with their publishers, or threatening them with a competing paper if they didn't toe the line. Indeed, wherever papers continued to oppose one man or another, competing sheets bloomed, financed obscurely, and devoted to polemics and stealing away advertising.

Now, with the turn of the century, things had slid back to peacefulness. Some of those phantom papers vanished. The larger dailies continued sedately. Marcus Daly took the waters in Europe, hoping to prolong his failing life and health. Montana became the watchword for corruption, unbridled graft, and the domination of public affairs by powerful corporations, most plainly the Anaconda company.

How corrupt everyone was! J. Fellowes Hall marveled that a good newsman like John Durston could let himself become a mouthpiece for the Daly interests, without any compunction about his paper's independence. Rumor had it that Clark had simply paid the owners of the *Bozeman* c *Chronicle* twenty-five-hundred dollars to switch their support to him for the duration of the election. Daly, on the other hand, had bought papers all over the state. And what of those editors? How easily they had been bought. What were their considered views beforehand, and what had they become when a little cash changed their minds? It amused him.

He was the best newsman in Montana, though Durston might give him a run for his money, and he had maintained the integrity of the *Mineral* through thick and thin. It never varied. It was a Clark paper. It opposed the octopus corporation gradually choking Montana. Yes, he had never wavered, the paper had never weaseled, the editorials had never shifted ground, and the paper's integrity was intact. Now that was an achievement in a state when almost no newspaper had gone unscathed by the money flowing into politics and elections. It was said that Clark had spent a million, and Daly had spent a couple hundred thousand, but not a nickel had flowed to the *Mineral*.

That knowledge intoxicated him. He was the only newsman left in Montana whose integrity and virtue were intact. He was true to the highest calling of his profession. He was the survivor. His conscience was intact and unchallenged. Everywhere else, there were editors and publishers who could not look themselves in the mirror each morning. He thought he would celebrate with a dinner at the Chequamegon, or maybe an adventure a little farther down the slope.

Thirty-one

There wasn't much time left. Marcus Daly knew that. The doctors had opinions, but no cures, and there was little to be done. He knew it when he arose in the morning, knew it all day long, knew it when he went to bed, knew it in church, in his dreams, at the dinner table, and when he shaved each morning, knew it when he eyed his daughters.

The real questions arose from his business. The company he and James Haggin had built over many years was suddenly under siege, and from two parties. The first was the abominable Fritz

Heinze, whose staff of thirty lawyers, led by his brother Arthur, were attempting to steal the most lucrative mines in Butte, using apex litigation and bought judges. It was theft pure and simple. The courts would decide who owned what, and Heinze owned or influenced the sitting judges.

All his life Daly had avoided litigation as much as possible; he and his partners well knew that mining litigation enriched only the armies of lawyers that bled the profit from mining corporations. But now the Anaconda Company was under assault from every direction, flimsy lawsuits, frivolous lawsuits, absurd lawsuits, all designed to bleed the company white. They were rising from Fritz Heinze's army of buccaneers.

But there was worse trouble brewing, this time in the cozy warrens of East Coast capitalists who had suddenly discovered that the Anaconda Copper Mining Company was one of the richest prizes in the United States. There, a cabal of financiers was scheming to own Butte Hill by one means or another. They had first focused on the two mining and smelting companies operated by Boston's copper men, the Boston and Montana, and the Butte and Boston, but Heinze had tied them up with various lawsuits, mostly dealing with apex issues. So the financiers turned, instead, to the main prize, the Anaconda company. These were no ordinary Wall Street financiers. These were men whose own fortunes derived from Standard Oil, and indeed one of them was William Rockefeller, John's brother, and their colleague H. H. Rogers, a man as powerful as the Rockefellers themselves. It might not be Standard Oil that was eyeing the richest hill on earth, but it was the same cabal. And they were slowly, carefully, and furtively buying every share of Anaconda stock they could get, at any price, and were edging toward control of the company.

Daly and Haggin had watched it closely, and with a certain foreboding. For Haggin, in California, it might mean profit. But for Marcus Daly, it might mean loss of control of the company he had built from his initial purchase of the lackluster Anaconda mine, which he had turned into an incredible bonanza just by steering his miners toward the ore that lay in plain sight within.

Rockefeller and Rogers were not Irish. Anaconda was Irish. Its future executives would be Irish. Its hiring men and accounting men were Irish. Its miners were Irish. Its managers were Irish. Daly had made it so. He wanted the company to stay Irish. He wanted to limit the influence of others. He especially wanted to keep Rockefeller out. The brothers were not noted for their acceptance of the Irish, or for treating their employees gently. They were ruthless, and their vision didn't extend beyond making the fattest profit they could. They would not be good for Butte.

But Augustus Heinze would be worse. Already, his injunctions had thrown five hundred miners employed by the Boston companies out of work when the mines were forced to shut down. Heinze was simply a shark, devouring whatever he could eat.

The Rockefeller interests were buying shares of Butte mines and placing them in a giant trust, called Amalgamated Copper Company, capitalized in New Jersey at seventy-five million, with seven hundred fifty thousand shares outstanding at a hundred dollars each. Into this vast holding company would go every Butte mine and smelter that the financiers could snatch. Daly saw it all coming, saw the financiers move closer and closer to control, and knew that the days of his independence were numbered. If Standard Oil was created at just the right time to fuel horseless carriages and lamps, Anaconda had come at just the right time to wire the cities of America and bring electricity into every home and business. Both had ridden a sudden upswing of demand; both had glowing futures.

Daly thought about all that, talked to his friend James Ali Ben Haggin about it, and both knew the time had come to bend. For Haggin, there would be cash to invest in South American mining ventures. For Daly, control of the new company for as long as he lived; maybe time enough to keep it Irish. So they sold out. Haggin got fifteen million dollars. Daly got shares in the holding company in exchange for his Anaconda shares, and remained president and manager of the Butte company, while William G. Rockefeller became secretary-treasurer and Henry H. Rogers became vice president. Anaconda had been swallowed by one of the largest holding companies in the world. Anaconda was owned in New Jersey. The directors were Wall Street financiers, except for Daly. Suddenly, Easterners owned Butte, Montana. Swiftly the holding company acquired the Boston mines and anything else it could snatch.

Marcus Daly knew he was merely a figurehead, but he would use whatever power he had, for the rest of his days, to protect his Irish associates and workers and their families, and to protect Butte. Even as he struggled, the holding company shares skyrocketed and plummeted as speculators bought and sold at huge profits. Daly's Anaconda Company was buffeted month in and month out by rising value, dropping value, collapsing value, regained value. And each day Marcus Daly felt the worms crawling through his body, eating life away.

And there were all those lawsuits in Montana's district court, each intended to bleed some of the company's wealth. Heinze had gone from brilliant mining genius with the best eye for ore in the business to a buccaneer. And nothing illustrated that better than his outrageous Copper Trust.

Daly fumed every time he thought about it. Heinze's brother Arthur had been going through the countless claims that covered Butte Hill, looking for flaws in them all, looking for anything the Heinzes could exploit. And in the course of his close study, he found a tiny patch of land, irregular in shape, squarely on top of the Anaconda hill, bordering the company's great mines, including the Anaconda and St. Lawrence. The total unclaimed area was only nine one-thousandths of an acre, only a couple hundred square feet, only the size of an average parlor in an average home. But it was not claimed, and Augustus Heinze claimed it, and named it the Copper Trust, with his own brand of perverse humor. And then the Heinzes filed apex suits against the greatest Anaconda mines, proclaiming that all the surrounding veins surfaced, or apexed, on his patch of land. It was so brazen, so ludicrous, so bizarre, it might have been dismissed —except that Augustus Heinze owned one judge entirely, and influenced another. And all of Daly's efforts to have the suits dismissed came to nothing. Heinze was a menace, not just to the company, but to Butte.

Daly had his trap brought around. There had been a day when he would have walked from his great Washoe smelter to the *Anaconda Standard*, but that day was gone now, and would not return. He threw a scarf around his throat and ventured out. The trotters were waiting for him, sleek and ready. His heart always lifted at the sight of his own fine horseflesh.

At the newspaper, he slid out, dropped a carriage weight, and entered the newspaper he had founded and built up from nothing. A gust of cold air swept in on his coattails. His old friend John Durston was in his lair, looking grayer now, but still lean and alert and keen-eyed. The man had stayed with him through everything.

Durston eyed his visitor with pleasure, and nodded toward a wooden swivel chair, and Daly settled gratefully into it. He couldn't stand up for long anymore.

"I've been reading what I can find about the Standard Oil Gang," Durston said. "I always like to know who owns me."

Durston laughed, but it was tentative.

"They own me, too," Daly said. "But I own a piece of them."

"I like the name Anaconda better than Amalgamated," Durston said. "Anaconda is poetry. Amalgamated sounds industrial."

"It's all consolidation," Daly said. "They consolidated a lot of small oil producers into Standard Oil. They're consolidating a lot of copper companies now. It's supposed to be for the good of everyone."

Durston smiled. "I'll know it when my paycheck improves."

"You've fought my battles, John. They may be wanting you to fight theirs. Not just now, but soon." He was referring to his demise, but wasn't sure the editor understood that.

"Scallon will replace you?"

"I've arranged it. There's some others, like Con Kelley and John Ryan ready. Scallon's doing my legal work against Heinze. He's ready. Are you?"

The surprise question baffled Durston.

The editor finally asked whether there would be a shift in viewpoint.

"You know the score better than I do," Daly said. "We don't think much of Heinze, and he's already paralyzing the city, throwing people out of work with his legal maneuvers."

"He's not an uplifting influence," Durston said.

They laughed at Durston's delicacy.

"Amalgamated may not be a good influence on the state," Daly said. "The company passes from local hands into East Coast capitalists—and with it, the state government."

Durston didn't say anything, and sat waiting.

"You'll have less independence, and probably less budget. The new board of the company sees the press differently; a mouthpiece, not a news gathering organization. Not that I am so different, but I've stayed out of your way mostly."

"We're a company paper, and I'm prepared for that," Durston said.

"You may not be when the time comes."

Durston stared into space. "I'm old enough to retire. We have a fine country place near Bozeman. There are lines I don't cross, and at the same time, I'll usually find ways to put my employers in the best light."

"They'll be saying that Montana's about to be owned by the Standard Oil Gang."

"I'll be saying that Heinze's ruining the court system of Montana and corrupting its government."

"They'll be saying the company's Irish and shouldn't be, and Montana should welcome others."

"I'll be saying the state already has and always will."

"Maybe you could talk about Heinze's thirty lawyers and pliant judges."

"I have libel laws to watch out for, Mr. Daly."

"They'll want to shrink your editorial staff, fire some of your cartoonists, spend less on syndicated material, hew the line. They might send a man into the newsroom to check a story in advance, or pull something, or hide something. They might want to keep the company's acquisitions secret, its profit and loss secret."

Durston settled back in his chair and gazed upward, not quite focused on his visitor. "I've been a loyal company man from the beginning, fought your wars, struggled with the whole sordid business of electing William Andrews Clark. I've been all that not because you told me what to do here, but what you didn't tell me to do. I've never been forced to violate the integrity of the *Standard*, or myself, and you've never cornered me with such demands."

Daly smiled. "I'd hire you all over. And when you retire I'll try to find a man to fill your shoes."

"There are several here, Marcus."

"I would need to do it soon, John."

The two stared at one another.

"Soon?" Durston asked.

"A few months, a year, maybe two."

"Then I am lucky to have you in the president's chair for as long as you wish to be there."

"We'll whip Heinze good and proper, John. He's overstepped, and soon he'll be wearing a ball and chain at Deer Lodge."

Daly rose, unsteadily, and Durston eyed him closely, perhaps only then registering what Daly knew about his health, and his future. Change was coming.

Thirty-two

The consumptive Orangeman lived on, damn him. William Ward actually rallied, which annoyed Red Alice. Some color returned to gray flesh. He downed his gruel, and his throat didn't torment him as much. He lay abed, day after day, without the strength to stir. He barely made it to the stinking outhouse behind her cottage.

The children annoyed him and he annoyed them, and they all annoyed Alice Brophy, but there wasn't anything she could do about it, and besides, being annoyed by the Protestant in her bed was more interesting than not being annoyed. The con killed everyone, if miner's con, silicosis, didn't kill them first, but William Ward was making fate take a vacation.

She knew why he still lived. Some men, and he was one, were domestic. Men were supposed to be wild hares, barely able to endure the cottage and kitchen and a wife and children, but it wasn't true. Some men were just the opposite, wanting nothing more than a snug haven from the world, and a mate who might be a friend and lover. Ward was like that. Once he escaped the big boardinghouse and got settled in a cottage, with rambling roses in front, his eyes grew less desperate, his breathing got better, the wheeze subsided, and he even slept through the nights instead of coughing himself to death. Singing Sean Brophy wasn't like that. Singing Sean could barely stand to be in the house; give him a saloon and other males, and he was in heaven. But not William Ward the heretic.

She hated it. She had counted on him croaking so she could get on with her life. She had pamphlets to pass out and a mission to fulfill. She intended to turn every working stiff in Butte into a Socialist, and get rid of the corporate system, get rid of it all, string up the rich capitalists at the nearest tree—which would be far away from Butte because arsenic smoke had killed them all. But weirdly, William Ward was still her income. She still took her sign to the mine headframes, asked for coins for a sick miner, still passed out tracts and collected her dimes, and still made enough to feed her family from it. That made her even madder. William Ward's sickness was her piggy bank.

If keeping an Orangeman alive wasn't bad enough, Augustus Heinze was worse. Red Alice couldn't master the whole of it, but it was all bad, and it peeved her. Heinze owned a good mine called the Rarus, which was next to some mines owned by the Boston and Montana Company, with all those rich Boston financiers behind them, and they were throwing lawsuits at each other, and claiming that the ore apexed on their own properties, and they were accusing each other of hauling ore out of the mines that didn't belong to them, and a lot more. Heinze's top men owned some shares in the Boston mines, and that enabled Heinze to file stockholder suits against the management, alleging this or that. It didn't matter what. The whole business was intended to throttle the other side, steal ore, and defeat mining in Butte. That was capitalism for you. Heinze was a courthouse miner. That's how he stole his ore. He had a judge named Clancy there who saw things his way, and never wavered in helping Heinze along. And the other judges helped too, and Heinze was becoming a fatter and fatter capitalist in the courtrooms, rather than by building up productive mines. And the more all these capitalists did this, the madder Red Alice got. This was what was supposed to be the way to make the world prosperous? Ha!

The only one she felt a little kindness toward was old Marcus Daly, who buried Singing Sean, and didn't like lawsuits. But she didn't excuse him, either. He starved his workers and raised Thoroughbreds. His racehorses were treated better than his miners. It was the system, rotten and greedy, that needed replacing, and she was trying hard to get people to do just that.

Then the day came when all the courtroom struggles spilled over into the streets. Heinze got an injunction shutting down the Boston and Montana mines until ownership of the ore could be settled, so the Boston-owned mines complied, and suddenly there were five hundred miners out of a job, and a lot more grocers and saloon keepers and clothiers and coal merchants feeling the sudden loss of income all over Butte. Red Alice hoped the whole rotten system would tumble down, but it didn't.

William Ward was amused. "You can't make over the world," he said from his bed.

"I'll make over you, if you don't shut up," she said.

"It's not the system. It's the bad law."

"The system made the bad law."

"Congress made it. Apex law doesn't exist anywhere else. In other countries, the boundaries of a mining claim are the limits. No one goes chasing a vein into the next mine—at least not legally. So they don't have all these lawsuits."

She seethed at that. "You can get up and leave," she said.

He stared, and slowly got to his feet, and clung to the edge of the bed, and then caved back into the bed.

"You will have to help me, madam," he said.

Stricken, she pushed him into the bed, not out of it, her eyes averted. "You wouldn't be sick in a Socialist world," she said.

"In a Socialist world everything is divided equally, the good and the bad. I'll be glad to share my consumption with you, with your children, with everyone. Everyone gets an equal share."

She glared at him, full of retorts, but he was coughing again, and she whirled away. Equal share! She'd had more than an equal share of the bad. She'd be glad to share a few things with him, if he wanted.

He was eyeing her with fevered eyes. It had taken only one sharp exchange to set him back by weeks. He weakly tugged the worn blanket over him and turned away. What had been a fragile little companionship had withered in an instant, with abstract ideas tearing them asunder. She had her beliefs; he had his. They had ended up torn, and he was growing gray again, as if every bit of progress had fled him.

She was damned if she would apologize to him. He was just trying to make Socialism look foolish. He didn't like the capitalists any, but he wasn't sold on her views either. She edged up to him, and ran a hand along his shoulder, and squeezed. He coughed, and gazed upward at her, and almost as fast as the color drained from his gray face, it returned to him. He needed only a little love to live.

She was dependent on him. He was the source of the dimes and nickels she collected each day at the mines, at the gates of a different company each time. She hated that. Hated that William Ward had a wife far away, and children far away.

"You will see them someday, William," she said.

It took him a moment to catch her train of thought. "Not bloody likely," he wheezed.

But over the next days he got better again, and she began to think that he would be one of the few who stopped the consumption, who drove it back, who lived on.

She returned to the mines, choosing the Rarus the next day, wanting nickels from Heinze's lucky miners, who were busily at work in the pits. She carried her tin bucket and her hand-lettered sign and her sheaf of SLP pamphlets, and hiked up the well-worn trail to the mines east of Butte, and braved a bitter wind. She wondered how she would survive in midwinter, when subzero cold and whirling snow would engulf her. She would, somehow. She was Butte tough, and that meant she could weather anything.

As usual, men coming off shift eyed her sign, those who could read, and a few dug into their britches while their damp clothing steamed in the cold, and pitched pennies and dimes and a quarter or two into her little tin bucket, and gamely accepted her pamphlet. "Workers Arise!" That's what the headline read. Every few weeks she got a different batch in the mail. But this day her vision was suddenly darkened by two big men, each in a black bowler and a tight striped suit.

"Beat it," one said.

"I have a right to be here."

"You heard me," he said, and knocked her down, a giant shove of the shoulder that sent her sprawling. The metal bucket sprayed her few coins. She scrambled up, started collecting the coins, when the other goon flattened her, sent her sailing several feet. She hit the frozen ground hard. He yanked the bucket from her hand, stuffed the Socialist tracts in his pocket, and kicked her in the ribs. She howled. That toe shot pain clear up and down her chest, and into her hip and out her arm.

The first one laughed. "You got the lesson,

sweetheart? No more. Not here, not anywhere, got it?"

"You big goons, you get out of here!" she yelled.

She got another toe in the rib, which hit so hard she felt pain shoot through her whole body. The ground was cold. Her chest hurt. The big galoots above her grinned. One tipped his derby, and they hiked away, carrying her money and her pamphlets and her tin bucket.

Several miners stopped, stared, and hurried away, not wanting to get into trouble.

"Chickenshit," she yelled at them.

Red Alice managed to get to her feet, felt her bruised rib cage, and decided she could make it down the long dirt trail to Dublin Gulch. Every step tormented her.

She neared her little cottage in the gulch when she spotted Big Benny Brice, the flatfoot whose beat included the gulch.

"Benny, I just was robbed," she said, and told him the story.

"It's because of your politics. You're a Socialist," he said.

"Is that supposed to be bad?"

Benny sort of cackled. "Not for me it isn't."

"I'm going out tomorrow. Will you come along and protect me?"

He hesitated, eyed her, and nodded quietly. "I'll come along for a bit, Alice. Maybe I'll crack some heads."

He sounded worried, but game.

"I'll go to the St. Lawrence tomorrow," she said. "I'll be there."

She limped into her cold house. The brats hadn't built a fire in the stove. William Ward eyed her, taking it all in. "I can guess," he said.

Now, at last, she sank into the ratty chair, exhausted.

She hurt all that night, but that wouldn't slow her any. She painted a new sign, found a glass jar for the coins, and scavenged a few older tracts she had salted away, and then she wrapped herself in her ancient cotton coat, and headed into the bleak dark dawn. The shift started at seven; in winter, in Butte, that was still dark. No one noticed her. She would be going to the heart of the Amalgamated mining complex this morning. She discovered Big Benny waiting for her, a fine figure of a man in his blue greatcoat and earflap hat, a nickelplate badge on his chest.

"Thanks, Benny," she said, and watched the miners drift by. They eyed her silently, and mostly slid by, wondering about the cop standing off a bit. But a few picked up her tracts and dropped coins into her jar, and she thought things would be all right.

But then the two goons in their derbies showed up, headed straight for her, their meaty fists clenched and ready. Big Benny beat them to her, clobbered one and sent him staggering, but the

305

other slugged Benny in the groin, and Benny whoofed and folded, even as the pair of them unloaded on Benny. She saw one slide brass knuckles onto his fat fingers and start some serious work on Big Benny, who fought back impulsively and bravely, but was no match for two hooligans who knew exactly what they were doing. When Benny went down, they didn't quit. They kicked his ribs and kicked his face, even though Benny got a leg and yanked one down on top of him and let the hooligan have an elbow and a bite or two.

Red Alice screamed. This time miners rushed up, saw that the flatfoot was down, and pulled the hooligans off and held them at bay while Big Benny lumbered to his feet, weak and dizzy, and put his cap back on.

"I'm taking you in," he said.

But one of the hooligans slid a shiny little revolver from his breast pocket, and laughed. "Go tell the sergeant all about it, flatfoot," he said. "He'll sure be interested in your sad story." The other one worked free of the restraining miners, dropped his brass knuckles into his greatcoat, and retrieved his own little snub-nosed. The miners retreated. One of the goons snatched her jar and her sign and her pamphlets.

"Lady," he said, "next time you hand out this crappola, you won't be around to cry."

Thirty-three

F. Augustus Heinze wondered whether Katarina would show up on a bitter day. But she did. She was attired in a wine-colored woolen coat with Persian lamb cuffs and lapel, and a muff to match. It paid to be fashionable when genuflecting before the money machine. He smiled. The lady knew exactly how to appreciate what she was about to see.

"You came after all," he said.

"Why shouldn't I, Augustus?" She always remembered to call him that. Everyone else in Butte called him Fritz, much to his annoyance. That was worth a smile, so he took her elbow and escorted her up the Anaconda hill, past shanties, along worn dirt trails used by the miners, past sheds and eventually past the headframes and mills and boilers surrounding the Anaconda company's greatest mines, the Anaconda itself, the St. Lawrence, the Neversweat, and various outlying ones including his own Rarus. Her attire was so out of place it shocked the eye in that grim world of iron, rough-sawn wood, silvery rails, brick chimneys, black iron, and humming hoists.

The day only improved the scenery. It was bright and cold and not a cloud troubled the sky. It was also numbing cold, mitigated only by a lack of wind. But on any hill crest, such as this one, cold air moved constantly, no matter whether the air gusted through the works.

"I'll be the first lady to see the Copper Trust?" she asked.

He smiled. "I don't know of any ladies in my life. I'm taking you to show you how rich I am; it will inspire your gold digging."

"I'll clean you out of it," she said.

He laughed. If anyone was exploiting anyone, he was working her for all she was worth, which was plenty.

He threaded through the factory jumble atop the hill, and finally stopped at an odd patch of barren clay, marked by raw wood stakes in no particular pattern.

"The Copper Trust," he said, with a gentle wave of his kidskin gloved hand.

She stared, not quite grasping it. He intended that she shouldn't grasp it. The total surface of the Copper Trust came to nine one-thousandths of one acre.

"It comes to a couple hundred square feet or so," he said. "Welcome to my parlor."

"It's too small for my taste. I'd want a larger parlor," she said, eyeing the odd collection of surveyor's stakes.

"My brother, Arthur, and one of my engineers located it," he said. "Unclaimed land atop the richest hill on earth. So we claimed it. I own it.

The Montana Ore Purchasing Company has it."

"What's that?" she asked, eyeing a small hole where someone had shoveled away the thin clay topsoil down to the bedrock a couple of feet below.

"That's where all the veins of these mines apex, and that's what permits us to follow the veins wherever they may go, straight into all these great mines. That hole is the Pearly Gate. The ore is ours, not theirs, according to mining law. And we shall have it, and have payment for all they've stolen from us for years."

"Your brother found this?"

"Arthur, yes. Lines get drawn, boundaries are defined, and sometimes not every corner or piece is accounted for. I have a very gifted brother, a man with a sharp eye, a man who reads deeds and descriptions with a magnifying glass."

She yawned. "We're done now?"

"Ah, Katarina, how little your imagination is achieving at the moment. Inflate your brain to the size of your beautiful bosom. We are standing on the greatest bonanza in the history of mining. We are standing on wealth that dwarfs anything the world has seen. This little hole is the doorway to heaven. It requires reverence, a bowed head. You need to stand before that hole and receive a wafer on your tongue."

"I think you're daffy. It's too cold to make jokes."

He sighed. "I see through rock. I see ore radiating from right here, rich veins of copper, spreading into those mines over there, ore they are eating up each day. See how busy they are, steam hissing from their boilers, cages running up from the pits, with my ore loaded onto them."

"Let's go. I'm not buying it. You don't even have enough land here to sink a shaft or put up a works."

"No need. All the law requires is proof that the vein apexes here. That hole will do nicely. Two feet down, solid rock and copper ore, and I have discovered the apex of all those veins in the Anaconda and Neversweat. It's like finding the navel of the universe."

"You're a dope, Fritz Heinze."

He laughed, and escorted her away from that brown hilltop. "My attorneys are preparing the cases; we'll file soon. The newspapers will howl. The moguls will gnash their teeth. The opposing lawyers will yowl and whine and rage. The politicians will cluck. The financiers will recognize a new player. And in a while, we'll shut down the whole hillside. Anaconda's miners will be out in the streets. They'll put heat on Daly and Scallon and their new owners, Rockefeller and Rogers. I've never had so much fun."

He steered her along the clay trail, past cesspools, past yellowish water that smelled of urine, past rusty rails, with loose ore lying everywhere it had fallen.

"Why did you show me this?" she asked.

"Gold digger, meet copper digger," he said. "No, it's better than that. I'm a courthouse miner. That's what they call people like me."

"I'm a bedroom miner," she said, "and I'll own all of you. You're my slave."

"You're also a witness. You saw the claim. You saw the shaft and the vein in its bottom. Just in case Anaconda has notions of pulling up the stakes, filling the hole, and posting armed guards, I can always call on you," he said.

That amused her. "If William Rockefeller pays well, why would I stick with you?"

"I make ladies happy," he said.

He walked her to her flat, kissed her on the cheek, and headed for the Silver Bow Club, where his brother would update him on the lawsuits. Arthur was a genius. He could find a good lawsuit in anything. It was Arthur who advised that his subalterns purchase shares in all neighboring mines, which opened the door to all sorts of stockholder lawsuits that Augustus found valuable and amusing. He was clogging the district court with them.

Arthur was waiting for him at the brass rail. "Here's to our success," he said. "I filed about an hour ago. It'll probably be assigned to our friend Clancy."

"Oh, my, Vesuvius will soon erupt."

"I suggest you preempt it. A little story in the press. You are about to stop the Amalgamated Copper Company's massive theft."

Fritz Heinze smiled. "We'll give it to the *Mineral*. Hall's a pompous ass, but he'll fill his paper with it if we approach him."

Arthur sighed. "Sometimes, Augustus, you disappoint me."

Heinze grinned. He loved to cross swords with his wily brother, who was just as responsible for the Heinze fortune as Fritz was. He simply cocked an eyebrow. This would be Arthur's show.

"You need a paper of your own," Arthur said. "And I just happen to have one."

"Why should I need a paper? The less I'm visible, the better I like it."

"Some battles are fought in public, and elections are among them, and this state elects its judges. Issues before the legislature are another, and both Amalgamated and Clark have ways of making their views and agendas loud and clear. That's why they win."

"I can spend my money better on other things," Augustus said. "Papers are rat holes."

"Follow me," Arthur said.

F. Augustus Heinze downed his whiskey, wrapped himself in his greatcoat and silk scarf and kid gloves and flap-eared hat, and plunged into an icy late-winter night. His brother seemed to know just where he was going, and turned in to a gloomy Irish pub, and headed straight toward a massive, shaggy, ill-kempt, red-nosed, watery-eyed boozer who was scowling at the world.

"You, is it?" the man growled. "This better be good. I don't come cheap, pastyface."

"Augustus, meet Mr. Pat O'Farrell, a printer and founder of great enterprises."

"My enterprise is foundering all right. I can't sell enough ads to keep a flea in food," he said.

"Mr. O'Farrell has founded a weekly paper he calls the *Butte Reveille*, but it is overmatched by the big dailies and resting stillborn in his bosom."

Augustus Heinze was not impressed. The man was a drunk. He lurked here in this sleazy dark saloon downing ales and muttering to himself and any fool who'd listen.

"Mr. O'Farrell is a phenomenon," Arthur continued sedately. "He needs four ales, or at least two shots of Irish, to reach manhood. Anything short of that, he's a beaten-down dray."

"I'll buy the man some Jameson's and we'll see," Augustus said. He signaled the beefy barkeep. "Pour the man the best Irish whiskey in the house."

"You'll be paying in advance," the keep said, narrowly. "I don't know you."

Heinze laid a greenback on the bar, which the bartender scrutinized carefully, and reached for his prized bottle. He poured an exact, measured ounce in a shot glass, and handed it to O'Farrell, who sighed, downed it in a swallow or two, and smiled. Heinze nodded, and the keep poured another, and O'Farrell sipped that one at a leisurely clip.

"It takes a minute or two to catch hold," Arthur said. "And then he lights up."

It did take a minute. O'Farrell inflated. He sat taller. He stuck his chest forward. He eyed his drinking partners with a steely gaze. "The *Reveille*'s for sale," he said. "Fifty dollars a week will give you the loudest and most sublime and elevated and noble voice in this loathsome city."

"Can you spell?" Heinze asked.

"Infallibly, when I am writing papal bulls and royal edicts. More fallibly with names."

"Why should I pay you fifty dollars a week? For what?"

"I am a rottweiler, a terrier by profession, sir. I am a hangman by vocation."

"Who would you hang, and what would you hound?"

"The Anaconda company, now in the hands of the Amalgamated Copper Company, an infernal holding company, operated by nefarious pirates and vomiting dogs."

Augustus turned to Arthur. "Did you prime him?"

"Nope, this is his natural and infernal nature."

"And what do you think of me? Of the Montana Ore Purchasing Company, Mr. O'Farrell?"

"It was fashioned by saints, sir. It arrived to free

314

us from the tyranny of bankers and rich crooks and scoundrels. It arrived to keep the richest hill on earth from falling into the hands of a single greedy cabal, men who intend to suck the lifeblood from our fair city."

"Have you samples of your elegant and noble prose for me to examine?"

"Ah, sir, I have yet to publish, but I will make an arrangement with you. Finance me for two or three issues, and weigh the evidence, and if I don't fill your needs and expectations, we'll part company in peace and fellowship."

"Pour another Jameson," Fritz said to the keep. "The tab's on me."

They toasted the arrangement, and toasted it a few more times.

"Now, O'Farrell, I have just filed suit to stop the Anaconda Company from stealing any more of my copper and silver ore. Those rich veins apex on my property, the Copper Trust, right there on Anaconda Hill, and I intend to pursue the latter under the mining law of the land, and stop the theft, and win royalties for every ounce of ore that has been stolen from me."

O'Farrell licked his lips. "I'll drink to that," he said.

The next afternoon, the first copy of the *Butte Reveille* hit the streets and was instantly bought out. O'Farrell had poured it on: "Lawsuit Stops Plunder," the headline read. It went downhill from there. "At long last, the corrupt financiers and malefactors of wealth, in their whited sepulchers of the East Coast, will be brought to their knees by a new suit in Montana District Court alleging that these culprits have engaged in stealthy theft of such proportion as the world has never before witnessed," it said.

Augustus found it entertaining. O'Farrell was a genius of invective, and needed only a few facts to turn an event into a morality play. Augustus read O'Farrell's thunderous story with something like awe. Never had he seen words strung together in such biting cadences, such vast disdain, such eloquent indignation. The man might need a little guidance now and then, but Augustus Heinze now had his own rotten little tabloid, which would perfectly obfuscate his real designs, and make him all the more beloved among the ordinary people in town. He wished he had thought of it earlier, and was pleased that Arthur had seen the need. Butte had a new rag.

Thirty-four

Marcus Daly died a few days after the November election of 1900. When William Andrews Clark read it, he had his servants bring him several hot water bottles to allay the chill spreading through him. He knew he ought to rejoice, but couldn't.

The Senate seat was awaiting him now.

But he felt a chill, and set the hot water bottles about his person, tucked between the chair and his robe. The chill did not go away, but seemed to drain him of bodily comfort. Maybe that was Daly's last jest. There was no aesthetic pleasure to be found in a rubber bladder.

The man had been ill for some while, certainly ever since he collapsed while putting together the sale to Amalgamated. And after that, the man had declined steadily. Bright's disease, it was said, along with heart trouble. Daly had gone with his physician to one of the great spas of Europe, Carlsbad, to take the mineral water, but hadn't gained from it. By the time he got to New York and took rooms at the Netherlands Hotel, it was plain that he could not manage the trip back to Butte. And there he lay, life ebbing, his own staff tightly silent about Clark's huge victory at the polls. He and Heinze and the Populists had shattered the old man's grip on Montana.

Clark rang for the servants. The bottles were cooling much too fast, and he wanted them refilled, hotter. His imported London manservant and two Liverpool maids scurried to work. Clark had them build up the fire in the parlor stove as well. It was late November, not yet bitter, but much too cold for Clark.

He said nothing to Hall; he knew exactly what the editor would do. A bare-bones report of Daly's

317

death, a modest eulogy, and a lot of silence. Let Daly's *Anaconda Standard* fill its pages with Daly's squalid life and death. The *Mineral* would be decently quiet.

The refreshed hot water bottles arrived, and Clark tucked them in, but they didn't allay the cold crawling through him. He told himself he should rejoice: nothing stood between him and the United States Senate. Rogers, Rockefeller, and the Standard Oil Gang didn't care one way or another, and probably thought Clark could be useful. A fellow capitalist and mining magnate might be an asset in Washington. The company's new president, William Scallon, wouldn't care either. It had been Marcus Daly's private war, and now Daly was dead.

For some reason, Clark didn't rejoice. What passed through his mind was some aphorism he had heard somewhere: the death of anyone diminishes us all. The death of his enemy, the man who had frustrated, angered, insulted, and embarrassed him, only diminished everyone. It made no sense to Clark, but he was not used to thinking about lofty matters. The accounting ledgers were his home.

For the next days Clark lived in his own parlor, barely seeing anyone. It was almost as if he were grieving, though of course he was not. The Daly funeral finally took place in New York, at Saint Patrick's Cathedral, attended by three thousand, with Montana's and New York's bishops presiding. There were similar masses in the great churches of Montana. There were eulogies that annoyed Clark. There were tributes and toasts and remembrances that set Clark's teeth on edge. Everything Daly had done to make Clark's life miserable had been forgotten.

Except by William Andrews Clark. This 1900 campaign had gone better than the one in 1898 but it was more complicated. The unions were stirring. The Populists were fading. The Amalgamated Copper Company was a Wall Street shark worrying a lot of people. Clark had allied himself with the ever-entertaining Fritz Heinze, and between them they defeated Amalgamated without great difficulty.

It was said that Henry Rogers and the Standard Oil Gang had set up a war chest of a million and a half dollars, worried that Clark would carry an anti-Amalgamated government into office. That and two pro-Heinze judges in the Butte district court that oversaw the mining suits were ample to make the East Coast moneymen nervous. But Daly was listless, and not even present during the latter part of the campaign, off in Europe. And his lieutenants lacked the forcefulness of Daly. The one question mark was the unions, which had always been in Daly's camp. But now the working people were uneasy about the Standard Oil Gang, and its expanding presence on the Butte Hill.

Heinze exploited that, even bringing in vaudeville acts to draw crowds. The whole thing had cost Clark a bale of hundreds and five hundreds. There were still votes to be bought, papers to be influenced, and legislators to be pocketed. But by the time the election rolled around, the Clark and Heinze forces were unbeatable, and so it had proven to be. He'd won. He'd whipped Daly. He'd whipped all the money that Wall Street could toss at Montana. He and Fritz now enjoyed the esteem of two of the three district court judges that heard Butte's mining suits, Edward Harney and William Clancy; both the city and county government; and they had a solid command of Montana's government, too. Won. The trust spreading its octopus arms into Montana was whipped.

And then Daly had died. Some said he died upon hearing the bad news. The gossip was that those surrounding him at his deathbed in the hotel never spoke a word about the election. But maybe that was all the news that Daly needed to die in defeat. It was an odd thing: in the space of a year, the Anaconda Copper Mining Company had been swallowed whole, and Marcus Daly was gone. Clark shifted the hot water bottles around, trying to get some last heat out of them, but they were listless lukewarm bladders now. Nothing was a comfort anymore.

So, Washington it would be. That wasn't a comfort either. He'd be stuck there for six years.

He couldn't imagine spending much time in that damp and sticky city, listening to the drone of bores, attending dreary banquets, shaking the limp hands of limp ambassadors, changing sweaty clothes three or four times a day. He wondered suddenly why he had campaigned so hard, spent so many months of profit to capture that seat. Now that Daly was dead, the seat didn't matter. The awful truth hit him hard: he had run to oppose Daly, and now that Daly had perished, there was nothing to his victory except a title. He would be called Senator, and that was all he would get out of all those dollars.

He arose, leaving a welter of water bladders behind him. There was still the legislative session ahead, in January, and he would prepare to buy his way through that if need be. He wondered whether to bother. His mind had focused on the United Verde mine down in Arizona, and its rich promise. He was building a model workers town, improving his reduction works, finishing a railroad between the smelter and mine, and he was exploring other mining properties. He thought about more trips to Europe, buying art in Paris, sampling fine French wines, building a home or two elsewhere. Butte annoyed him. With Daly dead, what reason was there for him to stay on in the cold, mean, smoky, arsenic-laden iceberg of a city?

After he had groomed himself for the day,

taking great pains with his wiry beard to properly conceal his thin mouth, he retreated to his bank offices and dispatched a note to Anaconda's new president and manager, William Scallon. Clark barely knew him, but did know that Scallon was a gentlemanly Canadian lawyer who'd fought the company's legal battles. A quiet man, it was said; a man who listened and weighed all he heard. A perfect lunch companion. So Clark invited Scallon to a little lunch in a private parlor at the Silver Bow Club. It was time for some quiet talk, far from the ravenous ears of the mob.

Scallon arrived at the club promptly, almost as if he was responding to a command performance for a king, which was not far from the reality of the moment. Clark was king of all he surveyed, the ruler of Butte, Montana. But Scallon wasn't exactly kowtowing, either. Behind him were the most powerful financial men in the nation, men who could make or break companies, states, and even pocket-sized nations.

"A victory celebration," Scallon said, settling into the plush wing chair opposite Clark. The lunch would come later, after a fireside chat.

"Oh, yes, a perfect triumph," Clark said. "I'll sail right in when the legislature meets. But of course there might be opposition . . ."

Scallon declined a drink, and settled into his armchair, patiently. "Perhaps you are wanting some idea of our intentions," he said.

"Well, I was wondering whether Mr. Daly's interests spread through your company, and continue even now."

"Yes, there are some," Scallon said. "Mr. Daly was much loved, and his interests lie in the hearts and souls of those who served him."

"Yes, he commanded great loyalty," Clark said, and let it go at that.

"You want to know something of our intentions, and I don't mind telling you," Scallon said. "Will we attempt to impede your ascent to the Senate?" he asked. "No, it doesn't really matter. Neither will we agitate against you when you are seated. Why bother? We have other things on our mind. Fritz Heinze's various lawsuits hang over us like a guillotine blade. His friendly judges are fully capable of doing grave damage not only to Anaconda Copper Company, but its parent. There are many millions at stake, and also the company's effort to consolidate all the holdings in Butte, to create an efficient, prosperous producer not plagued by a swarm of lawsuits. That, Mr. Clark, is what absorbs us. Fritz Heinze absorbs us. His various lawsuits, shareholder suits, apex suits, ownership suits, intended to enrich himself and weaken or destroy us—that's what's on the mind of William Rockefeller, and I should say, myself."

"That's capital, capital," said Clark. "Shall we dine? I have oysters on the half shell, expressed in on ice, and a few other little treats."

Indeed, the Silver Bow Club outdid itself. There were Limoges tureens of soup, delicate filets of beef, candied yams, all in such abundance that the two men could barely taste each serving. They devoted themselves to exclamations, and small talk, while Clark evaluated what he had just heard. Scallon was known to be true to his word. There would be no impediments this time. Amalgamated would not pour Rockefeller boodle into defeating him when the legislature voted; Amalgamated would not take its grievances to the United States Senate and buttonhole senators about ethics, the thing that so embarrassed him the previous round.

Scallon declined a cigar afterward, which pleased Clark. Cigars were noisome, but seemed to be a fixture of dining at the Silver Bow. Port and cigars never quite appealed to him.

"You know, Mr. Scallon—may I call you William? You know, I have nothing against consolidation. It's rational business."

Scallon raised an eyebrow. "You and Fritz Heinze certainly voiced another viewpoint during the election campaign. Rather vigorously, I must say. In fact, in rather black-and-white language."

"Oh, that. That's when Marcus Daly governed Anaconda. His appetite for expanding the company simply knew no bounds. It had a, shall we say, negative impact on the honest yeomen farmers and independent businessmen, and politicians of our fine state. But that was then, and this is now, and we are looking into the future."

"So you have no objection? You don't believe the company is bad for Montana?"

"Well, I think Fritz Heinze always exaggerated. It doesn't bother me. In fact, I could easily side with you on various issues. I'm also committed to Arizona, where my operations are several times larger than here. No, William, I have no difficulties. I think there might be some advantage to a state government dedicated to keeping its mining operations profitable. And in the hands of experienced men."

"I knew this lunch would be a delight, Senator," Scallon said.

"It's just common sense," Clark said. "Make it all work. Consolidate. Give a firm a continuous supply of good ore for its reduction works, give it freedom from frivolous lawsuits, give it a retailing operation, offering the world wire and brass and finished copper. Give it stability. Give it a steady and economical supply of labor. Give it a good reputation among moneymen in the East. Oh, it makes a lot of sense, sir, and it's the way to go."

Scallon stared. "I think I'll have a drink after all," he said.

In moments, a steward brought two glasses of bourbon over ice.

"Cheers," Scallon said.

"Cheers and success," Clark replied, and they sipped.

Thirty-five

Watermelon Jones brought word from the bank, as Clark's offices and headquarters came to be known. J. Fellowes Hall tipped the fellow a nickle, and opened up the sealed envelope. It was in Clark's hand, but unsigned.

"Lay off Amalgamated," it said. Nothing more.

Hall studied it, vainly seeking a clue. But there was nothing to explain the directive. Hall headed into the composing room, looking for proofs of pages going into the afternoon edition. There was a front-page cartoon, in which Amalgamated was depicted as a giant octopus with its tentacles wrapped around a virginal lady with a sash labeled MONTANA. It actually was a revised version of an older cartoon in which Anaconda was the octopus, and resembled other cartoons depicting Marcus Daly as a harness-racing driver running over a prostrate lady labeled MONTANA.

Lay off. Well, all right, Hall would lay off. He instructed the compositor to yank the cartoon and fill the hole with something else. He studied the headlines of the stories in the galley trays, and found another about Anaconda's slavish papers across the state, and the coordinated propaganda issuing from them. He was tempted to let that stand, but decided to kill the story—for now. He needed to know what Clark was thinking before he made any decisions on his own.

What an odd thing. Ever since he came to Butte, he had kept the Anaconda Copper Mining Company in his gunsights. Daly's vast, swaggering, domineering company must not be allowed to capture Montana. The capital of the new state should never be the captive of Marcus Daly and his minions. The vast combine of copper mines, timber companies, rail and haulage companies, utilities, and allied stores posed a threat to every other business, every farm and ranch, every shopkeeper, every toiler and workingman in the state. He had published every detail of the company's grope and grasp, every earnings report. He knew the company better than he knew Clark's. He could write anti-Anaconda editorials in his sleep. He could commission new cartoons and remember a hundred old ones. His pay and his job depended on keeping the transgressions of the company, and Daly, and now Amalgamated, before the public.

Until this moment.

It puzzled him. He didn't even know whether to keep the change a secret. Neither did he know whether this was temporary, and he'd be back at his old stand soon enough. For the time being, he would talk to no one. Fritz Heinze was sometimes a good source; maybe he would find out what he could.

And then it struck him that Clark had yet to be elected a senator, and might wish to keep the opposition subdued until the legislators put him in office. Yes, surely that was it. The old man didn't want to stir up the hornets this time. Lay off the company. That made sense. Sometime after the first of the year, William Andrews Clark would become Senator Clark, and the wraps would be off.

But that didn't make sense either.

In truth, Hall couldn't fathom what was happening or why. He headed for the ancient desk where Grabbit Wolf was scribbling, his sharp pencil occasionally scrawling cursive letters into foolscap. Wolf had been his right-hand man, his assassin, his hatchet man, all these years. Wolf had been the bulldog who sunk his canines into Anaconda. Wolf had been the one who turned a routine earnings report into something sinister. Wolf had been the only reporter in Butte to ferret out Marcus Daly's expansion plans, and expose them. The man was a genius.

"What do you make of this?" Hall asked, dropping Clark's note before the reporter.

"Clark's sold out," Grabbit said.

"I doubt it."

"Of course he did. He's a rich man, and he's got the same worries as Amalgamated."

"But they're business rivals."

"Daly's dead. As long as Daly lived, Clark

would be on the opposite side. Now there's no need."

"But what about Heinze? They're tied together."

"Clark has just kissed him off." Wolf was relishing the idea.

"That's unthinkable."

"Heinze's no use to Clark anymore. The election's over. Amalgamated lost."

"Clark wouldn't do that."

"Clark doesn't give a damn. He's going to be an absentee senator. He'll live in New York, show up in the Senate now and then mostly for show, and devote himself to running the United Verde in Arizona, between trips to Paris."

Hall had the distinct feeling that Grabbit was right. "What are you working on?" he asked.

"Amalgamated insider trading. Rogers and Rockefeller bought a lot of Amalgamated stock, driving up prices, sold it off suddenly dropping prices, and now they're buying up shares again at bargain prices."

"I'm not supposed to run that stuff."

Grabbit was grinning at him.

"But I will," Hall said. "When'll you have it?"

"For tomorrow."

"It'll be on the front page."

That's how Hall crossed the Rubicon.

He couldn't help but feel the world was shifting beneath his feet, chasms were opening, ready to swallow him whole. He thought he knew Clark, but now he was less sure of it. Did the man have any purpose in life other than to oppose Marcus Daly? And with Daly gone, where was Clark heading?

Hall abandoned the newsroom, climbed into his greatcoat, scarf, gloves, and flap-eared hat, which he hated but nothing else was practical in Butte's cold months, and braved the sulphurous air affronting him every step of the way to the Chequamegon. He wanted a drink among fashionable people; mining engineers, capitalists, shift bosses, society. He resisted an impulse to crawl into a dark corner of McGinty's and drink himself into oblivion. But drink he would do, whether in a classy joint or a hole.

He ordered double bourbon on the rocks, and settled into a lonely corner. He didn't want company. He wanted to taste and rub a terrible thought that had been creeping into his head. Was he a journalistic whore or not? He had been a Republican back East, proud of it, before he became a Clark Democrat in Butte. But he switched parties, and lambasted the Republicans of Montana, telling himself they were not the same as the ones he had known. He had enthusiastically fought Daly's efforts to move the Montana capital to Anaconda. He had fought the Anaconda company, now Amalgamated, because it threatened to own Montana, dictate state policy, decide state laws, and operate the state as a fiefdom. But now his employer was telling him to lay off; the burgeoning company was just fine. Hall could readily obey, but what would that make him? What of his principles? What, at least, of his beliefs? Was he ready to trade them in for another set? Was tomorrow's paper going to tacitly disown everything in yesterday's paper? And what did that make of J. Fellowes Hall?

He could not answer that conundrum, so he sipped his bourbon and watched the rest of the people chatter and laugh through the dinner hour, untroubled by who owned their souls. Most of them worked for a copper company and remained loyal to it. What difference did it make to a mining engineer? Hall peered about, seeing people whose main preoccupation was money; the more the better.

He envied John Durston, over in Anaconda, faithfully advocating whatever Marcus Daly advocated, and faithfully laying out Anaconda's case on every issue, and faithfully pummeling Daly's opponents. Durston had never had to switch since coming to Butte, though Durston, too, had started as a Republican and a progressive before heading West. But even now, Durston's paper was faithfully carrying water for its new masters, the Standard Oil Gang, and it didn't seem to bother Durston any that these financiers were among the most ruthless ever seen.

But Durston didn't work for a man like Clark,

whose views and politics were whatever suited him at the moment. Hall suddenly loathed Clark, the dapper little man who hid his pursed lips behind a wall of shrubbery, so one could never quite see Clark himself, but only a lot of wiry hair that even seemed to hide his eyes from view.

Hall sipped the last of his double, and ordered another. He had large decisions to make, and these decisions needed lubrication. Some people he knew eyed him tentatively, but Hall glared at them until they retreated. He would not advertise for company this night; he would deal abruptly with anyone who tried to join him.

He eyed the throng sourly. The Chequamegon was usually crowded. He was the one who didn't fit. The rest sold themselves for money or acceptance or high status. But he was a newsman, and a good one, at least he used to be before the devil bought his soul. Newsmen were different. Newsmen tried to be the conscience of their communities. It didn't always work that way, but it was present, lurking inside of Hall's mind like a headmaster's ruler.

Was he a newsman or not? Were his opinions convenient to the day, or were they grounded in something larger? Was he the rottweiler of his master, or was he something more?

He sipped and knew that the truth was complex. He had ideals and he had betrayed his ideals. He had tried to be loyal to Clark, and now it was

Clark being disloyal. He had come to Butte in a fit of vanity, and his own vanity had betrayed him.

He didn't excuse himself. He thought of his abandoned Amber and children, still back East, where he had kept them far from sight with a monthly check. He thought of his own bleak secrets. Who was he to rebuke Clark's slippery ethics? What of his own?

He sipped steadily, but felt absolutely no effect from all that whiskey. His mind was awhirl, and no mere alcohol could slow it down. If anything, he was more alert than he could ever remember, full of loathing not just of himself, but of Butte, and Clark, and Heinze, and every newspaper in town, and every floozy he'd ever dallied with. Butte was rotten; no, he was rotten and every one of those greedy mining moguls was rotten, twisting every ethic they could turn into a pretzel.

He drank steadily but got no further along toward oblivion, and finally quit. He wasn't hungry. He went to his flat, prepared himself for a sleepless night, and fell into a dreamless night. He awakened knowing his life would change, though he couldn't say how. He was tired of being a mouthpiece, ever-shifting, for whoever paid his wage. It was a bitter day, so he bundled well and walked to work, his breath steaming.

Grabbit's story rested in a galley tray, set and ready to be nestled into a page. Hall read it closely. It was all about the way the financiers had milked other stockholders of Amalgamated for all they were worth, driving the stock up, collapsing it, and buying back in at lower prices. These were the games played by the big boys, the Standard Oil Gang, for whom Montana was a spot on a map, and the subsidiary Anaconda Company was simply a grape to be squeezed. A lot of Amalgamated's small-time shareholders had been bamboozled into selling, and the rich got richer. Grabbit had done his job.

"Headline it," Hall told Wiley, the compositor, "right across the top."

He didn't feel like killing the story. He felt good not killing it. He felt he was performing a public service by headlining it. He was ready to take his chances with the boss. Some stories needed to be told. Some papers needed to renew their integrity. Some owners needed to be told to back off.

He found some newsprint and scribbled a note with a proofing pencil. "Good one," he wrote, and placed it on Grabbit's desk. It dawned on him that it was the first time he had commended Grabbit Wolf for a story. He hadn't commended anyone at the *Mineral* since he joined it. Maybe it was time to celebrate good journalism.

He penned a brief introduction, simply saying that his reporter had written an outstanding story, worthy of wide attention, and that the *Mineral* was happy to publish it. He added his name to that, had it set, and dropped it into the page at the top of the story.

"Moneymen Make a Killing," ran the headline. The old press clattered, the copies piled up, and the newsboys hauled them into the bitter air. He wondered how long he would have to wait to get the response he was expecting.

Not long, he thought, as he settled into his office swivel chair and waited.

Thirty-six

They wouldn't leave Red Alice alone. She was out daily with her scrawled HELP A SICK MINER sign and her pamphlets and her money jar. She steered clear of the mines because the goons chased her off and stole her pennies and shredded her pamphlets. So she tried the miners' favorite saloons at shift time, when the men in the pits thirsted for a Shawn O'Farrell. That worked for a while because the miners remembered her, and opened their purse strings.

But then the administration changed, Clark and Heinze ran the city from their offices, and soon the cops were chasing her away, smacking her with their billy clubs, busting her collection jars, and pitching away her pamphlets. When she saw a bluecoat coming she usually tried to beat a retreat, but they often caught her. They knew where to look and what hours she'd be on the streets, and they lurked in waiting.

"You're a bunch of crooks!" she yelled, but they only laughed and pounded on her with their nightsticks. The money in her jar always disappeared.

But Butte was a big, messy city full of neighborhoods, and she survived by randomly picking saloons in unexpected places. Her flat-foot friend Big Benny Brice not only turned a blind eye, but helped her now and then when hooligans showed up and wanted to steal from her or punch her. She loved that copper, but he was the only one.

Somehow she survived. William Ward, her unwelcome guest, neither got better nor worse. He would die in a week if she put him out; he survived indoors, and even was able to help a little. Each day he got up long enough to perform some small service for her, and then fell exhausted into his bed. Whenever she wished he would go, she was reminded that he had become her livelihood. The miners remembered William Ward, who had gone into the worked-out pits to die, and that remembrance was worth a nickel or a dime; enough to keep Red Alice's household afloat.

It would end someday soon. The goons would find her and pound the life out of her. The mines increasingly had their own police, even if none of them wore a badge or was a sworn peace officer. There were rumblings in Butte. There were rumblings in every mining town in the West, including Coeur d'Alene, Leadville, and Cripple Creek. Big trouble was brewing.

One bitter day, when the light gave out at four in the afternoon, she found Ward sitting up, with an ancient blanket over his legs. She thought of him as an intruder, and an Orangeman at that, stuck in her house, ruining her life.

"Twenty-two cents," she snapped.

"It's below zero," he said in that gravel voice that bespoke a ruined throat.

"Maybe you should try it," she said.

"I've overstayed. I will go," he said.

"No, no, no, you're stuck with me," she said. "Stuck with a Green."

"A kind woman."

"I don't care what you believe," she said. "It's all hoodoo."

"What do you believe?"

"I don't believe in anything. It's all somebody's way of controlling the rest of us."

She was worn. It was cold and she had her frail heat blown out of her, and the air stank of sulphur.

"I've got to leave you," he said. "You've helped me more than anyone should expect." The last of his words dissolved into that barking cough again. He couldn't talk much without a rebellion in his throat.

She was weary of him, and didn't reply. Politeness could only cover so much.

"I'll be gone in the morning."

"You go to hell, Orangeman."

"The air is bad. I'd do better in Arizona, place like that."

She didn't argue. She set aside her cardboard sign, emptied her bottle, and stared at the kitchen drainboard.

He stared mutely from his bed, and she read his thoughts. "No, they won't take you down the shaft. I won't let them."

"It's a good place to die."

"No! You shut up."

She wondered how many dozens of sick miners had wandered into the abandoned levels and hid themselves until they died of the con.

He looked feverish. The confrontation had set it off again. "Alice Brophy, you're barking up the wrong tree," he said.

"Just shut up."

"You're trying to start a political party. Socialist Workers Party. You're competing against the old ones here. Republicans, Democrats, Whigs, Federalists, Populists. There's a better way. It's got a weapon, strikes. The Western Federation of Miners."

He fell into another spasm. She knew all about the WFM. They'd been around for years. The Butte Miners Union was Local Number 1 of the

WFM, but different, more cautious. The WFM was radical. When they struck in Coeur d'Alene in 1892 company guards shot five strikers. The strikers disarmed the guards and marched them out of town. Governor Willey asked for help, and President Harrison sent General Schofield, who declared martial law and threw the strikers into a stockade without right to trial, bail, or information about charges. In Cripple Creek there'd been another one, triggered by the mine owners' effort to increase the workday from eight to ten hours. The union won that one. Another strike, in Leadville, in 1896, sought an increase of fifty cents in the daily wage, restoring the wage that had been cut earlier. The strike resulted in a lockout, violence, and the National Guard once again. Blood on the streets. Men fighting for a decent life.

Butte miners had been sympathetic but none of that had happened locally, and there was one reason. Marcus Daly was one of their own. His deep pockets had paid their passage to Butte. He listened. He drank a beer with them. He had mucked ore himself. He knew what a day's pay meant to them. And now he was dead, and neither Clark nor Heinze had much sympathy for the men in the pits who broke their backs and ruined their lungs and died young while the moguls turned their labor into private fortunes. With Daly gone, anything could happen, and would. Both Clark and Heinze made a great show of fraternizing with the miners, but it was all for appearances. Only Daly could pour a beer with them, speak their language, share a yarn out of the pits.

"So?" she asked.

"Red Alice needs a new sign. WESTERN FEDERATION OF MINERS. WFM. That's all. All miners will understand. The Butte union may be Local Number 1, but it's not really WFM. And new pamphlets. And a crack at a union job. Secretary, or clerk, or whatever."

"Why not a Socialist party?"

"Parties can't strike. Parties can't shut down a company."

"One by one by one," she said. "Little strikes, big strikes, national strikes."

"See what happens tomorrow."

She felt so giddy she cooked up some eggs. They were costly, but she had two and she fried them and gave them to him, and he nibbled at them, tiny pieces that would stumble down his ravaged throat. The brats could have some oat gruel, like herself.

She found some pasteboard over at Malone's Butcher Shop and crayoned her new sign. All it said was WESTERN FEDERATION OF MINERS NOW. She made the letters big, and used red crayon and outlined each letter with black crayon until the sign seemed to shout. She didn't put anything else on. Let them ask her. She'd tell them

Butte needed a real union. She would take her money jar, but she wasn't sure anyone would drop a nickel in. They knew she collected for a miner with the con.

She headed out late in the afternoon, at shift's end, and steered clear of the mines. She'd try the saloons, especially O'Mara's, where there were plenty of men, half with miner's con, who'd like to string up the mine owners one by one. It was over near the union hall, where talk ran hot, even when the air was bitter. O'Mara's was the place for dying old miners whose lungs were quitting. Younger miners avoided the saloon. They believed it was like signing one's own death warrant to drink there—and maybe they were right.

It was so brutal outside she wondered how long she'd last. She had only a thin blue cotton coat, but she had an old gray sweater and scarf and mittens and she'd make do. The wind pushed the smoke from the seven Neversweat stacks down on the town, choking anyone who was outside. It wouldn't be a good day, but she needed cash, and she had no choice.

She stationed herself in the lee of the battered saloon vestibule, and waited out of the gale.

"What's this about, dearie?" asked a wiry man whose clothing was frosted because he hadn't changed to dry after his shift. "Where's the regular sign?"

"I'm pushing the WFM. Start a new local. Get something done around here," she said. "Fair wages. Better hours."

"What's Big Johnny got to say about it?"

"I don't care what he's got to say. We need a real union, not a kept one."

"That's tough talk, Alice."

"Help me feed a sick miner?"

"You bet. That's the Orangeman, eh?"

"I don't care what he is. He's sick."

The man pulled a dime out of his britches and dropped it into her jar. "I don't know about this," he said, and headed inside. A sharp shot of warmth struck her, and then the door closed.

That's how it went for a while. Once in a while she stepped inside, even though women weren't welcome at O'Mara's, but no one tossed her out. One time when she was warming, a bearded stranger approached. "Why the WFM?"

"Marcus Daly's dead," she said.

He nodded. "I'll vote for it. We need more muscle around here." He eyed her jar. "That's for Ward, like before? I'll keep the damned Orangeman alive." He dropped a whole quarter in, two drinks' worth.

She headed into the bitter air again, lest they get restless about her being there, and collected a few nickels more as miners studied her sign. Most didn't comment at all, but eyed her sharply. That was fine with her. She had almost three dollars in her jar, an amazing amount that said something about her new sign.

Then Big Johnny Boyle showed up and eyed her sign.

"What's this?"

"I'm pushing WFM. New local. It's better than your chickenshit union."

"The hell you are. Get out of here."

"I've got the right. It's a public street."

"You heard me."

"They want a new local. They want a real union, with balls."

That wasn't the right thing to say. Big Johnny yanked the sign from her and ripped it up. "Now get out, or I'll take your jar, too."

"It's a free world. I'm staying right here."

He grabbed her jar, poured the coin in his pocket, and smashed the jar. The glass shattered into bright shards.

She refused to budge. "You treat me like you own me. You don't own me."

He pushed her away from the door, but she refused to budge.

"You tried to sell me when Sean died. You lined up men who'd pay your price. So sell me now. Sell me, Boyle, sell me to the highest bidder. I'll choose my man if I want one, Johnny Boyle."

He gave her a shove. She dodged and fled into the saloon, where twenty men stared and grew quiet. The sudden heat shocked her.

"Boyle tried to sell me," she said. "After Singing Sean died. I'm not for sale. Now he's stolen my money."

Boyle came through the door, carrying the cold with him. "Out!" he yelled.

"He's got my money," she yelled. "Everything you gave me for the sick man."

"That so, Big Johnny?" said the bearded one.

Boyle ignored the miner and manhandled Red Alice toward the door.

"Hold up, Big Johnny," the old miner said so quietly it barely carried through the saloon. He headed straight for the union boss.

But Boyle kept on dragging her toward the door.

"Big Johnny, listen hard. We're all for a new local here. We weren't until you started pushing her around. We just voted. And we'll keep on voting."

"Fat chance you've got," Boyle said.

"Put her out," the barkeep said. "No women in here."

"Never another beer for me in this stinking place, then, O'Mara," another miner said.

The barkeep retreated.

Boyle dragged her into the cold and left her there and headed back in. The cold whipped her thin coat. She fumed. She had three dollars in that jar. Now she had nothing.

She headed back to her cottage. Lousy damned idea, William Ward! Now look at us!

But the bearded one caught up with her and held out his hand. Clenched inside of his hand was all the change that Big Johnny had taken from her.

"Word gets around," the man said. "We'll vote ourselves into a new local real quick."

She stood in the cold, a handful of coins in her hand, watching the big miner retreat into the sulphurous wind. She knew she had already won, and could hardly believe it.

Thirty-seven

Bad news from gruff Doctor Cockburn.

"Nothing more I can do, Maxwell," he said. "Wish I could help you."

Royal Maxwell absorbed that bleakly. The doctor had just concluded that Maxwell was suffering from several diseases, including syphilis, gonorrhea, consumption, St. Vitus' dance, trichinosis, corruption of the liver, jaundice, diabetes, piles, enlarged prostate, and bloody flux.

He'd been feeling worse and worse. His flesh had yellowed and grayed, and his hair was falling out, and his eyesight was going.

"How did it happen?" Maxwell asked.

"Messing around with bodies will do that to you."

"But they were dead."

"That's what everyone says about the girls.

Actually, they were little kettles of microbes."

"Could you supply me with a date?" Maxwell asked.

"I could supply you with a bill. You owe me for eleven visits. And I don't want any more brass tokens."

Doctor Cockburn was referring to parlor house tokens, Good For One Lay, handed out by the various establishments on Mercury Street. They had become Royal Maxwell's cash. He had more than he could use, even when he was more vigorous, so he sold them at half price for cash.

"I could pay you with a spare coffin. I've some fancy ones left over."

"Greenbacks, Maxwell. Or a draft on your bank account."

"I need some laudanum for pain, sir. A great deal of it, to subdue a great deal of pain."

Cockburn peered at him through wire-rimmed spectacles, and nodded. "Tokens will do for that," he said. He shuffled through his shelves, filled with mysterious carafes and bottles, some blue, some brown, found what he was looking for, filled a smaller blue bottle, penned the contents on the label, and handed it to Maxwell. "Ten tokens will do, Royal," he said.

"Ten tokens!"

"Opiates cost. I should charge you double."

Grudgingly, Royal Maxwell emptied his pockets of brass tokens, some to Minnie's, some to

Chicago Marlene's, some to Paradise, some to Shorty's Bathhouse. He knew that Cockburn was coining a fortune, but there wasn't anything Maxwell could do except grumble.

"You got the last laugh," he muttered.

"Repent, Maxwell," Cockburn replied, rattling the brass tokens. "Repent of your virtues."

That's how it always ended. Maxwell figured he had no virtues to repent of.

Clutching his bottle of painkiller, Maxwell hobbled into the street, and was blinded by sunlight. He normally worked nights. The restricted district had more or less accepted him, though not easily, and with occasional rank hatred. His decision years earlier to make himself the undertaker of the whores and pimps and madams and opium eaters and saloon men had gotten some sort of results, but not what he'd hoped for. He'd buried a bunch. The denizens of the restricted district were very good at dying. Some committed suicide, especially the older ladies with varicose veins and puffy faces. Others got married and escaped. There were a dozen miners ready to marry any lady who wanted a man.

His offer to bury anyone for free, or whatever came from passing the hat, still stood. It was the only way to bury some of those bozos like Stucco the Pimp. It turned out that the district had its own favorites, and Maxwell pocketed a lot of cash when one of them croaked. But the district had even more skunks, people so rotten that the whores gloated when one croaked, and then Maxwell ended up giving a free send-off, in spite of laying out cash for coffins, rental of draft horses, flowers, and the rest. All in all, he staggered along, collecting hundreds of brass tokens. But he could always sell tokens at half price, so they were as good as greenbacks. He should have guessed that once he took up with the outcasts, his regular business would drop off, and now he had no respectable customers at all.

But that wouldn't last long. He shuffled his way to his establishment, which had fallen into ruin. The syphilis had gotten to his nerves, forcing him into a halting walk, and making it hard for him to move muscles the way he wished. It would only be a short time now before he cashed in. But he already knew what he would do if he could manage it. He would stage his own funeral. He would witness it, too. That's what the laudanum was for. He entered his peeling-paint building, and headed toward the rear room, where the prize awaited. It was one glorious coffin that had never sold, with smoked-glass walls, walnut and brass furniture, and gold-plated handles. He would bury himself in it.

He would stage the biggest, best funeral ever seen in Butte, black horses with black pompons, his ebony hearse, the casket with the oval of smoked glass in the lid, permitting him to see out but not permitting spectators to see in, and then the planting in Mountain View. He'd watch them lower him into the hole, listen to the last words above, stare up at the teary faces of all the ladies of the night, and then hear the rattle of clay as the grave diggers began to shovel. And then, as light diminished and earth rained down on top of his coffin, he'd swallow his laudanum, enough to send him off in peace, having gotten the pleasure of his own perfect, magnificent, memorable planting.

He felt so nauseous he wondered whether he could manage it. He wondered why he wanted to try. He'd lost all his former friends, especially all the Republicans, since everyone in the district was a Democrat. He was simply washed up. He was broke. He'd enjoyed nearly every dolly in the district, but what did it get him but a lot of festering sores? It was mad, this scheme. Butte had led him into perdition. Anything could happen in Butte. Some men tried to corner all the money; other men wanted every woman.

He wondered who would be pallbearers, and marked it down as something to work out. He thought he'd ask Augustus Heinze and William Andrews Clark for starters. He could publish a list of the people he had asked, no matter whether they turned him down. He wondered who might get his estate, and then realized there wouldn't be any. Everything would be sold off.

It wouldn't work. He slumped in his morris chair, feeling his innards surrender hour by hour, and knew the whole idea of witnessing his own funeral was a fantasy. He would need confederates. He would need friends. He would need Republicans. He had nothing. He lacked a single friend. He lacked family. He lacked colleagues. He didn't belong to any church or fraternal organization. Once he had contributed to a home for unwed mothers, but that was forty years earlier, and he thought he was doing himself a favor. But now he was all alone. He was damned sick and headed for a pauper's grave at the rear of the cemetery.

He thought about the bottle of laudanum, with Cockburn's scratchy label on it, and thought of drinking the whole thing then and there. They'd find him eventually, even though hardly anyone entered his funeral home anymore.

He rested a while; it was hard to hike around Butte now, and bitter cold, too. Maybe he could beg. He struggled into his black topcoat, couldn't find gloves or a hat but set out anyway. Maybe Chicago Marlene would help him. She had always liked to give her dead girls a good send-off; that meant something to her. Once, when typhus swept through her parlor house, and seven of her ladies turned blue and life left them, he had buried them all. Most didn't have names, but Chicago Marlene had paid, and he had put the girls into a single plot with a biblical verse on it: LET HIM WHO IS WITHOUT SIN CAST THE FIRST STONE.

He scarcely made it half a block when he felt the nausea flood him again, and he sat down abruptly on the street.

"Here, now, you'll get run over by a trolley car," said a copper, who lifted Maxwell up and brushed him off.

Maxwell knew the man. It was Big Benny Brice; the one copper who didn't pound on everyone with his billy club.

"Say, Maxwell, you ain't well," Big Benny said.

Maxwell shook his head.

"I'll take you back to your parlor."

Maxwell didn't resist. Benny's big paw held the mortician upright, and soon enough Maxwell was slumped in his morris chair, still in his coat.

"You been drinking, Maxwell?"

Maxwell shook his head.

"Something wrong?"

Maxwell just stared, and slowly shook his head.

"Yeah, something's wrong; you're looking like a puked-out dog," Big Benny said. "Someone stick a shiv into you?"

"I'm dying. Cockburn just told me so. I've got more fatal diseases than there are in Equador or Madagascar. I was trying to get to Chicago Marlene to see if she'd bury me."

"Dying? You? Funeral directors don't die." Big

Benny stared. "Well, I guess they do."

"No friends, no family," Maxwell said. "All alone. Maybe Chicago Marlene would."

"You want a planting? I'll do that for you, Maxwell."

"You, a flatfoot cop?"

He was insulting Big Benny, but he didn't care. He didn't want to be buried by a beat cop. He wanted a copper king to bury him. William Andrews Clark would do. Fritz Heinze could deliver the eulogy. An important man needed important mourners.

"That's right, me boy, a flatfoot with a billy club. And I get to see the world, and I get to see things that people do. You done them a lot of good in there, with your fancy send-offs."

"Good? What are you saying?"

"Maxwell, those girls, they're mostly off the farms. They got treated bad. Bad husband, bad father, rotten mother, and they fled marriages, fled parents, wanting anything but the life that was put on them, got me?"

"What's that got to do with it?"

"They come to the district by the hundreds, mostly hating themselves, blaming themselves, alone, ready to swallow a bottle of carbolic acid and burn themselves to death, eh?"

Maxwell nodded, unwilling for this to go further.

"Alone they are, Maxwell. Buried in a potter's

field without a headstone, forgotten. Until you came along. Sure, my boy, you wanted some boodle for it, but for them it was a miracle. Someone cared. You put on a show every time, driving that old hearse around, letting the world know that whoever was in there was special. I saw it myself, boy. I saw the ladies weeping, like your send-offs were the most important thing in the world to them. You were remembering them. They wouldn't die alone. Even their pimps paid respect when you drove by. Call me a flatfoot, boy, but I've got eyes, and I saw the good you did around there, getting the gals buried proper."

He drew himself up. "Me and all the other coppers, we all saw it, and we all think you did a lot of good, boy. So we'll bury you proper, and we'll be proud to do it."

"Bury me?"

"We'll march on either side of you, sir. We'll be a line of blue, escorting you. We'll make sure all of Butte knows it, too. We'd be honored to do it, sir. We saw what you did down in the district. A girl could dream of a good send-off. That meant she was someone, not just a nameless female dumped in a corner of the graveyard. Yes, Maxwell, we saw it and we'll be proud to send you on your way—if you want it, sir."

There was a question in it.

Maxwell felt so dizzy he could scarcely stand.

"Big Benny, I think I'd like to be escorted by

353

your men in blue," he said. "I hope they're all Republicans."

"We'll all be Republicans for the occasion, Mr. Maxwell."

"You will, won't you? Bury me?"

"I think I can arrange it, sir. Should I be taking you to the pesthouse?"

"No, Mr. Bruce. Just leave me here, and maybe in the morning you can check in. The door won't be locked. You can see if I'm a bit better."

"Count on me, Mr. Maxwell."

"You won't let me down, will you?"

"Should I find someone to sit with you, sir? I can find someone, I think."

"No, no, my friend. I'll just sit here and sip some medicine I got."

"Well, good night then, Mr. Maxwell."

Royal Maxwell nodded, watched the copper retreat into the night, and pulled out the laudanum, which he fondled as delicately as he would a woman's cheek.

Thirty-eight

Nothing happened. J. Fellowes Hall waited for the doomsday notice. Waited for a pink slip. Waited for a visit from Clark's lawyer. But in the wake of the *Mineral*'s new assault on Anaconda, no rebuke issued from up high.

Maybe Clark didn't care. Maybe Clark didn't see the story. Maybe Clark simply planned to give Hall more time, probation as it were. Whatever the case, Hall remained on the payroll, for the moment. It wouldn't last, of course, and Clark would eject him eventually. But Hall felt almost heady thinking about it.

As long as Clark was holding off, maybe Hall could redress the wrongs the paper had done, mostly crimes of omission. It had failed to report all the news, or it had colored its reportage to fit Mr. Clark's objectives. That was the paper's offense against the people of Butte. It wasn't the thunderous editorials Hall wrote on behalf of the owner; it was twisting or hiding the news on behalf of the owner. The news didn't belong to anyone; it was something different, something attached to the public good, something that ought not to belong to anyone, not even the owner of the paper. Hall didn't condemn himself. He was simply no different from all the other editors of all the other kept newspapers in Montana.

The next day nothing happened, and the day after that nothing happened. J. Fellowes Hall remained the editor of Clark's premier newspaper. Well, then, maybe it was time to produce the sort of paper that Hall might be proud of. But how could he even start if the Damocles sword was dangling over his neck?

He burrowed into his topcoat and braved the

sulphurous cold air, something he had never gotten used to. He hiked east, finally turning on an obscure lane that would take him to Slanting Agnes. He had not visited her for years, and wondered if she even existed. Consulting a fey woman about the future was not the way J. Fellowes Hall now did things, but what did it matter? He was desperate for a peek, a clue, a snatched moment from times to come.

The cottage was still there, unpainted, worn, looking ready to cave in, or slide into the nearest gulch. He knocked and waited impatiently, the wind harrying him mercilessly. She opened and stared.

"You is it? I shouldn't let you in here, Clark's paid liar, but I will. Don't expect a thing from me, you who spread lies."

He was expecting something like that, and didn't try to argue. He just nodded and stepped into a cold kitchen. She looked more worn and thin than ever, and he doubted she was getting enough to feed herself and her two boys.

"I don't know about you," she said. "I don't know if I want to."

"Your house is cold," he said, leaving his greatcoat on.

"What do you expect it to be, me a widow lady with no money?"

"The mines should pay a pension or a death benefit," he said.

"Now is that something William Andrews Clark told you to say to me?"

He saw how this was going. "I would like to learn about my immediate future—if you're inclined."

She busied herself, stirring up coals in the firebox of her stove, adding wood, and starting some water heating. All the while she was eyeing him as he sat, waiting and wondering if this was a fool's mission. She would not be hurried. He needed fast answers.

"I don't charge for it. I don't have a gift. Some people have a gift, but I don't. I just have moments, little flashes, that's all, and only when I'm unwilling. I don't want this gift. It's from the devil. People shouldn't know the future. But there's nothing I can do about it. If you want to know when you'll die, then maybe I'll tell you, maybe I won't."

She fussed around her kitchen, brought water to boil, steeped tea, and finally poured some amber fluid into a chipped cup and saucer.

"How are your boys?"

"You're making polite talk. You don't care about my boys. They're just more hooligans, aren't they? Now if you'd asked me what county I'm from, maybe then I'd answer you. It's Clare, County Clare, you know, but you wouldn't know and wouldn't care."

"Madam, I'm sorry I came. Thank you for the tea—I'll leave now."

"Sit down, you jackass."

But he didn't. He only wanted to escape. He started to get back into his greatcoat.

She paused suddenly. "Mr. Clark doesn't like you," she said.

"That's not news."

"Do the things you have in mind. You've got time."

He paused. "What do I have in mind?"

"How should I know? Do them."

"How much time?"

She sighed, annoyed. "You think I have answers. I don't. Things come suddenly to me, and then the peek ahead closes off again."

That was it. A totally unsatisfying encounter. He thought to give her a dollar. She glared at him. Five, then. He reached into his pocket, and pulled out some greenbacks. There were three singles and a ten. He gave her the ten.

"Filthy money," she said. "Clark money."

"You told me what I needed to know."

"I wish I didn't have the gift," she said. "Now things'll be worse."

He left thinking she was crazier than ever, and wondering why he laid a lot of cash on her. She could live for a week on that. He stepped into the choking air, the smoke from the seven Neversweat chimneys lowering over town again. A man couldn't breathe in Butte, which is why so many died young, and not just miners.

He had time. He should do what he needed to do. That had cost him a sawbuck. He was nuts, visiting her.

He coughed his way back to the paper, pulled out some foolscap and began a list.

1. Clean up air. Higher stacks.
2. County poor farm. Shelter for the homeless and helpless. Tax the mines.
3. Pension. Widows' fund. Support for old miners and widows.
4. Clean air in mines. Fight miner's lung. No rock dust.
5. Better water. No arsenic in it. Keep it cheap. The poor need it.
6. Cobble the streets, less dust and mire. Slow down disease.
7. County rest home. Refuge for sick men and children.
8. Mining law. End apex law and litigation. Stop underground theft.
9. Tax mine profits for schools.
10. Clean up the courts. Impeach crooked judges.

There were many other reforms that came to mind, but these ten would be a start. He found Grabbit Wolf hammering at a typing machine, and summoned him.

"We've just become the reform paper," he said.

Grabbit started laughing. "Let me guess. You've been bought."

"Sure, William Rockefeller forked over."

"I'll want some whiskey money."

"A quart a story," Hall said instantly. "I'm serious. We're selling reform. We're going to be the paper that cares about everyone in Butte. Choose any one of these to start with. Do a piece on the problem. Get some quotations. Talk to someone who's hurting. Then write the story. New story every couple of days."

Wolf looked over the list. "You want to get us all fired?"

"Clark's too busy to notice."

"What's the one that gets us fired? I'll do that first."

"That would be a widows' fund, a pension, something for men with miner's con."

Grabbit lit a cigar. "I guess you're asking for it," he said. "I can write that one off the top of my head."

There were two younger men on the staff, both gifted cartoonists. "I want some tough cartoons," Hall said. "Tax the mines. Build a hospital. Start pensions. Start a widows' fund. Kick out the crooked judges. Start a poor farm for the needy. Clean the water."

"You trying to get us fired?" asked Potter.

"Yes," Hall said, and walked away.

He settled into his swivel chair and found

himself actually shaking. He seethed with some sort of feeling he had never experienced, something so piercing and urgent that he couldn't name it. There was pain, yes. What he was doing scared him. But there was something else, something heady, something that filled him with pride. For the first time since he arrived in Butte, he felt what, what? Honorable. Honorable! He didn't know how much time he had before Clark pitched him out, and the rest of his staff too, but from this moment on, he would run the only reform paper in Butte. And there was a lot to reform. And after he had tackled these, he would have another ten, and another ten after that.

Grabbit vanished from the grimy office, as if shot out of a cannon. The old souse looked inspired. By midafternoon, just in time for the evening edition, he was turning in copy for typesetting. He started with widows' funds. He interviewed three miners' widows in Dublin Gulch, all living hand to mouth after their men had perished from miner's con. He quoted all of them as saying they needed a widows' fund; miners' widows should be cared for by the mines. The mines had ruined the bodies of their men, and left the widows penniless, with children, and nowhere to go for help.

"Those rich men, they feasted on Mike's body, and won't give me two cents to feed my wee ones," said Margaret McCarthy. "In the Silver

361

Bow Club they don't eat all the food set before them, and my boys wait for the scraps."

There was more; homeless widows, sick children, suicides.

Hall published the story and waited for whatever would happen, while Grabbit set to work on the next. He tackled the apex law next. The 1872 mining law was a license to steal, and that was exactly what was happening deep under the streets of Butte. Grabbit found plenty of lawyers willing to talk, and not just Anaconda's lawyers trying to defend its mines from the onslaught of Fritz Heinze.

Not everyone thought the law was pernicious, and Grabbit collected some good quotes from a few who favored it.

"Apex law keeps me in business," said Gerald Jones, Esq. "It keeps most Silver Bow lawyers in business. No mine is safe in anyone's hands so long as it's legal to follow a vein into the next man's mine."

That made a fine story, which Hall discreetly featured on the bottom of the front page, where no one would miss it. It was sure good business. The edition sold out an hour after it hit the streets, and Hall cranked out some more copies just to gild his profits a little.

And still, no rebuke from Clark. It dawned on Hall that Clark tacitly approved. It enhanced his stature and inclined the legislature to vote him into the Senate. But what Hall enjoyed most was a sense that at least he was pursuing the mission of any good newspapers, which was to enhance the public weal. One might argue about what the public good might be, but one could surely seek to improve security, health, sanitation, wages, retirement, and medical progress.

Grabbit Wolf turned himself into a whirlwind, and developed stories that struck at the heart of Butte's neglect of its humbler citizens. Hall made a point to avoid sensationalism, and published each piece with a quiet headline that would inflame no one.

Opposing papers took notice and began jeering at Hall, accusing the *Mineral* of going batty in its rush to reform a world that could never be changed. The *Anaconda Standard* took issue with any reform that might raise the cost of labor, such as pensions, and Heinze's little weekly, the *Reveille*, heaped coals of scorn on Hall for suggesting there was anything wrong with apex law and litigation.

For the first time since coming to Butte, he began to feel like a man at the top of his profession. Even his perception of Butte seemed to shift. He had come to love the battered, filthy, chaotic, ugly city, the city that killed its own, the city where typhus and silicosis and tuberculosis lurked at every corner, the city where desperate children stole anything they could, just to get food. This was his Butte, ugly and shameful, and laden with vices. The *Mineral*'s voice would be drowned out by the greedy and calculating, but still it was a voice of reform. And that inspired Hall, and his bright employees, to wrestle even harder with the evils at every hand.

"My dear," he wrote Amber. "We've been parted a long while, and now I wish to bring you here, and make Butte our home. I was uncertain about it; Butte is raw and cruel, and unhealthy too, but it is also a place where determined people might prosper. Things get better. There are now pleasant places to live. Begin making travel plans and disposing of what you won't ship, and you will find funds forthcoming in the mail."

He couldn't imagine how it had happened.

Thirty-nine

The private railcar, discreetly enameled maroon, rested quietly on a siding below Butte, supplied with steam and electricity by an idling steam engine. It didn't attract notice. It was owned by William Rockefeller, and was furnished in the family tradition of great quietness. There would be no gold-plated faucets within.

But it was luxurious, nonetheless, with walnut paneled walls, a rear parlor with a cut-glass chandelier and overstuffed chairs, two bedroom suites, a galley and quarters for servants, and three water closets equipped with showers. From its curtained windows one could gaze upward upon a turmoil of seedy buildings, a solid brick-and-stone shopping area, and a forest of headframes and boilers, a hodgepodge of mining and smelting sheds sprawling over the crests of the slopes.

Rockefeller, John's brother, occupied one bedroom; Henry Rogers occupied the other. The richest men on earth had come to view the richest hill on earth. The enclosed ebony Rockaway parked discreetly near the private car belonged to William Scallon, president of the company, and Marcus Daly's successor. In due course, they would all climb into the Rockaway and see the sights, but for the moment they convened in the parlor where they could gaze out upon a hill that was not quite yielding itself to them, as planned. For some years, this trio, and its allies, had pursued consolidation, the euphemism for driving rivals out of business and combining all their assets into a single company, of course owned and operated by the three who were sitting in the parlor, enjoying whatever their hearts desired. William Rockefeller was being abstemious; Rogers toyed with a scotch, and Scallon sipped a bourbon.

Rogers was the most striking of the three. He was sixty-one, graying, jut-jawed, handsome, robust, hale, commanding, and amiable. He spoke in flawless cadences, well-honed by a careful upbringing and improved by wealth. Rogers, rather like the Rockfellers, was a devoted churchman who endowed public buildings and congregations in his hometown, Fairhaven, Connecticut. His geniality was legend. His host this trip, William Rockefeller, operated in his brother's shadow but was a forceful man in his own right. Scallon felt vaguely diminished by two of what the popular press called the Standard Oil Gang.

Matters had come to a head. For some while the Amalgamated Copper Company had been buying Butte mines. Famous names fell under the company's direction. Those owned by the Lewisohn brothers were gradually being eaten up, as were the famous mines of the Boston people, the Boston and Montana Consolidated Copper and Silver Mining Company, and the Butte and Boston under the control of Albert Bigelow, and many smaller mines as well. There were scores of mines and reduction works on the hill, stretching to Walkerville and beyond, and far to the east and west. Many of these independents still shipped their ore to the Heinzes' Montana Ore Purchasing Company, which reduced their ore more efficiently and at less cost than any of its rivals. The ore flowing into it was crucial to its profitable operation. Bit by bit Rogers and his colleagues had brought the smaller mines into Anaconda's orbit, or at least control, steadily diminishing the rich copper ores that the Heinzes could process and send away for final refining in the East. But Rogers's noose failed to tighten entirely, which was an increasing annoyance to him, and to the rest. If Standard Oil could distribute two hundred fifty million dollars in dividends to its lucky few owners over several years, the copper trust could yield even more. The potential was there, before their eyes. But what had stymied this great strangle of the industry was F. Augustus Heinze's staff of legal beagles, who fought the chokehold with a variety of lawsuits.

William Scallon eyed the other gentlemen in the private car with some reserve. He might be the president of Anaconda, but he had never encountered men like these. He was a Canadian and a lawyer, and a gentleman. These two visitors to Butte had conducted themselves in a manner almost beyond his imagining. They had induced panic selling of Amalgamated stock, and then bought back in at bargain prices, making tens of millions in sheer profit. They had capitalized their trust with stock that was grounded in thin air, and made many more millions out of nothing. At will, they could make Amalgamated stock rise or fall, sell out or buy into it, and pocket the loose change. But their absolute mastery of the Butte mines was less certain now, thanks to the machinations of F. Augustus Heinze and his vest-pocket judges. That is what brought them in their private car across the continent to this ugly place. Scallon was perfectly familiar with mining magnates like Clark and Daly, but he had never understood men like this who gave little thought to consequences.

"Well, then, gentlemen, let's proceed," he said.

The visitors nodded. The October day was mild enough, but for some reason the East Coast men bundled up before descending the iron stairs and climbing into Scallon's elegant Rockaway, where Scallon's liveried coachman waited patiently.

The Rockaway, a square, enclosed coach with large glass windows, would be a perfect vehicle to see the sights. It would at once insulate the passengers from the rawest smells, while affording them a perfect view. Its black lacquered exterior bespoke quiet elegance. Spectators would not mistake the eminence of those within as it passed through the streets of Butte.

Scallon's coachman knew the route and the schedule, and without direction he turned the handsome drays up the long slope to the great hill east of town where the Anaconda mines clustered as well as Heinze's Rarus mine, and the Boston and Montana group.

"We'll begin with the comedy," Scallon said.

The driver would take them to that patch of land in the midst of the great mines that Heinze had christened the Copper Trust, and where, according to his lawsuits, the rich veins all apexed. It was a good joke. Heinze's suits had languished in Montana courts for years, too frivolous even for the friendly judges to cope with. But the site would entertain these calculating men from the East, in their black coats and monogrammed silk scarves.

The Rockaway gained the hill, and the city fell away into a chaotic and unpaved district, jammed with rails, dirt paths that took miners to the pits, sheds, flapping laundry on lines, headframes, great stamp mills, hoists, boiler rooms, and heaps of industrial debris, all grim against a bright blue heaven and serene mountain slopes. That was the paradox. So much beauty just beyond this junk pile perched on the hill.

Scallon's coachman took the coach as far as he could, and then opened the door to the substantial men within. They stepped daintily into the grass-less mire, eyed the smoke lowering from the Neversweat stacks, and edged gingerly toward the offending claim, which was marked by iron stakes and a NO TRESPASSING sign, as well as an elegant masonry edifice that supported a gilded sign that said COPPER TRUST. It was amusing on sight. The Copper Trust commanded land barely large enough to support a two-hole outhouse.

Henry Rogers stared pensively. William Rockefeller smirked. Neither said a word. This was a sideshow. They looked vaguely annoyed by the waste of time visiting here. Scallon hurried them back to the Rockaway, and the coachman drove the lurching vehicle toward a nearby cluster of rough buildings lying farther east.

"That's the Rarus," Scallon said. "And that's the Johnstown. And beyond, the Boston and Montana's Pennsylvania."

These gentlemen were familiar with the case. Heinze's apex suit against the Boston and Montana declared that the veins being mined there apexed on Rarus ground. The suit had been heard by Judge Clancy and had bounced up to the Montana Supreme Court and back even as Heinze's miners were feverishly gouging the disputed ore out of the ground and shipping it to Heinze's smelter. The courts had forced Heinze to post a bond in the event that the case should go against him. Heinze, in turn, had invented a phantom East Coast finance company with ghostly assets that bonded him, and persuaded the gullible courts to accept the arrangement. If Rockefeller and Rogers could conjure something out of nothing, so could Fritz Heinze.

"Here's the boundary line. Unless you wish to enter the pits, you'll want to observe that beneath our feet, Fritz Heinze is cleaning out the disputed ore as fast as he can, and lifting it over there." Scallon pointed to the works at the Johnstown. "The ore from here's being lifted there."

"We'll stay aboveground," Rogers said. "It's our ore. Amalgamated ore."

"Correct, sir," Scallon said. Amalgamated had not yet folded its newer acquisitions into its subsidiary the Anaconda Company.

He steered his guests a little farther, to the line separating the Rarus from the Michael Davitt mine, another of the Butte and Boston properties. The Bostonians had claimed that Rarus veins apexed in the Michael Davitt; the court had eventually shut down all operations in both mines that involved the disputed veins. But that was all the opportunity Heinze needed to gut the veins and smuggle orc out while awaiting the court to decide. He had sent hundreds of miners into the forbidden ground, where they were hollowing out the rich veins, sealing off the depleted chambers, and feeding the contraband into the Montana Ore Purchasing Company smelter by lifting it from adjacent shafts. Now Heinze's theft was Amalgamated's problem because the trust had bought a controlling interest in the Boston mines and had pushed their primary owner, Albert Bigelow, out the door.

"Somewhere, at several levels under our feet, sirs, ore from here is flowing to the Heinze smelter."

"He's violating the Ten Commandments," Rogers said.

Next they drove to Meaderville and viewed the

Minnie Healy mine, which was at the heart of an apex suit with the various surrounding mines, especially the Piccolo and Gambetta, owned by the Boston and Montana firm. The gifted Heinze had discovered rich new veins in the Minnie Healy, and argued that they apexed there and ran into the Boston property, so he had filed suit to claim the ore. The Minnie Healy was thus one of the keys to controlling the veins in several surrounding mines. It was this suit that had drawn Henry H. Rogers and William Rockefeller to Montana that mild afternoon. It would be decided in Judge Clancy's courtroom that day of 1903.

Rogers and Rockefeller walked the boundaries, felt the earth shudder beneath their feet, studied their works and Heinze's, and climbed into the ebony Rockaway once again, while Scallon's driver took them to the next locale. That proved to be Heinze's Nipper Consolidated, which lay next to the Little Mina, which was owned by Amalgamated's subsidiary, the Parrot Silver and Copper Company. Heinze's favorite judge, William Clancy, had put the Little Mina into receivership, further threatening the Standard Oil Gang's copper trust.

Rogers and Rockefeller paced the boundaries, eyed that cluster of headframes and hoists, and examined the bright black foothills of the Rockies, not far beyond. Pockets of snow had collected in the upland valleys, and purple shadows crawled with the sun across the high country.

It was time to go to court. The impending verdicts were so important that they had drawn these princes of finance west. The trust was under siege, and might fail under Heinze's endless assault, which was tying the trust into knots. Stockholder suits filed by Heinze's lieutenants, Lamm and Forrester and MacGinnis, who held shares in opposing corporations, had prevented the Amalgamated Trust from absorbing the Boston properties, and threatened to unravel the entire consolidation of mines in Butte within the Amalgamated holding company.

Scallon's man drove the Rockaway to the ornate courthouse, which looked more like a church than a public office, which may have been intended. Judge Clancy would deliver his decisions at four this twenty-second day of October, 1903. These were simply two more in a string of them issued by the district court in Butte, but these intelligent men well understood that companies crumble under the weight of such edicts, empires collapse, dreams shatter.

They found Judge Clancy's courtroom nearly empty. Scallon nodded briefly at Amalgamated's lawyer, Dennis Jones, and Heinze's lawyer, Albert French, and settled on a bleak bench at the rear. Heinze was not present. It was quiet. Four o'clock came and went and the room remained muffled in silence. Clancy enjoyed doing that. He no doubt knew who were sitting on his pew-like benches, and a little discomfort was in order for all the litigants. He had kept them uncomfortable for years.

Then at last, the clerk of court appeared, and the bailiff, and the handful of men rose as his honor emerged. Judge William Clancy was as disheveled and grimy as ever; food stains darkened his unkempt gray beard. He peered about, his cunning gaze settling on the visitors, and he let them all remain standing. He smiled slightly while the court was called to order, and settled into his chair.

Rogers started to sit down, but Clancy rebuked him. "You will respect the court," Clancy said, gesturing Rogers to return to his feet. And so they all stood, while the judge yawned, shuffled papers, and waited for the clerk to ready himself. Clancy scratched his beard. Scallon thought it must itch, and was probably teeming with vermin. It showed no sign of having been washed. A faint odor drifted through the hushed courtroom, and Scallon thought that none of the rest of Clancy's person had enjoyed the comfort of soap and water, either.

And so they stood, while Clancy enjoyed himself by doing nothing. Then at last, he invited the opposing counsel to step forward.

"Gentlemen," he said, leering slightly. "Let us begin. In the matter of *Forrester and MacGinnis v.*

Boston and Montana Consolidated Copper and Silver Mining Company and *Lamm et al v. Parrot Silver and Copper Mining,* I find as follows."

He droned on for a few minutes. The upshot was that the Amalgamated holding company could not legally absorb the Boston or other properties in Montana; that the trust itself was an attempt to create an illegal monopoly; that the holding company would be prohibited from owning stock in the Boston companies or their subsidiaries. In essence, Clancy was ruling that the holding company could not consolidate mines in Montana.

That brought the slightest of frowns to the faces of the Standard Oil men.

But there was more. Judge Clancy licked his lips, which were largely hidden beneath his soup-strainer beard, and continued. The Minnie Healy mine, whose ownership was disputed, belonged to the Johnstown Mining Company, which was a Heinze property. Thus was ten million dollars of ore passed to Heinze, plus the opportunity for Heinze to file more apex suits against all the properties adjacent to the Minnie Healy.

The Standard Oil Gang heard its empire collapse.

"And there you are, gentlemen. The court so rules. Tomorrow I'm heading for the woods to hunt for elk and jackrabbits."

Forty

William Ward finally died of consumption. Alice
Brophy knew it was coming. He had turned
waxen, was coughing up blood constantly as his
lungs surrendered, was struggling to breathe, had
turned feverish, and stared at her from onyx eyes
that sometimes seemed to hide the flicker of life
itself within him.

He had been a long time dying. The con had
waxed and waned. There were months when he
seemed on the brink of recovering, only to slide
back into desperate coughing, spitting up pieces
of his lungs, and utter weakness in which he could
not even get out of bed.

Her bed. He had been the unwelcome visitor for
three years. Her family had adjusted itself to his
presence, sleeping anywhere, or not sleeping at
all. He'd been the Orangeman among the Greens.
Not that she believed any of that religion stuff, but
she felt a special loathing of the Orange Irish.

He had left a family behind and she didn't know
how to contact them. Maybe the union would
know. In his healthier moments he had tried to
help out; cook, clean, anything to ease her life, but
it had come to very little. Butte lacked places to
die. No one wanted a consumptive, because they
infected those around them. Maybe she had the

con now. Maybe Tim and Tommy too. They weren't exactly in the prime of health. They looked like ghosts. They were mostly stealing, and were good at it. So far no one had caught them. They saw opportunities, sometimes to trade one stolen item for another; a coil of rope for an apple. They were a part of gangs, lifting anything they could and then trading it for whatever they needed. The gangs roamed freely from Meaderville to the flats below the hill, and their shifting membership was drawn from all over Butte. Timmy often returned to Dublin Gulch carrying something odd, something he said he'd found, but he wouldn't say more, and that odd item would vanish the next day. She didn't like that, but mostly because she feared he would get pinched.

Alice Brophy stared at her still, cold guest, not knowing what to do. Then she decided he was a union man; let the union bury him if they would. Big Johnny Boyle wanted nothing to do with her. She was too radical for him, though radical wasn't the word she used. She wanted justice. She eyed Ward, oddly tender about him. He had given her good ideas. He had tried to help. He had at least been a friend. But now he lay still and cold and green of flesh.

She donned her worn coat and braved the cold, hiking slowly toward the union hall, the headquarters of Local Number 1, Western Federation of Miners. Only this union wasn't like the other locals. Big Johnny and mine management were tight as could be, so this local alone, among all the locals, was actually silent about all the red-hot issues burning through the miners of the West. There were a few firebrands, mostly stirred up by people like Red Alice, who demanded more: mine sanitation, cleaner air, better hours, better wages, a sick fund, a widows' fund, a pension. And Big Johnny had made a show of getting these things, and so had the managements, but it was only a show. The union's sick fund simply paid the hospital to care for the miners who walked in. The widows' fund paid brief death benefits—and then nothing.

Big Johnny wasn't in the union hall, so he had to be next door at the bar. She invaded that all-male sanctum and found him nursing a mug of ale.

"Who let you in here?" he asked by way of greeting.

"I let myself in. William Ward is dead and needs burying."

"So? Bury him yourself."

She was afraid of that. "He was a brother. He paid his dues for years."

"Not for the last three, he hasn't."

"You owe him one."

"Alice, you butt out. Get your skinny ass out."

"I'll make sure the whole town knows about it, Big Johnny."

That gave him pause, if only for a moment. "He

wasn't a member," he said lamely.

"You wouldn't even know that. You don't know who's a member. You got three thousand members and you don't know who's one and who isn't. You need a clerk. Like me. I keep track. I'll make sure your dues are in."

For an answer, Big Johnny turned his back on her and sipped ale, and started nudging his neighbors, as if it was all a joke. The barkeep started frowning at her, meaning he was about to pitch her out on her ear.

"Guess lots of people gonna hear about this," she said.

"I don't give a rat's ass," he snapped.

"We need a new union," she said, just as the burly keep started to round the far side of the bar to chase her out.

She ducked into the street, thinking she was clear, but the man followed her outside and booted her in the butt.

"Some friend of miners you are," she snapped.

She stood in the cold wind, letting it cut through her thin coat and chill her heart. Lousy, whoring union. Maybe women should run it. At least women cared. It was said that Big Johnny was in thick with Anaconda's management. He never lacked any beer money, that was sure. And he lived fancy, too. After Marcus Daly died, they kept up the game. Once in a while some bigwig in the company would buy a little brick house for a miner's widow, and make sure it got talked about. Heinze and Clark did the same thing. Tame union, no strikes, no pressure to have pensions or sickness benefits or money for miner's con. No sanitation. The pits were cesspools, full of human waste, every puddle down there teeming with sickness. No wonder so many miners died of dysentery. The miners didn't get poorer; they got dead. The rich got richer and lived long lives.

She needed that job. She hated to say it, but William Ward had been her livelihood. Every day for these years she had handed out tracts and collected cash for the sick miner. The miners knew about Ward, chipped in dimes and nickels, and she had survived. And now he was lying stone cold in her house. She thought maybe she could bury him herself. She had half-grown children now, big enough to help her wrap Ward in a winding sheet and take him somewhere. Maybe drop him off in front of the Episcopalian Church, the damned Church of England, and let them plant him.

She felt a new sadness wash her. She liked William Ward, and she liked him because he wasn't so full of shit as the rest. Sometimes when she was mouthing away, he just smiled at her, as if to say cut out the crap, and she knew she was talking a lot of hot air. But now he was dead, and he was filling up her house. She sure as hell didn't know what to do, and the wind was howling. She wished she could burn him in her stove.

Then she remembered her flatfoot friend, Big Benny Brice, and thought she knew where he'd be skimming along, twirling his billy club the way he did. He'd be over on East Broadway. So she braved the sulphurous smoke and headed into the commercial district, looking for some flash of blue.

She found her flatfoot standing on a grille that vented boiler heat, while a forlorn mutt waited to return to his favorite spot.

"Well, if it isn't Alice Brophy, and how are you?" he said.

"I need a little help," she said. "William finally, well, quit."

"Quit?"

"Died. I always have trouble saying it. He's lying in my bed. No one wants him. The union won't bury him."

"Ah, I see. Well, let's go have a look, Mrs. Brophy. There's a few things need to be done."

She was startled. It was the first time anyone had called her Mrs. Brophy in many years.

They hiked toward Dublin Gulch, and Alice had trouble staying even with Big Benny.

"Now I've been meaning to have a word with you, and about that boy of yours. Timothy is it? That boy's heading for trouble."

"Then let him get into it," she replied.

"Could it be, madam, that he's a bit starved?"

Red Alice started to rub her eyes.

Big Benny Brice said nothing more as they slipped from commercial blocks into humbler ones, and finally into the gulch, with its crowded cottages and endless odors. They turned to Alice's decaying cottage, and the flatfoot stood aside while Alice opened. The room was stone cold. She drew a curtain aside to let in some light, while the copper studied the remains lying in the alcove bed.

The cop touched Ward's face and neck, and nodded.

"Let's walk over to the courthouse, madam, and we'll do what needs doing. Silver Bow will lay him to rest, and I'll see to it. And I'll come with you, if you choose to see him to his grave."

The flatfoot studied the barren kitchen, the lifeless stove, and the lampless interior before he stepped into the smoky winter air.

"He was a good man, I imagine," the constable said.

"He was an Orange—yes, a good man. A miner. When he first got sick he tried to die down in the pits. It's warm there."

"There's a lot of bones down there, Mrs. Brophy. They fed a lot of rats."

They trudged into town, pushing against the bitter wind, until they got to the station house. "This'll do," he said.

She made her report. Time of death, name, next

of kin, cause. She couldn't give them an address. Wife and children in Belfast. Cause of death consumption. No estate that she knew of.

"We'll send a man, madam," the desk officer said.

"That's it? That's the end of William Ward?"

"I'll take you home," Big Benny said.

She followed him as he trudged back. He stopped at a coal dealer and paid for a small bag of Montana coal, and carried it with him. When they got to her place, he built a small fire from kindling, and then added some coal. It would take a long time to heat up the cottage, but the flatfoot settled easily in a shabby armchair and waited. She was colder than ever, but had nothing to pull over herself.

And there wouldn't be anything soon, she thought. Her only source of money lay in that bed. And she couldn't find a job, and likely never would, given that she was Red Alice.

It took an hour before a man with a black hearse showed up, and he and the flatfoot loaded William Ward into it. The cottage was finally starting to warm.

She didn't know the funeral man. There were more undertakers in Butte than there were preachers.

"We'll head straight out to Mountain View," the man said. "I put two diggers on the grave, and all we need to do is wrap him. I take it you're not a relative."

"He's my brother," she said, wondering why on earth she said it.

"Kin?"

"In a way. In a way."

"You are welcome to ride with me, madam."

She wondered about it. The cottage was just starting to be warm, heavenly warm.

"I guess I will," she said.

"I'll be going with you," said Big Benny. "Seems the best thing."

The mortician expertly wrapped William Ward in a white winding sheet and tied it close and tight, while Alice and the flatfoot watched. Then he nodded, and the mortician and copper carried the Orangeman out to the ebony hearse.

So they sat in the open seat, while an ancient dray clopped down the long grade to the flats, hastened along by the wind at their backs. True to his word, the funeral man had a grave ready for William Ward. It was nowhere near six feet deep, though.

Big Benny and the two grave diggers lifted William Ward from the hearse and set him gently in the shallow grave, a long white bundle.

"Anything you wish to say? A moment's reflection?" the mortician asked. "A prayer? A verse of scripture?"

Alice couldn't think of a thing. "I'll have a mass said for his soul," she said. "He was a good man. And don't be billing me because I don't have it to give you."

So the grave diggers shoveled, and Alice and Big Benny rode back, into the bitter wind.

And Alice wondered why she missed Ward so much.

Forty-one

Victory called for a party, and F. Augustus Heinze knew how to create one. That evening at the Butte Hotel he threw a corker. There were gold rosettes for the women at the long table; there were gifts of stock shares for the gentlemen, who were dressed in dinner jackets. The women were drawn from the demimonde as well as society, and the ladies eyed one another cheerfully, as if to acknowledge they were not so far apart.

Fritz Heinze knew how to celebrate, and this evening there would be much to celebrate. So the bubbly flowed, the whiskey glasses were filled and refilled, and the ladies glittered in their finery.

It was time for a toast. He stood, an impressive figure, muscular and trim, still youthful. He eyed the assemblage, his gaze pausing at Katarina Costa, wearing scarlet this evening in wanton celebration of her status, and then he lifted a hand to quiet them all, which actually took some while because no one was very sober, and he raised a glass.

"We have something to celebrate," he said

quietly. "We have slain the anaconda. We have slain the giant constrictor, the snake that grows fifteen feet in length and devours its prey, including mortals, by squeezing them to their death. We have slain the trusts, the monopolists, the holding companies. We have slain the Rockefellers, Standard Oil, and all their legions of lawyers and kept judges. We have slain them all. Let us drink to that!"

He downed a glass of whatever he was holding; it didn't matter.

"Hear, hear," someone yelled.

"We have spared Montana from becoming a vassal of Standard Oil! We have protected the integrity of our government and our courts! Anaconda is finished!"

He wasn't quite sure of that, but what did it matter? They drank to that, drank to Heinze's gaudy staff of lawyers, drank to Heinze's Montana Ore Purchasing Company, and drank to drinking.

The evening passed in heady pleasure, and Fritz Heinze refrained from excess. Tomorrow would be a day of last-minute appeals, hurried injunctions, and legal maneuvering as the great constrictor snake writhed to free itself from the court's decisions. He knew just what the company would seek. A change of venue on the ground that Judge Clancy was prejudiced. A new Montana law empowering the company to reject the jurisdiction of biased judges. And of course a hundred petitions that would pile up on Judge Clancy's desk. No wonder the judge decided to go elk hunting. If he stayed around town, he was likely to be the elk.

The gala broke up in the small hours, and he summoned a hack for Katarina, and then accompanied her out to the mud-splattered vehicle. The horse's breath steamed in the silver lamplight.

"Good-bye, Augustus," she said.

"Good-bye? What do you mean?"

"You have another mistress," she said.

"I'm lost, my dear."

"Her name is Standard Oil, and she has captured you. Thanks for all the lovely times. You'll do in a pinch."

He was puzzled, but her wry grin illuminated the moment.

"Well, good-bye then," he said.

He opened the door of the hack, she pecked his cheek, and slid in, adjusting her cape. Then he watched the dray clop away with his prize.

She was right. He had another aphrodisiac.

He returned to the banquet room and found his party had dissolved. It was late. A yawning servant in a white apron toted glasses and napkins away. Empty bottles littered the tables. He had whipped the most powerful combine in the world, and now life was empty bottles and a weary waiter. He didn't feel elated. He had imbibed, but was cold sober. It was odd, how hollow he felt at the moment of his greatest triumph.

He decided to stay at the hotel. He headed for the desk, awakened a sleepy clerk, and took a room. He found his coachman outside and sent him off, telling him to bring a fresh suit of clothes in the morning. He told the clerk he didn't wish to be disturbed. He would get up whenever he got up.

He headed up the stairs to a corner suite, quite at home. He never had been interested in showy palaces, and could enjoy himself anywhere. He was amused by Clark's thirty-six-room brick pile a few blocks west. The man wanted to be important and show it. Heinze didn't want to be important; he wanted to enjoy life. So he let himself in, doffed his tuxedo and undid the rest and plunged into a cheerful summing up of this notable day. His particular pleasure was comparing himself with great figures. He admired Alexander the Great, he sometimes thought of himself as Hannibal, he decided he was occasionally Napoleonic, but more likely he was like Frederick the Great, which reminded him that people still called him Fritz despite his best efforts. Augustus was fine, as in Caesar Augustus, the finest emperor of them all. Or maybe he was Genghis Kahn, sweeping the world before him.

The only thing that worried him was that he had

triumphed too young. He had a lot of life ahead, and no more Matterhorns to scale. That meant he would fight boredom the rest of his life, which wasn't the most palatable way to squander his days. And so he drifted through the wee hours, and finally slept. And the new day came and waxed and still he slept, until a furious and unaccustomed knocking awakened him. That made him cross.

It was Arthur, his brother.

"What?" Fritz asked.

"You fiddle while Rome burns," his brother said, mysteriously.

"I'll meet you in the dining room. Order my breakfast."

As good as his word, Fritz settled into a dining room chair, still attired in the evening's glad rags, and began sipping coffee, eyeing his nervous brother.

"Amalgamated's shutting down," Arthur said. "They've laid off everyone here and in Anaconda and Great Falls, the only exception being the pumping crews in the mines. Six thousand five hundred men laid off so far. And they're shutting down the smelter furnaces. They've locked the gates. You know what that means. This isn't short term. And the layoffs are falling cards. Everyone's laying off people or shutting down. We may have trouble getting supplies for our own mines. The lumber camps are shutting down and laying off.

The coal mines are shutting down. The railroads are laying off men. It's the whole state."

"It's just a ploy, Arthur. The snake's angry."

"Not a ploy. They're lifting the mules out of the mines. The mules are delirious. The mules are coming up, Fritz, rolling on the grass, dancing in the light."

"So what?"

"I don't seem to get you to understand that this is dangerous."

"They can't stay closed for long. They own businesses, and you've got to operate your business or lose it."

"They've told the papers they have no choice. They can't do business here."

"Well, this is fun," Fritz said, digging into eggs Benedict.

"There are crowds gathering. They know you're here."

"Why here? I didn't lay them off."

"Don't make foolish arguments."

F. Augustus Heinze was not intimidated. "They're playing their aces, but it's still a game. The Standard Oil boys are showing muscle. Give in, or we'll shut down Montana. Look, Arthur, they've got surplus copper. Thousands of pounds of it, and it's depressing prices. This is a slick way to keep prices up and reduce their stockpile by a hundred thousand pounds. You have to give Rogers credit. He knows how to stay profitable."

Arthur didn't much like that. "Try telling that to all those men out there with no paychecks and winter coming on."

"Oh, I'll do that in time. But we'll need to see what's happening in the courthouse."

They slipped out the back door of the hotel, in cloaks, and headed for the Silver Bow County Courthouse, hoping Judge Clancy would not be anywhere in sight. The wind was blowing. There were knots of surly men outside the ornate building. But Judge Clancy was there, with armed guards.

His court was in session. He was hearing motions from Anaconda's lawyers, one of them being that he vacate his earlier decisions because of prejudice.

Judge Clancy yawned, revealing yellow teeth. "I have a prejudice, all right," he said. "It's lawyers that offend me."

He lifted a newspaper in his bony hand, and waved it in front of the crowd. It was a Helena paper, and the headline was "Fair Trials Law," and the kicker above it was "Special Session." Heinze couldn't see the text, but he didn't need to.

Clancy licked his chops. "Your people have been busy," he said, staring at Anaconda's legal talents. "Call a special session, pass the Fair Trials law. That means if you think a judge is biased, all you need to do is certify it and you get another to try your case. Now that's entertaining."

It was more than entertaining. It was blackmail. Amalgamated wanted to pitch out any judge it didn't like and choose its own, and only then would the mines reopen and the miners and smeltermen go back to work.

The courtroom was jammed. One of those present was Big Johnny Boyle. There were other union men listening too.

"I'll take it into consideration, gentlemen," he said, and vanished into his chambers. The mob of unemployed men stirred darkly. A wall of policemen stood between the judge and the mob. The room was stifling. The bench was empty. The guards carried shotguns. The mob stared helplessly at the closed chamber door. The union men studied the Heinze brothers, and Fritz could not fathom what was in their heads.

"We'll lick 'em," he said.

But the remark seemed to fall to the floor somewhere between himself and Big Johnny Boyle.

"The mules are up," Boyle said. "The mules are up."

F. Augustus Heinze wished he weren't wearing last night's glad rags.

That was the sum of the troubles for that day. The Heinze brothers passed through the silent multitude, and headed for the relative safety of the Butte Hotel. Augustus wanted only to get out of his tuxedo, which hung forlornly on him now.

Back in his hotel suite, he found a change of clothing and freshened himself. There was work to do. The hotel seemed deserted, and the streets of Butte seemed empty. The streetcars had quit. The provisioners who supplied saloons and restaurants and stores were not present. It was as if an economic knife had fallen, severing Butte from its commerce. It was quiet, much too quiet, even as the storm clouds hovered over the town, threatening to bring winter down upon it.

He could weather this. He knew what to do which was nothing at all. This would be a waiting game, but the waiting was between Amalgamated and its miners and suppliers. Let them sweat it out. Let one or another crack.

"What are you going to do?" asked Arthur.

Fritz smiled. "Let them stew."

"Is that a good idea?"

"A few thousand miners can bring the most powerful holding company in the world to its knees. All we have to do is watch."

"But isn't it the reverse? The holding company's bringing Butte to its knees. And sooner or later, Fritz, those miners you think you've got in your pocket are going to turn on you. You can bet that Amalgamated is working on it. You can bet that Johnny Boyle's listening to them."

"Then we'll deal with it when we have to. Good afternoon, Arthur."

The evening passed quietly except for the

thundercloud hanging over the city. Fritz Heinze had a fine time in the hotel's barroom, listening to the gossip. The worse it sounded, the better he liked it. When the rumors were catastrophic, he thought for sure he had won. He headed to bed early, feeling quite chipper about it all.

But the next morning before he had even finished his eggs Benedict and coffee, a peculiar delegation sought him out. They were men he knew, bankers and union men. There was a man from Senator Clark's bank; and John D. Ryan from Daly Bank and Trust, and A. J. Davis, II, banker son of a banker and mining father.

Fritz invited them to coffee, and they settled around him. Ryan apparently was the delegated speaker. Ryan was Daly's man, and deep in the Anaconda hierarchy.

"Fritz, the union miners met last eve, and agreed unanimously on a simple matter. The union would be pleased to purchase your stock, and that of your colleagues, in the companies in the stock-holder lawsuits, the Boston and Montana and the Parrot. We've agreed to lend the Butte Miners Union the means to do so. Then those shareholder suits can be dismissed by Judge Clancy."

Fritz Heinze was startled. He hadn't expected that. The stockholders' suits filed by his lieutenants were what had paralyzed the Amalgamated holding company. Rogers and Rockefeller could do little or nothing with their

Montana properties, including the Parrot and all the Boston and Montana mines and smelters, so long as Clancy's verdicts stood and Heinze's men could paralyze the managements of those companies.

"The union would be pleased to resolve this conflict. Isn't that the case, Mr. Boyle?"

Big Johnny nodded. "This is one hell of a winter coming on," he said.

If the union owned the stock it would agree to whatever the Standard Oil Gang required to put the men back to work. Rockefeller and Henry Rogers would win, and win spectacularly. There would be champagne corks popping on Wall Street. And Fritz Heinze's mining empire would fall apart under the pressure of the monopolists.

"No," said Fritz Heinze. "I won't sell out myself or my company or my colleagues or the people of Butte, or Anaconda, or Great Falls, or the state of Montana. I won't sell out."

"That's set in concrete?" asked Ryan.

"It is," Fritz Heinze said, sensing what lay ahead.

Forty-two

The crowd stood silently waiting for Fritz Heinze to speak. There were more people jammed into the courthouse area than Heinze had ever seen in Butte. More people than lived in Butte. They stood there in a deep quietness that might be despair or might be anger, but wasn't indifference. The quietness stretched to the quiet mines, the quiet boilers, the quiet smelters, the quiet trolley cars, and the quiet mountains rising in virgin grace not far beyond. Someone thought there were ten thousand who had come to this place.

Heinze was not fooled by the quiet. He had guards behind him. Before him was a mass of desperate humanity, people out of work and facing winter and starvation. They waited with solemn faces, wrapped against Butte's mean air, which for the moment was free of sulphur and ash and arsenic.

It was not just the working stiffs who waited. The business people listened intently. The newspapermen listened closely. The captains of industry and mining moguls listened from their carriage seats. Lumber barons and railroad men listened. Heinze hoped he was up to the task. Somehow, he had to make his fight their fight, and he meant to try.

And how better than to go on the offensive?

He began with history; his struggles to get a foothold; the efforts of the Anaconda Company to drive him out, which he resisted in all ways and by all means. He talked of all the ways he had been pressured and browbeaten and threatened. He had a fine, sonorous voice and a command of the language, and he put these to good use. He knew he was well liked in Butte, especially by his miners, and he put that to use too.

"They fought me in every possible way. They have beaten me a dozen times in one way or another, and I have taken my defeats like a man. I fought my own battles, explaining them to the public when I had the opportunity, and asking their support at the polls . . ."

"My friends, the Amalgamated Copper Company in its influence and functions, and the control it has over the commercial and economic affairs of the state, is the greatest menace that any community could possibly have within its boundaries."

He talked about the cases just decided, but knew he wasn't gaining much traction with these silent auditors. They wanted their jobs. They wanted to be able to buy coal for their stoves, and food for their tables. But he was not yet done with them. He knew their fears and the things they were struggling to avoid.

"It is true that I am deeply interested in the

outcome of this struggle. My name, my fortune, and my honor are at stake. All have been assailed. You have known me these many years. You are my friends, my associates, and I defy any man among you to point to a single instance where I did one of you a wrong. These people are my enemies, fierce, bitter, implacable, but they are your enemies too. If they crush me today, they will crush you tomorrow. They will cut your wages and raise the tariff in the company stores on every bite you eat and every rag you wear. They will force you to dwell in Standard Oil houses while you live, and they will bury you in Standard Oil coffins when you die. Their tools and minions are here now, striving to build up another trust whose record is already infamous. Let them win and they will inaugurate conditions in Montana that will blast its fairest prospect and make its name hateful to those who love liberty. They have crushed the miners of Colorado because those miners had no one to stand up for their rights.

"In this battle to save the state from the minions of Rockefeller and the piracy of the Standard Oil, you and I are partners and allies. We stand or fall together."

He saw the softening in their hard gazes, and swiftly laid out the conditions of a settlement: his lieutenants would sell their stocks to the union at cost if Amalgamated would turn over its claim to the Nipper mine. The rest could be arbitrated. And as a capstone, he demanded the company guarantee a three-dollar-and-fifty-cent daily wage for three years, which surely would please the miners who worried about wage cuts.

The crowd drifted away thoughtfully. He could not tell if these people were really persuaded or were just waiting. They didn't get their wish, which was to go back to work to feed their families. Their thoughts didn't go much further than their empty cook pots. But he had made an offer, offered arbitration, and given them hope. But even as the vast crowd broke into knots and slowly trudged into the cold, he knew he had only delayed the next stage of the crisis.

He made his way back to the hotel, still under guard, and waited. The city of Butte waited with him through the night and day, its shops doing little business, its homes without sustenance, its saloons empty.

Then word came: Henry Rogers, and his head of Montana operations William Scallon, turned Heinze down flat, and demanded a special session of the legislature to enact their pet "fair trials" law, giving them the power to choose the judges who would hear their suits. That was what they had been after all the while, and had not bent an inch. They did not seek a change-of-venue law; they sought a law permitting them to select the judges of their choice. And so the shutdown continued day after day, while miners pinched and starved and moved out of state.

Governor Joseph Toole tried to put together an arbitration committee which included Senators Clark and Gibson, Congressman Joseph Dixon, and the railroad man James J. Hill. But these worthies failed to bring the two sides together to talk. And so it failed.

Amalgamated had all the advantages. It alone could put the thousands of unemployed back to work. The next weeks saw the wars of the press release, the cannons of propaganda, but there was no progress. Governor Toole refused to call the special session. He would not give the holding company the power to choose its judges merely by certifying that one or another was biased. He would not let a powerful Wall Street company rule the sovereign state of Montana. Fritz Heinze had a point, and everyone knew it. It was shaping into a hard, cold, bitter winter, and as it deepened the unions ramped up their pressure on the governor, along with interested parties across Montana. People were starving.

Then Toole surrendered and called a session to begin on December 1, 1903. And the trust responded by reopening some of the mines and smelters. By the tenth of that month, the legislators enacted the "Clancy Law," as it was being called. The haunting reality of fifteen thousand men across Montana being jobless as winter closed in was too much even for independent legislators.

"They got it," Fritz complained to his brother. "Not even a change-of-venue law. They got the right to pick their favorite judges," he complained. "That's what being a Rockefeller gets you."

"We've got forty or fifty lawsuits that are about to drop down the outhouse hole," Arthur said. "And they'll have the judges to push us out the door."

It was odd how swiftly everything changed. Fritz Heinze was a courthouse miner, and now the courthouse had changed hands. The craven legislature had knuckled under. Amalgamated had just bought the sovereign state of Montana.

But he was determined to gouge out whatever he could. The struggle wasn't over. There was rich ore lying in disputed veins along the edge of his Rarus mine, ore whose ownership had not yet been settled, ore both sides were forbidden to mine until the apex suit was settled. He would go after it.

"It's simply retribution," he told his dubious brother. "It will repair some of the injury they've done us."

"And put a ball and chain around our ankles," Arthur replied. "They own the courts now."

"Aw, Arthur, you keep on being a lawyer, and I'll keep on being a geologist. I know where the ore is."

"And between us we'll practice law and geology in Deer Lodge," Arthur replied.

Fritz Heinze grinned. Adversity simply got his juices flowing.

He sent his miners to the forbidden zone and they were blasting out the ore night and day, and were bringing it to the surface far away, up the Johnstown shaft, thanks to the interconnecting crosscuts and drifts. But it was not a secret for long. Amalgamated miners heard the blasts, and sneaked into the Rarus mine through a dismantled bulkhead and saw for themselves the feverish removal of rich ore. Amalgamated attempted to stop the plunder in court; Heinze defied the court, dodged injunctions and summonses, and dug harder and faster.

"Quit worrying, Arthur. We're fast; they're slow. We'll have it; they'll never touch it. By the time they get in, they'll find empty cuts." But he wasn't sure of that. There had been brawls deep underground. Rival crews had fought with their fists and steam hoses and even with dynamite. It had been worth it; the Montana Ore Purchasing smelter was reducing some of the richest ore ever, hundreds of thousands of dollars of rich ore.

"What if someone is killed? That's dynamite they're tossing down there. That's steam hot enough to scald a man to death. What about that, Augustus?"

"This is the richest hill on earth. The richest hill

on earth! So quit worrying. The prize is worth the risk."

But Arthur Heinze couldn't shake his foreboding. Over in Helena, the fury of the courts was exploding.

"Looks like we'll be hauled into federal court," he told Fritz.

"It won't matter. By the time that happens, I'll have the ore out."

It took sixteen days for Amalgamated geologists to gain access to the disputed bodies of ore adjacent the Rarus. For that length of time Heinze had defied Federal Judge Hiram Knowles and dodged summonses. But Heinze's crew hadn't been idle. When the geologists did gain entry, they found the cuts loaded with waste rock. It would be all but impossible to ascertain how much ore Heinze had stolen without massive effort to open the drifts and crosscuts.

The war continued underground even while the litigants were duking it out in federal courts. Then two Amalgamated miners died when Heinze's men were blasting out a bulkhead. But not even that stopped Heinze's gang from disemboweling a disputed vein in the Pennsylvania mine. And even as the battles raged around the Rarus, Heinze's men were pouring into Amalgamated mines adjacent to the Minnie Healy and looting ore over there. Heinze's miners were swarming through the richest hill on earth, cleaning ore out of obscure corners with breathtaking speed and audacity. Any ore was Heinze ore. Any mine was a Heinze mine.

Injunctions had no effect. It was war in the bowels of hell, and crews were employing any tactic at hand, including flooding crosscuts, burning trash and fouling the air, and dynamiting barriers perilously close to opposing gangs. The war raged through the rest of 1903 and into 1904, but finally abated when large numbers of miners were almost trapped by flooding. The judges dragged Heinze and his lieutenants into court, fined them for contempt, and dressed them down.

Fritz Heinze didn't really mind. He just smiled. He had, in the space of a few months, carved a fortune out of the disputed lodes. The whole escapade had cost Fritz Heinze only twenty thousand dollars in fines, and his foremen got off for a thousand apiece. And in that time he had lifted half a million dollars' of ore out of the disputed lodes. Maybe more; he wasn't even sure himself how much ore he'd snatched.

It was time to throw more dinner parties at the Butte Hotel. He had money to spend, and friends to spend it on. He had lady friends to invite; he had colleagues to thank. There were businessmen whose patience he had tried, and now he wanted to restore all those bonds of friendship and obligation that had buoyed him through his life in Butte. He had come to town as an obscure geologist and had parleyed a nose for ore, and some advanced knowledge of smelting, into a fortune. He had taken his licks, but now he survived, still a major independent, still a man with several mines, a giant smelter, a web of contracts with suppliers of fuel and mining timbers and chemicals. He was still in tight with the union men, still a man to drop down the shafts and visit the stopes and crosscuts and enjoy the company of those sturdy men who braved the bowels of the earth each shift.

He might not have a whole victory, and the great snake writhed and threatened, but did not strike him dead. He had more millions than he had ever dreamed of possessing. He had taken modest family wealth and parlayed it into one of the nation's greatest fortunes. He enjoyed that. He enjoyed the thought of good wine, good Havanas, and luscious ladies. He thought it was time to toast everyone who sat at his tables. He was bloodied, and the holding company owned the courts, but he would celebrate no matter.

Forty-three

If Red Alice had believed in God, she would have thought the great lockout was heaven-sent. But she settled for the idea that it was fortuitous. It proved she was right. Socialism was the answer. If capitalists could put thousands of hardworking and loyal men out of work on a whim, then it was time for the nation's industries to be publicly owned.

She took heart. After years of being ignored, suddenly she had plenty to say, and a finger to wag, and an audience to hear whatever she said. She hadn't made any progress with Big Johnny Boyle, but plenty of miners and smeltermen were listening.

She had sold pencils and distributed tracts for years, occupying a certain patch of street in the heart of Butte where a steam vent released heat. She shared the prize ground with a yellow dog, which made its living from the local restaurants. They both stayed warm, at least on most days, but there were subzero times when not even a grille releasing warmth could make her sentry post bearable.

Most days she sold five or six pencils for a dime each. She had her regulars, who dropped a dime into her bowl, took a pencil, and a tract. Big Benny, the flatfoot, kept a benevolent eye on her, and sometimes chased hooligans away when they threatened to clean her out. He was equally solicitous of the nameless one-eyed yellow dog who shared the patch of warmth, and protected the mutt from cruel kicks. It was said that a bratty boy had poked a stick into the dog's eye.

She rarely got enough cash even to keep her in food, but it somehow didn't matter. Her boys,

Tommy and Timmy, were geniuses at snatching whatever was needed, or bargaining what they had for what they needed. Somehow there would be a meal each day, if only gruel or soup made from bones gotten at the butcher shop. If Timmy lifted an item or two now and then, what did she care? It was all part of making an unjust world more just, and distributing what had been taken by the predatory and giving it to the needful.

Big Benny didn't turn a blind eye to all that. Sometimes when Timmy or Tommy slithered by, carrying something, Big Benny would corral the boy by the scruff of the neck, confiscate the loot, and return it to the shopkeeper, saying he had relieved some punk of his boodle.

"I caught a brat, turned 'im upside down, shook him until it rained out his loot, and here it is, ready to put back on your shelves," he would say.

That kept him in good stead with the shop-keepers, and it also allowed Big Benny to ignore the boys on other days, especially when it was cold and the parlor stove was empty. If the shopkeepers thought that Big Benny was just fine, Red Alice's boys thought he was even finer. Most days Big Benny never saw a thing.

And somehow Red Alice and her boys received their daily bread. She hadn't seen Eloise in years, and had stopped wondering about her. She had heard that her girl was a rich man's household servant in Great Falls, but she couldn't say.

She viewed the shutdown more positively than anyone else in Butte. Now the miners would see! Now the miners would fight! It was chilly, but she harangued anyone who was willing to stop and listen, often arguing with people, usually under the benign eye of Big Benny the flatfoot.

"This proves it! The only way to keep your jobs safe is government ownership. You'd get your pay from Uncle Sam, not the Standard Oil Gang. You'd be getting paid right now, and working right now, if the government owned the mines."

They were listening this time. Before, they usually nodded, eager to escape the cold and wind, and eager to lift a pint in the nearest pub. Then one day a miner she knew, Star McSorley, approached.

"Come along now, Alice. I've a bunch waiting to hear you."

"Buy a pencil and I will."

"We'll buy all your pencils, Alice; come with me."

"If it's to a saloon you're taking me, I'm not allowed in."

"It's a saloon, and if Gold Tooth Scatt objects, we'll throw him out."

She liked that, petted the no-name dog, and abandoned her post. He led her down Broadway, and then right three blocks, to a little pub she didn't know existed.

He ushered her in. There were twenty, no thirty,

miners there. Anaconda men; somehow she knew that. Maybe Anaconda men tipped their hats a little differently. They were nursing their beer and studying her. They were just off-shift. Most had gotten out of their wet work clothes in the dry rooms; it was fatal to head into a cold evening in their brine-soaked work duds. They were pale, not having seen much sun, and some coughed constantly.

Scatt was actually smiling and rubbing his hands on his grimy bar apron. An invasion by a female was fine with him.

"Tell us what you think, Red Alice," McSorley said. "I brung her to talk to us."

It was warm there, and she was warmer than she had been in a long time. Butte was never warm except maybe in July, but this saloon's heat caressed her and pierced her coat.

"We've got to make a better world," she said. "We need a better world, where a man can count on a job and a decent wage, and count on it in the summer and winter, and in the best of times and the worst of times. We need a world where there's a fair wage for hard work, and hours that don't grind a man into his grave before he's lived half a life, and a safe place to work, and a safe place to retire.

"We need a world where a man gets a pension, where they don't just use you up and spit you out to die. We need a world where a man can open his brown envelope and take out enough money to feed his wife and children and keep them in a little place of his own and give them a chance to live. We need a world where there's help if we're injured on the job, where a man who loses his limbs, or his eyes, or his breath while mucking ore for rich men can get help.

"We need a world where we've got someone watching out for us. We're the poor, the forgotten, the ones down in the darkness who drill and shovel and lay up timber and cough our life away; we're the ones who are forgotten when the rich men fight to steal mines from each other and never think of the stiffs two thousand feet down in the earth who are shoveling their ore into cars and sending it up the shaft so that they can make still more money.

"We need a better world than the one we've got," she said.

She felt the warmth of the saloon pierce her clothing, and she unbuttoned her coat and let the warmth reach through her skirts. She hadn't known such warmth since the times when Singing Sean Brophy lived and worked.

They weren't skeptical, these tired men. They weren't arguing with her. They seemed as thirsty for her message as they were for their mug of ale after a hard day's toil deep underground. If the beer in its way was release, so were her words, so was her message. They too wanted a better world than the one they were trapped in.

"There's a way," she said.

No one responded, and maybe they would all discard whatever she said.

"It's the one big strike," she said. "It's when we all strike at the same time, and the rich men who have used us discover that they need us, need our labor, and that without our labor their own wealth falls apart."

Now she did see some skepticism. Who could imagine one big strike across America?

"We get there one by one, local by local, trade by trade," she said. "Not all at once, not tomorrow, but soon. We get there by taking over our own unions. We get there by putting fighting men in office. We get there by tossing out the ones who ride on our toil, who are cozy with the fat cats, who cut deals instead of defending us."

"Like Big Johnny Boyle," one man said.

She didn't reply, didn't even nod. But she knew they all absorbed that and agreed with it, and that from this moment on, Big Johnny would be on his way out of Local Number 1, Western Federation of Miners, and that soon, soon, the Butte Miners Union, as it was called, would lead the howling pack across the West.

She liked the warmth. It had been so long since she had been warm in winter. One of the men handed her a big pretzel from a bowl on the bar. She nibbled on it, licked the salt on it. She

411

hadn't had a pretzel in years. There were boiled eggs, too, and they encouraged her to take a couple and put them in the pocket of her cloth coat.

"What's a better world?" she asked. "A fair wage and a job you can count on. You've just been out of work for many days, all because the owners are fighting, and bribing judges. You were put out of work so that the company could put the heat on the state. You were put out of work and no one cared about you. They knew you'd be starving, they knew you'd not have anything to spend in the stores, they knew that putting you out of work would build up a lot of pressure every-where to put you back in the pits. And they were right. They got what they wanted by starving you, by throwing your job aside, by forcing you to live without your wage day after day. And now you want a better world, and you know how to get it."

She wondered where the words were coming from. She wasn't educated, but the words came from somewhere, like a stream of hot water flowing from her, and the heat and warmth made her almost dizzy.

She was suddenly tired. These days she barely had strength to walk from her Dublin Gulch cottage to the grille where the heat was, the place she shared with the yellow dog. She wished she could have the ordinary privileges of any man, and sit in a saloon like this and sip a beer that would dull the pain and case the weariness of

412

her muscles. A better world for women would be that much further away than a better world for men.

She rose to leave, and they watched her. McSorley escorted her to the door, and pressed his hands over hers, but no one said anything.

She braved the cold, glad of the hard-boiled eggs in her pocket. She carried her pencil jar, but the pencils were gone and a lot of silvery change lay in the bottom. She would buy more pencils, a cent and a half each, fifteen cents for a box of ten, and sell them the next day. The cold didn't bother her this evening because she was warm in the center of herself.

By sheer luck, both Timmy and Tommy were in the cottage. They stared at her, aware that she was somehow different. They looked sullen. She didn't much like the way they looked, mean and ungoverned and cunning. Maybe that was her fault. She'd never liked her children, and they had always known it. She suddenly felt stricken about that; a rush of motherhood bursting in her this odd autumnal eve.

She handed each of them a hard-boiled egg.

"Where'd you nip that?" Timmy asked.

"They were given to me. Some men in a saloon, they gave me the eggs and a pretzel. There's good things for workingmen who go there."

He immediately cracked the shell and peeled pieces off the egg.

"You're good boys," she said. "Now it's time to be a man."

"You been drinking?"

"No, you're fine strong boys, but now you'll get a regular job."

"You crazy?"

"In the pits. They let boys work. You can be nippers."

Those were boys who ran supplies into the mines. Boys could do that, even if they weren't old enough to be mucking. They brought in tools for the drillers, blasting caps for the powdermen, new shovels to replace broken ones, sometimes hay for the mules. They took worn drills out of the mine to be sharpened topside. And they hauled debris out of the pits. They did whatever a half-grown boy could do, and were vital to the smooth operation of any mine.

"What if I don't want to?" That was Tommy muttering.

"You will," she said, iron in her voice.

Timmy looked at her, and at his brother. "I think we're nippers," he said. "We get to nip what's in there." He started cackling.

"You're good boys," she said, and they looked bewildered, never having heard the like. "Big Benny's going to miss you. He won't have much to do."

Forty-four

The summons from Clark and Bro. Bank startled J. Fellowes Hall. He hadn't heard from William Andrews Clark in years. The *Mineral* had been profitable, and that had seemed all that Clark cared about. But now Hall faced a trip up the hill to the bank, and who knew what?

Clark wasn't even in Butte very much. He was in Washington off and on, occasionally attending to Senate business. More often he was in Arizona, or California, or France. But here was a green-uniformed messenger boy with a brief note:

HALL, BE HERE AT HALF PAST TWO. WAC.

Maybe it would be a raise. Not only was the *Mineral* profitable, but it had the best circulation. His coverage hewed carefully to solid ground through all the politics that swirled around Butte. He had been wary of the Anaconda Company and the Standard Oil Gang, and had said so carefully. He had been wary of Heinze's court-house gambits, stealing mines via lawsuit, and had stated the case. He had largely avoided discussion of Clark's senatorial career, where Clark was setting records for absenteeism. So if Clark wished to see him, it couldn't be anything bad.

But Hall wasn't sure of that. Clark was unpredictable. And Clark could take exception to anything at any time. It had been a good run. Hall had upgraded the staff, modernized the plant with a rotary press, produced a paper that consistently outsold the rest, and had won acclaim. So he wasn't really sure why the summons made him nervous, but it did.

Hall had finally imported his family from Pennsylvania, actually overriding their own wish to stay East. They had heard awful things about Butte and had no wish to plunge into such a poisonous and bleak world. But Hall had found a comfortable west-side house for them, sent money to ship furnishings and pay their rail fare, and had installed them in the two-bedroom house with a good view southward. The ugly mines were out of sight behind them.

He had welcomed Amber, who frowned for a month as she examined Butte, and welcomed Nicholas and Stanley, who promptly scorned Butte's wild and sleazy schools stuffed with children with foreign names. But now, a year later, they had settled in, and found delight in the rowdy and scabrous city. All of which meant that J. Fellowes Hall was in Butte to stay; he had no plans to move on, and wasn't restless the way he had been during his first years, when each day brought a new affront to his dignity.

He eyed the sky, found it clear, and decided a

suit coat would suffice, so he clamped his felt hat on his graying hair and set out on foot, soon arriving at the well-worn stairs to the second floor of the Clark bank. Upon presenting himself, a luscious raven-haired receptionist promptly ushered him into Clark's sanctum. The little man was perched, as usual, behind a vast well-polished desk, and bristling his whiskers in all directions as if each hair was a howitzer.

"Well, Hall, I've sold the *Mineral*," he said abruptly. "I thought you'd like to know."

"Sold?" The news astonished the editor.

"The whole thing. I'm not keeping a piece. I got a good price for it, a nice gain, and it's done."

"Ah, who's the buyer?"

"Why, who else could afford it? John Ryan of the Anaconda company. They prefer not to own the papers outright, so the papers are usually owned by someone high up. Word is, he'll replace Scallon soon. But behind Ryan is some real strength."

"Amalgamated owns the paper?"

"As of yesterday, yes. Thought I'd let you know."

"Are they planning any . . . changes?"

"I haven't the faintest idea. That's all, Hall. You may go now."

"Ah, am I still the editor?"

Clark smiled. "Haven't the faintest idea. I told them I'd tell you this afternoon."

"Well, thank you, Mr. Clark. Is there anything else I should know?"

"They're fine fellows over there, Hall. Scallon, Henry Rogers, Rockefeller. Just fine fellows, personal friends of mine, good God-fearing businessmen who love a good dividend."

Clark waved Hall off, so the editor retreated, slipped past Clark's cheerful assistant, clambered down the creaking steps, and into the smoky streets of Butte. His heart was racing. He was trying to think what he knew about the papers owned by the copper trust, and what sort of copper collar they wore, and whether there was any editorial leeway.

Durston's *Anaconda Standard* relentlessly hewed to the company's view of things, trumpeting whatever needed trumpeting. Durston didn't need guidance from above; he was usually a step ahead of the owners when it came to defending and promoting the Amalgamated holding company. Hall didn't know much about the rest, the company papers in Missoula, Billings, Livingston, and Helena. Neither did he know how various weeklies round about Montana fared. Often those papers weren't actually owned by Anaconda; the company had simply lent operating funds to the papers when they needed cash. That was all it took to influence the editorial direction of those editors.

So Ryan was the man. Ryan was a Daly protégé, a lawyer from Canada, a banker now, a company executive, and the heir apparent whenever Scallon left the firm. Ryan was tougher, harder, meaner, colder than Daly or Scallon; more like Henry Rogers, all piety and family and civility on the one hand, even while he was demolishing rivals and destroying or buying out opposing forms.

And Ryan spent much of his time at the Daly Bank. Well, good enough, Hall thought. He should find out at once where he stood. It all probably would be fine.

He found the Daly Bank up a way and marched in, hoping to meet the new owner.

Ryan was in, it turned out, surrounded by a sea of hair-oiled men in wire spectacles and black sleeve garters whose desks formed a phalanx that protected the great man from the public. He had heard these were Ryan's own legal assistants, all of them looking for loopholes and exceptions and badly drafted clauses.

"J. Fellowes Hall here to see Mr. Ryan," he said to a cadaverous fellow with a sleeve garter on both arms.

"Yes, he's expecting you. Mr. Clark rang up moments ago."

That was Clark, Hall thought. Still reading minds. He knew where Hall would go.

Hall found himself in the most orderly office he had ever seen, devoid of paper, or folders, or motes of dust in the sunlight. And behind an orderly desk was an orderly man, with chiseled face and cold, assessing eyes, all belied by a hearty smile.

"Sit," Ryan said. "Pleased to meet you. A most illustrious editor indeed."

Hall settled into a chair that looked virgin, as if no one had ever sat in it. It was an illusion, of course. Many a bottom had pressed the cushion, and yet Hall had the feeling that he was the first.

"Well now, we have the paper, and we are pleased with it. We have the best circulation and the best advertising in Butte."

"Yes, sir, I've worked hard to bring it to that level."

"And the most profitable paper, too. Our dear friend Mr. Clark always insists on it."

"Yes, sir, and that comes from selecting stories that draw readers to us."

"Well, Hall, we're going to make some minor changes, with your approval, of course."

"I'm sure I'll be happy to adjust the paper to your needs, sir."

Ryan smiled, or rather his lips did; the rest of his face didn't, and his bleak gaze didn't change at all. "You know, Hall, this is a deeply ethical and moral town, with many happy families and warm hearths. Yes, with churches on every corner. We have delicate and gracious women, embued with their duties as mothers and wives and exemplars."

Hall saw where this was going, and nodded.

"I think, Hall, the paper is a bit racy, shall we say, for Butte. This is a sober and quiet place, with neighborhoods suited for children, and high standards of conduct."

Hall nodded.

"So, we shall proceed without coverage of certain unfortunates and without sensationalism of any sort. We want the people of Butte to understand that their town is a haven for the upright and industrious and virtuous, and not a place for unbridled conduct."

"That can be arranged, sir."

"Good. I'm pleased that you are flexible. Some people in the press are difficult."

"I am always flexible, sir."

"Now, as for the paper's editorial opinions, there will be some changes. Henceforth, your opinion page should reflect what appears in the *Anaconda Standard*. Durston knows exactly what is good for the state, the industry, and of course for Amalgamated, and we wish our other papers to reflect his viewpoints, or reprint his editorials so that we may magnify our opinion statewide."

"Yes, sir," Hall said.

"Now, of course, if you are tempted to digress, check here first. You need only bring a draft of what you are planning to say to any of the fellows just outside the door here, and they will approve it or not, or make certain suggestions. We want to speak with one voice, of course, and not have diverse opinions rising from our company newspapers."

"Bring it here, sir, yes, it's just a few blocks."

"Good, Hall, you catch on quite handily. Now, Hall, we're going to change some of the content, also. We've found that some of the stories dealing with the mining industry are less than accurate or enlightening, and we plan to make some changes. There's to be no original reportage about the mining industry. We'll send along an occasional piece for reprint, or make suggestions. And oh, yes, there's a fellow in your paper that you'll discharge. He seems to get things wrong so often that I question his ability. Wolf's his name. I believe he has the odd nickname of Grabbit. Let him go at once, Hall."

"Ah, he's got no pension, sir."

"He should have thought of that before engaging in irresponsible journalism."

"Very well, sir, I will let him go. With a month's pay?"

"No, Hall, just out the door."

Hall wrestled with that and chose stillness. Life was sad.

"Oh, yes, the cartoonists. You have two, I believe."

Hall nodded. He had two brilliant ones whose favorite sport was taking shots at Ryan's colleagues.

"We'll be discharging them, Hall. You can use the ones that Durston employs. We can send over the plates for your press."

"They have families here, sir."

"We all have families, Hall. Now, the newsboys. You're paying them a penny more than other papers do. We'll stop that."

"It inspires them to sell more papers, sir. They're the best in Butte."

"Anyone can do it. You just stand there and wave papers at people. Sorry, but they should go into more productive work if they want higher piecework wages."

"Yes, sir."

"Now then, we'll have you back in a month to review your progress, Hall."

"Yes, sir."

Ryan rose, rounded his spotless desk, caught Hall's elbow, and ejected him, smiling all the way.

Hall stood in the street, breathing smoky air, thinking about quitting, knowing he couldn't, and that he would kowtow to his new masters. Meanwhile there was the immediate problem of carrying out Ryan's commands.

He headed for the paper, sucking sulphurous smoke from the gray air, bracing himself for the tasks ahead. But when he got back to the paper he was no more prepared than when he had left Ryan's office. Inside, he steeled himself to fire Wolf, but couldn't find his star reporter, so he slumped in his chair, relieved for the moment, and then took the sleazy way out. He penned a note and left it on Wolf's typing machine.

The cartoonists would be easier. He found them scratching out new burlesques and paused at their tables. "New owners, boys. Amalgamated. They're making some personnel changes."

Stoltz, one of the cartoonists, sighed, tapped the dottle from his pipe, and started collecting his stuff. Bertrand, the other one and younger, stared, and followed suit. Hall had the sense that this was quite ordinary for political cartoonists. He watched silently as the pair suddenly whooped.

"We'll buy you a beer, Hall," Bertrand said. And moments later the pair vanished into the smoke.

He decided he'd let the newsboys find out about the wage cut when they turned in their daily collection and the circulation man, Stu Billings, totted things up and paid them. Company policy, something like that.

Hall returned to his warren, and stared at the walls. He was no longer an independent newsman. But he still had a job for the rest of his life if he conducted himself in the approved manner. He would not have another.

Forty-five

Senator Clark avoided the New Year's Eve frivolities as being unseemly and beneath his station. He paid close attention to seemliness now, and cultivated dignity as carefully as he trimmed his bristly beard.

The occasion that he wished to avoid was the opening of the Silver Bow Club's grand new quarters on Granite Street, which occurred that first night of 1907, when two hundred fifty or so of the club's members began with a drink in the old fourth-floor quarters, and then carried their glasses the short and wintry distance to the new structure.

Not that Clark disapproved. He had fought for the new building for years. He had been one of the founders and the club's first president in the early eighties. He had railed at the old club because it wasn't suitable for men of station and achievement. So he was delighted to celebrate the opening of the new club, but had chosen to do it his own way, with the first banquet to be held there. That was the best way to avoid all the drunks and reprobates he didn't care to run into.

So the club had been christened without him, christened with Chinese firecrackers, and a waterfall of spiritous drinks that enabled the celebrants to maneuver from 1906 to 1907 without pain. By all accounts it was a rather inebriated crowd that toasted the new club and its grand future.

The new building was a marvel, the finest gentleman's club between the two coasts. It was clad in golden sandstone quarried in Columbus, Montana, and was fitted with the finest furnishings and appointments that money could buy. The building rose four floors and had an Otis birdcage elevator to lift people to their destinations. The servants lived in the basement next to the boiler and coal bunker. The top floor contained bedroom suites for guests or members who wished to stay over. Below that was the grand ballroom. Below that were the club rooms and the saloon and dining room. There were reading rooms, and a separate parlor for the ladies. Members entered through their own grand doorway up slightly from the street, while servants and service people had their own entrance around the corner. The hidden stairway system was intended to shield servants from view as they moved from place to place. It was all just and fitting, and William Andrews Clark heartily approved of it all, including the quarter-million price tag.

The club was ready for princes of industry and commerce, kings, queens, presidents and senators and politicians of all stripes. Senator Clark certainly would entertain there, and enjoy the company of his peers there, and maybe do a little business there. But his exuberance at the completion of the Silver Bow Club was tempered by something else: he didn't plan to stay in Butte. Now that his Senate term was concluding, he was not bound to Montana in any particular way, and could reside anywhere he chose, and that choice would be New York City, where he would build a mansion, collect art, collect accomplished friends, and sojourn in California or Paris if he felt like it. But all of that he set aside for the moment. He had finally gotten a gentlemen's club in Butte worthy of members and guests as prominent as himself.

He had acquired real estate in Los Angeles and Santa Barbara, plantation property in Mexico, assorted urban lots in places he visited. His Arizona mines drew him there, especially the United Verde mine, which was a fountainhead of new wealth. And even as his properties expanded, so did his family. In 1901 he had secretly married his beautiful young ward, Anna La Chapelle, whose Paris education he had been funding. They had a girl in 1902, but they did not announce the marriage until 1904, which created a great stir and a few raised eyebrows. In 1906 a second girl was born. So there was a young second family residing in Senator Clark's Butte mansion, at least some of the time.

It wasn't that Clark disliked Butte; it was that he was drawn into a larger world from coast to coast, and was embarking on the life offered only to the very rich. He enjoyed the city that made his fortune, and bestowed upon it Columbia Gardens, a beautiful trolley park in the foothills east of town, and delighted to host great parties there for all of the people of Butte. But Senator Clark simply had other interests that stretched farther and farther away from Montana.

Now it was his pleasure to celebrate the opening of the Silver Bow Club, and to celebrate Butte itself, which had finally transformed itself from a raw frontier town into a great brick-and-stone metropolis. It really was his city. He had nurtured it and still employed a large part of its labor force. He wasn't at all disturbed by the reality that it was owned by the Standard Oil people. Or that those people dominated the state government, Silver Bow County and Butte government, most of the newspapers, and many of the state's other businesses.

He chose his guest list carefully. There would be all those fine fellows over in Anaconda, including William Scallon, Cornelius Kelley, and John Ryan. And of course, Henry Huddleston Rogers and William Rockefeller, if they cared to come out to Butte. There would be one person who would definitely not be on that list, and that was F. Augustus Heinze, now a resident of Manhattan, and not welcome at such an event as this.

Fritz Heinze had sold out in early 1906. He had taken his time about it, and probably had tried to keep options open for himself through the long negotiations. But in fact, soon after the election of 1904, and the enactment of the "fair trials" legislation demanded by the trust in December of that year, Fritz Heinze had seen that the end was approaching. He no longer had friendly Montana judges available to keep the Amalgamated

Copper Company at bay. He continued to engage in boisterous politics and legal maneuvers, even while he began cloistered talks in Butte hotels with the trust, most especially John Ryan. Eventually the talks were moved to New York because of Heinze's fear of discovery. He did not want to be seen as selling out to the very trust and monopoly he had assailed so virulently all those years.

And in fact, when the deal was finalized, the whole thing was an elaborate ruse. Heinze sold his Butte copper properties to a brand new trust, which in turn was controlled by Amalgamated people, so the nature of the transaction was well concealed to everyone—and no one. The swashbuckling Heinze walked away with ten million dollars for nearly everything he owned or controlled on Butte Hill, and also for the dismissal of his hundred and ten lawsuits against Amalgamated. Heinze still had mining properties in Canada and Utah, and he kept an interest in the Pennsylvania mine in Butte, but in truth he was out. His acerbic little newspaper, the *Reveille*, died too. He was gone.

And now, Senator Clark was hosting a banquet. It wasn't a large one, but it would include everyone who was someone in Western mining. It would be exclusively male, of course. The Silver Bow Club's discreet servants greeted the gents as they arrived, helped them out of their topcoats and silk hats, and directed them to the ballroom, which was fitted out for the banquet. The gents were uniformly attired in dinner jackets for the gala affair, and had snowy starched shirtfronts on display beneath their black bow ties. The senator greeted them and eyed their attire critically. Nothing annoyed him more than slovenly attire or grooming. Not even William Rockefeller would be seated if his glad rags weren't up to snuff.

Fortunately, on this fine winter's eve of early 1907, the assembled princes of mining and commerce were perfectly attired, and therefore welcome to Clark's soiree. He would, following a spiritous hour devoted to camaraderie and a sumptuous dinner of roast duck and truffles, address these captains of industry and finance. Just briefly. This was, after all, to be a celebration, an acknowledgment. He simply wished to make it known that Butte was the most important place on earth.

The senator surveyed his guests benignly. He was especially pleased to see a fine contingent from Amalgamated. These splendid gents were the wave of the future, and the suppliers of copper to a nation that was even then gradually electrifying its cities and in great need of the wire to do so. It was strange, Clark thought, how timing could be everything. The Rockefellers had built Standard Oil on the kerosene that lit the lamps of the nation, but now Standard Oil was fueling the horseless carriages that were crawling across lands once traversed by horse. And copper entrepreneurs like himself had arrived just in time to make electrification possible.

The banquet proceeded decorously, and after crème brûlée and port and cigars, Senator Clark had himself introduced by Henry Huddleston Rogers, and proceeded to address the brilliant assemblage.

"My purpose this evening goes beyond introducing you to the finest gentlemen's club on earth," he began. "The Silver Bow Club is a place of unparalleled comfort and privacy and distinction. Its opening symbolizes something else. The rock beneath our feet, often called the richest hill on earth, has recently become a lot richer.

"This is not the result of vast new discoveries, although we continue to find copper in endless quantities, but in the new efficiencies of extraction. It does us little good to sit upon the most fabulous body of ore since history began if we cannot get a decent profit from it. And only recently have we achieved our goal to get a splendid return on our heavy investment in machinery and labor. As of now, there is nothing to stop us from getting undreamed-of returns out of our investment here."

They were all listening carefully. Clark noticed that some of those starched shirts were well stained by the evening's imbibing, which he duly noted. Such men would likely not be invited next time. He checked his own starched bosom, which harbored not the slightest speck of disorder.

"I am talking, of course, about the consolidation of the copper industry here. At long last, the mine operators are not at war; the courtrooms are nearly empty. The countless apex suits and minority stockholder suits have been dismissed. The lawyers making a living from this heap of litigation have gone elsewhere. The great flow of ore moves uniformly and efficiently to smelters whose very size makes them more efficient and profitable than before, when there were numerous smelters competing for ore from dozens of independents. All this, in short, is the way to wealth. We have ended the litigation and rationalized our production," he said. "Every pound of copper is cheaper than ever to refine."

There was a polite scattering of applause.

"I haven't the exact figures, but the litigation was taking several million a year out of our pockets," he said.

"But things have improved in other ways. First, the government of Montana, on all levels, has become far more accommodating to business, and by keeping taxes and regulation to a minimum, and by giving mining corporations access to a fair and unbiased judiciary, the prospects of greater profit are very bright. We are in constant contact

432

with Montana's officials, advising them and assisting them to help build the state's economy.

"Likewise, the industry and state are benefitting from a friendly and cooperative press at last, a press eager to present the public with the best available understanding of mining and its needs. This ensures that the government will treat copper producers with some equanimity. I am pleased to say that as a senator I was able to influence the federal government along the same lines, and this is already reflected in our profits."

"Of course," he said, delicately, "consolidation is not yet complete, but perhaps someday it will be, and meanwhile there is nothing but amiable relations among the proprietors." That was signal enough for the moment that someday, if the price was right, he would abandon his own holdings on the hill. But that was for the future. He knew that Henry Rogers would take note, and make plans.

"Now, my friends, take it from me: the opening of this splendid Silver Bow Club signifies the beginning of the most profitable mining on earth, a time when copper is the true gold. The richest hill on earth has only just begun to yield its treasure. If you think you've seen a lot, I'll leave you with this. You haven't seen anything yet."

That was it. They saluted him. They toasted him. They toasted the Silver Bow Club, and headed out into the wintry night.

He was among the last to leave, and happened to depart with Anaconda's John Ryan.

Outside, in the cold of the eve, a wraith of a woman stood, with a hand-painted sign pressed to her bosom.

Clark examined the sign, which read CAPITALISM IS THEFT.

"Who's that?" Clark asked.

"That's Red Alice," Ryan replied. "She's nothing to worry about."

Epilogue

After selling out to Amalgamated, F. Augustus Heinze established himself in the Waldorf Hotel, where he entertained lavishly while expanding the Heinze brothers' empire to include banking as well as their own shaky trust, United Copper Company. But in New York he was in over his head, and his empire collapsed, in part because of the shareholder maneuvering of his old adversaries, the Standard Oil Gang. That collapse triggered the recession of 1907 and inspired bank reform, in particular the Federal Reserve System.

He married Bernice Henderson in 1911, and they had a son, but she died of spinal meningitis in 1914, ending a brief, bitter marriage. He died soon after, from cirrhosis of the liver, having shortened his life through high living.

William Andrews Clark died in 1925 after a long life devoted to expanding his business empire into one of the nation's major fortunes. He sold his Butte holdings to the Anaconda Company in 1910, but continued to pursue mining and other enterprises on a global scale.

The Anaconda Copper Mining Company gradually consolidated its holdings in Butte, absorbing the Heinze and Clark properties as well as virtually all the remaining independent mines. Eventually it owned the twenty-six copper mines on Butte Hill, along with transportation and reduction works. By 1915 there was no longer a need for the Amalgamated copper holding company, and it was dissolved. The Anaconda behemoth reigned supreme until the late twentieth century. It owned most of Montana's daily press and had an outsized influence on Montana's state government and several local governments. It was brilliantly managed, enormously profitable, and politically powerful. In the late fifties it sold its daily newspapers, which were no longer needed to promote the company's well-being. By the 1960s Montana finally had a vigorous independent press. The company moved most of its operations to Chile where labor was cheaper, but was eventually bought out in 1977 by Atlantic Richfield Company and no longer exists as an independent company.

In the period following this novel, Butte was riven by labor unrest and radicalism as well as managerial arrogance. The Industrial Workers of the World, better known as Wobblies, arrived in Butte to agitate for better working conditions. And the Pinkertons arrived in town, hired by the Anaconda Company to do its dirty work. One of these was Dashiell Hammett, who wrote a vivid novel, *Red Harvest*, depicting the period.

There is still abundant copper underlying Butte, and it is being mined on a small scale even now. Much of the city has vanished into the Berkeley Pit, but enough remains to retain its character.

Author's Note

Historical novels come in many forms, ranging from the dramatization of actual events and characters and history at one end of the spectrum to novels in which an entirely fictional story is set within an historical period and place.

I have chosen a middle ground here. The copper kings and their minions are drawn from history, while actual events form the narrative spine of the novel. I have dramatized conversations and events that could well have happened and are consistent with history. On the other hand, most of the other characters, such as miners and shopkeepers, are entirely fictional. My intent was to portray people in all walks of life as they struggled with the maneuvering of the copper kings. William Andrews Clark's paper was actually the *Butte Miner*, but I have fictionalized it to the *Butte Mineral* for story purposes.

There is an abundance of superb literature about the rivalry of the copper kings and life in Butte in the last decade of the nineteenth century and first decade of the twentieth. Preeminent among them is *The Battle for Butte: Mining and Politics on the Northern Frontier, 1864–1906* by Michael P. Malone. I have quoted F. Augustus Heinze's famed speech to the miners directly from this outstanding history. Another valuable source is *The War of the Copper Kings* by C. B. Glasscock. *Copper Camp: The Lusty Story of Butte, Montana, the Richest Hill on Earth* is another fine resource rich in anecdote. It is a Writers Project of Montana work with uncredited contributors. Butte is remarkably Irish, and that aspect of the city is exhaustively covered in *The Butte Irish: Class and Ethnicity in an American Mining Town, 1875–1925* by David M. Emmons. The domination of the press of Montana by the Anaconda Company is superbly examined in the splendid, award-winning *Copper Chorus: Mining, Politics, and the Montana Press, 1889–1959* by Dennis L. Swibold. Mining town sociology and tradition is examined in *Tracing the Veins: Of Copper, Culture, and Community from Butte to Chuquicamata* by Janet L. Finn.

These were my primary sources, but there are many other fine resources in magazines, newspapers, and academic papers. I wish to acknowledge the assistance of my wife, Professor Sue Hart, and a distant cousin, Jack Gilluly, in supplying me with valuable research material.

—*Richard S. Wheeler*

Center Point Publishing
600 Brooks Road ● PO Box 1
Thorndike ME 04986-0001 USA

(207) 568-3717

US & Canada:
1 800 929-9108
www.centerpointlargeprint.com